DARK REFLECTIONS

Pauline S Wright

DARK REFLECTIONS
Published by Cambuslea Publishing

Copyright © Pauline S Wright 2014

This novel is entirely a work of fiction.
The names, characters and incidents portrayed
in it are the work of the author's imagination.
Any resemblance to actual persons, living or dead,
events or locations, is entirely coincidental.

ISBN: 978-0-9929759-0-6
eISBN: 978-0-9929759-1-3

Acknowledgements

With thanks to Suzanne for her help
and patience.

The cover is from the portfolio of Carolyn Smith.

CHAPTER ONE

Flash! She blinked. Like defective fairy lights, the sun pierced the branches for a nanosecond. Flash! Her hand went over her eyes. The fairy lights went out one more time.

Mid-May, reasonably warm, still Corinne Pallin's teeth chattered as she followed the man through the woods. The back of her neck rigid, a pounding headache was on its way. Relax, she told herself. Enjoy the walk.

The path was cavernous green. Silence reigned except for the cushioned crunch of pine needles under their feet. Neither spoke. Uncomfortable, but Corinne was in no mood to make the effort of polite, useless conversation with a stranger.

In the tunnel of branches it was cool and dim. A very few metres only separated them from the bright day beyond the thick canopy.

It was Kate Menzies who, with a smile that came and went as fleetingly as a nervous twitch, had said her husband would carry Corinne's bags.

'He'll show you the way to your cabin.' The woman had voiced no particular interest in Corinne's last minute booking, only reciting a jaded-by-repetition hope that she "have a good stay".

Knowing that was as likely as the day turning out to be just a bad dream, Corinne gave no response.

Eight hundred metres from the shop, a left turn, two minutes walk, and Corinne emerged from the moist, green cover into the sunlight.

A wide expanse of water, flat and steely-grey lay in front of her.

'Oh!' The heat pricking her skin, her eyes travelled over the smooth loch.

'It's… breathtaking.' She felt small, inadequate in the face of this unexpected panorama. Mesmerised, she shaded her eyes against the glare. 'Everything is so still.'

Her guide was watching her. 'Loch na Duroir,' he told her. 'It's certainly at peace right now.' He held her bags, one in each hand, waiting with no sign of impatience, to show her the accommodation she had rented unseen.

'Loch na Duroir…' Corinne dropped her hand from her eyes. She faced him. 'Sorry, I guess I'm holding you back.'

'Don't worry, I'm in no rush.' There was no smile but his square face, devoid of any artistic stubble, was pleasant enough. She believed him when he said, 'I do the same. Just stand and watch.' His eyes formed two narrow slits as he gazed out over the water. 'There's nothing much to see but you can't stop yourself.' He paused, his face showed no embarrassment at having voiced this very personal trait. Nor did he shift his eyes as he murmured, 'You'll find the loch's got a strange way of drawing you in.'

They stood, not moving. Nothing, not even the interminable lick of water on the loch-side pebbles disturbed the stillness of the warm afternoon.

Corinne shuddered. In the face of this magnificence, she felt exposed. Had she been in her right mind when she'd chosen this place? Too remote, too… overpowering, she decided. A bad choice. Vulnerable as she felt, this openness crushed her.

'Right, then,' Ross Menzies cut into her thoughts.

Corinne flushed as if he'd heard her damning assessment. This was his home ground after all.

'Right,' she repeated a tad too quickly. 'Lead on.'

Ross Menzies dumped the bags on the planked walkway that acted as footbridge from the path to the cabin door. 'You first.'

With no idea of what to expect, Corinne went past him in into the cabin.

This wooden box would be her home for the next two, three days? That's if she stayed. She wasn't sure yet. But then right now she wasn't sure of anything. This uncertainty was new. A new bewildering state, frightening, to one not used to it. And she wasn't.

Inside the cabin there was relief. Bigger than she'd assumed at first sight, half was taken up by the square living room plainly furnished with cane chairs and sofa and a low table.

One glance took it all in; bedroom on the right at the back; bathroom next door. A galley kitchen was squeezed into the remaining space on the left.

Sticking her head into each, she saw everything she would need. The place was small, a cleverly scaled-down version of real life. She smiled; a play-house for grown-ups. Grown-ups – plural. She dropped the smile. On her own, she wasn't here to play.

'There's a heater there if you get cold tonight.' Ross Menzies' voice intruded in her head.

Well-built, attractive, not yet in middle-age, he was standing watching her. He had a way about him – talking without moving his head or flexing a muscle. He appeared to know what she was thinking. Intrusive, it unnerved her.

He pointed to the iron stove perched on four squat legs. 'I'll bring wood and make it up for you tomorrow in case you want that. Anyhow, it'll be ready if you need it.' He glanced around the living room. 'Are you sure you'll be all right here by yourself?'

Grabbing one of her bags, Corinne swung it off the floor and dumped it down hard on the table. What she didn't need right now was sympathy. The pounding in her head was loud, her skull felt ready to explode. She was just managing to hang on to what was left of her sanity. 'What makes you think I won't be?' Belligerent. This wasn't like her. Dear God…

'Oh, no reason. Only it can be lonely up here. It takes a little time to get used to. That's all.'

'Thanks for your help, Mr Menzies. I'll be fine.' She

moved the second bag beside the first, placing it with infinite care this time. 'You don't have to worry about me.' She waited.

'Right, then, Miss Pallin.'

'Thanks again for bringing the bags.'

His work done, the owner of the Four Hills Lochside Cabins left cabin number 1.

Alone, Corinne wondered a second time what had possessed her to pick this place. She scowled at the empty room. *Picked? Picked* implied taking time to choose it over others. There had been no others. One advert on the back of a magazine – and she had been in a hurry to get away. Away from *him,* away from that room where he'd taken her pride, her self-worth, her trust, leaving her emotionally crippled.

Not a soul knew where she was. Home, that's where she should have stayed, to be told by friends and family that everybody hits a bad patch occasionally. But then it would be followed by all and sundry going over and over it until the bones were picked clean.

Not yet. Not while she was here; in the middle of nowhere, delaying the dissection of her life.

At her office they would find it hard to believe. Veering so far off the agenda just wasn't her. Her life was structured, organised – well organised – and she admitted it, predictable. So what? It's who she was.

She admitted, too, if she'd stayed even for one day, Noel would have been right in there, coaxing and pleading. Then, if she didn't forgive him, the whole thing would get turned on its head and end up being her fault for not giving the marriage another chance. That's why she'd *picked* here and not there.

The cane chair creaked softly as Corinne lowered herself into it. Space. That was exactly why she was here. Lots of space – for the screaming in her head to be let loose.

She stared at the two bags. Their soft green leather

criminally misshapen, crammed full, they seemed to mock her. Had she brought the right things to wear? No matter; the days were fast easing into summer.

Summer… Corinne leaned back. Congenial creaking surrounded her as she settled down further.

Last summer… The last time the bags had been used. A month in Antigua. Mr and Mrs Noel Anderton on their fifth wedding anniversary. Four weeks of pure heaven. But even there, away from their rented beach-house, he was recognised. She hadn't minded. She never minded. But it always surprised her since his photo, full back sleeve on every one of his books, was five years old. That seemed to make no difference. Still they knew him.

Did Ross Menzies or his wife read Noel's thrillers? The thought had first flashed through Corinne's head as she signed in to Four Hills. It was a little guessing game that was harmless if she guessed wrong; satisfying if she got it right. The Menzies? No, she didn't think so. Not them. Still, they might know his name. Hence her signature half-way down the page in the archaic dark blue covered register. *Miss C Pallin*. Anonymous and safe.

Another check through the cabin satisfied Corinne everything she needed was there. A small fridge in the corner of the kitchen was stocked up, bread and cereal in the cupboard. This suited her fine. When stressed, she didn't eat much. A sudden thought came. If this is what Kate Menzies fed her husband he looked fit on it.

She swung the bags off the table and chucked them in the bedroom. Her headache still niggled away. In the kitchen she filled the kettle and flicked the switch.

'Hi!'

Corinne swung round. 'Oh… Hello.'

The tall girl leaning in the doorway scarcely spared Corinne a glance. 'If it's coffee you're making, I'll have one.'

5

'Yes… It's coffee.'

A long sleeveless top over a couple of bright tee-shirts hung straight on the visitor's thin frame over tight black leggings. On her feet, a pair of silver pumps, the toes scuffed and devoid of their silver coating. Without waiting for an invite she swaggered to the sofa and slid down in a fluid, boneless movement. Glancing over her shoulder at the loch, she threw one stroppy word at Corinne. 'Well?'

'Well, what?' Corinne placed two mugs beside the kettle and waited for the water to reach boiling point.

'Don't you want to know who I am?'

Corinne glanced at her visitor's profile. The girl's eyes were still trained on the loch. She could be no more than nineteen, if that, tall and much too thin with an insolent pout on her beautiful, angular face. And – Corinne searched for the right word – uptight. That was it. So uptight you could feel the tension waiting to burst out of her. No amount of summery clothing could disguise it.

The kettle clicked. Corinne poured boiling water onto the coffee granules and stirred. 'Well,' she hesitated, 'in the space of half-an-hour, in the radius of… let's say, half a mile, I've come across two tall redheads…'

The girl scowled. 'No brainer!' She wriggled straight and took the mug Corinne held out. 'Louisa. Louisa Menzies.' She gave a disparaging laugh. 'No hiding it, eh?'

'Corinne Pallin.'

'Wow! Corinne! Well… Who stuck you with that?'

Corinne sipped her coffee. This abrasive creature was strangely intriguing. 'If you don't like it, don't use it,' she said easily.

The girl's pale fingers circled her mug as if seeking warmth from its contents. She scrutinised Corinne. 'You're not easily riled, are you?'

'Is that what you're trying to do?' Corinne asked. 'Rile me?'

'Oh, for God's sake!' Anger flashed over the girl's face.

6

'It's only a name!'

Corinne thought that she was about to take off but Louisa Menzies sank back hard on the sofa. It creaked loudly. 'I'm only here because they thought you might need a hand getting settled in.'

'That's good of you.'

'Not me! Oh, no, don't get any idea I've got anything to do with it.' The scowl was back. 'But you might as well know before you start wondering, there's nothing much to do up here. They wouldn't tell you that!' The negative piece of intelligence appeared to engender a degree of satisfaction.

'So I'm giving you something to do? Is that it?' Corinne said, adding, 'Glad to be of use.' She waved vaguely to the great outdoors. 'Don't you help your mother? With the cabins I mean. There must be other visitors here at this time of the year?'

Louisa pulled her legs up under her on the sofa. 'Oh, we get them coming well before this. Even in the dead of winter. Idiots! But then,' she paused, 'they come up here for privacy. You know – no prying eyes…'

Corinne considered the implication. 'Good idea.' Concentrating on her coffee mug, she waited. The question had to come.

'Game over!' the girl gave in. 'Why are *you* here? Don't say it's for a holiday.'

Corinne scrutinised her visitor. *Friend? Confidante?* She was old enough to be the girl's mother – just – and, her problems were her own.

'I needed a break from work,' she said simply.

'What do you do?'

'I'm the editor in a publishing firm in Edinburgh.' There was no harm in telling her.

'What's it called?'

Too late to hold back, Corinne told her, 'Pallin-McCall.'

'Huh! Keeping it in the family!'

'Pierre Pallin is my father.'

'What's that called…? You know…? Nepotism! That's it!'

'You think so, do you?'

The girl's eyes widened. 'Slave-driver, is he?'

Corinne laughed. 'No. He's not. But we've had a real busy time of it recently. What with getting the company set up on the web.'

'Easy enough,' Louisa scoffed. 'What happened? Did your old man not go for it?'

Corinne moved her head slowly and gazed across the loch before she answered.

'Oh, yes. He went for it all right.'

'So…?' Louisa leaned forward eagerly.

Corinne swallowed the last of her coffee. 'That, Miss Menzies, is another story for another day.'

In one slick move, Louisa was off the sofa. She glared at Corinne. 'That means "get lost" right? Oh, don't you worry. I can take a hint.' Her mug crashed down on the table. 'Ten minutes with me and that's enough for anybody!'

Corinne saw Louisa's face turn sour. A minute before it had been alight at the thought of someone else's problems.

'That's not what I meant,' she told the girl. She flicked a finger towards the two bags lying in the bedroom. 'You can stay if you want. I'm just going to unpack. That's all. Stay. I really don't mind.'

'Huh! Don't do me any favours!' Louisa made for the door. Seconds later it rattled in its wooden frame as it slammed hard behind her.

Corinne shot across the floor. Pulling the door open, she stuck her head out certain that the girl would be lingering sulkily on the walkway waiting to be invited back to resume their nipping banter.

She was wrong.

Louisa Menzies was moving fast. Already at the end of the walkway, she jumped off and made for the trees, her long legs as gracefully frantic as a deer that's heard the click of the gun.

Corinne watched her disappear then reappear between the trees until she reached the turn in the path and vanished completely out of sight.

The image of her visitor lingered as Corinne emptied her bags and the few randomly packed things were put away. She was unsettled by this encounter with the daughter of Ross and Kate Menzies. There was a fragility about that defiant green-eyed gaze as though the girl was waiting, expecting to be cut down, even by a complete stranger. And she invited it.

About one thing, Louisa was right. Just ten minutes in her company had disturbed Corinne. And this her first day. Not what she'd expected and definitely not what she'd come here for.

In the bathroom, half her makeup fitted into the tiny wall cabinet. In the bedroom, she opened one of the drawers in the dressing-table and tipped in the rest. Everything she normally used she'd brought. Crazy! There was no one to see, no need for expensive creams and foundations here. As far as she could tell, at Four Hills, among the high trees and dim paths, she would have no need to put on any sort of face at all.

She shut the drawer and confronted herself in the mirror. Not many lines fanned out from her brown eyes – usually bright – today dull. Brown, thick hair, decent enough skin. Her reflection stared back. Thank God there was no comparing her with the Menzies genus. No contest there. Grabbing her shoulder-length hair she twisted it onto the crown of her head and jammed a vicious, toothed clasp over the top.

Bags emptied, clothes put away, she sank down on the sofa. On the table was a pile of brochures. Starting from the bottom, Corinne fanned them idly through her fingers.

An over-simplified map of the area showing woodland walks thickly and blackly outlined; train times – regular but not that frequent she noticed; a card illustrating a bird with a bold, piercing eye and a small but lethal, dark beak, asking visitors to respect the birds in the area. A sparrowhawk! She recognised it, reasonably positive. Last, on top of the pile, was a welcome from the owners of Four Hills.

Discarding the rest, Corinne examined the square card.

Set out above an invitation to buy provisions, and the usual warnings about the dangers of water (Loch na Duroir, she presumed), was a picture of her hosts.

Ross Menzies stood in the middle, his wife at his right and Louisa at his left.

Corinne's experienced eye picked out several faults. Her keen editor's sense initially offended, she relaxed as she realised, about this, she need do nothing. This was not her problem.

She leaned back with the card in her hand and enjoyed a ruthless analysis. Not well posed, the members of the Menzies family stood square-on, smiling into the camera. Three tall, handsome people. She examined their faces in turn. A trifle forced, the smiles were fixed. Having met Louisa – a very telling ten minutes – she could easily imagine that in the second after the lens clicked shut on the little tableau the girl had sprinted away to avoid any further ignominy.

Corinne realised she could hardly see the figures on the card's shiny, laminated surface.

The sun, beginning to dip over the loch, was fiery gold. It streaked through the cabin, penetrating and brilliantly harsh and caught Corinne's eye. Two seething, pink lava circles appeared on the insides of her closed eyelids.

Annoyed at her own carelessness, she nevertheless smiled. She hadn't done that in a long time, not since she was an unworldly little thing, much too young to know the importance a good pair of Bvlgari.

Certainly here, so close to the water, she'd need them. She glanced down at the table. A present from Noel, she had put them down – where?

Rifling through the pockets in her jacket, she came up with a folded tissue, her train ticket, a pound coin and a printed card from the taxi company she'd taken from home to the train station. No Bvlgari.

The zippered side in one of the bags, empty and leaning drunkenly against the wall in a corner of the bedroom, yielded up the sunglasses case – empty. Her handbag, tipped out impulsively onto the bed, a variety of detritus scattered across the cover but not the one thing she hoped to find.

Corinne reviewed her movements that day. She had worn them on the train journey up here. She was pretty sure she hadn't left them in the taxi. The driver had been very polite, serious, humourless, but polite nonetheless. He'd put her bags in the taxi, and set her, and them, down outside the Four Hills' shop.

The shop! God, why hadn't she thought of that right away? The bags had sat on the floor with her handbag on a chair beside her. But the sunglasses?

With the handbag contents back where they belonged, Corinne convinced herself the Bvlgari would be safe in the drawer of Kate Menzies' shop counter. There was her first sojourn – retracing her steps back the way Ross Menzies had brought her and her meagre luggage.

Grabbing her jacket, she locked the cabin door. Walking purposely, her thoughts centred on finding the Bvlgari. No Noel. No humiliation. No pain. A pair of sunglasses was her priority.

The prevarication failed. Noel was back in her head.

If he could see me now, she thought, trekking along a dirt path, he would have a fit. For him, a 'cliff shelf', smooth and equipped for sun-bathing, in the shade of a friend's villa on the south Italian coast was as rough as he wanted it these days.

Corinne slowed. Her feet dragged in the dirt on the path. If she were honest, she had gone along with him. Aware it was happening she had shut her eyes to what they were becoming. Even her grandparents beautiful house south of Nantes was not enough for him these days. Too out-of-the-way and old-fashioned, he said.

That was the first place he would try. She was glad she hadn't taken off there.

The image of the dusty, old stone house, took hold. Emotion welled up and tightened Corinne's throat.

The thought of having out-manoeuvred Noel was satisfying. It halted the threatening tears as she reached the shop.

The place wasn't big but with an eye to the needs of the cabin visitors, the Menzies had stocked the shelves well.

She passed a chill cabinet full of specialist cheeses and smoked salmon. A good variety but pricey, Corinne noted. In a narrow corner space was a wine-rack. Labels described what would have sat comfortably in a good city restaurant.

In two parallel aisles, customers were taking time to fill the small silver baskets provided.

An elderly, affluently dressed woman with a slightly younger man; a slim shouldered, middle-aged man with soft grey hair and a barely discernable patterned shirt was discussing the merits of bran cakes versus oat cakes with a similarly dressed young companion.

These people were not trying to 'hide away' as Louisa had hinted. They all seemed to Corinne to be quite comfortable to be here, and to be seen. The pricey provisions in the chill cabinet were obviously meant for them, not the passing back-packers.

'Are you all right, Miss Pallin?' The soft voice belonged to Kate Menzies.

Corinne had been standing staring openly at the other shoppers. The elderly woman was waiting patiently for her to move away from the front of the counter.

'Oh! Sorry.' Corinne stepped back. 'It's been rather a long day to be honest.'

Her basket now on the counter, the elderly woman smiled

at Corinne.

Corinne returned the smile.

The woman's purchases paid for, Kate Menzies came from behind the white marble counter.

Corinne said uneasily, 'I was wondering what to have for dinner.' Spontaneous little lies seem to come easily here.

'I put a few things in your fridge. I thought they might do you for tonight. But if you'd rather pick ...' Kate Menzies waved her hand at the rows of shelves. Strands of her copper-red hair had escaped its thick plait and twirled and frizzed about her face. Even more striking than her daughter, Corinne decided.

'Now I think about it, I'm not terribly hungry,' she admitted. 'But thanks for the things. I will use them.' She stayed where she was while Kate went back behind the counter and put the purchases made by the two men, oat cakes decided on, in an unmarked brown paper bag.

'Sorry about that.' Kate was back.

'Actually, while I'm here...' Corinne weighed in before Kate's attention was diverted again. 'It's my sunglasses. I think I may have left them on your table over there when I came in earlier to sign for my keys.' She glanced over at the three chairs and the small table set up in the shop's window.

The area, just a couple of metres square, made a convenient reception.

Corinne went to the table. 'I remember, I was here, and I put my bags down there. My handbag was on this chair... and my sunglasses...?' She spread her hands at Kate Menzies.

'I don't remember seeing them, Miss Pallin.' Kate pulled out the chairs one by one. Her search was meticulous. But from the start it was obvious the sunglasses were not there.

'You've searched the cabin?' she asked but without pausing went on, 'Of course you have.'

Corinne shook her head. 'Oh, it doesn't matter.' Lie! There, she was doing it again! 'My own careless fault.' True.

13

'They won't be far,' Kate Menzies said. 'I'll do a proper search later. When Ross gets back I'll ask him. He'll find them. I'm sure.'

Corinne held up both hands. 'Or they'll more than likely just turn up.' She managed a casual little laugh.

'Oh, but you will get them back.'

Corinne moved away. 'Don't worry about them.' Pointing to the wine-rack, she said, 'Can you recommend a nice bottle of wine? Nothing too grand. A white. I'll just scramble a couple of eggs, I think.'

The subject of the sunglasses was neatly shelved.

The walk back to her cabin didn't take long. After only one trip, Corinne covered the distance like a route travelled often, requiring no conscious thought or effort, which was just as well. Her head still ached.

In the cabin, she fingered the wine bottle. A drink? Not a good idea with a head like a pillow stuffed with a mixture of thistledown and barbed-wire. She knew the cause. There was no getting away from it. As much as she'd tried to keep Noel out of her thoughts, he'd been there at her shoulder throughout the day reminding her of the mess she'd left behind.

Although not cold in the cabin, Corinne rubbed her hands up her arms.

It had been one hell of a day. And telling Louisa Menzies so much about herself was a mistake. Taken off-guard she'd said more than was wise.

Doubts crowded back about this chosen spot. It was too beautiful, much too distracting. Really, what was needed, she reflected, was a faceless hotel, where she could draw the curtains and pick over everything said by Noel, as well as her own – she cringed at the memory – screaming reaction. But hadn't she had cause?

'Miss Pallin?' Ross Menzies' voice reached her in the kitchen.

'I'm here.' These people have a habit of sneaking up on you, she thought. 'What can I do for you, Mr Menzies?' Purposely, she changed her expression. A minute later and he would have found her a snivelling wreck.

'I brought these.' A soft spectacles case was held out for her inspection. 'If you could make do with them until we find your own...'

Corinne accepted the case and emptied the sunglasses out onto her hand. The thick black plastic frames had brown lenses. 'You didn't have to do that. It's very kind. Thank you.'

'Will they do?' He was waiting.

'I'm sure they'll be fine.' Conscious of his eyes on her, she unfolded the legs of the sunglasses and slid them on. 'Perfect!' Head up, she faced him through the bright brown lenses. Impossible for her to imagine this man wearing designer shades.

'Good. Kate was worried.'

'Is there anything else, Mr Menzies? It's... I've got a headache. I think I need food and an early night.' She slipped the sunglasses off.

'Well, like I said, it's quiet here. Get a good night's rest and we'll see you in the morning. Don't forget to lock your door. And, please, it's Ross.'

Unmoving, he waited for her to take this in. 'Right... Ross,' she said lightly. 'I'm Corinne.' Mistake, she thought instantly. He knew her name, now she'd just given him use of it.

'Goodnight, then.' Ross Menzies left the cabin without repeating her name.

Corinne shoved the sunglasses back in their case and laid it down within easy reach on the windowsill. The unexpected gift had distracted her just enough to get a grip on her emotions. Never having suffered from self-pity, she was not a maudlin type normally. However, her present situation was far from normal.

Everybody needs a good cry occasionally, she told herself.

But because of Ross Menzies, that moment, for her, was past.

Corinne woke several times in the night. She lay on her back listening to the moving branches on the huge pines close behind the cabin. The soft shushing was like night-time traffic in the city after rain. In the darkness, she morphed the two. This sound she didn't mind.

Once she thought she heard the murmur of voices. Feeling for her mobile, she flicked it open. Nearly three. Pitch black, anyone out in that would have a hard time moving easily. She slid further under the covers. During the day it had been warm, now it was as cold as a winter's night. The bed, however, was surprisingly comfortable.

Her last thought before she slept was that it was raining. Steady drops drummed on the wooden roof above her head. To Corinne, it sounded right. It should be raining in this place she'd found as her hideaway.

Corinne slept late – until ten.

In the little dressing-table mirror, she examined her face. After the rain started last night she'd fallen into a deep sleep. This morning it showed; smooth skin, wide eyes – and the barbed-wire in her temples gone.

Her breakfast included the butter left by Kate Menzies in the fridge. This was a place where a normal diet held no place, she reckoned, adding a little conscientious rider: a wander around the loch would walk it off.

Lacing up her trainers, she heard voices. Unmistakeable thin, high pitched childish tones. Grabbing her jacket and the pseudo Bvlgari, she pulled the cabin door shut behind her and locked it.

At the loch edge, several people were on the move. In the distance a couple of small boats, tied to a wooden jetty on the far side of the loch in the opposite direction to the

Menzies' shop, bobbed effortlessly on the water.

The childish voices had stopped. Like yesterday, the general air of remote quietness pervaded everything. There was nobody near her cabin.

In her right pocket she put the crude little visitors' map. It was simple, the thick black line encouraging you to follow the paths without deviating.

Sticking the sunglasses in her other pocket, she strode to the path. It curved its way through the woods with the loch out of sight on her left, half-hidden behind a thin barrier of trees.

In the cool, green gloom, Corinne was very aware of the solitude.

To her right, a branch high up in a tree snapped making her jump as it fell to the ground. Laughing at herself, she listened but could hear nothing more than her own feet scraping the dirt of the path.

The feeling of isolation built and she began to move faster. Again an unidentified missile hit the ground behind her. She swung round. Nothing. Nobody.

She began to hurry, her steps increasing to a comic power-walk.

Breathing fast, she slowed when she came up behind several cabins built just metres from the water's edge like her own.

Nobody in evidence, the sight of the buildings – habitation at least – reassured her. Calmer, and her leg muscles already starting to ache, she walked on.

Her breath, and her reasoning, was back by the time the path skirted out of the woods just above a little cove. Eager to get out from the trees and into the light again, she almost ran down to the edge of the loch.

The sun, trying hard to come from behind a bank of pale, grey cloud, warmed the air. Her jacket came off and she sat down on one of the huge boulders that seemed as if they had been placed there for that very purpose. She wondered at their authenticity.

Would anyone take the trouble to enhance a place like this? It was all too perfect.

Inhale, exhale, she drew the fresh air deep into her lungs. After her mad dash, she was hot and sweaty. Panic hadn't been far away. Idiot! In her heart she knew the fear had come from the vulnerability which was now, so unexpectedly, part of her.

She got up and wandered to the water's edge. The dark surface of the loch shimmered like black silk. She leaned down. The cold expression reflected back was hers – emotionless and vacant, like a death mask when all strife is past.

It shocked her. I'm alive, not moribund; she wanted to shout at her image. Inside I'm strong, confident, and hopeful! Noel, you will not destroy that!

She retreated back from the water. The sudden wash of tears had her reaching in her jacket pocket for the sunglasses. She slid them on. Bvlgari they were not, but they did the trick. They shut out the cruel dazzle, the reflections.

Shock seeping away, a feeling of peace washed over her. She gazed out across the smooth, flat loch. Where better to get her head around what Noel had done to her than right here, a million miles from real life?

CHAPTER TWO

Her body bent forward, Corinne sat very still on the boulder at the loch side.

An ache, intense, gripped her stomach, rose up and settled near her heart. Noel's image was vivid to the point of near paralysis.

Dark hair, blue eyes, with a deep guttural voice; when she first met him he was coarse and tactless, getting by on his personable looks. But there was more to him. Right off, she saw it. As did the agent that brought him to her. They'd come across a talent worth nurturing.

His first work was well received, tagged as more than mediocre. The second came with the confidence of one already under his belt, carrying with it the inviting aroma of success. The third was even better.

Media and magazine exposure called for, his agent insisted on a make-over. Subtle, it worked. The crass, coarse man disappeared. The brash, defensive voice was tutored, the right phrases learned, compliments carefully memorised for use on every occasion with the enhanced blue-eye twinkle.

This *creation* – and fourth book – established him. The reading public took to this polished man and an *affair* – Corinne could think of no better word for it – began with his voracious readers.

While this went on, Noel Anderton fell in love with his publisher.

Corinne didn't take long to make up her mind either. They weren't teenagers, both had been here before.

Working side by side, they fell easily into a world of celebrity and money that was impossible to draw back from once the gates were nudged open.

Ian McCall, her father's partner, was openly sceptical about it lasting. 'The piper's got to be paid,' was his prosaic take on it.

Corinne's father agreed. That *she* would be the one to pay the price was his fear.

'You... you have your own career to think around.' His English was almost, but not quite, perfect. The precise, hard edged diction was usually the only thing that gave him away as a resettled Frenchman. This time, it was his concern which tripped him up.

She smiled patiently, sure of what was coming. It did.

'Do not forget that the company will one day be your own,' he reminded her. 'I want that. So does Ian. If there is the need, we can buy him out. But I think there will be no need.'

She had heard it all before, the passing of time smudging over the harsh reality with a romantic finger.

1943. Ian McCall had been hidden from the Germans by her grandparents when trying to make his way back home to Scotland.

Her grand-mother liked to tell the story of how they were confused because he wanted to get to Scotland and not to England. Nevertheless, they were not much older than he and wanted to help. For weeks they hid him well. They played a dangerous game keeping him safe. But they managed it. Eventually, he had been smuggled in the black of night onto the back of a cart then a small boat. He reached the south coast of England with three other men, two Englishmen and another Scot. He had made it.

1945, and the unholy war came to its end.

Three years later Ian McCall travelled back to France to thank the couple who saved his life.

'You must all come to Edinburgh. I've a wee printing and publishing business set up there. It's not much the now, but I've great plans for it.' He invited the Pallins to bring their young son Pierre to visit him. But money was tight, travel not really on the cards.

Five years went by before the Pallins accepted Ian McCall's offer. Meantime, letters went back and forth. Ian added to his sketchy French while the Pallins tried their best at English, courtesy of Pierre's school-master.

The Scottish accent threw them more than just a little when at last they arrived at Waverley train station in Edinburgh to find Ian McCall waiting eagerly on the platform.

Totally different from their pastoral country life. the Pallins loved the old grey city.

After that first visit, the teenage Pierre came back every chance he got. He worked long hours with Ian in the business to help pay for his keep.

It came as no great surprise, the day Pierre told Ian he wanted to stay in Scotland.

'Are you sure about this?' Guilt swamped Ian McCall. The Pallins had one son. These were people he thought of now as his own family for he had none other. Grown so close, he could well understand how they would feel to lose their boy.

Ian thought hard and long.

Reaction from the Pallins was no less than he expected. Pain at the thought of letting their son go; joy at Ian's proposal. He would bring young Pierre into his business full time as his assistant if the boy was willing to work hard.

The reason for this generous offer was accepted by all concerned. Nobody ever put it into words.

Jean-Luc and Genevieve Pallin came to Edinburgh one more time to see their son settled into the little attic room of the tall Edinburgh building that was to be Pierre's home for the next ten years.

'It is what I want to do, Maman.' He kissed her tear-wet face.

In the cramped space accessed by a steep, worn staircase, he made them the first meal of many he would rustle up on the tiny gas cooker.

Ian McCall was there.

They laughed, and remembered, and tried to stop crying while they ate the slightly singed meal the young man served up.

Ten years passed before Pierre Pallin found the right girl to make him his supper.

Jean Fotheringham was a pretty primary-school teacher. On a wet Wednesday afternoon, she came into the printing office with a pile of neatly hand-written pages of poetry, put together by her fifth year pupils. They needed to be printed up to sell for school funds.

Pierre gave Jean a good deal on the printing. Later he delivered the box of booklets in person.

He was nearly thirty years old. Until then life had been good and without any ties. But after meeting Jean only twice he realised that this woman was the one.

Jean told him she was happy as she was, not ready to give up her teaching post to settle down.

Pierre Pallin was not a man easily put off. A year later, Jean was pregnant. She handed in her notice to the school and married him.

'I suppose it was meant to be,' Corinne's mother once told her.

Now, gazing out over the water of the loch, the faces of her mother and father came easily into Corinne's mind. It's true what they say, she thought. Things can go too smoothly. Just when life's plot is unfolding very nicely, the chapter abruptly comes to an end.

Not exactly true, that analogy. She knew, had known for years, her father wanted to go back to France, to the place he had been born. His parents, still alive, were too old to travel nowadays. Always happy to see any family who could spare the time, the old couple never complained if a visit had to be cancelled or cut short. There was always another day they said. Again, not strictly true. Their time was fast running out.

The miles she put between her and Noel, Corinne wished could have led her to them. But it was too much to put them through, all the tears and turmoil.

They would vigorously deny that of course, with Grandma Gena throwing up her hands and Jean-Luc nodding as always, agreeing.

But in her hurry to get away fast Corinne had gone north, not south. One phone call and Noel would find out she was not in France – if he bothered to make the call. Probably he imagined she was still in the city, near her home and her office, and him.

It's ironic, she thought. Just about to be handed the business, she couldn't stand to be around the place. Noel had a lot to answer for.

Viciously, Corinne skimmed a stone across the smooth water of the loch. All at once in her head, verbatim, that un-rescindable conversation – was it just yesterday morning. The moment her stable world – devious world – started to erupt.

Out of the blue it had come, 'You know you can buy a huge house right now in L.A. for just three million dollars.' Noel's face was animated, his cool blue eyes not so much looking at her as through her, as he pictured this fancied residence.

It was the first she'd heard of it. 'Who wants to live in L.A?'

'We do! We could move there, what… within a month if we got a move on. The lifestyle out there is just great.'

'Noel, our life *here* is pretty good.'

'Now's the time we should be striking out. Think about it. While things are about to change in the business, it would fit.'

'No!' Corinne contradicted him. 'Not change. You've got that wrong. Dad does want to give up his part in it soon. That's no secret. But you know fine he wants me to take it over. Uncle Ian's share too. Well, in time anyway.'

She glanced at him. 'You know all this, Noel. Nothing's *changed*. That's always been their plan for me.'

His enthusiasm waned. 'Don't I know it! And me? What does the great Pierre Pallin want me to do? Stay in the back-office scribbling away so that the money keeps rolling in?'

Corinne let that pass. Noel's study was a far cry from being a "back-office".

'We've got everything money could buy right here,' she pointed out. 'We don't have to move anywhere.'

Noel's expression turned sour. With no answer, his eyes slid away from her. Abruptly the topic was dropped.

The disagreement had delayed Corinne. She'd rushed away to a meeting with her father and Ian McCall at their offices on the far side of Edinburgh leaving Noel at home. Re-writes were waiting. He wanted to get on with them, he told her curtly.

'Fine. I won't make it back for lunch but I'll be home in time for dinner,' she promised him.

Her meeting at the office never went ahead. Ian McCall felt under the weather so with nothing pressing on the agenda the meeting was cancelled until later in the week.

Freed up, Corinne decided to pack up for the day. A surprise for Noel, she would make him his favourite pasta lunch and see if she could smooth over their earlier spat. Noel, behind his cool patina, was a sulker.

Fifteen minutes in her car, got her home.

In her usual parking space alongside Noel's black Porsche was another car. A silver Merc. At first she didn't recognise it. Then it struck her. Lynne Robertson, the IT consultant drafted into Pallin-McCall to get the business launched on the internet.

When it came to business, Corinne and Lynne got along well enough. Lynne was eight, maybe ten, years younger. Good at what she did, intelligent did not describe her. Ambitious, yes. They spent hours together in the office but there was never any rapport between them to kick-start any sort of friendship.

And Lynne never visited Corinne at home.

Parking her car next to Lynne's, she walked around the side of the house, through the iron gates to the rear.

As always, she hesitated for a second when she saw it.

Hidden behind black tinted glass, the lower level was one room running the entire length of the house. One end was the kitchen while a garden room spread through the other half. It faced out over the large flat lawn surrounded by hedges and trees.

Their favourite room in the house, this was where they spent windy days, or cold, winter Sunday afternoons with the heating going full blast. Purposely, there was no desk or computer, only a small television in the corner that Noel liked to have on, always with the sound down low but glancing constantly at it.

Corinne pulled on the sunken handle of the door. The glass panel slid silently, and she stepped inside.

She got no further.

On the wide sofa lay two people. Two naked people.

Bare legs twisting together, they heaved and shoved against each other, frenzied groans emitting from them both.

Corinne stared.

Noel's face was hidden. The woman's long blond hair swung in waves down over his head. But it was *his* hands that moved, grasping and pulling on the pale skin of her back.

Like a player in the children's game of statues, Corinne stood motionless. Unable to move, her feet seemed glued to the very shiny floor.

Urgent grunts reached her from the writhing pair. A ludicrous thought came into her head; how did she let them know she was there? Perhaps she should cough politely... or maybe just scream.

'Jesus...!' Noel saw her. Jumping up, he shoved Lynne away.

She lay back naked, sprawled and obvious. Her hand behind her head, she smiled across at Corinne, baring a row of unnaturally even, white teeth.

Noel reached for his trousers. 'Babe, this is nothing... nothing!' He gave a perplexed little grin. 'Listen to me...'

His words acted like a release on Corinne's locked senses. Forcing herself across the floor, she moved past Noel and took hold of Lynne Robertson's arm. Revulsion swept over her at the feel of the warm, moist skin beneath her fingers.

'Get out of my house.' She dragged at the naked woman. 'Now! Get out now!'

'My clothes...' Lynne struggled to her feet. 'Noel, do you want me to go?' She stood boldly between them.

Grabbing her clothes, Noel thrust them hurriedly at Lynne. 'Go on,' he nodded. 'You'd better go.'

Holding on to his arm Lynne slipped her legs into her trousers and zipped them up. She stood, her bare breasts glistening with sweat, her underwear in her hand.

'Can I use your bathroom?' She glanced at Corinne as she stuck her feet into her high-heeled shoes.

Corinne searched about her. The jacket of Lynne's suit hung on the back of a chair. She whipped it off and threw it at Lynne. 'No. You can't.'

'Corinne...' Noel appealed.

Fingers shaking, Corinne pointed to the open door. 'Get out,' she ordered again.

Wrestling into her jacket, Lynne Robertson picked up her bag and walked past Corinne out into the garden, her underwear still in her hand.

The following hour was one Corinne wished she could highlight, press delete and erase from her memory.

When she went over it, her stomach churned and she felt like throwing up.

Noel used every ounce of his wiles on her.

'I was gutted that you didn't want to come out to L.A. with me.' He came close and covered her hands with his.

Corinne flinched. Minutes before, his fingers had been caressing another woman. The soft feel of Lynne's skin was still on her fingers. She shuddered.

Noel felt it. He backed away. 'Why don't you go and make

us coffee. I'll be with you in a second.' Like it was just an ordinary day.

Corinne walked to the kitchen. Had she dreamed the last five minutes? She filled the kettle and listened intently to the hum of the water as it started to heat. Suddenly, light-headed, she grabbed a kitchen stool and sat down. This was real.

'Cory,' dressed, Noel was beside her. 'I don't know what I was thinking.' He hung his head for a second before lifting his eyes to hers. 'I was hurt I suppose.'

Corinne met his bright blue eyes, as contrite as she had ever seen them.

'Why, Noel? Why? We have one argument. The next minute you're in bed with someone else. Tell me. When did we become that shallow?'

'I was gutted! You wouldn't even talk to me about moving to L.A. It's like what I want doesn't mean much to you anymore.'

'That's rubbish! And you know it.' Corinne lowered her voice, 'I suppose Lynne listened to you?' Tight as a drum, she was trembling.

Noel threw her an injured glance.

'You're always too busy nowadays for *us*!' he accused her. 'How many times in the last year did I want us to get away? How many, Corinne?' He went on the attack. 'I'll bet you don't even know.'

'I take it you do? You've been keeping score? Tell me then. Come on, Noel,' she challenged. 'Tell me how many times.'

Noel moved uncomfortably on his stool. Leaning his elbows on the counter, he avoided Corinne's eye.

Corinne persisted. 'Go on! Tell me, Noel. I want to know. What's the count?'

'Okay, so you've been busy,' he conceded. 'Well, so have I. Working my guts out over that last book.' Fired up now, he glared at her and the flood gates opened.

27

'Remember last June? Last June, I wanted to get away. Louis Togniri offered us his yacht in the Greek islands. Just for a month. That's all I wanted. Four weeks!' He was shouting now. 'But oh, no! We had too much on, you said!'

Spreading his hand out wide, he began to tick off his fingers one at a time with alarming precision.

'That was one. Then South Africa had to be forgotten about because of the bloody book festival in Berlin. *You* had to be there. After that, Christmas, we couldn't get away because your grandparents wanted to see you.'

'So you *have* been keeping count.' Corinne nodded slowly. 'You could have come with me to France last Christmas and to Berlin. Not to was your choice. Did you take a note of that?' She shivered. The tears that threatened were stemmed by rising anger.

Noel scowled. 'There were plenty of other times besides when you just swanned off.'

Suddenly, Corinne snapped. 'You managed to amuse yourself no doubt!'

'Yes! I did!'

'Who with? Lynne?'

'Awe, Cory …'

'It's a straight-forward, simple enough question, Noel. I need a simple answer.'

Again he avoided eye contact. 'Yes.'

Shivers started in Corinne's legs and this time she felt them travel all the way up her body. She swallowed hard. There was a sour taste in her mouth. She'd put the question and gotten her answer. A quick calculation was called for.

'She's been with us for, what, eighteen months.'

'Yes, I guess. A little over a year maybe.'

'You and her…? From the start?' Her heart was thumping hard.

'More or less.' He waved his hand as if to erase what had been said. 'But it was nothing, baby. I love *you*. It's not the same with her. That was just a bit…'

'Don't you dare!' Corinne stared at him. 'Don't say it!'

'Cory, I needed you. You didn't seem to want me. Lynne wasn't with anybody. We just clicked. It just sort of happened.'

'Please, Noel, don't say anything else. I don't want to hear it.' Outwardly calm, her blood raced through her veins threatening to explode. 'In fact I want you to leave. Go to a hotel, anywhere, I don't care. I just need to be by myself.'

'If that's what you want.' He agreed, adding that he would be back tomorrow. They were a partnership, he reminded her. They could get past this. He loved her, he said. Couldn't she see that?

Corinne shifted on her cold stone seat. *Couldn't she see that?* Right then he'd begun to turn it back on her, chucking off any responsibility for his actions. Noel had developed a genius for easing himself out of sticky situations. For that she could thank his agent who'd taught him only too well how to wriggle out of uncomfortable spots.

He'd tried it on her.

'Corinne, I need more of your time. More of you.' An overnight bag packed, Noel was ready to leave. 'When your father and mother settle back in France, there's going to be just the two of us. Ian doesn't count. He's too old. And we don't have any kids.'

Corinne clenched her teeth. Did he know? No. There was no way he could have found out. It was just a handy stick to prod her with; he didn't want kids.

'Not now, Noel,' she said wearily. 'Please, just go.'

'Right. Whatever you want. But all I'm saying is that the time is right for a move.' He bent to kiss the front of her head and, too tired to fight, she let him, and he left.

For almost an hour there was silence in the kitchen. When Corinne at last climbed down from the tall stool, she felt cold and bloodless and exhausted. She made herself a second cup of coffee and stood with it in her hand gazing out through the tinted window to the garden. Clicking the lock, she pulled on the handle to make sure it slid into place. The door was solid. She hesitated then pulled on the handle one more time before walking slowly upstairs.

In the bedroom, she brought out her suitcases and laid them on the bed, side-by-side. She opened the lids and considered their empty interiors. Usually she knew her destination and what she would need for the trip. Everything would be fresh from the cleaners, hung on the front of the wardrobe by their daily woman, Emma, ready for her to do her packing. Energised by what lay ahead, she would be excited.

Not this time.

On the edge of her dressing table, Corinne had set down her coffee mug. As she swung round, her elbow caught the handle.

She saw it fall and tried to grab it but only managed to get warm coffee over her forearm. The mug somersaulted clumsily in the air before hitting the floor. In one piece, it rolled on the soft carpet spreading an unforgiving deep brown stain over the pale cream wool.

It was too much.

Corinne burst into tears.

Face contorted, she slid to the floor and gave way as she had rarely done in her life. Heartache times only: twelve years old and her dog Sammy died; three years ago, the day after her visit to the clinic…

Finally, it was over.

She stretched out her legs and rested her back against the side of the bed. Making no attempt to get up or to retrieve the coffee mug, she sat bemused, staring down at the sopping brown patch of carpet.

There are things, she thought, that just can't be undone.

Slowly she got to her feet. In the bathroom she washed her arm and splashed cold water over her face.

Burying her head in the towel, she patted her face dry.

Knowing her skin was red and her eyes blotchy, the mirror was avoided. Deliberately, she put her back to it.

Faceless, that's exactly what I need to be, she thought. I have to get to a place where nobody knows me, or Noel, or anything about us.

The idea spurred her into action.

She piled the three smart suitcases, each one inside its slightly bigger match, back into the cupboard. A couple of soft leather overnight bags were brought out in their place.

With no thought of preference, she opened her wardrobe doors and picked out several pairs of trousers and shirts and scooped up a pile of neatly folded sweaters. She grabbed a bundle of underwear and shoved it in a corner of one of the bags. Make-up went into a plastic bag and a couple of bottles fetched from the bathroom she put in one zippered side pocket.

Minutes later she was done.

Picking up the two packed bags by the handles she weighed them, one in each hand. Not too heavy; she could manage them on her own.

The taxi drew up at the house ten minutes after Corinne called for it.

It manoeuvred its way slowly back through the traffic to get her to Waverley Station at nine minutes to three. As soon as she got on board she noticed, thankfully, the train was only half full.

Placing the bags on two empty seats, one beside and one across from her, secured a relatively isolated space for the two-and-a-bit-hours it would take to journey north.

Four minutes after she got on, the train left the platform.

For a couple of miles it moved slowly, easing its route out parallel with the city, past Haymarket, through the suburbs, and on, away from home and Noel.

There was a moment of panic as towns and villages started to thin out. What was she doing? Alone, distancing herself from everything she knew?

The sun flickered in through the dusty window. She shut her eyes tight.

If only it were that easy to shut out the sight of a naked Lynne Robertson.

'Ticket, please.'

Corinne's eyes flew open.

The black clad, bulky figure of the guard stood beside her.

She saw him eyeing the two bags taking up space on the empty seats. 'Oh! Yes. I've got it here.' She searched through her handbag before remembering she'd put the ticket into her jacket pocket freeing up her hands to carry her bags along the platform.

'Here it is.' The orange and white ticket, and a pair of sunglasses, was pulled from her pocket. 'Sorry.'

Why was she apologising?

He reached out for the ticket, muttering under his breath what might have been 'Thank you.' He nodded through the window at the speeding landscape, his lips parted with a knowing smile. 'Looks like we're going to get good holiday weather for a change.' With a jerk of his pen he scored across her ticket and it was handed back.

Holiday! She should put him right. *Escape!* That was nearer the truth.

Corinne watched his broad, black-clad back as he moved down the aisle. Checking tickets, he distributed irrelevant remarks and information, earning pleasantries in return.

What was wrong with her? She should have answered his friendly chatter. Life goes on, heartache camouflaged by smiles and touché éclat.

At the far end of the carriage, the automatic doors opened, the guard went through and disappeared.

Putting on her sunglasses, Corinne leaned back and closed her eyes.

The moving red electronic prompt half way down the

carriage warned Corinne well in advance that the next stop was Blairkeld – her destination.

On the station platform there was no sign of a ticket collector. No evidence of *any* station staff. Nobody was waiting to get on the train and she was the only person to get off.

A space in the half-barrel plant tubs along the side of the wooden fence led her to the exit. With no turnstile or ticket barrier in operation alighting here was undemanding. At the same time it was unsettling that no one noted the comings and goings of passengers.

A concession to strangers, a small neatly painted sign, shaped like an arrow, pointed to the gap in the fence, telling travellers which was the *Way Out.*

On the other side of the fence, a very old car was parked up on a piece of waste ground. The ancient white Rover had a square cardboard sign in the back window professing its function as Taxi.

Corinne went to the driver's door.

'Do you know Four Hills?' She glanced through the open window at the driver reading a newspaper. 'I'm not sure exactly where or how far it is.'

The driver closed his newspaper. Very carefully, he folded it into a neat square and put it on the seat beside him. Ruddy faced, he stretched his fleshy eyelids wide before answering her.

'Four Hills? Aye. It's not far.' He nodded at the two bags at her feet. 'You'll not be wanting to walk with those, mind you.' He opened the door and got out.

Corinne backed up. 'No, I don't want to walk,' she told him. 'I don't know where it is, that's all.'

'Well,' he said, 'that's what I'm here for.' He opened the back door of the car, picked up her bags and placed them on the far side of the seat.

'In you get.' His hand on the door, he stood waiting.

'Thank you.' Corinne eased herself in onto the thickly

padded, leather seat. The interior of the vehicle smelled faintly of old-fashioned piny after-shave left too long in the bottle. No other taxi she had ever ridden in enveloped you like this one. The door facia was polished birds-eye maple with handgrips and mountings all in the same cream coloured leather, not as cracked as that covering the seats.

Climbing in behind the wheel, the driver repositioned the rear-view mirror. 'There, that's better. I can see you now.'

Corinne met his eye in the small rectangular mirror. 'Are you the only taxi?'

He nodded. 'There's not much call for taxis up here.'

Obviously not. Corinne glanced out of the window as they started to move. What she judged was a main road, deserted, veered away in the opposite direction to where the taxi was headed. She leaned forward to make sure the driver heard.

'Is Four Hills near the town? Near Blairkeld?'

'Near? Well... not near, no, I wouldn't say that. Mind you, not far neither. No. And it's not big enough to be called a town,' he informed her. His head came up and he spoke to her through the mirror. 'To the folk here it's the village.'

Corinne fell back on the mounds of creaking leather. 'I see.' What else was there to say?

'If you're any sort of a walker, you'll make it up to the village.' He sounded doubtful.

Corinne felt irked. Obviously, you had to be half decent on your feet in country like this. 'It's just I thought Four Hills would be part of the... village.'

Again he flicked his eyes up at the mirror. 'No. No. Four Hills – that's the cabins. They're dotted along the top end of the loch and halfway down yon far side.' His eyes were back on the road. 'The far side from the village, that is.'

'Ah, right.'

'If you've got yourself a place on that side it'll take you longer to get there.' Again his head jerked up. 'Mind, I don't take the car any further than the shop. The Four Hills shop, that is. After that you're on your own.'

CHAPTER THREE

Voices penetrated Corinne's day-dream, catapulting her back to the present.

Relieved to escape her thoughts, she none the less resented the intrusion.

Shading her eyes, she gazed over the loch. No boats were out on the water, no fishermen on the shore, nobody in the cove but her.

Up off her hard stone seat, she stretched her arms skyward, easing her back. Despite the morning sun warming her face, the rest of her body felt cold. She stuck her hands, curled tightly, into her jacket pockets, immediately glad of the warmth.

Again, this time behind her, muffled movement and voices grew louder. The smack of a stick whacked off a tree trunk was unmistakeable, bringing a high pitched girlish protest. A tussle of words, indistinct but passionate, drifted down to the cove before dying away as if the protagonists had agreed a truce and hostilities ceased.

Hearing nothing more, Corinne thought they – whoever *they* were – had walked the other way away from the loch and deep into the woods. She bent and picked up a smoky blue pebble. Aiming long, she launched it far out into the loch. A single muted *glug* resulted as it hit the water and sank into oblivion, its legacy, beautiful concentric rings of water, spreading slowly across the glassy surface. Success of sorts!

She stepped nearer the water's edge. Stones, all sizes, each a fraction of a shade different in colour from its neighbour, lay at her feet. She searched diligently. Most were smooth and silky to the touch while the rest were heavy and coarse as granite, their edges softened by the millennia. She gathered a selection in her hand, chose one, and drew back her arm and let fly.

Shorter travelled than the first, the effect proved not so impressive. But the simple action once more was overwhelmingly satisfying. Her next attempt went further. The precisely formed circles grew, expanded, and slowly disappeared, gratifying but fleeting.

The stones juggled back and forth against each other in her hand. They felt good. Tactile, she thought. Funny word, tactile. An artist's word. Artistic talent was not in her make-up. As a child, nobody could recognise what the drawings she brought home from school were meant to be. The nearest she could claim to having created anything was her design of the garden room…

The stones dropped from her hand. For a time she had forgotten the reason she was here. Remembering, the sickening feeling of disbelief engulfed her.

'What do you think this is?' Young and confident, the boy's voice came from close behind her.

Corinne swung her head as a grey-green scaly creature was placed on her arm. There was no time to see it closely. It scuttled up to her shoulder with lighting speed.

'Ahh…' She stayed still. 'I don't know. What is it?'

Two children stood, one on either side of her.

The girl cupped her hands together and reached out. She lifted the creature off Corinne's shoulder, sending a look of disgust in the boy's direction.

'It's only a lizard. I call them lazies. Lazy lizards. All they do is sun-bathe the whole day.' Her expression changed and she glared at the boy. 'You shouldn't have picked him up, Freddy. It's not hot enough, yet.'

Corinne began to breathe normally again.

Her hands clasped in a ball, the girl carried the tiny creature to the tree-line in the rays of the sun. 'Freddy, help me. Pick that flat stone up. I'll put him under there,' she instructed.

Freddy followed orders.

Opening her hands, the girl set the lizard down.

Freed, the creature darted away as Freddy let the stone fall back in place.

'Freddy!' The girl pushed him roughly.

The boy stumbled backward, executing a neat little skip to retain his balance.

'It'll be okay,' he said. 'They're hard to kill.'

'You'd better not have killed it! I'll tell Mummy!'

Freddy faced Corinne, the lizard, dead or alive, apparently no longer of any interest. 'Who are you? Are you staying in a cabin?'

'Yes. My name's Corinne.'

Already, Freddy had lost interest. Picking up a pebble, he bounced it several times in his palm.

'I'm Lucy,' the girl said serenely as though the little contretemps over the lizard had never taken place. 'Freddy's my brother. I'm older than him by four years, one week and six days. That makes all the difference you know – I'm the oldest. *I* have to take care of *him.*'

Corinne watched the two children. Lucy was a good half-head bigger than her brother. Both had the same mousy-brown hair and pale hazel eyes and, even this early in the year, their skin was sun kissed.

'How old *are* you?' Corinne asked.

It was Lucy who answered. 'I'm almost twelve. Freddy's only eight… nearly. Our birthday is in the same month. I'm the eleventh of June and he's the twenty fourth.' She gazed openly at Corinne. 'We always have a birthday party. We share it. You can come if you want to.'

'Well, I might not be here then. But thank you. That sounds fun. Where is it you live?'

'Told you!' Freddy shouted at his sister. 'Told you she'd want to know everything!'

Lucy ignored the outburst.

'Mummy and Daddy run the craft centre. It's not far from the village. Do you want to see?' Moving the pebbles into little ridges around the toes of her trainers, the girl was staring at Corinne waiting to hear the answer to her invitation.

'Not today, thanks. Today I'm just going to get my bearings. You know, find out where the paths lead. Maybe another time.' Corinne dusted her hands together. 'I think I'll get back now.' She glanced at the water. 'You'll be all right here, will you? You and your brother?'

Freddy threw a stone high in the air over the loch.

All three of them watched its descent. It came down a good way from the shoreline hitting the water cleanly. At once the smooth surface was transformed into one huge spreading circle followed by lesser but still impressive rings.

'See?' he said. 'You've got to aim it high so's it comes down straight and fast. Whoosh… That's how you get big rings. *You* need to practise.'

'Yes. I guess I do.' She watched him jettison another stone. 'But you're good at it,' she nodded, and the mysterious noises which made her scamper like a scared rabbit through the woods earlier suddenly made sense. She had not been as alone as she'd thought.

'Wait 'til you see me swimming.' Freddy did a dry land crawl. 'Can you swim?'

Lucy gave her brother another push. 'He thinks he's good at everything. But he's not.' She glanced at Corinne. 'We'll walk back with you if you like?'

Corinne smiled. 'Won't your parents be wondering where you've got to?'

Lucy ran nimbly up to the tree-line. 'We'll tell them when we get back.' Turning, she smiled sweetly at Corinne. 'Then they'll know.'

Freddy walked, arms outstretched like a tight-rope walker, heel-to-toe, heel-to-toe, in a wobbly line beside Corinne. Less than a minute passed and the lure of the woods was too much for him. He shot away into the undergrowth. Seconds later he was back, a piece of pine branch in his hands. Stripping it clean of needles, he was left with a short, limp stem. Disappointed, he threw it into the trees and was off again.

'He's never at peace,' Lucy confided to Corinne.

Corinne smiled at this quote from an adult, as yet unknown to her.

They walked in silence, the little girl occasionally picking up a leaf or a stone to examine it before returning it to the exact spot where she found it.

'Have you got any children?' Lucy picked up an empty bird's shell; delicate creamy-white, one end broken and jagged where the chick had struggled to hatch out into the world.

She balanced it precisely in the centre of her hand and continued walking.

Corinne swallowed hard. *I should have but I haven't.* 'No,' she said.

'Haven't you got a husband either?'

Corinne glanced at the girl. The innocent hazel eyes were watching her.

'Yes, I have a husband.'

'He's not come on holiday with you, has he.' The empty shell was not put back; it was being transported carefully along on Lucy's outstretched hand.

Corinne stopped. 'How do you know that?'

'Louisa told us. Well, she told Daddy and I heard.'

Just then Freddy bounded out from the trees. He caught at Lucy's arm. 'I'm starving!'

The two children stared at Corinne.

It dawned on Corinne that her cabin was only metres away. Two smart kids had manoeuvred her very nicely into a corner.

'Well… I suppose…' she hesitated.

'We have to go.' Lucy said. 'Our sandwiches will be ready.' Her outstretched hand folded over the delicate shell. Fingers curled tight, her knuckles strained white for several seconds. Slowly, she opened her hand. Tiny crushed fragments of white shell were stuck to her soft pink palm.

Carefully she brushed them off and pulled at Freddy's jumper. 'See you!' she threw at Corinne.

And they were away.

Corinne realised she hadn't thought about Noel for over an hour. The kids had done that at least. Progress? The point of being here was to think the whole thing through; turn it over in her head until she made sense of her situation, or at least came to terms with it.

Her lunch was unappetising. Coffee mug in one hand, she picked up her phone with the other.

Since getting on the train at Waverley Station, it had been switched off. Checking to find that people wanted to know where she was had been purposely postponed.

She flicked it on.

The screen glowed iridescent in her hand. Immediately, guilt struck. A good number of missed calls. Texts had followed. She recognised the senders, or most of them.

Scrolling down she stopped on a number and pressed. Seconds later the familiar voice filled her head.

'Cherie?'

'Yes, Papa. It's me.'

'You are all right? Where are you?' Her father's voice was inquisitive although not insistent.

'I'm fine. I needed space, that's all. I'm sorry if I worried you and Maman.'

'Noel said you argued.' He was letting her know he was aware of the facts.

Corinne closed her eyes. Not all of them, if she knew Noel.

'Look, I'm not far away. Tell Maman not to worry about me. I'm very comfortable.'

'Do you want her to come to you?'

'No. Not just now. I need to be on my own. Just for a little while. Will you explain to her?'

'Is it bad, Cherie? This rift between you and Noel?'

'I don't really want to talk about it. Not right now. I just need to think things through.' With an effort she brightened her tone. 'Am I permitted a couple of days off? You and Uncle Ian won't do anything drastic without me, will you?'

'If that is what you want, you must take the time you need. We will see to things here. Do not worry. Everything will be taken care of.'

This time the guilt consumed Corinne. She had downed tools without as much as a scribbled post-it-note of explanation.

'I'll ring you again soon. I promise.'

'Is there anything I can do, Cherie?' It seemed her father was reluctant to sever the connection.

He was trying hard not to pry, she knew.

'This is between Noel and me.' She hesitated. 'Nobody else.'

No Lynne Robertson. No sex. No deception. Don't complicate things.

'I need to sort this out for myself.'

'Can you do that? Without your husband with you, *can* you sort it out?'

There was a brief silence on the line.

'I expect I'll be home in a couple of days,' Corinne promised. 'Tell Maman, will you?'

'Won't you call her? Just to say hello?'

'You know her. She'll want all the gory details.' Corinne tried to laugh but the result was hollow and dry.

'Are there gory details?'

Corinne sighed. 'Don't, Papa. Please. I don't want to discuss it right now.' Even to her ears it sounded curt. It wasn't fair to him.

'Well, don't stay away *too* long, will you?' He let her go easily.

'I won't. I promise I won't.'

'Goodbye, Cherie.'

'Bye. Love you. Love to Maman.'

Corinne clicked her mobile shut. No more calls. Her father would soothe over her mother and let Uncle Ian know she was safe. Everybody else could wait.

While they'd talked her coffee had gone cold. Carrying the mug into the kitchen she put it in the tiny microwave oven. Ten seconds later it was warm.

Outside she sat on the edge of the planked walkway.

The sun was brighter now. Its reflection bounced off the loch, sharp and dazzling. Without her sunglasses she had to screw up her eyes.

Without your husband with you, can you sort it out?

Her father was no fool. His one piece of advice, he had put to her as a question. Going over that question, Corinne wasn't sure of the answer. But then to face Noel before she resolved things in her head was not an option.

The coffee was cold again. She emptied it out across the pebbles and got to her feet slowly but didn't move from the spot.

A small rowing boat eased away from its mooring far down the side of the loch and glided smoothly out into the water. In it were the man and woman she had seen in the shop on her first night at Four Hills.

Corinne watched the man paddle out a short distance, settle the oars, and head down the loch, following the shore line. Pulling strongly, he moved the light boat easily through the water, little waves lapping at its side leaving a short-lived disturbance in its wake.

The woman sat facing him, her head wrapped loosely in a white scarf that fluttered in the breeze suggestive of a Hemingway heroine. They gave the illusion, even at a distance, of complete harmony as they ventured further away from their mooring.

'The Taylors,' a voice said in her ear. 'It's all an act, if you ask me.'

Corinne jumped. Behind her Louisa Menzies, hands raised and shelved over her eyes, followed the progress of the boat.

42

'What makes you say that?'

'Oh, I don't know,' Louisa grinned. 'Only… Well, he's a lot younger than her. *And* he doesn't let her out of his sight. Not for a second. Frightened she gets away maybe.'

'They look happy to me.' Corinne didn't know why she was defending the couple.

'Oh, come on! It's obvious she's the one with all the money.'

'Oh! You mean, he's...?'

Louisa pulled a face. 'If you say so.'

'I didn't say anything! I don't know them!'

'God, you're touchy.' Louisa's eyes slid away from the boat. 'Is there any coffee going?'

'Is that why you're here? Coffee.'

Louisa flinched.

For a moment neither of them moved.

You, my young friend, like to do all the running. Corinne thought. She made for the cabin door but instead of following, Louisa sat down on the walkway.

'Forget it. Never mind.' The habitual flicking back of her red hair, occupied the girl.

Corinne didn't argue. The empty mug she pushed inside the cabin door while she grabbed her sunglasses. She sat beside her visitor.

'Do you have a job? Other than here at the cabins I mean?'

'I was at college for two years.'

'Oh. Where was that?'

'Glasgow.' Louisa glanced sideways at Corinne. 'Nothing brainy like you. Art and design.'

'Were you any good?'

'Huh! You've got a nerve!'

Corinne smiled. 'Yesterday I was under the microscope. You found out about me. Now it's my turn.'

Louisa glared at her. 'Yes! I was good at it!'

'What happened?'

'Who says anything happened?'

43

'You're here, aren't you?' Corinne waited. In front of them, the water sparkled like crystal shards. She put on the sunglasses which Ross Menzies had given her and tipped her face up to the sun.

Louisa was slow to answer her. 'My mother wasn't well. I had time off to look after her. Happy?' Wooden, the explanation was well-rehearsed.

Corinne didn't question it. 'I didn't know.'

'Why should you? Anyway, they try to keep it covered up.'

Corinne was taken aback. 'What do you mean?'

'She was a top model my mother.' There was a touch of bragging behind the mockery. 'Back then she was *the face.* So they say.'

'I can believe it. She's a very beautiful woman.'

From behind the dark lenses Corinne watched Louisa. The girl's hair was like burnished copper, her pale skin showing the beginnings of a cruel, pink sun-rash.

'You're very like her,' she offered.

'I don't want to be like her!' Louisa glared at Corinne but was met with the brown, opaque lenses. Her thin shoulders came up in a callous shrug.

'She's weak. She can't do anything anymore. Everything has to be run past *him* first. Breathing's a problem without his say so.' The long fingers sank carelessly into her brilliant hair and were pulled through impatiently, leaving deep furrows in the halo of red.

'I take it she doesn't model any more?'

'Up until six, seven years ago she did. But then she had a nervous breakdown.'

'Oh! I'm sorry to hear that. It must be difficult. Getting over that, I mean, as well as running a business.'

'Don't worry. Up here it's no great secret.' Louisa gave a laugh. 'Nobody says anything but everybody's in on it.'

Corinne removed her sunglasses. 'Still it can't be very nice for her to be talked about like part of the scenery.'

'Why not? She's used to it.' Louisa shot a look at Corinne. 'For God's sake, she strutted half-naked on the cat-walk for years!'

'That's a bit cruel, isn't it?'

'You think?'

'People can't help getting ill. It happens to most of us at one time or other.'

'What's wrong with you? Do you take medication? You don't seem ill.'

'I'm not. What made you think that?'

Louisa kept her eyes on Corinne. 'Yesterday you said you came up here for a rest,' she said edgily. 'Was your work too much for you? Was that it?' There was no trace of sympathy in the girl's voice, only triumph.

'No. I'm not ill. Things happen. I needed a break.' Corinne laughed. 'Hey, how did we manage to get back on to me? We were talking about you.' She saw annoyance flash cross Louisa's face. Ignoring it, she asked, 'Tell me, what do you design?'

'I was into fabrics. Hand finished. You know. Special occasion gear. That sort of thing.'

'Can't you take up your college place again now that your mother's all right? Won't your parents want you to go back, if you've got a knack for it?'

'Huh, you make it all sound so simple. Just pack my bag, jump on the first train and when I turn up they'll be waiting with open arms to take me back – I don't think so!'

'It's worth a try isn't it?'

Louisa did not answer.

Corinne put her sunglasses back on. 'I'd like to see your work if you've got any here.'

For a time they didn't speak. The air was full of soft blended noise; the lap of water, the rustle of birds and the great branches behind them creaking against each other. Tiny sounds which, as part of the woods, went un-noticed because of their constancy.

45

At last Louisa stood up. 'I'm going back to the shop.' She hesitated. 'Do you really want to see my stuff?'

'I said so, didn't I?' Corinne got up before the girl could change her mind. 'Wait a minute. I'll get my jacket.'

'They're really, really good.' Corinne held up a silk top. Cropped short, it was sleeveless with alternate folds of burnt orange and heavy pale lime green beading.

'Too young for me, I hate to say it. But I think they're beautiful. And original. You must be able to sell these. Individual pieces are always sought after.'

'Huh, if only it was that easy. What you've got there in your hand is part of the collection I was making for my degree.' Louisa scooped up a small makeup-bag, a hairbrush, sunglasses, and several other things lying scattered on her bed. She heaped them on the small bedside-table, making a show of rearranging them in an untidy pile.

Corinne watched the clear-up operation but said nothing.

They were in Louisa's bedroom. The girl had brought Corinne through the shop to the living quarters. This part of the building was built out and wide. Its one great drawback was that the windows faced into the tall trees at the back.

'We've got to keep the lights on most of the day or we wouldn't be able to see a thing.'

Louisa was standing beside her finished work hanging on a rail, talking fast to cover her nervousness.

The girl's work impressed Corinne. It was obvious she had talent. The rail-full of clothes was well designed.

'Who made these up for you?' she asked.

'I did them myself. We had the machines. At college, everything we needed was on hand.' Louisa shrugged. 'It didn't take me very long.'

'They're great. If I had that sort of skill, I would be heading straight back to college.'

The beaded top was snatched from Corinne's hand. 'I told you!' Louisa threw the white dust sheet over the clothes rail.

'I can't go back there.'

Ready to argue the point, Corinne changed her mind. It was none of her business. Right now she had enough hassle in her own life. She didn't need more. 'Well, I think they're pretty good, anyway.'

The little showing was over.

Turning to leave, Corinne found her way blocked. 'Mrs Menzies.'

The woman had been standing in the doorway listening.

'Miss Pallin.' Louisa's mother swung her eyes past Corinne and settled on her daughter.

'She's just leaving.' Louisa pushed Corinne, forcing her past Kate Menzies into the hall. 'She's seen everything there is to see.' There was a smirk on the girl's face.

'Excuse my daughter's bad manners, Miss Pallin,' Kate laughed uneasily. 'I saw you come in. I was wondering if everything is in order with the cabin.' She clasped and unclasped her hands. 'I should have been down sooner to check. I'm sorry.'

'No need.' Corinne smiled. 'Everything's fine.'

'Oh, I'm glad. People expect so much nowadays.' Kate smiled nervously. 'If you want anything…'

'No, really, I've got everything I need.'

'Well, if you…' Kate persisted.

'For God's sake!' Louisa pushed past her mother. 'What she doesn't want is the third-degree! I know what that feels like. I get enough of it!' In seconds she was down the hall and into the shop.

'I'm sorry about that,' Kate said. 'Louisa doesn't mean to be rude. But things at the moment are … well, you know teenagers.'

Corinne saw the hurt in Kate's Menzies' eyes.

'Oh, you don't have to explain.' She moved down the hall. 'I'll get out of your way now. I might see if I can find something easy for tea. I'm not much of a cook.' Not true; she was good in the kitchen. God, why did she say that?

47

She blamed Kate Menzies for the lie.

Despite her remarkable beauty, the woman was obviously insecure. Corinne felt for her and the throwaway remark was a spur-of-the-moment attempt to make herself appear equally flawed.

Kate followed her. 'Take your time. If you need me I'll be over there.' She moved to the counter.

There was no sign of Louisa.

Walking up and down the well-stocked aisles, Corinne was very aware of Kate. The tall slender figure stood, slightly bent, leaning her hands on the counter in front of her. Her head was bowed but even from the other side of the shop it was obvious she was breathing erratically. When she lifted her head, her mouth moved nervously as if she had words to say but was practising in case they came out wrong.

Corinne put her basket on the counter.

'I met two children this morning. Freddy and Lucy. I didn't get their last name.' She ignored Kate's vacant look.

The woman took the basket and held on to the handle.

'Yes... Oh, yes.' Kate came to her senses. 'The Coburn children.'

'I met them down by the water.' Corinne grinned. 'That was an experience! We came back through the woods together.' She was relieved to see Kate relax.

'They know every twist and turn in the woods here,' Kate said. 'But they're a pair of rascals. Especially Lucy. If they give you directions make sure you get them checked out.'

Corinne could well believe it. 'Thanks for the advice. Why aren't they in school? It's not the holidays yet, is it?'

Kate appeared not to hear. 'You can get lost easily if you haven't been here before.' She stared straight at Corinne. 'You haven't, have you?'

'Sorry? Haven't I what?'

'This is the first time you've been at Four Hills, isn't it? Tell me,' Kate leaned forward. 'You don't know the Coburns? Do you?'

48

'No, I don't.'

'No. Of course you don't. Ross would have told me…'

'Are you all right?' Corinne enquired softly. 'Do you want me to find Louisa for you?'

'No, no. Here,' Kate shoved the basket towards Corinne, 'take your things. You can pay for them later.'

Corinne gathered up her few purchases and replaced the basket in the pile at the edge of the counter aware that Kate watched as she did this. She walked to the door and out of the shop.

Knowing Kate's eyes were on her, Corinne steeled herself not to glance back.

Behind the closed door of her cabin, Corinne gave a little shudder of relief to be on her own.

She didn't want her problems added to by the Menzies family.

The tension between Kate and her daughter in that bedroom had been palpable. Not the slightest effort had been made by Louisa to hide it.

From the short skirmish Corinne could have sworn Louisa hated Kate.

And Kate? Too embarrassed to take issue with it, and too nervous to cover it up with any degree of success, she could only apologise half-heartedly.

I don't need this. Corinne fought down the idea of throwing all her clothes into her bags and heading south, away from Four Hills. But her mood see-sawed. The logistics of actually doing the simple deed put her off.

She started to assemble a simple salad. Another meal, another prevarication.

In the end, the meal she put together wasn't bad; cold ham and salad, then an apple.

Transported from a far sunnier place on the globe, she carefully peeled the skin from the fruit in two narrow strips. Paring slice after slice of the flesh, she ate it slowly, savouring the little ritual she rarely wasted time on at home.

It was satisfying, being able to lie back and gaze out over the loch without an urgent meeting or deadline cutting short this simple self-indulgence.

Corinne lay there as the sun began to come down and transform the water to liquid gold. Too brilliant to watch for any length of time, she averted her eyes from the amazing sight and reached for her mobile.

She felt ready now. This would be a good time.

More missed calls and messages sprung out at her as she flicked the mobile open. She pressed the screen.

'Cory?' Noel knew straight away it was her. 'Where are you?' he demanded.

She breathed in deeply. 'I'm at a hotel.'

'Where? Tell me which one. We've got to talk, Cory. You know you've got everyone worried about you.'

The blame was shifted effortlessly to her.

'I've already spoken to Dad,' she countered. 'He'll tell anyone who needs to know that I'm taking two or three days off. Nobody needs to worry.'

'Not worry! You've left me! People are wondering what the hell's happening to us. You can't do this, Cory. Already, they're beginning to talk.'

'Is that all you're concerned about? What people will think?' She wasn't worried. Master of the slick get-out, was Noel.

'I need you, Cory. Please, tell me where you are. I'll come and get you.' He hesitated. 'This thing with Lynne… it's over.'

Corinne closed her eyes. How easy it would be to believe him.

'Is she still at the office?' She hated herself for asking.

'Well…yes. I reckoned it would be best to leave everything as it was. It would be too obvious if she left right now.'

'So you've discussed it with her?'

'I had to! Believe me she's as sorry as I am.'

'Noel!' Corinne felt her self-control slipping. 'I don't care about her. Don't you get it?'

'Fine. No more talk about Lynne. I get it. Oh, Cory, we can get over this.' His voice rose, eager now. 'I know. Let's forget about L.A. For the time being anyhow. We can rent a house in France. A place near your grandparents. We could relax, and talk things through, just the two of us. You would like that.'

'Do you really think a holiday is going to sort us?'

'Awe, Cory, please don't do this. You found me out. I put my hands up.'

Corinne placed a hand on her forehead. It felt hot and clammy.

'Noel, I trusted you. Yes, trusted. More fool me! But I had the idea I was enough for you. Now… I have no idea. Your launch weekends away; your promotional trips…' She laughed weakly. 'That's it, isn't it? She was there every time! God help me, I never realised until this very second. I've been so blind!'

'Corinne, we've both got a lot to lose here.'

'Is that a threat, Noel? Because if it is, I wouldn't repeat it to my father. Or to Uncle Ian for that matter.'

'What do you mean by that?'

'You didn't get where you are on your own, Noel.'

'I know that.' His voice was flat. 'Like I said, I need you, Cory. Please come home.'

'Not now. Not yet.'

'Cory, listen…'

Her mobile clicked shut before he could utter another word.

CHAPTER FOUR

No way could Corinne face Noel. Not yet.

The image of Lynne Robertson, naked, made her back away from the idea. Emotions were still raw.

If a drinker, she might well be reaching for the bottle. So what if Noel had played away. He was no saint; she knew that.

The euphemism gave Corinne no comfort.

To hell with it! A glass of wine might just do the trick.

The black foil on the rim of the wine bottle ripped easily. Pliable, metallic, it scratched her hand as she pulled at it. She cursed mildly and the appeal of the wine drained away. Open the bottle or not?

In that moment of indecision she heard footsteps. Firm, purposeful, she tracked the tread over the walkway. It stopped outside the cabin door.

The unopened bottle in her hand, Corinne waited motionless for the knock to come.

Nothing. No voice, no shuffling, no knock. She slid the bottle upside down in her hand glad now that she hadn't opened it. Slowly she edged towards the door.

She jerked it open.

Ross Menzies stood there. 'Sorry, Miss Pallin.' He nodded at the wine bottle she held shoulder high.

'Oh, it's you!' Corinne laughed shakily.

Ross flicked a finger at the bottle. 'I didn't mean to scare you.'

'Oh, sorry about that. Please, come in. What can I do for you?'

'I'll do that for you if you like.' He took the bottle from her and went to the kitchen, opened a drawer and took out a corkscrew. 'You *were* going to open it?'

'Yes. I was. I picked it up at your place yesterday but then I didn't feel like it.'

'Not much of a drinker I take it?' The cork gave a soft, satisfying *chug* as it came out cleanly. 'There.' He handed the bottle back.

'Would you like a drink?' Corinne asked.

'Only if you're sure I'm not in your way.'

'There's not exactly a great deal to do here at night.' She poured the wine. 'Or am I missing out?'

'No, you're right. It's early in the season. If you come, say, July or August, there are usually things going on.' Ross accepted the glass Corinne offered.

'Like what?' She waved him to a chair and perched on the corner of the sofa.

'Oh, fishing trips. And the visitors like barbecues. We set them up on the far cove. Mid-night boat rides. It keeps them happy. You know the sort of thing.'

Corinne didn't know. She nodded but said nothing. She wasn't interested. A couple of days and she would be gone.

'Miss Pallin,' he set his glass down on the small table. 'Corinne…' He leaned forward, his face dispassionate. 'I've got this for you.'

Corinne's heart sank. What now?

Ross drew his hand from his jacket pocket.

'Ah!' Corinne put down her drink. 'My Bvlgari! She stroked the sunglasses. Glancing at him, she smiled. 'Silly, I know. But I did miss them.'

'Don't you want to know where I found them?'

Corinne focused on the sunglasses. 'I know where you found them.'

'How do you know?' Disbelief, suspicion – Corinne saw both flash across his face.

'Well, this afternoon I asked if I could see Louisa's designs and we went to her room.' She shrugged lightly. 'I don't know if she did it deliberately or not but there they were, lying on her bed with a jumble of other things.'

'Ah…'

'She tried to hide them. But she must have known I would

53

see them. Why would she do that?'

'Confrontation, I guess.'

'With me? Why? We barely know each other.'

'No, not with you.' He was emphatic. 'With Kate. The two of them tend to rub each other up the wrong way. What else can I tell you? They're so alike they see themselves in each other.'

The sniping between mother and daughter in Louisa's bedroom was vivid in Corinne's head. 'And they don't like what they see. Is that it?' Aloud her thoughts sounded cruel. Corinne wished she could retract them.

Her words appeared not to trouble Ross. 'You get the idea.'

He sighed so deeply Corinne could see his chest heave. Bizarrely, she felt sorry for this man she barely knew but she had an inkling what he was going through. Trying hard to stay loyal, while telling the truth, was no easy matter she was discovering.

'I've only been here for a couple of days so tell me to mind my own business but your Louisa, she seems bright. And talented. From the pieces I saw, I'd say she's pretty good. Yet she seems unsure where she belongs.'

'She told you then, about not going back to college?' His face was grim.

'Just a little.' Corinne instantly felt traitorous. Had she let slip too much of the girl's idle chat? 'She happened to mention it in passing.'

He raised his eyebrows. 'While she was stealing your sunglasses?'

'What did she say when you got them back?' Corinne asked.

'Nothing.' He tasted the wine. 'She doesn't know yet.'

Corinne was stunned. 'You mean you went into her room and took them!' She couldn't get her head around this devious act. 'While she wasn't there!'

'Yes, I did.' He stood up. 'Don't act so shocked, Miss

Pallin. That's better than us being branded thieves. Wouldn't you say?'

Corinne held her temper. 'So you said nothing to her about it?'

'No. I didn't. But then neither did you.' About to leave, he changed his mind. 'Do me a favour will you? Wear them tomorrow so she sees you've got them back. It'll save everybody a lot of trouble.' For a second time he backed away from her and this time he left, pulling the door behind him very deliberately as if to emphasise closure on the unsavoury episode of the Bvlgari.

Corinne stayed where she was. Glass in hand, she sipped the wine without appreciating it.

Ross's footsteps sounded until he was off the end of the walkway and onto the path. A moment later Corinne could have sworn she heard the murmur of voices. Low and muffled, the sound merged easily with the stirring of the huge trees in the woods until she was not sure she'd heard anything at all.

Friday morning dawned dull and overcast. The light wind that had blown since Corinne arrived at Four Hills was gone and with it the constant background rustling of pine branches.

Across the loch Corinne saw the water, oily smooth, and black, with hardly a ripple to lap over the stones at its edge.

She wasn't sorry to find the sun was not shining. With a headache during the night, today she could do without the constant glare. Admittedly, the eerie grey stillness that replaced it was heavy and oppressive.

She forced herself to eat a piece of toast and drink a full cup of tea. The headache might disappear if she avoided coffee for a while; that and fresh air might do it.

While she ate she listed phone calls that needed to be made.

It wasn't easy to start on them. Explanations, apologies,

and a throbbing head, was not a good combination. Urgent or not, they would have to wait.

Having dodged possible long distance verbal conflict, the moment she set foot outside the cabin, she was dismayed to come face to face with Kate Menzies.

The woman made no apology for hanging about waiting for her to appear.

'Miss Pallin, about yesterday.' Kate launched straight in. There were no preliminaries. 'I'm so sorry if we upset you.' The smile to Corinne was forced. 'You must come up to the shop and get whatever you want.' She put out her hand tentatively. 'Anything at all.'

'I've still to pay for the last lot.' Corinne breathed in the cool air. She wanted to be left alone.

'No. It's all right. You don't need to pay for anything.' With stiff fingers Kate Menzies fiddled with the end of the long plait of red hair hanging over her shoulder.

It dawned on Corinne what was going on. Taking the Bvlgari from her jacket pocket, she put them on. She faced Kate. 'Please don't worry about it. I'm fine with everything.' She motioned towards the path. 'I'm going for a walk. Which way gets me to the village?'

If Kate Menzies intended to mention the Bvlgari, she was distracted.

'Which way? Oh, you could walk up through the woods by the path just there. You'll come to the Coburns' craft centre first.' She stared at Corinne. 'That's about half-way between here and the village. It's not very far. The other way is back to the shop and then on to the road past the station and then on to the village.'

'Thanks. I'll maybe see you later.' Corinne needed to be away from Kate Menzies. Those green pleading eyes were unnerving.

She walked to the path and went left and then right, the direction Kate had indicated for the craft centre. Corinne walked briskly. No footsteps behind her confirmed Kate was not following.

Her headache grew worse, each step sending a jolt up through her shoulders into her skull and spiking the back of her eyes. She slipped off her sunglasses, put on partly to avoid eye contact with Kate Menzies. That earnest expectant stare could entice you to agree to anything. And, she noted, Kate had not been surprised to see her wearing the Bvlgari.

Last night, the Menzies had come to her cabin together, Corinne realised. Ross had faced her; Kate had stayed outside. Whose strategy was that?

Not long into her walk she found a makeshift seat. A couple of metres off the path, a tree had been felled recently. The stump, reasonably flat, with scored saw marks, had bright yellow sawdust scattered around its periphery.

Corinne sat down and closed her eyes. The Menzies lot were heavy going. She laughed silently. With them about you soon forgot your own troubles.

Scarcely moving, she sat on the newly created stump. Only a trickle of sound permeated down from the tall majestic trees overhead.

At first it seemed quiet but there was noise. Pine needles fell to the ground; insects and small animals scrabbled about unseen in the undergrowth.

Transcending these gentle sounds, Corinne was conscious of the blood pumping in her head. She wished she could press a button and lessen the sound as easily as dumbing-down the volume on a radio. Maybe this was what was meant by knowing yourself; listening to your own body.

She didn't know if she liked life this intense. The more she tried to ignore the sound in her head, the more obvious it got. Pump… pump… pump.

Corinne shivered and blinked. She rubbed her cold hands together and stood up. Her headache, beginning to ease, left her feeling fragile.

She glanced at her watch. She'd been there for the best part of an hour. Still it wasn't yet lunch time. If she went on she would reach the village and possibly get a sandwich.

Faster than when she'd started out, she walked on for another twenty minutes. At the top of a gentle slope she emerged from the trees into a large open space.

The clearing flattened out. In its middle was a huge log-cabin. The Coburns' craft centre. It gave Corinne a start. She hadn't expected anything quite so big.

Low and wide, the wooden building, with a purposely rustic veranda, had tables and chairs set out in front.

A party of visitors was gathered at a large table. Four children argued amongst themselves, while the adults ignored them and put their heads together to examine a map. A couple of the women looked up and smiled at Corinne as she passed into the shop.

The man at the counter grinned at her. 'Good morning.' His voice, light, nicely cultured English, was friendly.

'Is this a new face I see before me?'

'You're right,' Corinne answered. 'Well, nearly. This is my third day.'

'Hello. I'm Edwin Coburn. I run the centre with my wife, Tamzin.'

'Corinne Pallin.'

Straight away Corinne liked Edwin Coburn. Forty five she guessed, slim, his almost classical features had a healthy tan. His fine, pale brown hair was receding from his forehead but no attempt had been made to disguise the loss. This openness seemed to suit him.

'I'm staying in one of the Four Hills cabins. I've just walked up from there.' Corinne got the feeling he already knew who she was.

'Still trying to find your way about? Never mind. Now you've found us, we will expect you every morning henceforth.' He rubbed his hands together. 'Now then, what can I get you?'

'A coffee please – no, make it tea. And a couple of those energy bars.'

No sooner had Corinne given her order than Tamzin Coburn appeared.

Corinne was in no doubt who it was that breezed through from the back of the centre. In a long shapeless skirt and rainbow coloured top, the woman jangled as she moved. The ethnic bangles and necklaces were a throwback to the hippy era of the seventies, an age which Tamzin Coburn was not old enough to have experienced but seemed happy to embrace.

A grown up version of Lucy, a cap of soft silky hair framed Tamzin's face. She appeared hardly old enough to be the children's mother.

'Hi. Edwin's better half – Tamzin.' The woman introduced herself. 'How do you like it down there by the loch? Not too many visitors yet. Not too many midges either!' She laughed; a pleasant gurgling sound that halted abruptly.

'It's fine,' Corinne said. 'Very quiet.'

Edwin nodded to his wife. 'I was just saying, now she's found us we'll expect to see more of her.' He put the tea on a tray with a cup and saucer and the energy bars.

Tamzin picked up the tray from the counter. 'I'll take that.' She nodded to Corinne. 'Come on. Where would you like to sit? Over there do?'

Leading Corinne to a seat in the opposite corner of the veranda from the children, Tamzin unloaded the tray. 'You've met Lucy and Freddy, I understand.'

'Yes. They were down by a little cove at the loch when I was there yesterday.'

'Don't let them pester you, will you? Freddy can get over boisterous at times.' Tamzin smiled tolerantly. 'Most of the time actually.'

'Yes, I know. I was introduced to a lizard.'

'Yes, well…' Tamzin was amused. 'You'll have met the Menzies of course, Kate and Ross. And Louisa…'

Corinne recognised a probe when she heard it.

'Yes. Their cabins are very comfortable. They seem to

have provided everything.'

Tamzin's smile was still in place. 'They've put you in the one nearest their place. I suppose they want to keep an eye on you, being on your own.' She swung the tray under her arm. 'You should get Louisa to show you the paths around the loch and up the hills. It would keep her busy instead of hanging about all day.'

Corinne smiled but said nothing. She knew very little about these people and wasn't prepared to voice an opinion. Besides, bizarrely, she liked Louisa. She wasn't going to do the girl down before she knew what was behind Tamzin Coburn's barbed remark.

'I'll leave you to your tea. Enjoy.' Tamzin pointed through the door of the centre. 'Come and have a walk round when you're finished.'

'I will. Thank you.' Corinne watched Tamzin go inside and hand the empty tray over the counter to her husband. They exchanged a few brief words and his shoulders rose and his hands spread wide in a gesture of scepticism.

Corinne unwrapped and ate one of the sweet, sticky energy bars. Was she imagining it but was that little-girl image of Tamzin Coburn's just a trifle overdone?

She finished the bar and slipped the other one in her jacket pocket for later.

Drinking her tea, she watched the group of children invent a game they wanted to play in the woods. Excited, their voices grew louder until they were shouting. The oldest, about twelve, seemed determined to impose his ideas on the other three by dint of volume. One of the men in the group put a stop to the noise. Sullen-faced all four children trailed behind the grown-ups as they left the veranda, their own enthusiasm having killed their game even before it got going.

It was peaceful with them gone.

Alone Corinne felt self-conscious despite no one to see her. She got up without finishing her tea and remembered her promise to visit the craft shop before she left. In fact she was curious to see what the place had to offer.

Inside, Edwin Coburn was absent from the counter. Tamzin was in the back, talking to a couple of hikers.

Corinne went along the shelves of souvenirs. The display was good. Polished stones set in silver, small wood carvings planed as smooth as silk to the touch, thick woollen jumpers, hats and gloves; nothing very unusual, but no rubbish. All quality, and pricey, as in the Menzies' shop.

'What do you think? See anything you like?' It was Tamzin. The hikers had chosen, paid and moved outside.

'To be honest, I can't make up my mind. You've got some lovely things. I like your silver pieces.' Corinne picked up a bracelet. Highly polished, the links were of varying sizes, interspersed with solid little silver discs minutely decorated. She glanced at the price tag. For a trinket, it was expensive.

'If you like that, why don't you take it and wear it for a couple of days. If you don't fall in love with it, bring it back.'

The offer surprised Corinne.

Tamzin saw her hesitate. 'You don't have to pay for it now.' She untied the white price tag from the bracelet. 'If you decide you want it, pay for it then.'

'That's very generous. I don't know if I would be as open-handed if this were mine.'

'Oh, I believe I can trust you,' Tamzin laughed. 'Anyhow, I could easily track you down.'

Corinne jerked her head back. 'You know Edinburgh?' She could have kicked herself.

Tamzin smiled her little-girl smile. 'First cabin on the loch path, right? Any further than that and I would have to involve Edwin.'

'Sorry?'

'I don't drive. Nope. Even with the train, he trundles me down to the station. And away I go. Stirling, Glasgow. Edinburgh's my favourite.' The smile was still on Tamzin's face.

'Really?'

'Yes. Perhaps we'll bump into each other when I'm down.'

Gathering the silver bracelet neatly between her fingers, Corinne held it out to Tamzin. 'I think I'll leave this.'

'Oh!' Still smiling, Tamzin took the bracelet. 'Maybe another time.'

'Yes. Maybe.'

Corinne retraced her steps through the woods.

Only when she was well on her way did she remember she had meant to go on to the village. She wasn't bothered and grinned at her lapse of memory. In her office she would rail at herself for this slackness. Here, lochside, it was different. A curious mind-set pervaded the place, an awareness of people and surroundings raised to a different level from her norm.

Her mind toyed with the welcome she had received from the Coburns.

However lulled her senses might be she could have sworn they knew when she had arrived at Four Hills, certainly knew which cabin she had been allocated. Tamzin now knew she lived in Edinburgh. Neither of the Coburns asked if there was a husband, or a partner, or family. Both of them assumed she was on her own. Or they'd been told.

Did it matter?

There it was; too much thinking. Far too much thinking. The reason for this morning's headache. Used to working under stress, she should know better. Wasn't she in the business of sifting fact from fiction and putting each genre in its own little box, packaging it with a brightly accentuated cover to guide the reader's imagination to the right conclusion.

Until that moment she hadn't realised how much she missed work. Her office would be vacant without her, her desk undisturbed.

The vision stayed in her mind's eye as she walked back along the path.

In her cabin she settled down in her usual spot side-on to the window, overlooking the loch, her mobile in her hand.

In three days she had not spoken to her mother; her father just the one time. She excused herself; he would relay their conversation to her mother, keep her happy or at least *au fait* with Corinne's need for escape. And then there was Noel. Had she been fair to him, fleeing without letting him know to where? But then this place wasn't for him, it was for her.

'Papa, it's me.' A small bird landed on the water as her father picked up her call at the first ring.

'Hello, Cherie. Are you well?'

'I'm fine. Is everything all right in the office? Anything you want to go over?'

This was harder than she'd thought. The little bird on the water rocked from side to side. 'There were things on my desk.'

'Everything is being handled. Ian has stepped into your shoes. He is loving it.'

Corinne smiled at the image. 'Tell him not to get too comfortable.' The little bird flapped its wings against the surface of the water and settled further down the loch.

'Papa, did you know anything was going on between Noel and Lynne Robertson?' Her eyes went to her hand lying in her lap; it was trembling slightly. Curling her fingers she pressed her nails hard into her palm.

'Oh, Cherie… I did not know. I swear it. But since you have been away from us Noel has confessed to me that he has been unfaithful to you.'

The old-fashioned term struck Corinne as comical. She fought down the urge to scream that this was serious. It was no joke! And it wasn't about Noel. It was about her. 'He told you everything?'

'Enough. Your mother and I understand you need to take time to sort this out. Also Cherie…'

'Yes?'

'You must not let Noel's involvement with the company sway your decision. It is of no importance. Not to me or to your Uncle Ian. Your mother, she cares nothing except that you are happy.'

'Is she there?'

'She wants so much to speak with you. Wait a moment.'

Another little bird landed beside the first.

Corinne swallowed hard and braced herself. 'Mum?'

'Corinne.' Her mother's voice, so practical, demanded, 'Is it a decent hotel that you're staying at?'

'Yes, it's comfortable enough. It's quiet. Just what I need at the moment.'

'Corinne, whatever you decide to do about Noel – your dad told me what he did and I can't believe it! Anyway, I will go along with your decision, despite what I think of it.'

'That's good of you!'

'Corinne, it's you I'm thinking about, *have been* thinking about ever since you left without so much as a word of what went on between the two of you. You should have come to me.'

'I'm sorry about that. I just couldn't face anybody right then.'

'I understand that. Of course I do. It was a shock. It would be to anybody whose husband lets them down. Corinne, I don't blame you for wanting time on your own, but you mustn't take too long about it.'

'Just two or three days, that's all.'

'Oh, sweetheart, it's not for my sake, but I want you here, where I know you won't do anything –.'

'Stupid? No, I won't do that. I'm hurt, and to be perfectly honest, embarrassed. I couldn't see what was going on literally right in front of me.' Corinne paused. 'Do you know I caught them together?'

'Oh, Corinne, please don't dwell on that. It won't do any good. It certainly won't change things. Believe me, I know.

You've got to decide whether you want to split from Noel or take him back. But if you get together again what you mustn't do is hold this over him like a threat. That won't work, not for you and not for him.'

'You seem to know a lot about this. Mum, you and Dad never…?'

On the water, the second bird flapped clumsily and rose into the air. Abandoned, the first fluttered uncertainly. An instant later, it followed.

'This is about you, Corinne, you and Noel. All I'm saying is that you're right to take the time you need to think it through, yes, but don't take too long about it. I don't go along with what they say, you know, *absence makes the heart grow fonder.* That's a lot of rubbish! Left alone too long your husband will fill the gap.'

'Three days, Mum!'

'I know, I know. But be honest. Noel is easily swayed. You've just had proof of it.'

'What, the great writer has no staying power. Is that what you're saying?' Corinne's loyalty was torn. 'You don't think he can stand on his own two feet for any length of time. Is that it?'

'Corinne, this is not about what I think of Noel, this is about what's happening between you and him.'

'It never occurred to me before that you might not like him.' Corinne laughed weakly. 'It seems I've been blind on all fronts.'

'Corinne, I don't mean to upset you. Please, sweetheart, take time out to think. But don't stay away too long that's all I'm saying.' Her mother paused. 'He might not be here when you decide you want him.'

'That's just it. I can't make up my mind if I do want him.'

'Exactly my point. There are two sides to every break-up *and* every reconciliation. Corinne, usually the sex is only a part of it. Remember that.'

Corinne felt her stomach contract. 'Has he said anything

else to Dad? I know they've spoken. Maybe Dad didn't want to say.'

'No. Nothing more, as far as I know. Myself, I think Noel's wanted to spread his wings for a while now. There's always an attraction, bigger, better around the next corner for him.'

Corinne defended him. 'He worked hard on that last book.'

'Yes, he did. He deserves his success. Only now he wants more, Corinne. And if you don't want to move on with him you've got to tell him that.'

'What about the company? What would happen to that if I did throw it all up and move to the States? He says he wants to buy a house in L.A.'

'Ah...'

'Mum? What do you know about it?'

'Well, it seems he's already bought a place out there. Now, Corinne, don't get angry. I didn't know if you were aware of it.'

Corinne felt battered. 'How did you find that out?'

'Your father bumped into an old friend, Jimmy Grayson, in town. He's the solicitor helping Noel with the paperwork. Obviously, Jimmy thought we knew about it and wished you all the best.'

'Why didn't Dad tell me when he found out?'

'Corinne, you haven't been answering your calls. This only happened last night. We're only just getting to grips with it ourselves!'

'God, a house! Who in their right mind would buy a house in secret? Did he really think I wouldn't find out?'

A sketchy vision of a three million dollar mansion in L.A. rose up in Corinne's mind. Even as he'd put forward the idea he knew fine she would say no.

Fait accompli.

Was it just one more reason for them to split?

The sound of sighing came clear down the line before her mother's voice reached Corinne.

'To be honest I think things are getting out of control,' she said. 'That's why I say don't stay away too long or it will be too late to salvage anything out of this mess.'

The blunt words from her mother brought the same from Corinne. 'You think I should come home and face him right now?'

'That's up to you. If you're near – not *too* far away – it would be easy enough perhaps just for a few hours, just so you could talk things through face to face.'

'I feel too betrayed, Mum. Now this house thing… I can't believe it. I doubt if it would help if I came back just now. Anyhow, I'm not in the city.'

'You're not very far away, are you?'

'No. Just a couple of hours by train.'

'Would it help if we came there, your father and I?'

'No!' Corinne cut short her mother's suggestion. 'I don't think you two would care for Four Hills.'

If her mother was offended at the rejection, her voice gave nothing away.

'Whatever you say, Corinne. Take care.'

'I will.'

'And Corinne…'

'Yes?'

'Answer your calls.'

CHAPTER FIVE

Friday morning's grim weather dragged on into the afternoon.

Despite heavy skies, Corinne's headache began to shift.

Contrary to what she'd said to her mother, Noel was pushed to the back of her mind, to stay there for the rest of the day, she hoped. Not ideal. Not why she was here. And nothing would get resolved. Yet she couldn't face it.

She ate a sandwich and felt better.

One of her bags held a couple of unread manuscripts. Sent to her recently, she'd had no time to check them over. In her rush to escape Noel, she'd thrown them in, randomly, when she packed. No idea why except that it was work. Exactly the distraction she needed right now.

She dug them out. Feet up, she settled down on the sofa.

Usually, initial submissions came by e-mail. These two were the full monty, typed and clipped neatly together.

This was no chore. In editorial mode, she ploughed into the first piece of work.

The author was inexperienced. The raw novel needed a lot of re-work. Corinne read on as if it were a writing of great consequence.

Two hours later and still less than half way through, she lowered the manuscript.

Out over the loch a movement caught her eye. On the far shore what appeared to be a buzzard circled gracefully over a narrow, stony clearing. For a while she watched the bird dip and rise and dip again before flapping its wings and soaring high in the air out of her sight. The raptor's fruitless hunt was over.

She read another few lines of the manuscript.

Whatever evasion she found, whatever hideaway she found to crawl into, life was still out there, flawed and cruel. Nothing changed because she refused to face facts.

In an effort to stop the tears, she closed her eyes. 'Why! Why!' The tears came, hot and blinding. She swiped them away and lay back.

The manuscript, so carefully nurtured by a hopeful scribbler, fell to the floor.

Rain was running down the window in little rivulets when Corinne woke two hours later.

She shivered and swung her legs over the edge of the sofa. Her feet hit the floor before she was fully awake. In the same instant she felt a presence in the room.

'Louisa!'

The girl was sitting in the chair opposite, her long legs concertinaed under her. The manuscript Corinne had been reading earlier lay open in her lap.

'Hi!' Louisa's lips curved in the ghost of a smile. She tapped the bulky pages of the manuscript. 'This is crap. Right?'

'God, you gave me a fright.' Corinne blinked rapidly. Her eyes were gritty. 'What are you doing in here?'

Louisa smirked. 'I knew you wouldn't be out in this. You're not really the outdoor type, are you?'

Corinne grabbed the manuscript. 'How did you get in here? I'm paying for this cabin. I expect *the minimum* degree of privacy.'

'Going to rush up to the shop and tell on me… again?' Louisa reached out to the table and picked up Corinne's Bvlgari sunglasses. Slowly, she put them on and pushed them up onto the bridge of her nose.

Corinne watched the very deliberate, choreographed move.

In the late afternoon gloom Louisa's pale face shone with a curious luminosity. The dark sunglasses below her bright hair added to her extraordinary appearance.

Fully awake now, Corinne laid the manuscript aside. She knew the girl was baiting her, waiting, wordless and still, to see her reaction.

'They already know you're a thief.' It worked. She saw the shock on the girl's face.

Louisa's lips pressed hard into a straight line. Her long fingers gripped the arms of the chair. 'You… you…' The fine skin on her neck flushed red as she scrambled up. She pulled the sunglasses from her face and held them out to Corinne.

'Here. Take them. You would have got them back. It was only meant to be a bit of fun.' She sniggered. 'But I can tell you don't go in for that.'

Louisa pitched the Bvlgari straight at Corinne. They flew across the short space between them.

Corinne put out her hand, fumbled, and failed to catch them. The sunglasses fell to the floor with a feeble clatter.

Together Corinne and Louisa gazed at the fallen Bvlgari. Neither made a move to pick them up.

Louisa pushed at Corinne's arm. 'See what you've made me do!' The girl's shout was hysterical.

The childish accusation made Corinne gaze at the girl hard. Louisa's green eyes were awash with tears.

'Sit down,' Corinne ordered. 'I'll make us a drink.' Picking up the sunglasses, she put them back on the table exactly where Louisa had found them. Ignoring the girl's sulky face she went to the kitchen and put out two mugs and made tea.

When she set them on the table in front of the sofa, Louisa was sitting back in her chair.

Corinne asked her, 'Why didn't you give them back to me yourself? You wanted to, didn't you? Or would that have been too easy?'

Louisa, about to argue, appeared to change her mind. 'I'm not a thief.'

'I know.' Changing tack, Corinne flicked a finger towards the discarded manuscript, its edges starting to curl. 'Not your type of thing?'

'Reading, full-stop, is not my type of thing.' Louisa

glanced at Corinne. 'Is it any good?'

'Oh, it needs work, and lots of it. But I'd say it's got potential.'

'Potential… That's what they said about me, once upon a time.'

'Well, if you've got it, you'll always have it. It's just another way of saying you have the ability. Mind you, it means nothing if you don't actively use it.' Corinne motioned towards the manuscript. 'If that person hadn't tried to put his thoughts down on paper he wouldn't be using his potential.'

'Are you going to publish it then?'

'Like I said, it needs a lot of work.'

'Huh, you're going to knock him back. I can tell.' Louisa grinned. 'I'll bet you didn't even read it!'

Corinne's animosity rose at the girl's unfounded slur. She fought it down.

'That's where you're wrong,' she said. 'No, I haven't read it all. Not yet. Anyhow, I wouldn't claim it was all right if it wasn't. I don't tell lies.'

'Everybody tells lies.' Louisa was scathing. 'Even you!'

The girl left. Corinne felt relieved but inevitably wound-up.

It happened each time she came into contact with Louisa. Disturbing vibes came from that green-eyed sulky stare and those openly barbed comments. It wasn't just hostility. Despite having been found out over the sunglasses, Louisa kept coming back; back to the cabin, back to her. Was it the pure audacious nerve of a teenager, or was it the need to face her faults, her demons, that drove her back to Corinne?

She gazed out, unseeing, at the loch.

High, pale grey clouds thickened and darkened as she watched. Rain started falling again, lightly at first, hard and straight within minutes.

Corinne picked up the manuscript and flicked the pages through her fingers. Louisa was right; not very good. About it having potential, she had lied, and then tried to cover it up. Why? She had no idea. Louisa had seen right through her.

Corinne's jaw clenched. That's the reason she comes here, she thought. She feels we're two of a kind. How the girl got to her!

She snapped on a lamp and brought a throw from the bedroom. The next hour she spent reading the remainder of the manuscript. The last page gave her no more insight into the writer than she'd had after the first few paragraphs. At least she had finished it. She'd given it a shot. Vindicated, in her own eyes at least, she threw it down on the table.

It wasn't dark yet. An urge to stretch her legs got her to her feet. She was running low on milk. It wouldn't take long to walk up to the shop and back.

Under the trees the dirt path was protected from the worst of the rain. Her jacket had no hood and at varying intervals great water drops fell from the high branches. They managed to target her and run, icy cold, through her hair and down her neck. She found herself gasping then laughing in turn at the shock.

Her short journey to the Menzies' shop ended in a jog.

Defiantly, the Four Hills' shop lights shone out garishly through the gloomy evening.

Inside, Corinne came face to face with the Taylors who were about to leave.

'My dear, you're soaked through!' Mrs Taylor stood back appalled at the state of Corinne. 'Alec, would you see if you can get a towel for this poor woman.'

'I'm fine, really.' Corinne laughed it off.

'We were just leaving. Now…' Mrs Taylor's beautifully made-up face was full of concern as she waited for her husband to return.

'Still no Kate, I'm afraid,' Alec Taylor informed them. 'I found Ross. He's gone to fetch you a towel. He won't be a minute.' Glancing at his wife, he said, 'He doesn't seem to know where Kate is.'

'Don't worry about me. I'm not that wet. Anyway, I won't melt.' Corinne glanced down at herself. Her leather jacket was rain soaked to a deep brown and her wet trousers were stuck to her thighs.

'Here you are.' Ross Menzies appeared from the door that went into the house. He handed over a towel to Corinne. 'This should dry the worst of it.'

'Kate's not back yet, then?' Kim Taylor asked Ross anxiously.

He smiled grimly. 'Not yet. She's probably sitting out the rain in the dry.'

'Yes, possibly.' Mrs Taylor was not convinced. 'Alec and I could help you look for her.' She appealed to her husband. 'Couldn't we do that, Alec?'

'No,' Alec Taylor's refusal was curt.

Corinne, rubbing the ends of her hair, stopped.

Alec shot a cursory glance at her before he went on less brusquely to his wife.

'It's getting dark, Kim. You shouldn't be out in this. Nobody should. We must get back to the cabin.'

Kim Taylor accepted calmly what sounded like a rebuke. She smiled apologetically at Ross. 'We'll see Kate another time. Tomorrow, perhaps?'

'I'll talk to her about what you mentioned,' he said. 'I'll get back to you.'

Their thick padded jackets zipped up to their chins, hoods pulled well forward over their eyes, the Taylors left. Despite their disagreement on whether to stay or not, they went out into the rain arm in arm.

Deep in thought, Ross stared at their retreating backs.

Corinne watched his face. 'I suppose he's right. It'll get dark fast, what with the rain and the trees.'

'Sorry?' Ross dragged his attention back. 'Oh, yes. Alec's right. Mrs Taylor shouldn't have been out in this.'

Corinne wiped her face dry and handed the damp towel back to him. 'And Kate? Is she walking in this?'

Ross folded the towel before answering. 'I don't suppose you saw her on your way here, did you?'

'No. Sorry. I made a mad dash because of the rain. I was the only one on the path as far as I know.' Corinne looked down the shop. Now the Taylors had gone there was no one else there besides herself and Ross. 'Kim Taylor seemed to think there was a problem. Is Kate all right?'

'To be honest, I don't know.' He threw the damp towel on the counter. 'She went out, middle of this afternoon. Usually she would be back by this time.'

'Where was she going? If she was visiting, couldn't you give them a call?'

'That's the thing, she went round all the cabins this morning making sure everybody knew about the open-house up at Coburns' place to-morrow night.'

'An open-house?'

The worry was still on Ross's face. 'It depends a lot on the weather. If it's good, it's a barbecue of sorts. If it's too windy or it rains, it gets taken inside. An indoor picnic, you could call it.'

'She's been back here since this morning though? You've heard from her since then?'

'Yes. But the thing is she didn't get *you* in. You weren't there when she called at the cabin. She said she was going to try again this afternoon.'

'Well, that would be right.' Corinne detailed her day. 'This morning I walked up to the craft centre. I was in the cabin all afternoon right up until the moment I decided to come here. Your Louisa was with me part of the time. Kate never came near. Not as far as I know.'

Ross's face was a mixture of concern and annoyance. 'What do you mean, as far as you know? You said you were there all afternoon.'

Corinne felt she was being interrogated. She made allowances. Ross was obviously worried.

'I fell asleep. When I woke up, Louisa was there. Nobody

else. I didn't see Kate.'

There was no sign of surprise from Ross as he absorbed this. 'Louisa went back out about half-an-hour ago. She was going up to see the Coburns.'

'Probably where Kate is. Louisa will tell her you're anxious about her.' Corinne could think of nothing else.

'She's not up there. I've already rung Tamzin. They haven't seen her since yesterday.' He grabbed Corinne roughly by the arm. 'I need to find her.' He gave her a little shake.

His intensity shocked Corinne.

Just then, the door to the shop opened.

The two men Corinne had seen in the shop on her first day at Four Hills hurried in out of the rain. They stopped abruptly at the scene that met them. Dripping water, they stood silently eyeing Corinne and Ross.

Ross dropped his hand. He smiled disarmingly at Corinne. 'Sorry. I'm just worried, that's all.'

'What's going on?' The younger man stepped forward. 'Have we missed something? Come on. Tell all. What's up that we don't know about?'

His partner, a man with a finely chiselled face and grey-white hair, put his hand up peremptorily to stop the flow of questions. His eyes narrow, he asked, 'Is everything all right?'

The two men waited, their bright water-proof capes shedding shiny wet circles onto the shop floor.

Realising Ross was not about to confide in the two neat, pristine, partners, Corinne spoke up. 'It's Mrs Menzies. She's been out for most of the afternoon.'

She flicked a glance at Ross. 'Her husband is worried that she's been away for such a long time in this rain.'

The older man said, 'If you want us to lend a hand finding her just tell us what to do. We'd be more than happy to help.'

'You can count me in,' Corinne said. 'That would be four

of us.' To the two men she added, 'I'm Corinne Pallin by the way.'

'Phil Skinner,' the older man introduced himself.

His friend stretched out his hand. 'Ryan, Ryan Teacher. I'm game. We're soaked through, anyhow. Hell, what's a bit of rain?' His laugh trailed away when nobody joined him.

'Great!' Ross was re-energized. 'With four we could go in different directions. Cover the most likely paths. It shouldn't take too long.'

'Good idea,' Phil Skinner agreed. 'We could meet back here in, what do you think, an hour? Yes? Right. Let's get started then. Which route do you want us to take?'

Ross was getting into his waterproof. 'I'll go down the far side of the loch. That's the trickiest path.' He inclined his head at the two men, 'If you could take the road back the way to the station.' He glanced at Corinne. 'That leaves you on your own, I'm afraid.'

Corinne shrugged. 'That's fine. The dark doesn't bother me. The only thing is I don't know my way that well yet. I *could* take the path up to the craft centre. I've been up there already.'

'Right then.' Ross brought down a cardboard box from a shelf. He ripped four large torches free from their packaging. 'Here, each of you, take one of these.' He handed over the torches. 'Search along the sides of the path as you go. You never know, she could have wandered off, sat down… Christ, I don't know. Just check wherever you can.'

With a flick on then off, the two men tried out the strong torch beams.

Corinne copied them.

Ryan Teacher seemed to regret his earlier attitude. Real or sham, he showed concern for the missing Kate. 'Don't worry,' he told Ross. 'Between us we'll find her.' He included them all in this last statement and his partner and Corinne murmured agreement.

'Right, let's get moving.' Ross stepped towards the door.

76

Before he reached it, he stopped and gestured to Corinne. 'You'll need a waterproof out in that.'

'Oh don't bother.' Corinne felt she was holding up the search. 'I'm already wet through.'

'They're just here.' Ross pulled out a folded plastic cape from a pile on a shelf. He passed it to her. 'This should do you.'

'Thanks.' The three men watching, Corinne, a trifle embarrassed, threw the moss green cape over her head. 'Right, I'm ready.'

In single file they went out into the pouring rain.

Before moving off they lifted their hands and waved to each other as if setting out on a morning hike on a fine day.

'Don't forget,' Ross shouted. 'One hour then back here.' He strode out strongly and the light from his torch soon disappeared.

The combined white beams from the torches of Phil Skinner and Ryan Teacher headed in the opposite direction.

Corinne followed the same path as Ross as far as the back of her cabin and then continued the way she had walked earlier on in the day.

It was much darker now, the rain blustery and heavier; the noise of it set up a constant drumming on her borrowed cape. She was glad Ross had made her take it. Not only did it cover her head and most of her face, it went down well past her knees. The slit for her left arm allowed her to hold the torch and aim it down at the path in front.

Angling its beam, she checked her watch. Ten minutes to eight. It would take longer than half-an-hour to get up to the craft centre if she went slow enough to check each side of the path. She was not entirely convinced that they would find Kate on the tourist paths. The woman must know these woods like her own back garden. Corinne was going along with the plan because Phil Skinner, by offering his and Ryan's help, had put her on the spot. Not that she minded helping, even in this weather. Also, what she'd told Ross back at the shop was right. She wasn't afraid of being on her own in the dark. Now, in addition, she had the torch he'd given her.

The middle of the path was flat but in darkness this was no stroll along Princes Street. Raised tree roots spread like knotted fingers from the edge of the path. In daylight she'd hardly paid them any attention, her senses automatically guiding her past safely. Now, after a couple of stumbles, she was wary of these potential hazards. A twisted ankle wouldn't get her far.

She walked as steadily as she could, constantly training a low arc of light, first to her left then to her right. The powerful white beam penetrated the dark between the trees and showed up the thick dripping undergrowth.

Occasionally, she was aware of scuttling creatures, too fast for her to see let alone identify. Apart from that – nothing. Nobody. No Kate Menzies.

After twenty minutes, the fingers of her left hand were cold and stiff. She stopped and swapped the torch over into her right hand. The rest of her body, still damp from her previous soaking, was warm enough. The cape did its job.

Another five minutes walking slowly and she saw the corner of what she assumed was the craft centre, ahead and to her right. She shoved the cape back off her face. Blinking through the rain, she strained to see. Not a building, a vehicle. A Range Rover.

She recognised it as the one that had been at the side of the craft centre earlier. Where it was parked now was approximately eight metres off the path, in one of the small clearings which occurred here and there. Its engine was silent and the lights were out. From where she stood on the path, level with the vehicle, it appeared abandoned. She thought about ignoring it and carrying on to the centre, then changed her mind. It was not far off the path. There was no danger she could get lost.

Corinne stepped off the path and immediately her shoes

sank into the soft, spongy floor of the woods. Her weight left shallow imprints which filled with water when she picked up her feet. After a couple of metres she was used to the sucking sound she made with every step. She swung the torch down sharply a metre in front and up again to light the clearing.

The white beam splayed off the Range Rover's rain-drenched windows.

Corinne stopped. Slowly, she travelled the torch beam from the front to the rear of the vehicle and back again. It was empty. Her little deviation from the path had been for nothing.

Corinne hesitated. Had her eyes played a trick on her or was there someone there? Training the torch on the passenger-door window she peered hard through the slanting rain.

Slowly, a white face rose up and peered out into the light. Beside it another face appeared from the driver's side of the vehicle. Together the two sets of eyes stared out at Corinne.

Relief flooded through her. In the eerie glow from her torch, she saw the pale face of Kate Menzies. Thank god! She was safe.

Her relief was short lived. It was replaced by embarrassment as she realised her mistake. It wasn't Kate. It was Louisa. And the face, cheek by jowl to Louisa's, belonged to Edwin Coburn.

Corinne was standing just steps away from the side of the vehicle. Through the streaming window the two occupants continued to stare out at her, their eyes reflecting their surprise. She lowered the torch beam to the ground not knowing if they knew it was her they had in their sights. For a moment she stood motionless. With two options, neither of them pleasant, she had to make a choice. She could turn, ignore them, and leave, never to mention that she'd seen them. Or she could face them and ask about Kate.

The decision, in the end, was not hers.

The driver's door opened and Edwin Coburn jumped out.

'What the hell are you doing out in this?' He came to within touching distance of Corinne.

Pushing back her hood Corinne let the rain pour over her face. 'I'm looking for Kate.' She was shouting too. She couldn't help herself. A shoddy defence mechanism, she wasn't going to be put on the back foot by Edwin Coburn.

'She's been out in this all day. Ross is worried about her.' She saw his irritation turn swiftly to what she assumed was genuine concern.

'Well, she's not here.' He blocked her view of the Range Rover.

'When was the last time you saw her?'

'I don't know. Not today.'

'Do you think she could be up at the centre?'

'No. Not possible. The place is locked up tight. No point in you going up there.' He was staring at her.

No offer of a lift then, Corinne thought. It was obvious he was anxious to get rid of her. While it crossed her mind to ask him if Louisa knew where Kate was, his expression was telling her to mind her own business.

'Right, I'll get back then.' Directing the torch forward Corinne made for the path but Edwin Coburn grabbed her arm. His grip brought Corinne to a stumbling halt.

Edwin steadied her. 'I'm sorry I can't give you a lift.' He gestured back over his shoulder into the darkness. 'Engine over-heated, I'm afraid. I was waiting for it to cool down.' He let her go.

Corinne faced him, hardly able to hide her contempt at the lie. She suspected he was trying to smile at her.

'Don't worry. I think I'd prefer to walk.' In the fast increasing darkness and the pouring rain it was a ludicrous thing to say.

Corinne went back the way she had come.

Her neck was stiff and her body as tense as she had ever

felt it. Her mind, too, was shredded with many sharp, jagged thoughts.

By the time she got back to the shop she had reached a decision. Ross would not be told about the Range Rover in the clearing, not by her at any rate.

'Did you see her?' The two partners were already back. There was no sign of Ross Menzies.

'No. Not a trace. Nothing.'

The three of them stood together in the middle of the shop, dripping water.

'I spoke to Edwin Coburn,' Corinne told them. 'He hasn't seen her all day. Their place is shut up for the night.' With a start she realised that Ross had left his business unattended, the front door of the shop unlocked, open to any passer-by to put their hand in the till and take what they wanted. But everything, it appeared, was untouched, exactly as they had left it.

'I don't suppose she's come back?' Corinne asked. 'She's not in the house, is she?'

'Oh!' The two men glanced briefly at each other. Ryan made a face. 'Sorry! We didn't think to check. We've only just got back ourselves.'

'No matter.' Corinne slipped her cape up and over her head. She let it fall like a deflated tent to the wet floor. 'I'll go and see. Just in case.'

'We'll wait here.' Phil appeared reluctant to move from his spot by the counter.

In the long narrow hallway that was the back entrance into the house, Corinne passed a couple of store rooms and a boiler room. She knew which was Louisa's room and glanced in through the open doorway as she passed. She closed the door and tried the next one along; another bedroom – and by the look of it a woman's room – empty. Opposite were another couple of bedrooms and a bathroom.

At the end of the passage the narrow hall opened up. On the left through an open door she could see a large kitchen and on her right was a living room. She stuck her head in both. They were deserted.

Disappointment welled up in her. The emotion was almost overwhelming. Why, she had no idea, except that to have found Kate Menzies safe and sound in her own home would have been a small personal triumph.

She went back to the shop slightly dejected.

'She's not there,' she told Phil and Ryan. She need not have said it. Her taut face and the shake of her head gave them the news.

Ignoring Corinne, Ryan said to his partner. 'Should we wait around for Ross, do you think?'

Phil included Corinne in the decision. 'What do *you* think, Miss Pallin? Would Ross want us to wait until he comes back?'

'I've no idea.' Corinne scuppered any speculation the two men might have about her and Ross Menzies. 'I'm not sure what else we can do tonight.'

'It's just over an hour since we started searching,' Ryan pointed out. 'We did say an hour.'

Phil decided. 'We'll give him another fifteen minutes. I'm sure he'll be back by then. With his wife, we hope,' he added.

Corinne said nothing. What if Ross wasn't back in fifteen minutes? What if he was, but without Kate? What then? Go home to their beds and leave Kate out there all night? She could not see Phil Skinner getting a good night's sleep leaving it like that.

Ryan ended the silence. 'Does anybody know if there's a rescue team here?' he asked. 'You know, like mountain rescue when you get lost in the snow.'

'Ryan! There will be no need for rescue services.' Phil fell short of reproaching his partner. 'I'm sure Ross is coming through that door any minute with his wife, safe and sound.'

Thirty minutes later they were still there, waiting, Ryan eyeing his watch every few minutes.

Corinne was beginning to see the sense in his enquiry regarding a rescue team. About to suggest they contact the nearest police station, she almost cried out when there was a noise at the door and it swung open.

Ross, soaked through, was exhausted. A shake of his head told them. He had not found Kate.

It was a minute before he could speak. 'She's not here?' were his first words.

'Sorry, Ross,' Phil said. 'There's no sign of her.'

The others did not say anything at all.

CHAPTER SIX

Ross Menzies' hair was plastered to his forehead and trickles of water ran down the furrows on each side of his mouth. He accepted Ryan's offer to make coffee with a curt nod. 'Thanks. I'm sorry I've kept you all up like this.'

Phil dismissed his apology. 'We don't mind. This is no time to be on your own.' Seated in an armchair in the Menzies' living room with his partner on a stool at his side, he rewarded Ryan with a little pat on the arm as he got up to go to the kitchen.

Close by, Corinne sat silent. She watched Ross. His head was down, apparently bemused at finding himself sharing a crisis with people who were little more than strangers.

Phil murmured assurances about the nights not being cold and people already camping out.

Corinne was only half listening. She felt like an unwanted visitor, too polite to get up and go when things had not yet been resolved, equally not sure if she were doing any good by staying.

The conversation petered into silence. Second by second it stretched into an embarrassing void. The longer it went on the harder it was to breach.

Given a choice, Corinne would much rather have been back out there in the rain searching for Kate Menzies not sitting drinking the coffee Ryan brought them.

His return broke the tension in the room. 'Is there nowhere else you think she could be?' he asked Ross.

'No. Kate likes the woods. That in itself is a problem.' Ross got up and stood at the window. It was pure habit; at this hour the view straight into the woods disappeared into the darkness. There was nothing to see.

'We,' Corinne glanced in the direction of Phil and Ryan. She hesitated but it had to be said. 'We were wondering if there's a rescue service that operates in the area that might know what the next step is.'

Ross sat down, his eyes concentrated on his coffee. 'Rescue is for accidents. The police won't come out until they're positive a person is missing. Usually twenty-four hours. That's normal.' He kept his eyes down.

An exasperated gasp came from Ryan. 'Surely if you explained, they would see that this is not normal behaviour?'

All eyes swung in Ryan's direction. He did his best to cover over his gaffe.

'Well, it's not as if there are a lot of shops or houses where she could be. Is there?' he demanded. His arms waved dramatically. 'And we've checked all the obvious places.'

'They won't come out tonight,' Ross repeated. He sounded sure. 'Kate... Well, she's done this before. Twice.'

Once again an uncomfortable silence filled the room.

Surprised, Corinne put the mug to her lips and drank a little of the coffee. So twice before, Ross Menzies had gone through this. Tonight's incident suddenly escalated to a whole new level. Less scary? More scary? She drank more coffee.

Phil leaned forward eagerly. 'Well she came back safe then. The same will happen this time, I'm sure.' He stuck to his comfort line. 'People are camping out in this weather no problem.'

Head down, Ross admitted, 'One thing I do know is that the police won't take too kindly to coming here again.' The words were so soft the others could hardly hear them. 'Maybe if she's not back by the morning... I'll get in touch then.'

Corinne saw Ross struggle to get the words out. While he'd taken their help readily enough, he was finding it difficult to let them in on the turmoil he was going through. How she would have loved to ask about those other times when Kate had gone missing.

She glanced at Ross's ravaged face. What was the point of doing that to this anguished man? Instead, she asked him, 'Is there anything else you want us to do tonight?' She gestured to the obliterating blackness outside the window. 'I think the rain's eased a bit. We could go again if you want? If you think it would do any good,' she said gently.

'No. Not tonight.' Ross was clear. 'No, you've done enough already. Thanks, all of you.' He stood up.

Corinne got up and Phil and Ryan followed her lead. All three, tried not to appear too keen to leave.

To Corinne, Ross seemed deathly weary, not beaten by the unsuccessful outcome of the night's search but dejected that it had come about at all.

'Are you all right to get back to your cabins?' he asked.

They nodded.

'Good. Keep the torches. It's pretty dark out there.'

In single file they trailed out through the long narrow hallway.

As they made their way to the door, Ross asked Corinne, 'Will you be all right? I'd walk you back but I don't want to leave the place just in case.'

'We'll see Miss Pallin gets to her cabin,' Phil Skinner offered. 'We've got to go right past there anyhow.'

Corinne and the two men walked, a trifle self-consciously in her case, through the deserted shop and out into the black night.

Compared with earlier the rain was now a mere soft drizzle on their faces. With a silent nod, a grim-faced Ross closed the shop door behind them.

Watching his shadow recede behind the glass, Corinne felt guilty about leaving him. That Phil Skinner felt the same was obvious. Ryan – she wasn't sure what he thought.

On their journey through the woods, not a single word passed between them. All three torches were concentrated into one strong white beam of light along the path until they reached the turn-off towards the loch and Corinne's cabin.

'Thanks.' Automatically, Corinne smiled at them through the darkness. Her torch beam swung down and along the short distance of the walkway to the cabin door. 'I'll be fine from here. Goodnight.'

'Goodnight.' Ryan shortened his stride but kept moving.

Phil hesitated. 'Miss Pallin… You know there really was nothing else we could do tonight.'

'Yes, I know that.'

'She'll turn up safe and sound. I'm sure of it. Don't you worry.'

'I hope so. Goodnight.'

'Goodnight.' The two men moved off.

It took Corinne all of five seconds to reach the solid wooden walkway. Another couple of steps and she was at the door of her cabin. Juggling the borrowed torch and the door key, it hit her that she had forgotten why she went to the shop.

A lot had happened since she had set out for a quick stroll more than three hours ago.

Now, tired, and despite the camping-weather prediction from Phil, cold, she couldn't get the key to turn in the lock. Annoyance was immediately replaced by alarm as it dawned on her the door was already unlocked.

She pushed it wide. Gripping the torch, she manoeuvred the beam slowly, checking the cabin's dark interior. Nothing was out of place. Chair, table, magazine – everything was exactly as she'd left it. Or at least…

Corinne stopped. The edge of the light caught a movement so slight that at first she wasn't sure it was not a blink of her eye. Breathing fast, she swung the torch up.

Louisa sat curled up in a corner of the sofa. The girl's long fingers were fanned over her face shielding her eyes from the torch beam full on her.

Corinne slammed the door shut.

'What the hell are you doing in here again?' She reached for the lamp switch. With one click the place was filled with soft yellowish light.

'I needed to see you.' Louisa's voice was indolent, her

eyes half closed.

Corinne threw the torch onto a chair. 'You know that your mother is missing, don't you?' she informed Louisa bluntly. 'We've been searching for her.'

'Edwin told me.'

'Louisa, this is no game. She's been gone for hours. Your father's worried half out of his mind.'

'My father! Hah!'

Corinne balled her hands. 'Don't you care what happens to her?' Her anger rose steadily. The girl managed to rile her every time they came near each other.

'I'll bet she's back by now,' Louisa dismissed the crisis simply. 'She makes a habit of this.'

Louisa's *laissez faire* attitude oddly comforted Corinne. That it did so equally annoyed her. There was no getting away from it – the girl knew her mother. 'Well, I think you should get back and find out. Don't you?' she snapped.

Like a great agile cat Louisa stretched her arms out in front of her and uncurled her legs. 'I needed to see you first.' The pale face was artlessly presented to Corinne. 'I need to know if you're going to say anything about earlier.'

'About what exactly?' Her anger still bubbling, Corinne did not feel generous.

'You know… me and Edwin.' Louisa gave a little laugh. 'Don't tell me you weren't *shocked* when you found us like that?'

'Louisa, now is not the time. I'm wet, I'm tired. I don't know what it is you want me to say. That I saw you in the Coburns' parked up Range Rover? All right! I saw you. There! Now I want you to leave.'

'Fine.' In one bound, Louisa sprang up. 'I'm going.' She smiled at Corinne. 'I'll tell you the rest tomorrow.' Stepping out onto the dark walkway she disappeared.

Slamming the door shut, Corinne locked it.

As she gazed down at the key in the lock she realised her hands were shaking. These people were driving her crazy!

In the bedroom she rummaged in the drawer for her bottle of paracetamol. Why did she let Louisa get to her so much? She shook out two of the little white pills into her palm. Trembling she screwed the cap back on the bottle and tossed it in the drawer. At the kitchen sink she filled a glass with water, gazed at it for a second then tipped it out. She grabbed the wine bottle. Splashing the last dregs into the glass, she washed down the pills.

Cold and exhausted, she felt a complete wreck. Why was it she'd picked this place exactly? Tomorrow, first thing, she was on the train back to Edinburgh.

The hastily swallowed pills did their job. Next morning she had no headache; no chill from the previous night's soaking, not a trace of an ache.

Corinne lay, her mind vacant, her body completely relaxed before she opened her eyes. The first thing she saw was the sun streaming through the front window of the cabin. It penetrated across the living-room and sneaked its way into a corner of the bedroom.

She grabbed her watch. Half-past ten!

She flopped back against the pillow. When was the last time she had stayed in bed this late in the day? As her memory clicked on the answer, she closed her eyes again.

The image engulfed her like a warm tropical tide on a sandy beach.

A year ago, she and Noel had attended a dinner for the JFL Fiction of the Year Award. Not Noel but an old friend of theirs had won the accolade. Honestly pleased for him, they'd been carried away on a wave of *We know what it's like because we've been there before you,* bonhomie. Both drank too much and stayed on until the very end.

When they got home they were too tired to make love. Corinne fell into bed and was asleep before Noel finished undressing.

The next day, she'd wakened half way through the morning – alone. A short message on her mobile told her he'd gone to see to things in the office.

Now, Corinne sat up in the cabin bed, hugging her knees. The warm embrace of sleep which lingered was stripped away by the truth as that message dawned on her.

How naïve she had been. How trusting. And so sure of herself! All these months she had never doubted that the thoughtful little message, left by Noel on her mobile by her bedside, was not the innocent communication it purported to be.

Corinne suddenly realised the gushing reception from Lynne Robertson when she'd at last got into the office that day had been nothing more than smug arrogance. She'd been playing around with Noel right under Corinne's nose. He'd left their bed to go to Lynne.

What a fool she was! It had taken her all these months to see it.

Corinne sprang out of bed. The last thing she remembered thinking before she fell asleep last night was that she would get herself home today.

Not now! No way! There was still a lot of thinking to do. Unravelling, re-assessing.

While she made breakfast, images stirred up by last night's little escapade with the missing Kate Menzies, whirled about in Corinne's head, the Range Rover in the clearing paramount. How many times had her own husband met his girl-friend in similar circumstances? Noel worked at home almost every day. Time and opportunity, he had lots of. Had there been an occasion when some unsuspecting soul, dog-walker, jogger maybe, had come upon him parked up where he shouldn't have been, like she had with Louisa and Edwin?

What reason would Noel make up on the spur of the moment for his unlikely presence in a back-of-beyond spot? Without a doubt he'd come up with a tale more inventive then an over-heated engine.

For a second time, the absurd lie of Edwin Coburn's made Corinne wince.

It's the easiest thing in the world, lying. How many had Noel told her in their five years together? He'd blamed her for going away too often, but at the time he had been happy enough to stay behind, even pressing Emma, their daily, to take extra holidays, saying he was happy to be on his own. Returning back home, Corinne found him there, every time, waiting, the house as neat as it had ever been despite Emma's absence.

Corinne swore out loud. She threw her half-eaten toast down on the plate. He had gone as far as spraying her perfume, lavishly, over their bedroom.

The devious bastard! He'd been covering up the smell of Lynne Robertson!

The need to be outside, to be on the move, grabbed Corinne. She must clear her head. She had to take a long hard look at what was happening between her and Noel. Forget that she'd caught him, literally, with his pants down. Forget, too, all the good times they'd spent together. It was time she removed the blinkers. She needed to know what was real or was no more than a thin sham covering up the lies that she had been too loyal to suspect.

The morning was bright. The trees backing onto the cabin exuded almost human warmth after last night's heavy rain.

Ah, last night – Kate Menzies.

It all came flooding back to Corinne, sweeping her own problems to one side. She felt she had no option. First, she must go up to the shop to find out what had happened to Kate. After her part in the frantic search, futile as it had been, not to enquire would appear callous. In any event she did want to know if the woman was all right. Louisa's apathetic view of her mother's disappearance, she hoped, would be justified.

It didn't take her long to walk the short way to the Four Hills shop.

After yesterday's downpour, the fine day had encouraged people out. There was a long queue of cabin residents, walkers and hikers waiting at the counter.

Ross Menzies was on his own. Working as fast as he could he made time for a word with each person, gave receipts and bagged up their purchases.

Under the politeness were signs of tension.

As soon as he saw Corinne he waved her aside. 'Could you wait? I won't be long.' It was more an order than a request.

About to make an excuse, Corinne was jostled by a woman joining the queue. Ross did not see her hesitate, or chose not to.

Corinne waited. She was anxious about Kate. At the same time, she wanted to get out of there, or, if she were honest, out of the reach of the Menzies family for a while.

'Sorry to keep you,' Ross said. The queue was gone; the people who were left were browsing. 'I can't leave the counter just now.' He appeared uneasy talking to her. 'I wonder –.'

'Is Kate home? Did she get back all right?' All Corinne wanted was a simple yes or no, no detail, no deep explanations that would draw her in.

'Yes, thanks. She's lying down right now.' He glanced at her. 'Could I come and see you later on. Maybe this afternoon? I'd like to talk to you.'

'Me? What about?'

The lingering customers were foraging through the stacked shelves. None of them looked their way. Ross lowered his voice. 'I don't want to talk here. I'll come down to your cabin later. If that suits you?'

Reluctantly, Corinne agreed. 'Yes. Fine.'

The relief on Ross's face was obvious and Corinne was glad she had agreed. 'I'll be there.' Why he needed to delay it when he could tell her right now was puzzling.

But then, she thought, the people here are puzzling.

A humid heat was beginning to build by the time Corinne walked back to the cabin.

First, she tidied the place then changed into jeans and a thinner top.

Outside, she picked a spot on the edge of the walkway to wait for Ross Menzies. Warm and moist, the dreaded midges were about but not too many. Nobody was out on the water or on the lochside nearby and she was glad to be on her own. The few times she heard movement on the path behind her, she ignored it. Nobody came near the cabin.

Flipping off her shoes she tested her bare toes on the stones. Breathing deep, her lungs filled with the warm pine scent and she closed her eyes. It was ironic. She had come out of the city to be on her own. Here she'd landed right in the middle of friction and sleazy secrets that belonged to another family.

Annoyingly, what she'd seen in the woods last night had triggered off more suspicions about her own relationship; suspicions not just about Noel's affair, but her own part in it.

Loving Noel had never once blinded her to his faults. That much was true. As his celebrity grew so did his shortcomings. There was no arguing that. Every one of them she saw. But through it all she handled him with all the care and skill of a well-paid P.A.

Going over it, she pin-pointed exactly where she had let him down. Flattering him to build his confidence, complimenting him to avoid any potentially disastrous stumble on the hazardous path to fame; it had all worked, yes. But she'd put the spotlight on *him* not *them.*

Corinne bent and picked up a smooth grey pebble. Aiming skyward, *á la Freddy,* she launched it out into the loch. Leaning back, she propped herself up on her hands, her face raised to catch the sun. How hard she had worked for him. Damned hard.

He'd got what he wanted. Reached the pinnacle.

Yet the man she'd helped on his way up the ladder wasn't the man she'd found lying naked with another woman in their house. That wasn't the Noel she fell in love with.

What she didn't understand was what possessed him to take such a chance, such a risk, in his own home.

Like a snake emerging from a writhing mass, another question raised its head.

Had he wanted her to find them? Finish their marriage? His betrayal certainly made a pain free get-out for him. Confronted, he'd confessed quickly. Corinne smiled wryly – about as quickly as he'd packed a bag and left their house. All done with token resistance. That should have started the alarm bells ringing in her head.

Corinne straightened up. Her eyes flew open. My god! He'd set her up! How long had he been waiting to do this? *She* had come back unexpected. *She* had sent him packing. *She* had run away. On the face of it, it was all her doing. *She* had started the ball rolling by leaving. All heavy stuff compared with a little sex.

It was all so obvious now. It had been set up to get him out of a marriage that he didn't have the guts to bring to an end himself. His cheating on her – no crime – would let the charismatic writer keep his appeal. He was an attractive man after all, the faceless critics would say. And he would need to get away to recover and lose himself in a new novel.

Convenient – Corinne laughed out loud – he had a new home in L.A!

'Hi!'

Corinne jumped. Her heart pounded against her ribs. Still large in her head, she half expected to see Noel.

Ross Menzies was striding along the path towards her. His muscled body moved easily and relaxed, giving no sign of this morning's tension let alone last night's. If he was still feeling it, he covered it well.

He raised his hand. 'Thanks for hanging around for me.' He scrutinized her face hard. 'What's wrong?'

Corinne forced a smile. 'It's nothing. I was just taking it easy. Difficult when you're not used to it.'

Ross lowered himself down beside her on the walkway.

'You need to take it easy after all the running about you did last night.' He spread his hands condemning his actions. 'I shouldn't have got you involved like that.'

'I didn't mind. Really. I'm just pleased that Kate got back all right.' She glanced sideways at him. 'What happened? Did you find her or what?'

He heaved a sigh. 'She was up at the Coburns' place.'

'No! I was up there...' Corinne stopped. Cautiously, she went on, 'Or at least near there. I met Edwin just before I got to the centre. I didn't see any sign of Kate.'

'No. There wouldn't be. I found her in the woods way beyond the back of the centre.' He faced Corinne.

Close up, his bloodshot eyes betrayed the truth that Ross Menzies had been out most of the night searching for his wife.

'I need to ask you what Kate said. You know, when she came to see you about Louisa.'

'What do you mean? Said about what?'

'Well, why Louisa did what she did. Taking your sunglasses. Kate was strung-out about that. Until then she was herself, happy, calm, things were good, but that stupid trick of Louisa's set her off again for some reason.'

Corinne shot a look at him. *For some reason!*

'I would say any mother would be upset if her daughter attached herself to things that didn't belong to her.'

'Is a thief, you mean? Why don't you say it?' Ross drew in a long noisy breath. He gazed straight ahead, his face grim. 'Sorry. You're right, of course, Miss Pallin.'

'Corinne.'

His eyes were trained on the waters of the loch. 'I just didn't think it was that big a deal.'

'I said it wasn't,' Corinne reminded him. 'You made a fuss about it. You and Kate. Not me.'

'Yes, that was my fault. When I told her about those cheap sunglasses I gave you, she got upset. To her that only made matters worse not better. That's why she wanted to come and talk to you.'

Corinne shifted position on the hard wooden walkway. 'Did you know that Kate bribed me to say nothing about my sunglasses going missing?'

'Oh, Christ! You *are* joking?' His jaw clenched.

Corinne's raised eyebrows had Ross shaking his head. 'Sorry. The thing is, as far as Kate is concerned, Louisa is still her little girl.'

'Really? That's not what… Oh, forget it. It's nothing.'

'No. Go ahead. What were you going to say?'

'Well, that's not the impression I got when I was with them both. It blew up out of absolutely nothing. I hate to say it but they were hardly civil to each other. In fact…'

'What?'

'Louisa goaded Kate and Kate just stood there and accepted it.'

Ross was silent. He was gazing out over the loch, not at her.

Corinne knew she had stumbled on the crux of the problem. About to ask when it had all kicked off between mother and daughter, she was cut short.

Ross got to his feet. 'Can we go inside?'

There was no one nearby.

He saw her reluctance. 'Indoors would be better.'

Not knowing what was coming, Corinne got up.

Making no attempt to help her, Ross stood by, in the still way he had, waiting while she brushed the dust from her jeans and picked up her shoes.

Inside the cabin, the heat had built up. Drawing the chairs back from the window gave a little respite from the direct sunlight.

Pouring a glass of water for herself she motioned to Ross but he waved away her offer.

In the shade, they sat side by side, the two chairs a fraction apart, facing out onto the loch.

Ross was the first to speak. 'I think I might be taking

advantage of you.'

They were both staring straight ahead. It was a calm, idyllic waterscape that was spread out in front of them.

'At my age, I'm the only one who can say that.' Corinne smiled trying hard not to show that the quivering in her stomach was telling her something different.

'I think it's only right that I explain what's going on.' Ross's voice was low. 'After all, we seem to have dragged you into our affairs without as much as a *welcome to the mad house!'*

Corinne laughed. It came out dry and forced but released some of her pent up tension.

Ross seemed not to notice. 'Kate likes you.'

'She doesn't know me,' Corinne pointed out. 'And I don't know her. Louisa told me she used to be a model. It's not hard to believe. She's a very beautiful woman.'

'Top of the pile for over twenty years.' Ross sounded sad.

'When did she give it up?'

'Six years ago. She didn't give it up – it gave her up.'

'How so?'

In an instant the ghost of those six years passed over Ross's face. 'You think she's beautiful now? You should have seen her back then. Nobody else could come near.' He slumped back in the chair, his eyes half-closed. 'Then, she put on a little weight and found a few stray grey hairs… You know the old story.'

'It happens. I take it Kate couldn't handle it?' Corinne asked gently.

'Hah! Handle it? Oh, she handled it all right. And she had plenty of help handling it.'

'Ah…'

'Appetite suppressers, energy pills, painkillers…' He opened his eyes wide. 'The entire spectrum.'

'Should you be telling me this? It's Kate's business. I don't feel comfortable with this. It's not that I'm not sympathetic, but I'm not even a close friend of hers.'

'If you were, you'd know.' He gazed at her. 'I'll be honest with you. Kate has become a little reclusive since she gave up the catwalk.' He waved his hand from one side of the cabin to the other. 'I bought this place so that she could feel safe. You know, get completely away from the old life, the paparazzi snapping at her, always pulling her apart.'

'Well, she seems to like it here.'

'We had everything under control. She was happy. She practically lived in the woods, walking, running and canoeing even when she doesn't like the water much. All the time she had Louisa beside her. Thirteen years old and as like her mother as her twin. They were inseparable.'

'She had you as well as Louisa.' Corinne began to see beneath the surface of the conversation. 'I don't have kids but surely Louisa must have been a comfort to her when she gave up the catwalk?'

'I suppose she was – at first. Then, well, when you see yourself in the mirror twenty years older than the image in your head, it brings it home that the only one you're kidding is yourself.'

'And seeing Louisa there in front of her everyday wouldn't have helped either,' Corinne guessed.

'You've got it!' Ross sat forward, his elbows planted on his knees. 'When Louisa was seventeen, she got a place at College. She moved to Glasgow and lived there for a couple of years. She seemed to do all right.'

'Yes, I know. She told me. I saw her work.'

'They say it's good,' Ross shrugged. 'I don't know. I'd have been happy to market it in the shop. I mentioned it to Louisa but she knocked the idea back. Said that would just be playing at it. I could see what she meant. I suppose she was thinking on a grander scale. Kids do, don't they? You know, fashion shows, the big time.'

'Oh, I think she'd need to get a lot more experience under her belt before she set her sights in that direction. That would be way down the line.'

'You're right of course. But I think that's why she wanted to move to London. For the experience.' A deep frown pulled at Ross's brows shading his eyes. 'Kate didn't agree.'

Corinne was surprised. 'I would have thought she would be the first to appreciate Louisa's talent.'

'Glasgow was far enough for Kate. Louisa was out of sight – not here reminding her how she used to be – but not *too* far away.'

For a while they both sat saying nothing. Ross appeared lost in the image of mother and daughter, at opposite ends of their careers, at loggerheads.

Corinne felt for this man airing his struggle to a woman he'd known for only three days. 'Perhaps being away from her old friends wasn't the best thing for Kate?'

He glanced at her. 'I thought the same thing. As luck would have it, she didn't leave them *all* behind.'

CHAPTER SEVEN

The vital nucleus of Ross Menzies' story was missing.

Corinne couldn't figure it out but the vacuum was there. It was a tale with the revealing pages torn from its heart.

Walking along the edge of the water she weighed up her own problems against those of the family at the shop. She came out on top in the angst stakes. Her *life* had been ripped apart. Unlike Ross Menzies though, she would work through her problems by herself. As Noel had reminded her – did he really not know of her agonizing choice three years ago – she had no kids to screw up her decisions.

The cove where she first came across Freddy and Lucy and the sludge-green lizard was in bright sunshine.

Idly, she wondered what had been the fate of that small prehistoric remnant. The children, too busy arguing, had not checked on its survival, or otherwise, between the rocks.

Today the little semi-circle of stony space was already occupied.

A bulky middle-aged man in a white peaked cap and a straining yellow shirt, a credit to its makers as somehow its buttons held, was scrabbling about in the pebbles. His bumbling movements and the heightened colour on his face were uncomfortable to witness. A woman, short, and as rotund as the man, stood at the edge of the loch. Her bell-tent of a dress gathered above her knees, she defied the biting cold water as it lapped at her bare toes.

Further back in the cove, a man, a woman, and two small boys, were making a scanty day-camp. Running down the short length to the water, in and out of the shallows, the boys screamed when the water licked at their feet. The adults ignored them, trying to make the best of their stony seats with rugs folded under them, feigning a modicum of comfort.

When Corinne appeared, several "hellos" came her way. A

feeling that the bell-shaped woman, retreating centimetres out of the icy water, was about to engage her in small talk made Corinne return her greeting without stopping. Seconds later she was past the makeshift camp with the pair settled on their rugs, and up onto the path.

At the tree-line, Corinne stopped. The right-hand turn in the path went back towards her cabin; the left went to the farthest cabins where she had not yet ventured. She glanced at the sky. Early afternoon and the sun filtering through the pine branches was warm. She went left.

For ten minutes she walked on before catching sight of the first cabins.

The path, running along in front of the small buildings, narrowed before sloping slightly uphill. The scrubby bank to Corinne's left rose two to three metres back from the edge of the loch. It didn't bother her that she would have to scramble down if she wanted to get near the water. She was content to keep strictly to the path.

By the time she reached more cabins, Corinne had been walking for thirty minutes. Chevron patterned tyre tracks rutted the path before ending at a large clearing amongst the trees.

A dusty slope gradually eased down to the water to a broad, substantial jetty.

Halfway between the trees and the jetty, three cabins, bigger but styled much the same as her own formed a rough semi-circle.

As she cleared the trees, she could hear the low hum of machinery. A generator was fenced-off in a small flat patch on the far side of the cabins. Except for the constant mechanical whir the clearing was peaceful, also deserted.

Corinne walked to the far end of the jetty. It was broad, not high, and solid. She could hear the soft slap of the water against the uprights.

The sun-soaked boards were warm under her hands when she sat down and dangled her legs over the side. She shaded her eyes to stare out over the water.

Two canoes swayed in the middle of the loch. A race appeared to be in progress.

The shallow craft came close to each other then skimmed fast away down the loch, reversed, then repeated the process. One canoeist, much slicker than his counterpart, made his turns more precisely, his angled movements expert, if a trifle arrogant. He was no beginner.

With the sun warm on her face, Corinne watched the little vessels compete for a while. It was relaxing not having to put in any effort.

She lost track of how long she sat there and was surprised when her watch showed her it was a few minutes past four o'clock. The afternoon had gone.

She lingered for a last look at the water.

The two canoeists were still out there but no longer together. They had paddled away from each other and now seemed centred in their own particular stretch of the loch, plying back and forth at pointedly different speeds.

Corinne, her back to the water, walked towards the path. She noticed a silver Aston Martin sitting behind the first cabin. As she drew level with it, the cabin door opened.

Kim and Alec Taylor were talking earnestly; not an argument, an incongruous agreement on a distasteful subject it appeared.

The couple saw her and stopped. In the initial moment of recognition, Corinne caught a flash of relief on both their faces. Obviously she was more welcome than some.

Kim raised her hand and walked towards her. 'Hello, there. How do you like our little hamlet?'

'It's a fair way,' Corinne admitted. 'This is the first time I've managed to walk this far. I can see the jetty from my cabin window. It's a bit remote but it's lovely.'

Alec joined them in time to hear this. 'If you think this is remote,' he said, 'you should carry on another couple of miles. There are two more cabins further on and up the hill right back in the trees.' He laughed. 'Back to nature types like them.'

Corinne smiled. 'It sounds a tad primitive to me.'

Kim nodded. 'You're not wrong there, my dear. No electricity! They haven't even got a generator.' She shuddered, sorry for the hardy residents. 'Above all else I must have good lighting.' She laughed good-naturedly at herself and her little foible.

Corinne glanced at Kim. The woman's face was very pale, her makeup complete, and her fine blond hair immaculately styled if stiff and rather out of fashion. Even in a fitted-out cabin, Corinne wondered at her roughing it this far. 'You have a very peaceful spot here,' she said. 'I was surprised to see a car.'

Alec answered her. 'That's ours. I'm afraid we spoiled ourselves with that. Ross Menzies let us bring it down the track. We're in this cabin here. And Phil and Ryan – you've met the boys I believe – they're in the one over to the right there.' He pointed. 'And there's a young couple just got here this morning – we've only seen them but haven't met yet – they're in the other one.'

Kim touched Corinne's arm lightly. 'We're going to be quite a little party tonight,' she said with a hint of excitement.

'Ah...' Alec Taylor hesitated. 'About that, I was thinking... maybe too tiring?' His words wiped the smile from Kim's face.

'I think we'd better give it a miss tonight,' he said.

Kim caught his eye and nodded as if realising just then that she was indeed tired. 'You're right of course,' she said, adding softly as if abandoning the outing had been her idea, 'You won't mind missing it, will you?'

Alec slipped his arm through his wife's. 'Don't be silly.' He pulled her close.

Kim leaned against him and shrugged. 'Ah well, perhaps another time.' She raised a smile at Corinne. 'But you'll be going, I take it?'

'Going where?'

'It's the get-together tonight,' Alec said. 'Everybody in the cabins, any hikers, campers, anybody who's in the vicinity really. All are welcome. If they turn up they'll get a drink at least.'

It suddenly dawned on Corinne. 'Oh, the picnic! Ross did say last night.'

Kim was puzzled. 'Didn't you see Louisa?' She glanced hastily at Alec and hurried on. 'She was here earlier. When she left she was on her way to your cabin to make sure you knew about it. So she said.'

Corinne was confused. 'First Kate then Louisa. Why them? Isn't it up at the Coburns' place?'

'Yes, it is,' Alec confirmed. 'But you might say the Coburns and the Menzies are, well, working together. You know, buy a bottle of wine from the shop to take when you go, then while you're at the craft centre…'

'Buy a souvenir,' Kim finished for him. 'Nothing at all wrong with that.'

'No, of course not.' This thin chitchat back and forth between the Taylors had Corinne puzzled as if they knew something she didn't.

'They are very close, the families,' Kim said.

'Too close if you ask me,' Alec Taylor voiced his opinion. 'That young woman needs a firm hand.'

Kim said wistfully, 'She's not found her niche in life, yet. That's all.'

Her husband wasn't convinced. 'If you ask me, she's going a dangerous way about it.'

'Oh, Alec, she's not bad,' Kim smacked him softly on the chest. She glanced at Corinne. 'Not really.'

Corinne smiled. 'Well, I must start back. It was nice to see you again.'

'And you, my dear,' Kim echoed the sentiment. She gazed earnestly at Corinne.

'You should go this evening,' she said. 'You'll probably find it charming in a countryish way.' It was said without a hint of patronizing Corinne or anybody who might eventually turn up at the Coburns' picnic.

'Yes. I might give it a go.' Corinne raised her hand briefly and went up the path and into the trees. She had the distinct feeling that Kim and Alec Taylor had not moved.

The sun was still shining when Corinne reached her cabin.

Real barbecue weather, she reflected as she stripped and went under the shower.

She wondered if it was like this down in the city. Back gardens filled with smoke and the unmistakeable aroma of hot coals and charred steaks. She could almost smell it. Normally she would be doing the same. Noel would set up the barbecue and she would open the garden-room door...

Second-hand invitation or not, she would go to the Coburns' picnic.

Dressed in thin dark trousers and a loose white top, she got ready without much fuss. The one bottle of wine she'd bought at the shop was finished but there was a tin of savoury biscuits in the cupboard. Grabbing that, she opened the cabin door.

For a second she stood and over her shoulder glanced at the living-room. Every time she went out and came back she had this very uneasy feeling.

What was needed, she reckoned, was a good burglar alarm.

Switching off the light she reasoned there was nothing much for anyone to steal, on the other hand it would be good to know.

Before she shut the door she picked up a stone found on her walk that afternoon. It was roughly half the size of a golf ball. With the door open no more than a couple of fingers width Corinne shoved the stone just inside. Gently she pulled the door closed and locked it.

The music reached Corinne through the trees before she got to the craft centre.

People sat at the tables talking and laughing. It made for a good sound, a lively prospect that Corinne didn't know if she could match.

The semi light of evening descending, a couple of spotlights attached high up on the back wall of the veranda were on, shining down on the crowded tables.

Corinne did a cursory count as she went up the steps. It appeared the entire population of Four Hills was already there. She knew Phil and Ryan, and some hikers who'd been in the Menzies' shop at the same time as her.

The man who drove her from the station in his old white Rover taxi was there. Despite wracking her memory, for the life of her she couldn't recall the man's name. He was at a corner table with another man and two women. They sat, paper plates with odd scraps of food in front of them, not eating, waiting expectantly.

Through the doorway, Corinne caught sight of Tamzin Coburn. The woman's short hair was covered with a long, thin scarf which floated about her head like a hovering mist. Moving out into the spotlights, her rainbow-striped dress emanated a simple life, but with a designer label.

Corinne crossed the veranda. 'Hello.' She held out the tin of biscuits. 'I bit paltry, I'm afraid. Best I could do.'

Tamzin laughed. It was light and genuine. She was enjoying herself.

'Just exactly what we need. We've not nearly enough nibbles.' She shoved the tin back at Corinne. 'Would you be a pal and offer these to our visitors. Oh, and the cheese…' She lowered her voice. 'We've been landed with a sketching class from the village. I don't mind. The more the merrier.' A smile, conspiratorial, was flashed at Corinne. 'It's all good for business.'

A sketching class. That accounts for the numbers, Corinne figured. And Tamzin had shown no surprise at seeing her.

Alec Taylor had been right – all, apparently, were welcome.

Opening the tin, Corinne offered it and the cheese board to the tables. Half way round, the volume of conversation rose. Seconds later, a burst of clapping spread across the veranda.

Edwin Coburn emerged from the centre brandishing a couple of bottles of champagne.

'Now, we can get the party going!' He motioned to Corinne. 'Pass those glasses out will you? Four bottles only I'm afraid. We'll see how far it goes.'

Corinne did as he asked and Edwin followed behind her with a bottle in each hand, splashing a measure of champagne into every glass held out.

'Sorry about press-ganging you into this,' he said in her ear. 'But I think Tamzin's gone to make sure the kids are settled down for the night.'

'Oh, don't worry about it. I don't mind.' Corinne gave out the last of the glasses.

Leaning back on the rail of the veranda with her glass, she was joined by Phil Skinner and Ryan Teacher.

Phil held up his glass. 'Cheers.'

'Salut,' Corinne came back at him.

Ryan tilted his glass at her. 'It was you, wasn't it? This afternoon, watching us?'

His accusing tone rattled Corinne. 'I don't know. What were you doing that was so interesting?'

Ryan's lips tightened. He glanced briefly at his partner then away. 'Nothing untoward, if that's what you're implying.'

'Now then Ryan, Miss Pallin didn't mean any such thing.' Phil smiled at Corinne. 'It was us on the water when you were at the jetty.'

Corinne nodded. 'Yes. I was there. I didn't know it was you in the canoes. I must say, you seemed pretty expert.'

'Expert!' Ryan sneered. 'It was like teaching a moggy to swim!'

Corinne didn't comment but glanced at Phil.

107

The man was shocked. 'I'm much better on dry land, I'm afraid,' he told her.

'You gave it a go, anyway.'

Phil smiled at her. 'Miss Pallin, you are a woman who knows how to make allowances.' He ignored his partner. 'If you'll excuse me.' Placing his glass on a near-by table, Phil walked away.

Ryan and Corinne watched him go.

'I've upset him. Will I never learn?' Ryan questioned his own conduct.

Feeling she'd added to the disagreement between the two men, Corinne said, 'It must be dangerous, canoeing. I imagine you've got to have nerve even to try it.'

'Yes, you're right. Absolutely!' Ryan flashed Corinne a smile and promptly followed his partner.

Corinne stayed where she was. Several people talked to her then Tamzin appeared and asked if she wanted anything more to drink. She refused. Soon after she saw Ross and Kate Menzies arrive with Louisa trailing in their wake, with them but not with them.

Kate saw Corinne and headed straight for her.

'I just wanted to say sorry about last night.' In the beam from the spotlight, Kate's face was alarmingly white. Her cheeks were hollow, her eyes darting and pink rimmed. She was holding fast to her contribution to the party – a large box of chocolates.

Corinne did not want to go over last night. 'No need.' Nodding to the assembled company, she commented, 'A great party they've got going.'

'Where did you go?' Kate continued, ignoring Corinne's comments.

'Sorry?'

'To look for me... Which way? Where did you go?' Kate was pleading with her.

'I walked up here as it happens.' Corinne saw the cardboard lid of the chocolate box bend in Kate's grip. 'It was dark as you know. I didn't see you. I'm sorry.'

Kate continued to blink at her. 'No… I was… I was…'

Over Kate's shoulder Corinne saw Ross.

He was edging away from a noisy table of hikers hoping for their glasses to be filled again *gratis*. Corinne caught his eye as he glanced up.

Pushing his way through the crowd, he came up behind Kate and draped his arm over her shoulders.

Kate jumped at his touch. Visibly shaking, she tried to smile at her husband and held out the dented box of chocolates as an offering to nobody in particular.

'Give me these.' Ross glanced behind him. 'Louisa!'

On the other side of the veranda, the girl pulled away from a group of hikers and sauntered over. She ignored her mother and addressed Ross and Corinne. 'Having fun?'

Ross passed the box to Louisa. 'Make yourself useful. Give these to Tamzin.'

Corinne expected Louisa to refuse. But the girl laughed and grabbed the box out of Ross's hand. 'Edwin loves chocolates!' Again she laughed, this time louder. 'I know exactly what he fancies.'

Several people nearby stared and, without knowing why, joined in the laughter.

When Louisa went in search of Tamzin, Corinne was glad to see her go. In the short time her daughter had stood with them Kate Menzies had been silent and noticeably wary.

Kate, wide-eyed, turned expectantly to her husband. At that moment she wasn't concerned about Louisa. 'You didn't tell me Corinne came up here last night,' she accused him, her voice soft but urgent.

His hand tightened on her arm. 'Kate, forget about last night. It's over.'

For a long moment Kate studied Corinne. 'It was raining, wasn't it? You got wet.' she stated. 'I'm sorry you had to go out in the rain.' In that moment, the green eyes were no longer timid. 'It won't happen again. I've promised Ross.'

Corinne hung on for over an hour.

With less on her mind she might have enjoyed herself more because, on the face of it, it was a very uncomplicated, carefree party. Hikers and campers talked about places and people they'd come across on their travels. People from the cabins listened and added their tales of Munros climbed and highest mountains attempted. It was all civilised and amiable. Everybody was relaxed.

The exception was Louisa. With a face that got her noticed, she demanded centre stage, drank too much, and got increasingly loud and over-familiar with the men on the veranda.

Corinne guessed what was coming. She could see it unfold in front of her.

Louisa was noisy. One minute she wanted to sing, the next she wanted to dance.

The music was loud and two of the young men were up on their feet without much coaxing. Not put off by heavy boots they began their own thundering jig until the dust rose, the veranda trembled, and the sweat beaded their bright red faces.

Standing between his wife and Corinne, Ross watched. 'There are going to be a few sore heads in the morning,' he predicted.

Corinne agreed. 'They're having a good time. We've all been there.'

Edwin Coburn joined them. He carried a tall glass of sparkling water for Kate.

'I thought you might like this.' He passed it over. 'Tamzin's got this music far too loud.' He raised his voice but did nothing about the blaring noise.

They stood in a tight little group, not talking, just watching the gyrations of the dancers in the middle of the shuddering veranda.

Then it happened. In a frenzied movement, one of the

hikers lost his balance. His foot shot from under him and he pitched sideways. As he fell, he grabbed onto his partner for support. His partner was Louisa. She screamed loudly as the man thudded heavily to the floor, dragging her on top of him.

She shrieked with laughter as the man's friend pulled her to her feet. Startled, the other dancers stopped dead as the hiker scrambled up. The two men faced each other and a fight threatened to break out.

Louisa, moving elusively around the veranda, clasped onto one young man and then his friend. In their own clumsy fashion they followed her in a bizarre conga, the threat of a fight averted.

People got up and joined the swaying, snaking column with Louisa at its head, making its way off the veranda and into the darkness.

'Ross,' Kate's trembling voice could just be heard above the music. 'Stop her. Please.'

'No.' Edwin thrust his glass at Ross. 'You stay here. I'll see to it.' He smiled at Kate. 'Don't worry. It's just high spirits. They're enjoying themselves.'

He crossed the veranda. Hooking arms with Louisa, he joined the conga and led her back up the steps. He motioned to Tamzin standing in the doorway to turn the music down and she disappeared inside.

The music stopped and a strange, pervasive silence shrouded the veranda as if signalling an untimely halt to the night's proceedings.

The conga broke up and people sprawled exhausted in their chairs.

The music started again, a new track, softer, slower and gentler. Tamzin got it just right.

It encouraged couples up into the middle of the veranda along with Edwin and Louisa. They shuffled in time to the music, slow and easy.

From the side, Corinne was aware of Kate staring hard at

Louisa. The girl's arms were clasped around Edwin's chest. Eyes closed, her head was cradled deep in his shoulder.

Valiantly holding her up, Edwin slowly manoeuvred her in a circle on the makeshift dance floor. Once, Louisa lifted her head and smiled up into his face. She uttered to him and he shook his head. That was his only response.

Watching, Corinne gave a little laugh. 'I think the champagne's gone to my head, too.'

Neither Ross standing alongside, nor Kate on his far side, answered Corinne. Kate's eyes were riveted on her daughter, the glass of sparkling water untouched in her hand.

Ross removed the glass from her. 'I think we've had enough for tonight.' He nodded at Corinne. 'If you want, we can all walk back together.'

'Yes, I'm ready when you are.' Corinne realised that she did feel a little light-headed and was glad she wouldn't have to negotiate her way through the woods on her own.

Kate was not so eager to go without her daughter. 'We can't leave her.' She grabbed frantically at Ross's arm. 'Make her come home,' she appealed to him. 'We mustn't leave her here.'

Anger flashed over Ross's face. His fingers went through his hair in an unconscious gesture of exasperation. Then he patted Kate's hand and glanced at Corinne. 'This won't take a minute.'

'That's fine. There's no –.' Corinne was cut short by Tamzin appearing at her side.

'Sorry about all that noise earlier.' Tamzin gathered up the glasses. 'Have you had a good time?' She wasn't looking for an answer. 'I'll turn the music off now and shoo them off to their beds.' Without waiting for any agreement she went inside.

Seconds later, the music stopped abruptly.

People started to make tracks back home to cabins, tents, to the village. In a short time, save for cries of 'goodnight', the place was relatively silent.

112

Corinne and the Menzies were the last to make a move. Alone now on the make-shift dance floor, Louisa was proving difficult.

Edwin and Tamzin between them persuaded her to stop dancing.

'Even if you don't need your sleep, I do,' Tamzin made light of wanting Louisa gone.

Louisa yawned. 'I'm too tired to walk all that way back. Edwin, let me stay here. I promise I won't be any trouble. Please. Please.'

'You're coming home with us.' It was Kate. Her pale cheeks had two hot spots of colour and she appeared on the verge of collapse. 'Edwin and Tamzin want to get to bed.'

'Tamzin, I can stay, can't I? Please Tamzin.' Louisa was determined to get her own way.

Tamzin refused, making the excuse, 'We've got a real busy day ahead of us tomorrow.'

Urging Kate on in front, Ross held Louisa by the arm and walked her to the edge of the veranda. 'Let's go.' He took a small torch from his pocket and threw it to Corinne. 'We'll need that.'

Corinne switched on the torch and headed towards the path. Behind her she heard Louisa's plaintive grumbling as Ross dragged her down the veranda steps, ignoring the girl's protests.

Before they'd even left the steps behind, Louisa twisted out of Ross's grasp and faced Kate.

'Jealous cow!'

Kate gripped Ross's arm for support. She stared hard at her daughter, drunk, screeching obscenities.

Tamzin and Edwin went inside the craft centre, closing the door behind them.

Corinne felt removed from the little scene supposedly brought on by a splash of champagne.

The three Menzies and Corinne were silent on the walk back

113

to Four Hills.

Ross kept a firm hold on Louisa. It was doubtful whether, if he let go, she could have stood on her own. He did not give her the chance to find out.

Corinne walked side by side with Kate. Neither of them said a word.

At the turn in the path, Ross took over the torch from Corinne. He still had Louisa by the arm. 'We'll wait here until you're on the walkway,' he told Corinne and pointed the torch in the direction of the loch.

Before she reached the end of the walkway, Corinne had her keys out ready. She raised her hand to the three Menzies standing watching her but she could not bring herself to call out 'goodnight'.

She unlocked the door. The second before she pushed it open, Corinne remembered the small stone she'd placed strategically behind it and glanced towards the path. The family were already turning away.

Bending down she pushed the door open just enough to slip her hand inside and spread her fingers on the floor. Feeling nothing she opened the door a fraction wider. The little white stone wasn't there. Straightening up she slipped into the cabin through the restricted space.

She felt for the lamp and flicked the switch. The white pebble had moved to the front of the bedroom door. She picked it up and cradled it in her hand.

At the dressing-table, she toyed with the little pebble. It was telling her she should check nothing had been stolen. She caught her reflection in the mirror. At this moment possessions didn't seem to be so very important.

Corinne got up, crossed the living room, locked the door, and threw the bolt hard into its socket.

CHAPTER EIGHT

The bee-like drone of the light aircraft was loud. The plane descended at a steep, eye-bulging angle. Noel helped her out onto a narrow dusty runway on the edge of the Kenyan National Park. It was searingly hot, blindingly bright.

Corinne heard the droning grow louder, almost suffocating in its persistence.

Her dream receded at the appointed hour. Eight o'clock and she grabbed the quivering piece of technology and punched the alarm button silent. Half-awake, she glanced through her messages on the small bright screen. Guilt raised its head. Yesterday morning was the last time she'd checked.

Arranging her pillows into a prop, she sat up and scrolled through the list. First, her father, then Noel followed by an unfamiliar number, then her father again. Two more from Noel, a couple of business numbers she recognised, her father, a friend, her father yet again, Noel one more time, then, the last, her mother.

Corinne leaned back, her eyes closed. Of all the names on the rolling screen, the last one disturbed her the most. Her mother had called, once. It needed no explanation. Corinne knew her; she wouldn't call again until she got a response to her original message. It was the way her mother worked, family not excepted.

How could Corinne make her understand? She was not deliberately shutting her out, or any of them. But this was her problem. At arms length was where she had to keep them for the present. The final decision had to be hers.

Corinne was not keen to deal with the calls this early on a Sunday morning.

Thankfully, the business numbers would have to wait until tomorrow. As for the others, she doubted if any were so urgent they could put things right in her life.

In the shower, the warm water ran over her back, her

thighs and down her legs. The soft cascade felt good. She stood there lost in the primal feel of clear water on bare skin. At home, in a hurry, she showered quickly. Here she went slower.

Finished, she felt alert. The list on her mobile niggled away. Her parents, her friends; everyone would know by now. What did they think she was trying to prove by staying away?

Her hair half dry, she threw on warm clothes and did her face. It was a day for decisions. As she tumbled cereal into a bowl, she determined to face up to it. Pressing the speed dial, she put her mobile to her ear and waited.

Seconds later her father's voice, smooth and calm as ever, came at her.

'Hello, Cherie. How are you?'

'I'm fine, Papa. I didn't wake you did I?'

'No. Of course not! Your mother and I, presently, we are having breakfast. I take it you have been served with yours wherever you are?'

'Papa,' Corinne gulped a mouthful of orange juice ignoring the hint. 'I've been thinking. Would you mind if you and Maman held off going back to France?'

'Oh, until you and Noel have resolved your difficulties there is no question of us leaving. No. That we have already decided.' He did not pause to discuss it. 'Now, Cherie, tell me, what you have in mind?'

'Well, nothing definite yet.' Corinne breathed out slowly. 'What would you say if I went away for a time? Not very long, just a week or two.'

'A vacation! Why not?' His tone brightened. 'You and Noel. Yes? Time together. That might be the best way.'

'No, Papa. Not with Noel.' Corinne kept her voice level. 'On my own. Not with Noel. It's so I can get things straight in my head. With him along, well, that wouldn't be possible.'

'That is what you are doing, is it not?' He was blunt. 'Are

116

you not on your own now? What would be different on this holiday?'

'Right at this minute it's all about me and Noel, the two of us. I know I dodged out of it. I was wrong. I shouldn't have done that. But ever since I've been here I've realised things weren't how I saw them. I've had my eyes opened to a lot of things.' Corinne laughed feebly. 'No doubt I was the last to know what was going on.' She swallowed fast and rushed on, 'Now that I do, there's no going back. That is the one thing I don't have to decide: I know. Things haven't changed. It's just, I know the truth. I've got to take it from here on my own.'

'Cherie, is it wise to come to decisions before you have seen Noel? You have not spoken face to face with him since…'

'Since I found out what he's been up to? Is that what you were going to say, Papa? My God! I don't know.' Corinne tipped up her head and shut her eyes. 'Men seem to take these things in their stride. I'm not sure I could do that. Put up with a patched up marriage, watching and wondering what's going on every time he's with another woman. Never sure if… No, I would rather be on my own than live with a sham of a marriage like that.'

'All couples have their problems, Corinne. You and Noel are no exception. There are no exceptions.'

'So what are you telling me? Accept it, say: fine, you had a little *divertissement* but I forgive you? Go on as if nothing had happened. Is that what you're advising?'

'No! No! Cherie! I am not saying what it is you should do. You are a grown woman. Of course you must decide for yourself. I don't want to interfere. However, I can tell you, Noel is devastated. He has not been to the office except for one hour on Thursday.'

'He was probably too preoccupied!'

'Do not do that, Cherie.'

The pause that followed built up.

117

Corinne breathed deeply and broke the impasse. 'What makes you think he is devastated?'

'I called at the house yesterday,' her father informed her.

'I take it he wasn't alone?' Corinne wished she'd held her tongue.

'Yes, he was alone. He was sitting in the kitchen surrounded by his old manuscripts.'

'What?'

'His manuscripts. Old letters also, papers. Everything was out of the cabinet. It was as if every word he had ever written, it was spread out on the table.'

'Why? What was he doing?'

'Reminiscing? I do not know. Maybe. I cannot tell you. Corinne, what I do know is that he was upset. He was not his usual self. When I tried to speak to him he became very defensive.'

'Towards you, Papa? Are you sure? You two always got along all right.' She stopped. 'Or am I wrong about that too?'

'Corinne, this is not helpful. No, you are not wrong. Noel and I, we were very amiable together.'

Corinne smiled grimly. 'I know, Papa. Sorry. But this doesn't sound like him.' She poured more orange juice into her glass. 'Now he's got this new house in the States – I'm not being facetious – I wouldn't have been surprised if he'd left before now.'

'Well, he is still there, in your house, by himself. From the little he did say he is very anxious to see you. He wants to talk things over.' Her father paused. 'Why don't you see him, Cherie? Even to say that you need more time. Would that not be easier? Better than this… what…? Stand-off?'

'You make us sound like we're fighting a war. You don't see it like that, surely.'

'That is how it will turn out to be. Believe me. However amicable a split, there are always two sides to the story. And there will be a winner and there will be a loser.'

'Papa… You and Maman, do you blame me for any of this?'

'Cherie, it is not for us to say such a thing. If you are to blame then we, too, are to blame. You are what we made you.'

'No! I won't have that!' Corinne was adamant. 'Like you said, I'm all grown up. Whatever I've done, it's down to me.' She gripped the phone. 'None of this is down to you two, you and Maman.'

'She is here, beside me. Do you want to speak to her?'

It was what Corinne had dreaded. 'I'll have to go. Tell Maman I'll phone her later… soon.'

'Very well. Goodbye, Corinne.'

Corinne clicked her mobile shut. Every word her father had told her, she believed.

Nevertheless, it needed a lot of imagination to see Noel as a broken man. He had too much ego and was far too absorbed in his own importance these days for reminiscing.

She felt slightly comforted. From her father's account Noel was not having an easy time of it either. She wondered at him staying on at the house. Was he waiting for her to go back? Those papers dad had seen? What was so important?

Corinne shrank from the idea of packing her bags and getting on the train south to face Noel. Not ready for that yet, and also the fact that her father had not pressured her, gave her leave to stay on at Four Hills. She needed to believe that, otherwise what good was it keeping herself separate from the people she should have been able to rely on?

She flicked her mobile and her finger hovered over one particular number. Eating breakfast by her husband's side, her mother would know Corinne had declined to speak to her.

She should do it now. Even if only to say she was fine. But that was the trouble – she wasn't fine.

Corinne could not help compare her parents' marriage with her own. Whatever had gone on between Jean Fotheringham and Pierre Pallin over the years, her mother had always been able to make it right. Strong and so certain of herself.

Corinne closed her mobile. The click was hardly discernible yet decisive. Never once when she was growing up had she had an inkling that things were anything but perfect between the two people she loved most in the world. Now she got the sense they knew exactly what she was going through. Had they hit a rocky patch along the way?

Her mother was strong. Corinne doubted she herself had her strength.

At this precise moment, she was feeling too raw and fragile to be generous to Noel. Not enough time had passed to be rational. He had hurt her badly – he should not expect forgiveness so soon.

Corinne flicked her mobile open a third time. 'God help me! I *am* a grown woman!'

She pressed the screen. The name *Noel* stood out alone, bright. The digits danced along the airwaves and she listened to it connect.

'Hi! Noel here. Just say your name. I've got your number!'

So slick, so patronizing, Corinne hated that message. She shut it off before it finished. Either he was in a meeting or in the middle of rewrites. Whichever, she had avoided him for the time being.

At the top right of her mobile screen it read 9:42. Uncle Ian would be up by now. Corinne smiled and visualized him; stoic, sensible, a down-to-earth Scot. She loved him. His name was not among the list of calls she had received. She knew why. A man to listen if you approached him, he would never presume.

It was to him Corinne had turned when a teenager trying to work her way to a degree in English Literature. There were times she felt guilty about that. It had transpired because her parents had been too close, too anxious to be objective about her choices.

Ian McCall had let her talk it through, back and forth it

rumbled between them, until she eventually made her decisions. How badly she needed that now.

'Uncle Ian.'

'What took you so long, eh?' Ian McCall was sharp. Ten years older than her parents he was plain speaking. 'Did you lose my number or what?'

'Just things to think about.' Suddenly, Corinne felt shaky as she heard the deep voice. 'Have you seen Noel? I take it Dad's filled you in?'

'I had dinner with him and Jean two nights ago. They're worried about you, lass.'

'I can't help that.'

'You and Noel, can you patch it up? This, whatever it is?'

'Have you seen him?'

'No. I've not seen hide nor hair of him since you left.' He laughed dryly. 'You're costing us money, the pair of you. You know that?'

'Sorry about that.'

'Ah, well, I'll make sure it comes out of your salary.' A barely audible grunt reached Corinne.

'Dad says Noel seems to be working. When he went to the house Noel had practically emptied out the filing cabinet. He was going through all his papers.'

'Well, there's nothing in the pipeline other than those few rewrites he's to get on with. They wouldn't be a problem to him. Other than that I didn't know he had anything urgent to be getting on with.'

'Neither did I. This doesn't sound like Noel – work for work's sake.'

A silence settled on the line. It was Ian McCall who ended it.

'How did you leave things with him? I take it you didn't think to tell him where you were going?'

'No. I wanted to get right away.' Corinne sighed. 'I couldn't bear staying in the house. Not after…'

There was another silence. Blunt as he was, Ian McCall

was not a man to let his mouth run away with him. He was not insensitive. 'Well, he's still there all right. Your dad thinks he's waiting for you to come back.'

'I think he wants out,' Corinne admitted.

'How do you mean, lass?'

'He wants me to kick him out.'

'Out of the house?'

'No. Not just that. Everything; the house, us, the business.'

'Oh, is that right?' Ian McCall pulled in a long breath. 'Now that would cost him a pretty penny,' he said practically. 'We've got him contracted for another three books not counting the one that's just about due. If he wants to walk out on that as well...' He left the consequences hanging.

Corinne sucked on her lower lip. 'I believed between us we had more than that.'

'I would say that you did. But then people change.'

'Noel certainly has!'

'And you.'

'Me! Changed? You really think so?'

'I do that. Neither one of you is the person you were five, six years ago. None of us is. Mind, don't let what I'm saying upset you. You've moved on yourself. There's not a soul comes into the office who doesn't heed what you've got to say.'

'That's different!' Corinne dismissed his logic. 'That's business.'

'That's how you met Noel,' Ian reminded her, 'through business.'

'Thanks for that.'

'It's a fact.'

'Uncle Ian, was any of this obvious to you?' While it might open up new wounds, Corinne needed to delve deeper. 'Did you see this coming?'

'Like I say, people change. Occasionally they grow on each other. Ah, dare I say it; even get to like each other.

122

Then there are times they drift apart without ever knowing why. I could see *you* were content. You were satisfied with what was between you.'

'Noel wasn't. That's what you're saying, isn't it?'

'Be honest, lass. You must have got a suspicion of it yourself. He's become restless of late. He wants more. He's used now to being near the top of the pile. It's where he likes to be – way up there. Now he wants that bit more.' The smack of his lips sounded in Corinne's ear as Ian McCall asserted, 'It happens to most folk tasting success. If Noel's straining to move on, and thinks you're holding him here, well, that's not the way to keep him happy.'

'What we have is not enough?'

'For you, maybe, but once a body's got his eye on the top it's hard to draw back without going for it.'

'I should have seen this coming.' Corinne ached to have Ian McCall's rough bearded face in front of her, to see his thatch of grey hair bounce over his brow as he nodded sympathetically and feel the squeeze of his great clumsy hand on hers.

Eyes closed, she swallowed hard. 'He's hurt me,' she said. 'I can't undo what's happened. Yet I won't be made a fool of.' She was getting hot just thinking about Noel, naked and grunting, with Lynne Robertson astride him. 'I won't let him get away with that.'

She opened her eyes. 'If he wants out, he can. But there's no way he's walking away scot free. No way!'

'You intend to make him pay for his peccadillo then?' Ian stated.

Corinne's face flushed. 'Don't you gloss over it like that! Like it was nothing! It wasn't nothing!' Glad he could not see her, she lowered her voice. 'This is not my doing. Anyhow, it's the business I'm thinking about, not me. If we let him go it's going to cost us.'

'Maybe. It depends.'

'Depends? On what?'

'On how we, you, handle it.'

'He's our biggest name. If we lose him…' Corinne waited. She heard Ian McCall draw in a long breath through his nostrils and let it out again noisily through his mouth.

Corinne had an idea.

'Will you check out a couple of things for me?' she asked.

It was eleven o'clock before Corinne ventured outside on to the walkway.

Already the day was warm, the sky blue.

Arranging her Bvlgari on top of her head she went left at the junction of the path and started towards the little cove.

Before she covered a hundred metres she saw Louisa with the two Coburn children. As usual Freddy was darting in and out of the trees in the demented way that was uniquely his. Lucy walked beside Louisa, talking earnestly, a rapt expression on her small, intelligent face.

It was Lucy who saw Corinne first. The little girl immediately stopped. What she said to Louisa caused her to stop and they both gazed at Corinne.

Corinne saw that Louisa was going to walk on but Lucy was waiting.

Her hair like a flaming beacon in the dappled light, Louisa was forced to wait too.

Corinne reached them. 'We've all had the same idea,' she said. 'You going along to the cove?'

'These brats pulled me out of my bed,' Louisa drawled.

'We're going to see how many different kinds of stones we can find.' Lucy's clear eyes fixed on Louisa. 'You *said* you would help,' she reminded her.

'I'm here, aren't I?' Louisa gave Lucy a little push. 'Go and see where Freddy's got to. Go on!'

'Oh, all right,' Lucy hesitated before explaining to Corinne. 'This is very important. It's for a project Mummy set us.' The small bright eyes fixed on Corinne then swept back to Louisa. 'You *promised* you would help.'

'I know! I know! Go!'

Lucy, shoulders squared and head up, marched away towards the cove.

Louisa pulled a face. 'You couldn't put one over on her.' She flicked her hair back from her face.

A glance sideways and Corinne saw the deep blue shadows under the girl's eyes. She wondered at Lucy being able to persuade Louisa out of bed on a Sunday morning after a night like the one just past.

It was as if she had said the words aloud.

'Before you ask, yes, my head is aching, the mention of food makes me want to spew my guts out, and I could quite easily kill those two and bury the bodies to get a little peace.'

'That's sorted then!'

'God! You are a superior bitch!'

The venom in the girl's voice alarmed Corinne. She felt hammered by the words. Recovering somewhat, she asked, 'How's your mother this morning? Last night Kate…'

'Kate! Kate this! Kate that!' Louisa rounded on her. 'Not everything is about Kate bloody Menzies!'

Corinne stopped. 'If you can't stand it here, why do you stay?'

Walking on, Louisa brushed her hand over her face and flicked her fingers up through her hair. 'I didn't say I couldn't stand it.'

'No, but you'd like a way out?' Corinne caught her up and matched the girl stride for stride.

Louisa forced a laugh. 'You think you're so smart but you really don't have a clue.'

'Well, it seems to me that the only person you get along with is Edwin Coburn. Is there a clue *there*?'

'Very clever,' Louisa smirked. 'Girl from the big city comes to sort out the local yokels.'

The next instant she was serious, her eyes wide above the tell-tale blue shadows. She stared at Corinne. 'You told her, didn't you? About seeing the Range Rover up near the centre on Friday night?'

'Who?'

'Who do you think? My mother.'

'No, I didn't,' Corinne denied it. 'Oh, I saw you. Both of you. But I didn't say anything to Kate about it. It never came up.'

'I don't believe you!'

They reached the cove. From the edge of the water, the children saw them and, carefully toe-stepping over the pebbles, came to meet them.

Corinne tugged Louisa back by the arm. 'It's true,' she said in an undertone.

Freddy grabbed Louisa's hand and pulled her towards the water.

'I never mentioned it,' Corinne shouted after them.

As the little boy dragged her stumbling towards the water, Louisa glanced back at Corinne. Her face flushed an angry pink. 'You're lying,' she mouthed over her shoulder. 'You're lying!'

In that moment Corinne saw doubt in the girl's eyes. Louisa wasn't angry; she was scared – scared that she'd got it wrong.

Corinne's resentment dissolved into pity. She knew why Louisa had attacked her so vociferously. Kate had found out, or been told, that Louisa had been with Edwin. It explained Kate's nervousness on Saturday night watching her daughter's every move.

It wasn't the conga-ing pack-packers that had posed the problem, it was Edwin Coburn. Louisa revelled in taunting her mother. Like the disappearing Bvlgari, she pushed things to the edge gambling on not getting caught. It excited her.

'You're a slowcoach.' Lucy was beside Corinne. The little girl stared up at her. 'You look funny.' She had all the assurance of a child who knows if she tells the truth she will always have the upper hand.

'Do I?' Corinne was aware of the clear eyes scrutinizing

her. 'I was just thinking.'

'*I* think a lot. I have huge long conversations with myself. I can say anything I want and nobody hears me.' Her arms outstretched, Lucy balanced on one leg on a large boulder. 'What were you thinking about?' Her bare foot, white and soft, wobbled on the camber of the boulder.

Corinne put her hand out to steady her.

'I was thinking about hurting myself on these pebbles. That's what.' She held on to Lucy's arm while the girl edged off the boulder. Corinne regarded her own feet firmly encased in sturdy trainers. 'I'm not as brave as you.' She gave a little self-deprecating laugh.

Lucy did not join in but eased out of Corinne's hold. Cautiously, she moved over the pebbles. 'You'll have to take them off when you get to the water.' She halted her tentative movements to glance at Corinne. 'You're not deformed or anything, are you?'

Corinne's jaw dropped. 'No! I'm not deformed!' She bent her knees slightly and leaned sideways. She put her arm across Lucy's back. 'Come on. I'll give you a lift,' she offered. 'Maybe I'll dunk you in.'

A ghost of a smile flitted across Lucy's face. Obeying, she clasped her hands around Corinne's neck and hung on as her feet were lifted clear of the pebbles.

'Freddy likes you,' she whispered into Corinne's ear. 'He told me so. He hopes you stay for a long time.'

Fighting the urge to respond to this blatant piece of flattery, Corinne lowered Lucy near the water's edge.

The loch was flat and benign. Freddy was wading about, now and then giving a shout, 'Got one!' and plunging his arm into the water in the hope of discovering the one stone that was different from the millions of others.

Louisa, leggings rolled up to her knees, was doing the same. Between them they had already accumulated a mound of pebbles, all different in size and colour, in a small wooden crate which sat clear of the lapping water.

'Do we give them a hand or have you got to get your own pile?' Corinne asked Lucy.

'No. We share,' Lucy told her. 'He's all right at picking them up but I'll have to choose the best to show Mummy.'

Corinne nodded. 'Division of labour.'

The little girl paused, unsure.

'That's good,' Corinne confirmed.

The soft mouth firmed into a hard line. Lucy moved away to wade into the cold water beside her brother.

Corinne watched. Even at the tender age of a few days shy of twelve, and without knowing it, Lucy Coburn did not like to be patronised.

'Come out!' Lucy shouted.

Freddy was still in the loch searching for that elusive extraordinary pebble. 'We'll move some of these big boulders,' he was instructed by his sister.

Obediently, he searched on dry land, but with the colours of wet pebbles more eye-catching, Freddy tried to go back into the water. Despite his bravado, his second foray into the cold loch lasted for only seconds. He gave in.

Corinne straightened up. She had done her bit. Her trainers off, she'd suffered along with the children and Louisa in the cold, shallow water until she could stand it not a second longer. In the freezing loch it was only minutes until their toes turned numb.

At last Lucy was satisfied. 'That's enough.'

An inspection of their haul was called for. They gathered around the wooden crate and, taking great pains, Lucy picked a variety of stones, each one a slightly varying shade of bluish-grey.

'These will do,' she said, and dumped the rejects back into the loch. With care, she placed the chosen ten stones in the box. 'Come on, Freddy. I'll carry them.'

Corinne rolled down the legs of her jeans. Nodding towards the children she asked Louisa, 'Shouldn't we see them back to the centre?'

'I suppose so.' Louisa made no move to get up. Seated on a flat boulder with her legs stretched out in front of her, she was gazing out over the loch. Only when Lucy and Freddy reached the path, and Freddy made a dash in among the trees, did Louisa turn her head. 'You two, wait!'

Both children stopped.

'Hurry up then.' Lucy was impatient. She glanced at Corinne. 'Everybody doesn't need to come.'

Corinne heard the hint. 'Right. I'm going back to my cabin. Does the shop open on a Sunday?'

'Yes.' Louisa's reply was short and brusque. 'How long are you staying?' She feigned a grin. 'Shouldn't you be getting back to that important job of yours?'

Before Corinne could think of a comeback, Lucy shouted again. 'I'm not waiting any longer.' The crate carefully positioned under her arm, the little girl assumed a haughty manner and started walking towards her home.

Passing Corinne, Louisa flung at her, 'I'll see you later.' Neatly avoiding Corinne's eye, she ran the few metres to reach Lucy and draped her arm companionably over the child's shoulders.

CHAPTER NINE

He was turning off the path to the walkway when Corinne caught sight of Ross Menzies.

He was moving fast, a breath away from breaking into a jog and making for her cabin.

She caught up with him seconds before he reached the cabin door.

'Hi!'

'Ah! Good.' His expression was grim, the grooves on each side of his mouth pulled tight by the clamp of his jaw.

If it was meant to intimidate her, Corinne ignored it.

'You've got a visitor,' he said. The annoyance on his face increased. 'He's up at the shop.'

So she had misread his expression.

'A visitor?' Corinne's heart sank even before she asked, 'Who is it?'

Standing, hands on hips, Ross studied his feet. 'It's your husband – I think.' He brought his eyes to rest on her face.

'What?'

'Noel Anderson?' Ross spread his hands.

'Noel Anderton.'

'Yes, that's him. Well, he's waiting for you. About ten minutes ago he walked into the shop asking for you.'

'Did you say I was here?'

'He already knew you were here, just not exactly whereabouts. I told him I'd find you.' Ross gazed hard at her. 'If you don't want to see him…'

Corinne thought quickly. 'No, no. It's all right.' She smiled grimly. 'This isn't your problem.'

'So there is a problem between you and him?' Standing very still, he continued to scrutinize her.

Corinne shrugged. 'You could say that.'

'I could get rid of him, if you want.'

'No, he *is* my husband.' She glanced briefly at him without catching his eye. 'I'm sorry about, you know, the Miss Pallin thing.'

'Don't worry about it.' Ross Menzies was giving nothing away. 'You're right. No harm done. Anyhow, it's none of my business.' His tone of voice told her he was not as dismissive of her and her problem as his words implied. 'I'd better get back. What do you want me to tell him? That you're not down here or what?' He waited with that same patience Corinne had noticed he used with Kate and Louisa.

'I suppose I'll have to see him now he's here.' Corinne hesitated. 'But not down here at the cabin. No. I'll come to the shop. That would be best, I think.' She smiled up at Ross. 'Is that all right with you?'

'Fine by me,' Ross agreed readily. The conversation should have been over but he made no move to leave.

Reaching out, Corinne touched his arm lightly.

'What?' Ross jerked back as if she'd attacked him.

His reaction made Corinne jump. It was seconds before she recovered enough to ask, 'Did he say how he knew where to find me?'

'No.' Ross shrugged. 'He didn't say. Mind you, he did mention that we were on sat nav. "Thank God for that", was how he put it.' He raised his eyebrows at her. 'So he definitely knew you were at Four Hills. No doubt about it.'

And it was no surprise to you that he was my husband. So much for anonymity!

'Did he give you a hard time?' Corinne grinned. She knew the attitude Noel could assume if ever he was faced with a less than effusive reception. 'Knowing Noel, I expect he did.' Her grin changed to a grimace as she tried to make light of it. 'I'm sorry if he did.'

'Cory!'

The shout came from the path.

Corinne and Ross Menzies whirled around in unison.

Noel was striding towards them. 'Cory... Cory...' His hands outstretched, he was shaking his head at his wife like a parent at a recalcitrant child not wanting to go home after a day at the sea-side.

'Noel!' The supercilious smile on Noel's face irked Corinne more than his sudden uninvited appearance. The surge of anger which suddenly engulfed her at the sight of him shocked and surprised her. This was the man she thought she loved!

She swallowed the emotion. Inanely, she greeted him with, 'What are you doing here?'

The surprise on Noel's face fooled neither Corinne nor the person standing beside her.

'You have to ask? I've come for you. Why wouldn't I?' Noel chuckled, and for the first time he acknowledged Ross Menzies. 'You're done here. Thanks for your help.' It was said with acerbic sincerity.

Ross didn't move. He stood nearer Corinne than Noel. 'Are you all right with this?' he asked her. 'I can stay if you want.' His eyes didn't leave Corinne's face despite the long breathy gasp that emanated from Noel.

Corinne forced a smile. 'I won't bother coming up to the shop now. It'll be fine.' She glared at Noel. 'My husband won't be staying long.'

Ross strode past Noel without making eye contact, brushing against him as he went as if he did not exist.

Forced to do an on-the-spot tap dance, Noel narrowly avoided stumbling off the walkway. He threw Ross a black look as he walked away but Ross Menzies' back was impervious.

Corinne watched until he reached the turnoff. She fought down the strange feeling of being abandoned with the last glimpse of him through the trees. How could she feel any link with this man she barely knew? She swallowed hard and watched him disappear. There was no backward glance in her direction.

Without waiting for Corinne, Noel walked to the cabin door.

He threw it open hard. It crashed against the wall and bounced back in his face and he caught it and held it. Sticking his head inside, he checked out the cabin.

'Well! Well! It seems you've managed to make yourself very... eh... comfortable. A right little home from home, I must say.' He straightened up and glanced over his shoulder at the path. 'Roughing it, are we?'

'Noel, what do you want?' Corinne squeezed past him into the cabin. She made for the kitchen. 'You know I came away to get time on my own. I wanted to think about things. Why couldn't you just wait until I was ready?' She filled a glass with water from the tap and drank it down in several gulps.

'That's exactly why I'm here.' Noel was prowling about the living room. He did not touch anything. 'I want to see if you've come to your senses yet.' He sat down on the corner of the sofa, the favoured spot occupied by Louisa on her visits. Unlike Louisa when she draped herself there, Noel did not seem to fit his surroundings.

'Don't glare at me like that.' He held up his hands. 'I admit it. I told you I was in the wrong. But believe me, I've learned my lesson.'

Corinne felt a rush of disgust. She knew him better than that. But she said nothing. It was too soon. No arguing; no shouting. She sat down at the other end of the sofa.

Noel was smiling. It was all for her. Coercion by charm. She'd seen it work. Now she listened.

'These last few days have been hell without you. I need you to come back home with me. That's where we should be right this minute, talking this thing through. Get it out, finish it. Then we can move on. This is no place for you. Please, Cory, be sensible,' he cajoled her.

'You really think it's going to be as easy as that, don't you?' Corinne felt calm. It was a good start.

Noel's protest was tempered with justification. 'I don't see why not. I've told you, Cory, I've learned my lesson. I know I screwed up big time.'

'How did you find out I was here? Who told you where to find me?' She put him off his stride. His well prepared speech was halted in mid flow and he fumbled his lines.

'I… Awe, Cory. What does that matter?' His face was tight and the telltale sudden bite of his top teeth on his lower lip, a childhood habit that had taken years to conquer, told Corinne that he was not so sure where this visit was going.

'Nobody knew where I was. At least nobody in Edinburgh,' she said.

'It makes no odds, does it? I'm here now.' Noel shifted in his seat.

Corinne continued to watch him.

Under her gaze, he was uncomfortable.

'A woman,' he offered at last. 'I don't know who. She phoned the office and they gave her the house number. That's how.'

Corinne pounced on this breach of confidentiality. The office would never do that. 'I don't believe it!'

'Well, it's the truth,' he raised his voice. 'This… this woman said she had an urgent message for me and that stupid bitch of a so-called receptionist, she gave out our home number.'

His pithy description of the temporary receptionist confirmed it was no lie. Noel had never taken to the teenager who, while intelligent, was plain in appearance and inexperienced and, unfortunately from Noel's account, this time had slipped up.

Noel sat forward. 'In the end it wasn't such a bad thing. Was it? She just might have done us a big favour.'

'A woman phoned? What did she want?'

'Oh, for…' Noel threw himself back on the sofa. 'Corinne, forget about it. I'm here now. That's the main thing. We're together. Between us we can get this sorted. We could be back home before dark.' He tilted his head at her. 'I could mix your favourite whisky sour. We could take a long hot bath…'

Corinne laughed.

'Noel, you appear to have forgotten a few things. Despite what you seem to think, there's no way we can get back to how it was. Things have changed – for both of us.' She watched his expression alter subtly. 'Oh, I'm still the same person I was last Wednesday. I still want to do the job I've always done. It's you. For you it's different. You want to move to another life, another country.' With a shrug Corinne went straight for his dream. 'With a mansion in L.A.' She flicked her eyes over his face and away again. No puerile sarcasm; no bitching, she told herself. Keep it clean. She drew a steadying breath. 'What I said three days ago still stands. I'm happy with what I've got.' She stopped. Her eyes on his face, she said, 'No, scrub that. I *was* happy with what I *thought* I had.'

'You mean me – my fling with Lynne? Awe, Cory, don't let that end it all for us. I was a complete shit. I know that. Nothing, nobody, could compete with what we had going.'

'Is that right? Well what happens if I don't want to up sticks and move to the States just like that?' Watching him closely Corinne added, 'Would you still go ahead? Go out there by yourself?'

'Out there you could do exactly the same as you do here.' Noel leaned forward eagerly. 'Even try a new job if you wanted.' Sensing an opening, he seized it. 'Just think! We'd be right in the thick of things. The opportunities are fantastic out there.' His face was animated at the supposed abundance of riches that could be his.

'Abandon my father's business, just like that?' Corinne asked. 'You were eager enough to get us to take you on, get you started when you couldn't get anybody else to even read your work. You sit there telling me Pallin-McCall doesn't figure in your future?' Corinne was extremely calm. She didn't know how long she could keep it up.

'Cory, I don't know what you're worried about. Your father and Ian would be able to keep things going. They don't need you here.'

'I suppose you need me out there?'

'Of course I do.' His voice was low and warm. 'That goes without saying. You've got to come with me. It would make all the difference with you there.' Again the coaxing expression settled on Noel's face. 'You're my other half; the half that makes all the cogs go round. You make it all work for me, Cory.'

'You haven't answered my question, Noel. Would you go on your own to start this new life, this new career of yours? That's what it would be you know – a completely new life.' She watched intently for his reaction.

'No new career, baby. The same old me, but fresher, more dynamic – with all the punch L.A. would be able to give my next book.' His eyes grew wide; his face eager at this newly conceived paradise. 'We could make it big out there.'

Corinne glanced away. 'You know if you move out there, Pallin-McCall still has the rights to your next three books.' She gambled. 'The contract you were trying to find at home? Did you manage to get your hands on it? You shouldn't have bothered. I'm sure if you'd asked him Ian would have obliged with a copy.'

Just on the outer edge of her vision, she saw her husband jerk back in his seat like he'd taken a blow to the stomach.

'Well, I knew you could take care of that.' His words were measured. 'If we're to set up in the States your father won't hold you to any contract surely?' The bluster, momentarily, had left his voice.

Corinne couldn't take her eyes off him. 'Hold *me* to it? No, Noel, I don't think there's any clause that says that. Uh, uh. Pallin-McCall's contract is with *you* not me.'

'It's three more, Corinne! It would take me what? At the rate I'm working right now, maybe three, four, even five years.'

'Don't forget the rewrites,' Corinne twisted the knife.

Noel ignored this. 'That's too long to be tied down.' He

edged nearer her. 'If I can start afresh – with nothing to hold me back – I could try out new mediums. A screenplay maybe? They adore the Brits out there. Right now they're clamouring for our stuff. They can't get enough of it.'

'You're selling out there already. They love every single thing you've written. What you're working on now will be the same. I know the figures. They're lapping up *your stuff* faster than you can write it. Where your desk is won't make a scrap of difference to the distributors in the States.'

'Being over there, it would boost my profile with the American public.'

'You're wrong. It won't increase sales. I know what I'm talking about. We went over this when you did that tour of the west coast.' Corinne was getting tired of it.

'Your face is in every bookstore window. Part of your appeal is that you live in Scotland. It adds colour, a sort of charm. There is nothing to be gained by moving out there.'

'That trip was three years ago.'

'Noel, accept it. Right at this moment you're at saturation point. Push it any further and you'll turn people off. There's only so much the public will take before they move on.'

Noel grasped at the slim chance of pushing his case. 'So then if I try my hand at –.'

Corinne cut him short. 'A screenplay? Yes, you said.'

'Exactly! A screenplay. Yes. And I'd have a good chance of it getting accepted while the books are still selling.' He suddenly fidgeted with renewed confidence as if the concept had occurred just then. 'I'm right. Admit it.'

'Admit what, Noel? That you're successful? I know that. I was there, remember?' Corinne felt herself tense up. 'Every step you made I was right behind you.'

Noel edged his way a little further along the sofa. 'And you know, Cory, that I appreciate it. If I've got anybody to thank, it's you.'

If! If!

'What about Moira?' She reminded him of the none-too-

137

mean contribution his agent had played in his pole-vault over the top of other struggling writers to the front of the bookstore displays.

'Yes, and Moira too,' he agreed. 'But you, Cory, you can get me sorted out. Talk to your old man and Ian and get them to see how good it would be for me to try it out there.' His smile was wide, expectant.

Corinne drew her head back to allow her to see directly into her husband's face.

'You are unbelievable! That's the real reason you're here.' She saw his wounded expression and was off the sofa in one leap. 'I know better than you, Noel, what's in that contract. So if you think I'm going to help you wriggle out of it you can think again.'

Bluffing, Corinne hoped he wouldn't get down to the nitty-gritty details in his contract. Confident she knew its basis, Ian McCall had not yet called her back to remind her of exclusions and penalties. Still, her knowledge was sound enough; Noel was not one for reading, let alone memorizing, the small print.

Noel, however, was not about to give up.

'No, Cory. No. I want this for *us*. Honest! We can get past this last week. I know it and so do you. You're my wife.'

'Is that the best you can come up with?'

'I'm begging you. Let's get back to how it used to be with us.' He reached out and grabbed her. 'Come home with me now, please. We'll put this behind us. We'll forget this ever happened.'

Corinne extricated herself from his grasp. 'It won't make any difference. I've discovered too much about myself and about you to pick up things like they used to be.'

Noel's lips curved. 'Vindictive, right to the bitter end,' he sneered. 'You always had a touch of that in you. Since the day we met!'

Corinne was shaken.

'What! I was never mean with you, Noel. Never. I gave my

all to get you where you are right now – at the top.'

'It's always business with you, Cory. Isn't it?' His expression tightened and he laughed mirthlessly. 'That's really how all this started.'

'I pushed you into it, I suppose.' Petty words. She regretted them. It was the wrong tack to take. 'Noel, whatever brought this to a head has done its job well. We can't ignore it.'

Guardedly, Noel asked, 'What do you mean, done its job?'

'Let's be honest with each other. If it hadn't been Lynne Robertson it would have been some other woman. Am I right?' She held up her hands. 'If there were others, I don't want to know. Not now. Not at this point.' Keeping her eyes down, she went on, 'What I'm saying is that you really wanted a way out. I couldn't see it, but our marriage was over.'

'No, Cory. No it wasn't. It isn't. I love you.'

'You knew it, Noel.' Corinne raised her eyes straight at him. 'You knew it and didn't have the guts to face me with it.'

'You were never there to face!' he shouted.

'You might be right about that. But if I hadn't worked day and night, week after week – deserting you as you saw it – you wouldn't be where you are today. And don't you look at me like that. It's true. It's fact. You could have the guts to admit that at least.'

'Okay! But you weren't the only one slogging away. I didn't just sit back and do nothing. I worked hard. While you wandered about Europe, I was shut up in that back room in *your* office bashing the keyboard 'til I couldn't see straight. Working to *your* schedule!'

Corinne smiled grimly. 'How conveniently you forget. You came to us with a bundle of dog-eared pages of a half-baked idea.' Now *she* was shouting. She couldn't stop. 'You had nowhere decent to work. Moira gave you eating money. I *gave up* part of my office because I saw what you had was

139

special. Now you think I shoved you in a back room while I swanned about setting up all the promos. You think that was how I wanted to spend my days? My God! Have you got that wrong!'

'Well, it was your doing. You set it out. Nobody else got a say.'

Their voices had risen as long-dormant differences surfaced like bubbles from a slow sinking ship.

For a time they sat in hostile silence. Avoiding eye contact, they aimed their sights directly on the calm loch. The discomfort was too much for Noel. He got up and stood close to the window, his back to Corinne, his face hidden.

Despite her anger, Corinne felt a fleeting pity for her husband. Noel hated confrontation. With a tendency to exaggerate, he'd been known to introduce white lies to hide his unease if the media got the better of him. It was a trait she constantly covered up for him, usually with a blatant exaggerated lie of her own in order to expose and obliterate his perjury and render it harmless.

Noel slewed his eyes away from the loch and resettled himself on the sofa.

'What's past is past. That was then. We've moved on since. At least I want to.'

'Well, at last we agree on one thing.' Corinne managed a weak smile. 'It's going to be in different directions from now on.'

Noel shifted again. He was very close to her.

'Don't say that. If I give up the L.A. house, and Lynne – look at me Cory – will you stay with me?' He was gazing pleadingly into her eyes.

Corinne stared back. 'You mean you and her, you're still…?'

'Don't worry!' Noel patted the cushion between them. 'She went out there to furnish the place, that's all.' He defended himself. 'Well, I wasn't sure what was going to happen.'

Corinne couldn't believe what she was hearing. 'So all that, *I'm sorry,* and *come to L.A. for a bright new start,* that was in aid of what, Noel?' Her face flushed. 'Did you want me to smooth your way out there? Do all the ground work for you? Is that what you thought I would be good for?'

She stood up. Her inside was quivering as she studied him but her words came out calmly. 'I think you should go now.'

'Can't I stay here?' Ignoring the bedroom, he gestured at the sofa.

'No.' She went to the door and opened it. 'I don't think we've got anything more to say to each other, do you?'

He got up and stood inches from her. 'You were always special to me, Cory, from the first,' he said softly. 'I didn't mean to hurt you.'

'Get out, Noel.' She lifted her chin. 'This is over.'

He walked slowly past her and out onto the walkway.

'You'll regret this, you know,' he called back. 'If I were you I wouldn't make my mind up so fast. A good lawyer can unravel a contract until you don't know where it starts and where it ends.' He nodded at her. 'You might be smart, Corinne, but I'll have you and that company of your old man's tied up in so much red tape…'

'Goodbye, Noel.' She closed the door softly and deliberately, clicking the key firmly in the lock.

Corinne leaned against the door until the sound of his footsteps ceased to echo on the worn wooden planks. Pulling back the curtain from the side window, she glanced out. He was gone.

Her legs were trembling, her hands cold, and she felt slightly sick as she moved away from the window. That was the man she had loved, had built a life with, believed she was going to live with for all of her lifetime.

She swallowed hard. Tears flooded her eyes and she collapsed onto the sofa. Her face in her hands, she screamed into the empty room, 'No! No! No!' Hot tears rolled down her face as her hands beat at the seat he'd vacated.

In a flash her misery dissipated and was instantly replaced by rage so fierce that her face flushed hot and her body trembled. Blinded by tears, she lifted her foot and struck out viciously at the table. The light piece of furniture tottered on two legs before crashing onto its side.

Books, papers and the accumulated minutiae of everyday life in a cramped space rose from the table top and scattered in different directions across the cabin floor.

Corinne stared at the mess. Reminiscent of her life right now; one blow and the whole structure collapsed in chaos. It was like a doll's house she'd had as a small child. With wanton fury she had stamped on it because her parents had not bought her the toy she'd wanted. They had not given in to her and the doll's house – she remembered the incident clearly – was never replaced, or mended, but the broken pieces occupied a heap in the corner of her bedroom, a constant reminder of what she had destroyed. Hard as she tried she could never recall what it was that she had wanted so badly, only the doll's house that she had wrecked.

This time I'm not to blame. Not this time.

Wiping her face, she happened to glance through the side window. She was just in time to see a figure disappear away through the trees at the turnoff to her cabin.

A man or woman, she couldn't tell which, had heard, and possibly witnessed, her despair.

Sliding to the floor, Corinne sat there righting the table. Nothing destroyed except her pride, she realised. She began gathering up the couple of paperbacks that had fallen flat on their tightly packed pages and showed no sign of damage. The little black voice recorder she carried everywhere with her, likewise was undamaged. Her pen, her wallet, everything had survived the fall. The plastic sunglasses which Ross Menzies gave her were no worse off for their tumble to the floor. They went with the other things back on the table. Stretching to reach it, she drew the manuscript she had been reading along the floor towards her. The weight of the four hundred or so pages dragged against the top sheet which tore from its temporary binding with a fatal ripping sound.

'Oh, shit!' Corinne was left with the lone top sheet in her hand. Smoothing it out on the floor – the zigzag edge beyond repair – she examined it as if seeing it for the first time.

Her name, her position, and the Edinburgh address of Pallin-McCall, stared up at her. It was the sheet the writer used to send in his completed work. The details, strategically positioned, would show through the window in the A4 envelope he used.

She could see it. Carefully, he would have spelled out her full name, *Corinne Anderton,* to ensure that it reached the right person. The address would have been meticulously tapped out fearing a careless mistake might lead to the work not reaching the right desk and so deny any hope of publication.

The entire manuscript, front page intact, had remained on the table since she'd pulled it from her bag and began to read it. Purely a distraction, Corinne admitted to herself, to fill her mind with characters playing out their feelings on paper to help shut out the pulsating image of Noel with Lynne Robertson.

It had been picked up by Louisa when she'd let herself into Corinne's cabin on Friday afternoon. They had discussed it briefly when Corinne woke.

Had the girl read further than a couple of pages? Corinne guessed not. While Corinne had skimmed the manuscript with fast, easy detachment, Louisa had no doubt read the *cover* page, if not with eagerness then with avid interest at the details she found there. How simple to find out the telephone number and ring Pallin-McCall and ask for Mr Anderton.

Still on the floor, Corinne picked up the decimated page. She gazed at it. Louisa knew she worked at Pallin-McCall. She knew nothing of Noel. Nothing of why Corinne was here at Four Hills to escape seeing him, nothing of his involvement with Lynne Robertson. She had worked it all out for herself, or at least taken a chance that she was right. Clever girl!

Corinne's sigh sounded loud and laboured to her own ears. She didn't want to believe that she could be fathomed so easily. But she had. And by a flaky girl with a grudge.

"You're lying!" Louisa had mouthed at her in the cove.

Why had Louisa been so adamant that Corinne had told Kate what she had seen that night in the rain? Did she just need to offload her guilt and Corinne was conveniently there and so irrelevant to the lives of the Menzies family that she could be used?

'God damn her!' Corinne got up stiffly and retrieved the manuscript and laid it on the table scrunching the single page tightly into a tiny ball in the palm of her hand. Louisa had been trying to get back at her for what she thought was a betrayal. The girl had picked up the phone and purposely given away her whereabouts.

Now that Noel knew where she was, was there any point in prolonging her stay at Four Hills?

CHAPTER TEN

'Papa.'

'Corinne.' Pierre Pallin's voice had Corinne clutching her mobile hard against her ear. He felt so near.

She stopped walking, her rapt attention solely on him as if she'd met him unexpectedly in the street. She drew a huge wavering breath and cleared her throat.

'Noel was here. He came up this morning to talk things over.'

'You did not call him to come to you?' Her father sounded sceptical. 'No.' He answered his own question.

Corinne closed her eyes. He didn't know about Noel's visit. She was glad. There had been no conspiring. If she could, she would have hugged him.

'Then it is very unfortunate that he has done this.' His voice was wary. 'Cherie, you know that we had no knowledge of this?'

Corinne, eyes blinking, started to move again. She was on the short stretch of pebbles between her cabin window and the loch, a tiny hidden beach of only five metres by four, where she had not set foot thus far.

She picked her way over the pebbles, stopping just short of the lapping edge, and gazed out over the flat expanse of water.

'A complete waste of time, him coming,' she said slowly. 'All we did was argue. Inevitable, I suppose. I should have stopped it.'

'Ah! Now you have seen Noel, you will come home?' There was a barely concealed eagerness from her father.

Reluctant to say yea or nay, Corinne fixed her eyes on a yellow canoe swaying gently in the water on the far side of the loch.

'Cherie, are you still there? Corinne?'

'Yes, Papa. Sorry.' She drew her eyes away from the

yellow canoe and walked slowly back to the front wall of the cabin. The wood was warm and rough to the touch. She leaned her shoulders against it and breathed the sweet resin in the humid air.

'I'm near a village called Blairkeld. Four Hills is the name of it.'

'Yes.'

'You knew!' Corinne slumped against the wooden wall.

'Corinne, you mean too much to us. We had to know where you were. Your maman and I only. We did not tell Noel. That I can promise you.'

'No, I know you didn't.'

Everything came back to the same thing; Noel. It was all about Noel. Her life it seemed had been all Noel. She didn't want to talk or think about him any more.

'How did you manage to find out I was here?'

'Do not be angry,' her father warned. 'We hired an investigator.'

'What! A private detective!' Corinne straightened up. 'What on earth made you do that? Papa, you knew I would be all right.'

'We were worried about you, Cherie.'

'So you've known all this time. Tell me, when did you hire him? I want to know.'

'Corinne…'

'When, Papa?'

'It was on the day you left. I had no option. Your maman was worried. After you quarrelled Noel came straight to us and told us everything. He confessed he was in the wrong.'

'I'll bet he did!' Corinne gasped. 'Don't you see? He wanted to get to you first. Did he manage to get you feeling sorry for him? God, I can't believe this!'

'You did leave him so soon. Too soon perhaps, Cherie. There was not enough time. How could you know that it was not the end? How could you?'

Corinne kicked out savagely with her toe at the loose

146

stones. A scattering lifted dustily into the air and settled again, immediately unrecognisable among the millions of others.

'That's what I wanted to get away from. That dribbling of lies he tells, the half-truths. He's probably told you just enough to paint me as the one in the wrong.'

'No one is in the wrong. Husbands and wives, they have many disagreements, they fall out. It is not irreparable, Cherie.'

'I see it worked then.' Corinne gripped her mobile tight. 'Oh, I'll bet he was good. Did he turn it on, his old charming and vulnerable poor-boy-made-good act? That'll do it every time.'

'Corinne, do not say this. His success is nothing to be ashamed of. Noel has worked hard. You both have. Do not destroy all you have built in the last six years for a moment of weakness.'

'Oh, *a moment of weakness!* Well, he didn't use that one on me!'

'Corinne, this is becoming tiresome.'

'You think this is an act?'

'No. I did not say that.'

'Well, his *moment of weakness* is out in L.A. as we speak furnishing his house so that he can move out there with her.'

'That cannot be true, Corinne. You are making up this story.'

'No. I got it from the man himself. He didn't tell you that when he was running down all the times that I couldn't be at his beck and call, did he?'

She heard the long intake of breath before her father admitted, 'Well, he did mention there were painful times for him when you and he were apart.'

'Papa, he memorised it all. Everything. Dates, places, events. Doesn't that tell you what's been going on? He's been building up to this for ages. Me? I was too busy building up his career to notice.'

147

'I don't know what to say, Cherie. How to comfort you.'

'As long as you didn't say anything to him about his contract because at this precise moment that's all I'm concerned about.' She was now gripping her phone so hard that her clammy fingers stuck to it. 'He's not going to walk away from that.'

'He did mention that he did not think he had another book in him.'

'*Papa!*'

'That was all that was said on the matter. Nothing more.'

'You're sure? Tell me you didn't agree to anything or waive anything from his contract? Please tell me you didn't do that?'

'No. I did not. But, Cherie, he was very sorry that he could not produce anything new, truly sorry.'

'Papa, he was playing with you. And do you know why? Because he wants out of his contract. If it wasn't for that he would have been off to the States on the first available plane. It's not *me* it's his *contract*, that's the only thing holding him back right now.'

'You underestimate yourself, Corinne.'

'No, I don't. But he does.'

A vacuum on the line had her pricking her ears. She thought the connection was gone.

'Corinne.'

'Mum!' The cross-over of the mobile between her parents had been soundless.

'Corinne, are you ready to come home now? Your father and I want to get on with our move to France. This silliness has got to stop.' The stringent command struck hard at Corinne, harder than anything her father had said. 'You need to face up to things,' her mother continued. 'Hiding away is not the answer.'

'From what I hear, it seems I wasn't as well hidden as I intended,' Corinne said.

'Your father did what he thought was best in the

circumstances. We just had an agency trace your movements, that's all. Don't make such a big thing of it. If you were in the city we would have brought you home straight away.'

'I'm not a child, Mum.'

'Well then, stop acting like one. Get back to your husband and your business.'

Corinne laughed wryly. 'It sounds like he got to you as well.'

'If you mean Noel, of course we listened to what he had to say. He came here to see us. The man was distraught when you threw him out.'

'I threw him out!'

'Don't deny it, Corinne. Noel told us all about the words the two of you had. You're acting like you're the first woman in the world whose husband cheated on her. Well, you're not that unique. I don't believe you're that naïve either.'

'About what exactly?'

'You were too quick to condemn him. If I didn't know better I would have said it was you who wanted a way out.'

Stunned, Corinne couldn't bring herself to answer.

The silence on the line between them dragged on.

'Well, clearly I've upset you,' her mother half apologised.

Corinne did the same. 'I'm sorry if I'm holding up the move to France. It's not deliberate. I…' She hesitated. 'Say good-bye to Dad for me. I'll phone later.'

'Corinne, when do you intend coming home?'

Corinne heard, pressed the button and cut her mother off.

The phone conversation gave Corinne a lot to think about.

She stayed where she was, in the sunshine, alone in her secluded stony world, so drained she found she could hardly move.

Unthinking, she slid down the wall of the cabin.

'Ah!' Needles of pain pricked her skin. The wood was

149

rough. Sharp splinters pierced through her shirt and into her back.

Ignoring the pain, she sat on the hard uneven pebbles. Weighed down with self-doubt, she wanted to stay hidden in this isolated square of lochside.

Was her mother right? Was she secretly glad of the excuse Noel's cheating had thrown up? Was it an unforeseen chance to put space between the two of them that she'd grabbed at willingly – too willingly? It was the exact tactics she had accused Noel of using to end things. Was she as equally guilty?

Corinne sat with her eyes closed. Her mother's accusation played over and over in her head. She had to be honest. What if it were true? Had she blinded herself to the reality of her life? Their lives? She loved her job, loved the excitement that came with each new book release, each launch and the scurrying activity that went along with it. There was hardly one part of her business that she did not relish. The icing on the cake was she had done it for her husband. Or had she?

Corinne tipped her head back and immediately regretted the sudden movement.

'Oh!' Pain struck again. Another splinter sank through her thick hair and stabbed at her scalp. Her eyes watered. Blinking fast, she saw a blurry image step off the walkway onto the pebbles beside her.

Louisa was staring at her. 'Are you okay?'

Corinne struggled to her feet. 'Yes, I'm fine.' Head down, she brushed past Louisa and climbed onto the walkway.

Backing away, Louisa eyed her curiously.

Corinne returned the glance. 'What do you want?'

Shaking her head, Louisa did not answer right away.

Corinne noted the hunched shoulders and the constantly moving hands. 'Are you coming in or staying there?'

'I'll stay out here.' Louisa indicated the walkway.

'I'll be back in a minute.' Corinne went into the cabin. She made herself a coffee convinced her visitor would be gone by the time she went back outside.

She was wrong.

Louisa was standing in the same spot Corinne had left her.

The girl was shivering despite the warm sunshine that had burned off the last of the thin, white cloud and now was reflected blindingly from the surface of the loch. The fragile detached aura that always hung over Louisa was painful to watch as the girl clasped her arms across her body.

Corinne did not succumb. 'Did you come down to see my scars?'

'What? No. It's not my business.'

Corinne swung round full circle. 'But that's what you were hoping for? Right? Getting your own back?'

'It's got nothing to do with me!'

'Then why did you call my husband and tell him I was here?'

Louisa did not deny it. 'I'm sorry. There – I'm sorry.' Her gaze was defiant. 'But you wanted him to come, didn't you?' Childlike in her eagerness, she attempted to justify her interference. 'That's why you left that script thing lying where everybody could see it. I know I'm right.'

Corinne stared at the wide green eyes. 'You can't just turn things round to suit yourself. If we want to get technical, you broke into my cabin. That's a criminal act, you realise. Do you want to go down that route again?'

Like a huge flapping bird, Louisa flung her long arms out in Corinne's direction.

'So who's getting their own back now? Go on. Call the police! What do I care?' Her arms flopped to her sides.

'You think that I should just let you get away with this? Is that it?' Corinne asked.

'I've never gotten away with anything in my life,' Louisa complained.

'You seem to be doing all right. That little phone call of yours might have wrecked a lot of plans for a good few people.'

Louisa's head jerked up. 'What people?'

'Well, Noel for one, my parents for another. My grandparents. People you don't even know.' She nodded. 'If you were trying to stir it, you certainly succeeded.'

'He came for you, didn't he? Are you going back to him?'

Corinne shrugged. 'Maybe *you* can tell *me*. You heard us. You work it out and let me know.' She gave a bitter little laugh. 'Right at this moment I don't seem to know anything much.'

Louisa was shaking her head. 'I didn't hear anything. I saw your husband when he first got here. That's all. I was helping in the shop. I didn't even speak to him.'

'So you followed him down here, and got an earful. Right?'

'No! You're wrong!' Louisa was indignant. 'I was in the shop all the time he was down here. I only came when he got back from seeing you.'

So honestly said, Corinne instantly felt guilty about bullying the girl. Whoever had been listening to her and Noel, Corinne decided that person was not Louisa.

About to make amends she stopped when the girl sidled away from her across the walkway. Instead she asked her, 'Why *did* you come?'

Louisa glared at Corinne. 'It doesn't matter now.' The elegant figure hunched her shoulders and bounded across the walkway, her long legs covering the ground like a frightened animal fleeing for cover.

'Wait a minute. Louisa! Hang on!'

The girl was moving fast. Seconds later, she disappeared.

Corinne dodged inside the cabin and grabbed the door key. She locked the door and followed Louisa through the woods. With no chance of catching the girl at the rate she'd taken off, Corinne hurried but did not run.

But she was angry; angry enough to march straight up to the shop and tell the Menzies clan exactly what she thought of their little games.

152

When Corinne strode into the shop, sharp words marshalled at the ready to set the family straight, Louisa was nowhere to be seen.

She found only Kate and Ross. They were standing close, facing one another behind the counter, unaware they were being watched.

From the doorway, Corinne could see things were tense.

Ross was tight-lipped. Kate, her face more marble-white than normal, was gripping the counter for support.

Ross put his hand over Kate's. 'I'll sort this,' he said. 'You go in the back and take it easy.' His face softened. 'Don't worry about it.' Gently, he steered her through the doorway to the house.

Corinne, her anger still bubbling, advanced on him.

'Louisa brought my husband here,' she blurted out. 'You know that, don't you? The other day she was in my cabin, uninvited I might add, where she read things, private things. You need to keep a watch on her.' She was in full flow now. 'She says *she* didn't listen in on our conversation but somebody was there. I saw them. Is there anyone here that doesn't go about sticking their nose into things that don't concern them? Because if there is I would love to meet them!'

In the sudden silence that settled on the shop, she realised she had been, if not ranting then pretty close to it. The colour crept up her face. 'I'm sorry. But bringing my husband here wasn't in the plan. Not for the time being, anyhow. Louisa had no right to do that.'

Ross made his way out from behind the counter.

'She didn't mean to cause you any trouble. My daughter tends to act before she thinks.'

'And that excuses her? That's a dangerous way to live.'

'I guess it is. I'm sorry.'

In the face of Ross's candour, Corinne's temper started to subside. 'Well, it's done now.'

'Well, no. I'm afraid not.'

Corinne stared. 'What do you mean?'

Ross had the look of a man about to put a lighted match to his last boat.

'While I was down at your cabin, well, Kate, she gave your husband a room for the night.'

Corinne gaped at him wide-eyed. 'You mean he's staying here?'

'She didn't know that you didn't want him to stay,' Ross defended his wife.

Corinne was incredulous. 'I'm booked in here, *on my own,* and he comes asking for me. Wouldn't that start alarm bells ringing? And he's given a room – where? Oh yes – here! My God!'

'Calm down, will you!'

'Why should I?' Her voice was a decibel below a scream. 'I don't know what's in the water here but calm doesn't seem to be a state of play for you people. Get off me!'

Corinne found her arm in a firm hold.

Ross propelled her sideways past the counter and through the door into the narrow hallway to the house.

Gripping both her shoulders he forced her back against the wall.

'Kate's not well,' he said. 'She just didn't think. That's all. She didn't set out to cause you any trouble. She wouldn't do that.' He screwed up his eyes as if the concept was inconceivable.

'Let me go!' Corinne struggled. 'You're all crazy!'

'Shut up!' Ross slammed her hard back into the wall. 'Don't you dare say that!' He held her fast, increasing the pressure on her shoulders.

Neither violent nor abusive, it had the desired effect nevertheless. Corinne stayed very still.

'Please don't say that. Kate made a mistake.' It was a cry for understanding.

Corinne's body slumped slack in his hands. 'Let me go,

please.'

For a moment his fingers continued to grip her hard. 'It was me,' he said at last.

'It was you what?' Corinne asked.

'Me, outside your cabin.' He shrugged. 'I shouldn't have, I know. But I wasn't spying on you. It's your business.' His fingers loosened. 'I just wanted to make sure you were all right.' His hands stayed on her shoulders. 'It was difficult to know how things were between you when *he* arrived. Then when I saw the way the two of you were with each other... Well, split-ups can bring out the worst in people. It didn't sit right with me. You two alone.'

'Nor me. Believe me. Louisa arranged that little rendezvous all by herself.' Corinne grinned apologetically. 'That's why, when I saw the person in the woods, I guessed wrongly it was her. I'm sorry. It was good of you to wait. There really was no need.'

'Fine,' Ross nodded. 'What goes on between a couple is nobody's business but their own. But your husband has a sour way with him. He's not a happy man.'

'Kate obviously didn't see it,' Corinne said lightly. 'I shouldn't have kicked off like that.' Suddenly she let out a yell.

Ross froze. Slowly, he lifted his hands from her shoulders. 'What the...?'

'Splinters. In my back.' Corinne flexed her shoulders and eased herself away from the wall. 'I got them when I leaned against the cabin wall this morning.'

'Let me see.'

Turning, Corinne presented her back to him.

Ross lifted up her shirt. 'I see them. I can't do much in this light.' He let her shirt drop. 'I'll get antiseptic and cotton-wool and bring it by the cabin as soon as I can.' With a pat on her back he said, 'They need to be cleaned up.'

'I know. Just get me the stuff. I can do it.'

'No, I'll do it. That is unless you're a contortionist?'

Neither of them heard the door to the shop open.

'Well, cabin No. 1 occupant.' Louisa stood in the doorway, her face split by a broad smile. 'Being served personally by the owner.'

Ross's attitude changed instantly. 'You, young lady, have a lot of explaining to do.' Moving away from Corinne, he gripped Louisa by the arm and shoved her back out into the shop.

'Let go!' The girl struggled as he almost lifted her off her feet.

Ross's interrogation of Louisa was halted, not by the girl but by Ross himself. As he glanced back at Corinne his jaw hardened and a look of pure anguish settled on his face.

At the far end of the hallway Kate Menzies stood watching him. At her shoulder was Noel Anderton.

The smirk on her husband's face told Corinne all she needed to know. The two at the far end of the hallway had been watching her and Ross. How long for, she had no idea. And what they had made of it she didn't dare think.

The white faced stare she got from Kate Menzies tore at her conscience.

'Kate,' Corinne wasn't bothered what conclusion Noel was drawing. 'Kate, I need antiseptic, if you have any,' she said simply.

For what seemed an age, Kate continued to stare at her. She turned back into the house before Corinne could offer up any explanation.

Corinne thought better of going after her. She tried to steady herself.

'Why are you still here, Noel?' She didn't wait for an answer. 'Go home, please. Whatever it is you hope to achieve, you won't. Believe me, this is not a place for rational thought.'

Noel walked down the hallway. 'Well then, why are you staying? Isn't that what you came here for? Rational thought. At least that's what you've made everyone believe.'

'I wasn't thinking clearly at the time. You saw to that!'

'Ah, the blame game, now.' He smiled. 'Well, I intend to stick around just until you come to your senses, my love.'

'Go home, Noel.'

'No way! I'm staying right here. If you're not thinking straight, I need to keep an eye on you.' His smile disappeared. 'Make sure you don't do anything you'll regret.'

CHAPTER ELEVEN

'You must be kidding!' Corinne was incredulous.

'We want to make it up to you, me and Mum.' Louisa merged family misdeeds. 'I didn't know that phone call would cause you all this agro. Mum, well, putting him up was her way of trying to make things right. I suppose she thought you two might get back together given half a chance.'

Interspersed with little sideways skips, she was walking ahead of Corinne. Like a child enticing an adult to her way of thinking, she went on, 'You'll love it. We build a huge bonfire on the beach, and a barbecue. It's great.'

'I'm not in the mood right now.' It was no lie. Corinne didn't feel well. The niggling start of a headache was making her tetchy. It would probably only get worse.

'Believe me, I won't be very good company,' she warned.

'Oh, don't be like that,' Louisa coaxed. 'Please. Mum will take it personally if you're not there.'

Corinne surveyed the prancing, skipping figure. In no more than ten minutes the girl had altered. From the sarcastic trouble-maker Corinne faced in the shop hallway to a sweet, enticing young woman to whom anybody would be hard put to say no.

In the middle of the path just clear of the walkway, Corinne stopped. 'Don't come any further, Louisa. I'm going to lie down for a while. When does this thing start tonight?'

Louisa laughed out loud. 'Good!' Enthusiasm spilled out of her. 'Eight o'clock over the other side of the loch at the jetty.'

'Eight? Isn't it getting dark by then?'

'Not too dark.' Louisa's hope surged. 'If it's calm enough we could take a canoe out. I'll teach you how to paddle. It's great fun!'

'I *might* come,' Corinne cautioned. 'No promises. Right?

To be honest the last thing I need right now is to be sociable.'

'Just wait and see. You'll love it.' Louisa pledged a successful party as if it were in her power. 'See you over there.'

Corinne walked to her cabin. She did have a headache and the last thing she wanted was to sit al-fresco with people she hardly knew and, she was fast discovering, wasn't sure she liked.

Her world was falling about her and she was going to a party! Four Hills; it was like living in a parallel universe where no rules of logic applied.

Corinne drew down the bedroom blind and stripped to her underwear.

She lay on the bed and pulled the throw up to her chin. It was a relief to close her eyes and block out the piercing spikes of light that constantly bounced off the water whenever the sun appeared. She blamed that for her the headache. That and the never-ending images in her head of Noel, Lynne, L.A. She should have worn her Bvlgari. Where had she put them? She'd get them later…

Within seconds Corinne was asleep.

The loch sparkled sharp as diamonds hiding the black depths. She reached out to touch the precious gems and they shattered, cold, freezing over her reflection. Below the surface her face was smooth, the waves washing over her, lapping at her head… louder, and louder…

Corinne shot straight up in bed. The dream receded but the pounding she could still hear. It came from the cabin door.

In a scramble, she pulled on her shirt and jeans. Half-way across the living-room she glanced through the side window.

Noel! His hand was raised once more to ensure his arrival was noticed.

Barefoot and shivering, Corinne opened it. 'For God's sake stop!'

159

'Sorry.' He saw her rumpled hair and loose shirt. Without a word he dashed past her to the bedroom. He scanned around the room and behind the door.

'Just checking.' He grinned pleased his cursory search had revealed nothing.

Finding her trainers, Corinne put them on before facing him. 'You are the limit! What right have you to go poking about? So what if there was a man in there; it would have nothing to do with you.'

'Yes it would. We're still married, Cory.'

'Right, when it's convenient.'

'I want it always to be convenient for us.' He edged towards her. Before she could take evasive action, he had put his arms out and pulled her against him.

'No, Noel.' She resisted hard against his chest.

'Come on.' He held her in a tight circle. 'A little afternoon snack. Like being on holiday.' His grin softened. 'Oh, you are warm and you smell real good.'

'It won't work, Noel.' She tensed as he thrust himself hard against her. 'Not on me. Not any more, it won't. Keep it for your characters.'

He laughed. 'Don't play the wounded wife; you know you want it.' His grip tightened, pinning Corinne's arms to her sides.

She pulled her head away and his mouth came down and collided with the side of her face.

'Stop struggling, sweetheart.' He drew his head back and looked into her furious eyes. 'Oh! Ho! This is new. Such reluctance! You want to earn your goodies, do you? Well then, let's see what games you've learned up here in the woods.'

'Let go of me!' Corinne struggled to free her arms.

Noel slammed her back against the cabin wall, searching for her mouth with his. 'Cory, Cory…'

Corinne jerked her head sideways and again his mouth missed hers. He sank his fingers into her hair and snatched

160

her head back. It was his undoing.

One arm free, Corinne balled her hand. With all the force she could muster, she swung hard, aimed at his temple, missed, and collided with the corner of his eye.

With a yelp, Noel released her.

'You…' He bit off the abuse, his hand raised ready to strike.

'If you do,' Corinne's voice wavered. 'I'll make sure you regret it for the rest of your life.'

Noel lowered his hand. There was a glimmer of a smile on his face. 'You would too.' He laughed and stepped back. 'You keeping it for somebody else? That country bumpkin out there? Or, 'he sneered, 'does dear Uncle Ian do it for you?'

'What?' Corinne gasped. 'What are you talking about? You are disgusting. Get out. Go back to Edinburgh out of my sight. Go away Noel!'

Did she want to leave Four Hills? Corinne thought not. That was the reality. Back in Edinburgh they knew where she was – had always known apparently. If she went home now, she would have to go over it all again, reliving every minute of that day when she'd found Noel and Lynne Robertson together. The trite questions would come. When had the affair started? Had she no idea? How had she found out? In the middle of the day! What a shock that must have been…

She wasn't ready to face the inquisition.

Because Noel couldn't keep his mouth shut everybody knew about it, albeit his version. Titillating details would be exhausted to satisfy people's curiosity before amazement slid first into sympathy, then into gossip and finally into cold reality that, thank God, it wasn't happening to them.

Corinne lay back down on the bed.

Noel was only a couple of hundred metres away through the trees. No escaping *that* reality. When he'd left the cabin, she had locked the door and sat gazing out over the water.

Her insides trembled but she didn't cry. If she'd given in to him, he wouldn't have hurt her. Sex for Noel had always been about gratification; self-indulgent and while at times unrestrained, she knew he was not fundamentally a cruel man.

Nevertheless, the tussle between them had brought on another headache.

She hoped the weather would get worse during the afternoon. Just wet enough for the night at the jetty to be cancelled. If she could stay calm long enough her headache would go, and, with any luck, Noel would get fed-up being away from his usual haunts, get in his car and head back down to the city.

Lying awake, when Corinne heard knocking her first reaction was to ignore it, pretend she hadn't heard. Again it came; no thunderous banging as had destroyed her dream; this time a polite, timid sound, tapped out apologetically on the cabin door.

Guilt more than anything made her get up to answer it. The person waiting on the walkway – not Noel she guessed – they must know she was there.

Corinne found Kate Menzies standing tall and elegant as ever, on the wooden walkway.

Neither of them greeted the other. A diffident smile only came from Kate. They eyed each other briefly before Corinne waved her inside.

In the middle of the living-room, Kate waited as if she were not the owner of the cabin more a casual caller unsure of her welcome, uninvited and, consequently, not completely at her ease. Her delicate, wraithlike appearance was so akin to Louisa that it was if it were indeed the girl who now stood before her, aged it seemed, in the blink of an eye by some massive misery.

A bottle of antiseptic in one hand, Kate carried a white plastic packet containing cotton-wool in the other.

'Are these for me?' Corinne reached out to take them.

'I can do it for you.' Kate held tight to the things she had brought. 'I asked Ross if I could.' Embarrassment passed over Kate's face. 'If it's all right with you?'

'Yes, sure. It was a really stupid thing to do.' Corinne made for the bedroom. 'I've no excuse for it. I just wasn't thinking. Not about that at any rate.' Over her shoulder she said, 'You can put the things down there.' Corinne touched the back of her head and grimaced. 'I think we might need my tweezers to get this lot out.'

A little smile touched Kate's face. She said nothing to counter Corinne's self-confessed stupidity. The bottle of antiseptic she put on the edge of the dressing-table, and the tweezers that Corinne held out, she accepted between her long fingers. Opening the plastic packet, she fluffed up several bits of cotton-wool ready to start.

'I'll be as careful as I can,' she promised. 'If you want to lie down on your front, it might be easier.' She stood by the bottom of the bed, waiting.

'Oh, right.' Taking off her shirt, Corinne eased onto the bed and lay flat on her stomach. 'I don't know how many splinters are in my back. It feels like I've got at least a couple in my head as well.' She angled her head to one side to watch Kate unscrew the cap from the bottle of antiseptic and dampen a pad of cotton-wool.

With the bottle back on the dressing-table, Kate sat on the edge of the bed, the cotton-wool in her left hand the tweezers in her right. 'Tell me if I hurt you.'

Corinne gasped as the cold dab of antiseptic met the heat of her back. An almost imperceptible tug on her skin had her biting her lip in anticipation of the shoot of pain to come.

Kate was gentle. Her touch was the least needed to extract the little splinters on which Corinne had been careless enough to impale herself.

Kate went on with her inspection.

Apart from little gasps from Corinne, the room was silent for a while.

Corinne was waiting for it. Ever since Kate stepped through the door she had felt the tension in the woman. Moving hesitantly, speaking little, she was building up to something. It had to be the girl. What else?

She was right.

'Louisa is very impulsive, I'm afraid.' Kate dabbed at the tiny wound left by another recovered splinter.

'Weren't we all when we were young?' Corinne went along with Kate's excuse for her daughter.

'You think I make too many allowances for her, don't you?' Kate said bluntly. Not accusing, her tone was level and her attention to Corinne's back continued as gently as when she first started.

'That's not for me to say,' Corinne replied. 'You know your daughter best.'

Kate reached for the antiseptic. 'You do think that, though. I can tell.'

Pulling more cotton-wool from the packet, she soaked the soft pad and applied it low down on Corinne's spine. 'You're right,' she went on, 'I do make allowances for her. Mostly it's because she's always been highly strung, even when she was a tiny little thing. As a toddler she would get far too excited about the slightest thing. It would take us hours to calm her down. By the time she went to college she'd grown out of it,' Kate manipulated the tweezers, 'or so we believed.'

Flat on her stomach, Corinne twisted her head so she could see Kate.

'Kids get up to all sorts when they are away from home,' she sympathised. 'You can't do anything about that, even if you are a parent – especially if you're a parent.'

Kate's hand wavered. 'That's the thing though. I could have.'

'In what way?' Corinne was curious.

'Could you lie back? There are more little bits I have to get.'

Corinne did as she was asked. Sharp little arrows of pain stabbed her back where the tweezers and the antiseptic did their work. In the ensuing silence, she thought the conversation had died a natural death and felt relieved. Surprised when Kate started up again, Corinne had no way to divert her from her cathartic confession.

'I should have put her to boarding school all along. I regret that now. It would have been so much better for her. It might have made all the difference. I just couldn't do it. Several times I tried. I just couldn't send her away. I wanted her with me. She was beautiful, even as a little girl, and sweet. By the time I realised I wasn't as good a mother as I thought I was, she was her mother's daughter, as they say.'

'You let her go to college to do her own thing. No parent can do more than give their kids a bit of slack and let them get on with it. Maybe it'll work, maybe it won't.' With no children of her own, Corinne felt a tad sanctimonious. Increasingly, she was getting out of her depth.

'Louisa's designs proved you did the right thing.' Corinne felt on safer ground. 'She's very talented. And original.'

'Yes. And it seems she's taken to you, Miss Pallin.' The title instantly erected a barrier between them. 'Did she tell you why she left college?'

'Well, not exactly, no.'

'It was down to me.' Kate gave a nervous self-deprecating laugh. 'Oh my, I'm at fault again.'

Corinne propped herself up on one elbow. Kate held a cotton-wool pad gently between her long fingers. Highly strung she might be but there was no self-pity on her beautiful face. *That* was not a constituent of her fragile nature.

Kate met Corinne's gaze without a trace of duplicity. Talking appeared to be Kate Menzies' way of ridding herself of the bane of her existence – guilt.

About to sit up, Corinne was stopped.

Kate's hand on her shoulder pressed her gently back down.

'I'm not finished yet,' she said softly.

Whether she meant talking or seeing to her splintered back, Corinne wasn't sure.

'Just one more in your shoulder,' Kate said. For the first time she gave a relaxed smile. 'And then your head.'

Corinne stayed silent. Just one word might upset Kate or set her off again, talking, unburdening herself. Corinne wanted neither. A confessional would be more in keeping, she thought. And it was draining her.

'The college threw Louisa out.' Kate dropped the bombshell quietly.

Corinne had to be careful. 'I didn't know that.'

'Not her fault. Mine.' Kate eased herself further along the side of the bed. 'Now, can you tip your head that way?' Her fingers parted Corinne's hair, exposing her scalp. 'Ah, I see it. There. That's it. It's only a tiny scratch. Your hair will cover it.'

The antiseptic-soaked pad was pressed gently against Corinne's scalp.

'I missed Louisa very much when she went to Glasgow,' Kate went on. 'Oh, I knew for her it was right thing. Yet up here, in the slack months, I was very lonely without her.'

'You had Ross.' Corinne sat up and let the pad fall from her head onto the bed.

'Ross. Yes I had Ross,' Kate murmured. 'I'm a great disappointment to him, you know.' Her narrow shoulders rose in a dismissive shrug. 'I missed the London life, my career, my friends... Yes, I had Ross. I'm sorry to say, I let him down.' She said defensively. 'I was naughty, Miss Pallin. Very naughty. I needed that little extra to get me through the days. Oh, please don't be shocked. I knew what I was doing. I'd been there before. Back when the catwalk roundabout got too fast, too frenetic,' Kate smiled. 'I used to pop a little pill to keep up. Had to stay on the merry-go-round with the rest of them. Oh, we all did it. Nothing really bad. Harmless really. Nobody got hurt.'

'Ross disapproved, I take it?'

'Ross? No. Not Ross, not him. He understood. He always understood. Then,' Kate gazed past Corinne's head at the blank wall behind the bed as though a snapshot rifled from her youth were posted there exposing her past misdemeanours. 'I did the unforgivable.'

Corinne buttoned her shirt and waited.

'The college half-term is when it happened. Easter it was. Louisa came home to Four Hills for a full week – the holiday break. She had been working so hard to prove she had what it takes in the fashion world. Oh, her designs were good, really good. But she had lots and lots of competition.' Kate's face clouded as she recalled the hard time her daughter had gone through while away from her. 'She was so very tired, drained by all the effort she'd put in. I couldn't bear to see her like that. Like she was beaten before she'd even heard the results of that second year's hard work. It broke my heart.'

'What happened?'

Kate drew a long breath. 'I gave her my anti-depressant prescription to perk her up.' She pursed her lips so hard they disappeared into a straight hard line and the skin tightened over her high cheekbones. She caught Corinne's eye. 'She didn't tell you, did she?'

'No. She didn't.' Corinne swung her legs to the floor to sit beside Kate. 'If they threw her out, it had to be pretty bad for them to go to those lengths.'

'Yes.' Kate avoided Corinne's look. 'I didn't mean it to go like it did. I only wanted to make her feel better about herself while she was home with us. Her designs were wonderful. She had worked so hard on them. I couldn't bear to think that all her effort would come to nothing in the end.' She sighed so heavily that for a second Corinne thought she was about to cry.

No tears came. 'When she went back after the Easter break,' Kate continued, 'she was healthy and we assumed she felt good. She seemed ready to take on the world. Then her exams didn't go all that well. Her tutor tore her work to pieces. Oh, not literally, no, no, nothing that drastic. Nothing so blatant. Just sly comments, you know, a dig here, ridiculing her ideas, scoffing at her work. It destroyed Louisa's belief that she could produce anything that would be of interest to anybody.'

'They let her go on, continue her course? She did a third year?'

'Oh, yes. Ironic the way things happened. My daughter, Miss Pallin, worked like a Trojan. About a month before the summer break, the college had an open day to show their work for the year. They'd put the day together very well. The college got an extremely good turn out. Not just with friends and families. Local designers were there, and I don't know how they did it but several London fashion houses sent up their people too. It's so hard to get started in the fashion business even when they're always on the look-out for any special new talent. It was such a chance.

'I went down to Glasgow with Ross for the day. Louisa's designs were a hit. She got praise from several fashion scouts. So we knew her designs were no one-off fluke. The best thing was the tutor had no option after that; she had to retract her mediocre assessment and give Louisa a decent report.'

'Or else she would have appeared pretty provincial,' Corinne guessed.

'Exactly,' Kate smiled sadly. 'Well, anyway, after that things seemed to settle down. A chance that one of the fashion houses would pick up on her results and take her on, well, it was a possibility. We left Louisa that day feeling really positive about her work. That night she went out celebrating with the rest of the people from the college. For the next two days, she and another girl didn't turn up for their class. When they eventually did put in an appearance the tutor guessed they'd been drinking. She gave them a warning, which was fair enough, and we thought that was that. Then the next week, the same thing happened. Louisa and this other girl got a second warning from the tutor, again, nothing more.'

'Mindful of the talent she nearly missed out on.'

'Yes, possibly. Whatever, the warning she gave didn't do the trick. The woman phoned us the following week when Louisa didn't appear on the Monday morning.'

'Did Louisa not keep in touch with you?'

'Oh, we got a phone call, now and then. In line with the code of the teenager – you know how it is – enough to keep us happy.' Kate twisted a ball of cotton-wool into a long uneven thread on her fingertip. 'That same tutor let us in on what was really going on. I guess she had the right to be the one. Ten minutes after we got the phone call, Ross went straight to Glasgow. Oh, that was an awful day. He found Louisa in her flat, alone, comatose. She was stoned. It was a whole day before he got any sense out of her. A week-end cocktail of drink and drugs takes time to wear off. I know. Plus the result is not a pleasant thing to see. She was still suffering when he brought her home that night.'

'Sounds like the city life really got to her.' Corinne could only imagine.

'Now, Ross insists she has to stay here even though that's not what she wants. She hates this place more than ever. The idea of working with us, well, it's repugnant to her.'

'Her designs won't get seen up here,' Corinne said. 'She feels she's got a grievance.'

Kate nodded. 'Yes. And her grievance is against me.' Her red hair bounced and danced about her pale face. 'She blames me for it all, for everything that's happened to her.' She appealed to Corinne. 'I know I shouldn't have given her my pills. I assumed all she needed was a little help to get over a difficult patch. I'd no idea that it would get as bad as it did.'

'Kate, it might have happened anyway, whether or not you

169

started it. No, not started it, that's not what I mean.' Corinne groped for kinder words. 'Kids get into all sorts. As for her blaming you, she's picked on you because you're her mother – when she hurts you, she hurts herself. It's a form of self-abuse because, at the moment, it seems to me that Louisa doesn't like herself all that much.'

'She has no regard for anyone else, either,' Kate said. 'Lately she's started stealing.' An apologetic smile was thrown at Corinne. 'Sunglasses, jewellery. She hangs around the cabins.'

Recalling the knowing glance that went between Alec and Kim Taylor on Saturday afternoon when Louisa's name had cropped up, Corinne experienced a sudden sinking feeling in her stomach. 'Do you know that for certain?'

'She puts the stuff in her room. We try and make excuses when we give it back. I'm sure people know what's going on. They're not stupid.'

'Why does she go to all that bother just to have it handed back? I don't get it,' Corinne admitted.

Kate stared at her, astonished. 'You just said it: she wants to hurt me. Humiliate me.'

'Tell me, has she taken anything from the Taylors?'

'The Taylors? Why are you asking about the Taylors?' Kate's eyes widened. 'What have they said?' Mention of the wealthy couple on the far side of the loch horrified Kate. Her face crumpled. 'Oh, no! She mustn't. She mustn't. Not them. Not from that poor woman!'

'Kate! Kate!' Corinne grabbed Kate's flaying hand and held it still. 'I'm not accusing her. Nobody's accused her. Nothing's been said. They're the only people besides Phil and Ryan that I know. As they seem to be pretty well off, I just wondered that's all.'

'Oh, I see. It's only that Kim Taylor has... She's... Oh, it doesn't matter.' Kate lowered her head so that Corinne couldn't see her face.

Silence followed, during which Corinne let go of Kate's

hand and the woman relaxed.

Corinne asked, 'Better?'

A bemused Kate nodded. 'Yes. I'm fine.' The question about the Taylors went unanswered. Once her mouth opened and she was about to speak then she changed her mind. She flicked her eyes in Corinne's direction then away fast.

'Your sunglasses; it was good of you to forget about her taking them. She does it just to get attention. You saw her at the party up at the craft centre. That little display with Edwin Coburn? Entirely for my benefit. Oh, I understand why she does these things all right – to hurt me.'

'And Tamzin too.'

'Tamzin?'

'Edwin's wife.'

'Yes, Tamzin. How would Tamzin be hurt?' The implication suddenly became clear to Kate. 'You think Louisa and Edwin? No!' Kate shot up off the bed. 'No! You're wrong. There's nothing going on between them.' The tweezers were dropped onto the dressing-table with a clatter. 'No. I won't allow it.' Her mouth tight and trembling, Kate was visibly shaking as she left the bedroom.

Corinne followed her. The woman appeared to be talking to herself, muttering under her breath, the words so low that Corinne couldn't catch what she was saying.

'Kate,' Corinne caught her arm. 'Don't be upset. Please. You're likely right about that. Probably it's nothing.' Corinne was determined to rid the thought from Kate's mind. 'Louisa was having a good time last night, that's all. Nothing more,' she insisted.

Kate faced her. 'Anyone except Edwin. Not him.'

Before Kate had the chance to escape, Corinne blocked her way. 'Please, stay and have coffee with me.'

Sheer lack of space forced Kate to sit down. Immediately the distress that had erupted at the mention of Edwin Coburn faded away. But Kate appeared drained.

Corinne left her and went into the kitchen. She talked

loudly over her shoulder.

'When I was young, if you didn't dance on a Saturday night friends imagined you were ill!' She laughed out loud so Kate would hear. 'How crazy was that?'

Kate was sitting on the edge of the sofa, her eyes fixed on the loch. Corinne had no idea if she'd heard her.

'Here.' Corinne put the coffee mug into Kate's hand. 'Even at my age, I do silly things.'

No response came. Kate, holding the mug on her knee, appeared not to be listening.

Corinne tried again. 'She certainly lent a lot of life to the evening. The hikers had a great time.' It seemed her words fell on deaf ears.

'Kate,' Corinne leaned forward. 'Young people need to let their hair down now and again. It doesn't necessarily mean anything.'

The green eyes swung away from the smooth black surface of the loch and fixed on Corinne.

'You don't understand.' Kate's gaze went back to the loch. 'I've known Edwin for a very long time. Long before he met up with Tamzin and married her. Edwin and I, we started out in London together at exactly the same time. We went through everything together. You know, trailed the streets trying for jobs, for a place to stay. When I needed him he was always there for me.' She sighed. 'There were times I was sure I wouldn't make it. We even shared our dole money to get through the week.'

Corinne smiled. 'Long before your catwalk days, then?'

'What? Oh, yes. I was fresh out of school then. When I did get an agent we went our separate ways for a while.'

'Did you manage to keep in touch with each other?'

'Oh, always.' Kate smiled. 'We always met up whenever I was in London. On the move, I would send him the occasional postcard from Rome, or Milan, or wherever, and he would send one back.' Her face was sad as she remembered. 'His were always of towers. The Empire State

Building. The Eiffel Tower. The leaning tower of Pisa. Strange…' She pursed her lips. 'I asked him once about it. He said they reminded him of me.' Kate turned bewildered eyes to Corinne. 'I didn't know what he meant.'

'Men *are* strange like that. The first thing to hand,' Corinne said. 'It must be great to have him up at the craft centre.'

'You don't understand!' The accusation rang out – right before the trembling started. At first Kate's hands trembled then the tremors travelled up her arms to her shoulders until her whole body seemed to quiver as if an unseen giant hand were shaking her.

It scared Corinne to see the fragile figure struggle to overcome the emotion that swept over her. She eased the slopping mug of coffee out of Kate's shaking hand.

'Come on. It might be best if I walk you back to the shop. Ross will be wondering what's become of you.' Her hand went over Kate's long, trembling fingers. 'You can talk to him. Between you you'll work out what's best for Louisa.'

Tendrils of red hair bounced frantically as Kate rejected Corinne's offer. 'No! I can't! I can't tell him.'

'Kate, he already knows what Louisa gets up to. The sunglasses – they were nothing. Believe me. But if you're afraid she's going off the rails again, he'll want to stop it before it gets out of hand, before it's too late.'

Kate drew her hands away from Corinne's clasp. 'No. It can't be too late.' She shook her head emphatically.

Corinne feared Kate's control, holding by a mere thread, was about to snap.

Kate sat staring at her with only despair on her face as if she didn't know Corinne or why she was there in the cabin. Gradually, the trembling in her body eased away and she sat very still. 'You don't understand. I have to stop Louisa.'

A chill went through Corinne. 'Louisa might not take too kindly to being told what she can and can't do.' She considered for a second. 'She comes down here to the cabin.

173

Do you want me to talk to her about the sunglasses – see if I can find out what's behind her taking them? It might help. She might open up.' The rash offer was made.

A tentative smile flickered across Kate's face. Recognition of Corinne was there all right; a remote reticent recognition, with a touch of formality like she would afford to any one of Four Hills' visitors.

Despite the shared confidences, Corinne recognised that's exactly what she was as Kate said, 'That's very kind of you, Miss Pallin. But I need to put an end to what I started.'

CHAPTER TWELVE

Corinne rested her arm across the sofa's curved back, her head full of Kate Menzies' disclosures about Louisa. The animosity between the two was mind-blowing.

Kate had opened up to reveal what lay at the heart of it.

Corinne was doubtful about her rash offer. Talking to Louisa might help. It might not. Made on impulse, in hindsight she knew it had been a bad mistake to get involved.

She let out a frustrated shriek. She should steer clear. How ludicrous was this? *Her* trying to sort another person's problems when her own life was crumbling about her ears. She must be going mad! Earlier, she'd almost lost it. Desperate to wipe out the last days, how easy it would have been to give in to Noel's coaxing. *That* had been a life changing moment.

A shudder ran through Corinne. She felt weak and vulnerable. Arms gripping her body, she hugged herself protectively. Noel knew only too well how to play people, using his charm. Like an expensive accessory, he used it. Even in his early days as a novice writer he had done it. Clumsy it had been then, now honed to silky smoothness Corinne usually fell for it – knowingly. Well, not this time. This was no tiny, hard to detect fracture, easily mended with an hour's naked cavorting on a Sunday afternoon while the thing that triggered the rift was smothered by mutual satisfaction and never mentioned again.

No amount of charm was going to heal this break.

It wasn't that she didn't want to make love. She did. She was selfish. Part of that selfishness was to know he was hers, only hers, and knowing that he wasn't, hurt. She ached in a place deep inside her she'd not known existed, never before having been violated. The rift between them was all the more galling because they had been good in bed – she had thought. She was no prude. Obviously, it had not been enough for Noel. But she was confused; he wanted her still.

Corinne gritted her teeth and gazed unseeing over the loch. There were other men, men who would bring no history with them into the bedroom. Their lives, her life, could be separate, save for the occasional meeting, touching, loving. Other women she knew did it, why not her?

She slammed her way into the kitchen. A pile of dirty dishes lay on the draining board. Messy, slovenly, this wasn't like her.

She made a start. One on top of the other, she stacked the crockery as would a Parisian waiter in a busy pavement café fully aware of the admiring glances from his patrons at his daring and skill. She had seen it done; there was nothing to it.

The stack growing, a rogue plate slipped. Her carefully constructed tower tilted sideways and Corinne spread her hands wide. Stretching a finger, she straightened a couple of bowls sitting one inside the other. The bowls, with traces of limp salad, cradled a coffee mug. The coffee mug moved. The wine glass, departing from the coffee mug, tipped sideways. A spoon clattered into the sink as her delicate tower swayed perilously.

She stood, her hands frozen on the misshapen tower. It wavered beneath her over-stretched fingers. If she let go now it would tumble and smash.

What would that Parisian waiter do?

With a yelp that she didn't recognise as hers, her temper snapped. She let go.

The fragile tower swayed, doomed. Before it fell of its own accord, she scooped the wobbling pyramid off the draining board with a swipe of her hand.

The whole lot went down. The nerve jerking sound of breaking crockery filled the small kitchen. Corinne closed her eyes and listened as glass fragments tinkled delicately as they fell through the devastation, and decimated plates and bowls settled haphazardly in the bottom of the sink.

She stood back. This complete loss of self-control was foreign to her. She was definitely losing the plot. This little bit of domestic carnage, she could easily have prevented. Certainly, she wasn't thinking straight.

Ignoring the mayhem, Corinne grabbed her jacket and made for the door desperate to get out of there. The place was beginning to get to her.

At the open door, she hesitated. The sun, starting its downward dip over the loch, shot her through with a searing golden light. Her Bvlgari were lying on the windowsill behind the sofa. She picked them up. They felt smooth and cool. When she ran her fingers over the shiny black rims, she felt comforted by the familiar luxurious feel.

Staring down at the sunglasses, she raised her hand to her face and closed her eyes. When had she become this person – so materialistic, so avaricious? Had they all seen it: her parents, Uncle Ian... Noel even? Nobody had said a word to her.

Did it matter? Not now, she thought. It's too late. Not one person had picked her up on it or hinted at her being self-centred with her bulging diary and her weeks at a time away on business.

Corinne's defences rose as she visualized her family ranked against her. It was for *him,* for *them,* for the *company.* The plain truth was it was business. That wasn't selfish.

In her mind's eye she saw each of her many returns from abroad as a replica of the preceding one. The same bee-line for the office as soon as she cleared customs; the neat and precise report handed to the board the following morning, so proud of what she had achieved while she'd been away; her recommendation on what they should or shouldn't do with it.

The one person missing from that scenario was Noel.

With a reckless aim Corinne threw the sunglasses back on the sill. They hit the wide window and fell carelessly on their lenses, the two legs sticking straight up in the air like a bird whose natural radar has deserted it and crashed at speed into an undetected window.

Corinne swallowed the urge to scream. With a false calmness that did not extend to her seething insides, she picked up the sunglasses. She closed the legs slowly and carefully, one folding in precise harmony with the other, behind the lenses. Gently she placed them back on the sill, opaque lenses shining up at her. Did she care that much? Maybe she did. Maybe she cared too much.

Locking the door, she glanced at her watch. Seven thirty. Louisa said eight o'clock the party was to start.

Instead of heading for the path, Corinne left the walkway and crossed over the few metres of pebbles in front of the cabin window to the water's edge.

Shading her face with her hands she narrowed her eyes and gazed across the loch.

Against the brilliance of the golden sun she could make out the jetty, its straight outline grey and softened by distance.

Four small boats were tied up at its side, each shifting gently and randomly with the lap of the water. On shore, spiralled the telltale grey-blue tail of an open-air fire. Several figures moved around it. They had the preparations for the night's festivities well underway.

Corinne swung her eyes away from the loch and the far shore. How bad would it be if she did not put in an appearance? These people living or visiting the loch had no hand in her situation; they were not to blame for the break up of her marriage. She thought of Kate Menzies, misguided enough to try to put things right with a stranger for her daughter's sake, desperate in her efforts yet totally out of her depth.

And Louisa, resentful that everything that might have been hers had slipped away so easily, and blaming everyone for it except herself.

Then Ross – a man pulled this way and that. He seemed to be always at the run in an effort to make amends for the two beautiful women in his life. Shouldering the responsibility; a man not free.

Corinne sighed. Let them all get on with it – let them deal with their own problems. She would do the same. Broken dishes, broken marriage, she could handle it!

A laugh erupted from her and the anger of the last fifteen minutes melted away.

Buoyed up, she jogged back to the walkway, jumped up and unlocked the cabin door. Inside, she hesitated for a second – the Bvlgari or the thrift pair?

Smiling, she grabbed the Bvlgari and slipped them on her head.

The path to the jetty was no mystery to Corinne now. Knowing how far it was, her tread was slow and she was in no hurry to get to the party.

About halfway there she stopped.

A car was revving its way through the woods. From the mechanical growl, the vehicle was edging its way in low gear. Clearly, it was coming up behind her. It sounded a fair way off still but she moved from the path and waited in amongst the trees for the vehicle to pass.

It was only seconds later that the Menzies' Land Rover came swaying towards where she stood behind the trunk of an ancient pine.

Camouflaged well in the gloom, Corinne peered into the dim interior of the vehicle as it passed.

In the front passenger seat Louisa's face was pressed up against the window. On the girl's right sat Kate, stiff and upright, staring straight ahead. Beside her Ross was driving. As he coaxed the vehicle along the track it gave a violent shudder and threatened to grind to a halt just where Corinne stood.

As it passed her, she gaped, amazed.

Squeezed in the back, shoulder to shoulder, sat three people: Noel and both her parents. All three, like Kate, were

179

staring ahead, eyes trained hard on the path in front. No conversation went on. Everyone appeared to be concentrating hard on the vehicle's laboured progress along the path.

Struggling to believe her eyes, Corinne stood rooted to the spot in the shadows while the vehicle, just metres away, regained traction.

It moved on, making its way grindingly up the track.

Corinne moved out from the trees. No one had seen her. She laughed silently to herself. She might have known. Noel guessed she was out on a limb, what with her holding up her parents' move to France and leaving Ian to take care of the business. *She* was creating the disruption to all their lives.

Everything he could, Noel was bringing to bear on her. Anything and anyone – her mother and father included – he would use to get her to change her mind. It was a sly, underhand tactic to get his own way and no doubt he would put a gloss on the reason they split for her parents. She could practically hear him; the caring, contrite son-in-law going to any lengths to get them on his side.

Well, it seemed he had done that all right!

Did he want her back that badly? She couldn't understand it.

Corinne drew her fingers through her hair, and resettled her Bvlgari on her head. She had her own role to play in what was fast becoming a fiasco.

Corinne strolled the rest of the way to the jetty, as if she had no destination in mind and was in no hurry to get wherever.

In her head, she made up little speeches for that one moment when she came face to face with her parents. It wasn't going to be easy.

The cove had turned into a campsite, and it was crowded. Three people, at least, had been watching for her.

Emerging from the trees into the clearing, her family saw her and hurried to meet her.

'Cherie!' Pierre Pallin, with all the abandon of a continental, enclosed her in his arms and kissed her.

'Dad, Mum.' Corinne touched her mother's cheek with her own. It was routine.

Immediately, banal and meaningless, the carefully rehearsed words started rolling from her lips.

'How do you like it up here?' Corinne smiled at her parents, ignoring Noel. He stood back and to the side of Jean Pallin watching the little scene intently.

'It's a lovely spot,' her mother answered. 'For a short stay, I dare say.'

'Yes. It is. Dad, did you come by car or did you take the train?' Corinne was determined there would be no head-to-head in front of the strangers populating the campsite. They had no part to play in this.

'We drove up, Cherie.'

'That's a pity. The station taxi here is an old vintage piece. It takes you to another time and place.'

Her mother was not interested. 'We're here especially to see you. That's all. Nothing more.'

'You should have let me know you were coming. Never mind,' Corinne shrugged and paused before adding, 'Ross told you about the barbecue?'

'Yes.' Her mother dismissed the gathering with a fluttering hand. 'Corinne, your father and I need to talk to you, seriously. That's why Mr Menzies brought us here in his vehicle when you weren't at your lodge.'

'Cabin, Mum. They're called cabins. Dad, your car would never have made it along that path.' Corinne stated the obvious knowing her father's large indulgent vehicle, of which he was very protective.

'No, Corinne, I would not have managed that,' her father agreed. 'Cherie, we have not come to join in the fête. We need to talk to you. That is why we are here.'

'So serious on a party night!' Corinne injected a note of teasing she didn't feel into her voice.

Her parents as well as Noel, who had said not one word, were staring at her.

Corinne felt the smile on her face harden into a comic mask.

Noel stepped forward. 'Cory, please.' The corners of his mouth curved into a smile while he aimed his words towards Corinne's mother. 'Jean and Pierre have made the journey up here so that we can all sit down and put an end to this nonsense.' The smile was gone when he hooked his arm in Corinne's. 'You could at least hear them out.'

'No!' Corinne jerked away. 'You came here, all of you, without being asked. Well, stay if you want to, talk together if you must, but count me out.' She glared at Noel. 'Tonight, I'm going to do exactly what I want. I'm going to enjoy myself.' She turned to her mother. 'The entertainment is limited up here. If you don't like it you should go home.'

The glance that went between her parents wasn't missed by Corinne. She ignored it. Over her mother's shoulder, she fastened on the bonfire, sparking and flaming with orange ferocity.

'Wow! What a blaze.' Brushing past Noel, she headed towards the jetty.

On the wooden planking sat Ryan and Phil. They had supplied cushions and placed them in a line on the jetty.

'Hello, you,' Ryan greeted her. 'Family come to join you, have they?' His head tilted to one side.

Corinne realised her family had followed her, in Indian file and cautiously, across the pebble beach.

'Yes.' She had no option. 'Mum, Dad, this is Ryan and his partner Phil. They have that cabin up there.' The introduction was short and impersonal. 'This is my mother and father. They're here just for the evening.'

'Hello.' Phil reached out. Hands were shaken and brief smiles exchanged.

Ryan raised his hand and waved theatrically. 'And,' He nodded in Noel's direction.

'This is Noel Anderton. The writer,' Corinne said loudly.

'Well, a celebrity honouring our little gathering,' Ryan exclaimed. 'Whatever next!'

Corinne left her mother and father perched ignominiously on the edge of the jetty.

'I'm going to see if they can use a little help.' She crunched over the pebbles to get nearer the blazing bonfire.

'Cory,' Noel followed closely at her back. He grabbed her arm, drawing her to a halt. 'They obviously wanted to come. I didn't make them. I didn't even ask them. But now they're here, well, it might help us.'

Corinne faced him. 'Get it right, Noel. You mean it might help you.'

Noel ignored her glare. 'How do you know that if you won't hear them out? Maybe it could help us both.'

'God, you must have done a really good job on them!' Corinne spat out the words. 'Two days. Two days and you've got them ticking every box in your favour. The son-in-law every parent wants – *you*.' Her head went to one side. 'How did you do that, Noel? Tell me. Or more to the point – what version of this sordid little tale did you spin them?'

Corinne saw him bite down on some snide retort. She'd hit home. His version had been selective.

Noel gave a derisory laugh and stepped back. 'Come on, Cory. We're all family. Jean and Pierre, they want us to get over this.'

'Oh, I know they do!'

'Well then,' Noel's smooth, coaxing tone was back. 'Why don't we all get together? Talk things through. Come on, that's what you really want isn't it?'

Whether from the heat of the bonfire flames or from the tension inside her, Corinne felt her cheeks flame. 'Everybody has their own agenda.' She smiled sadly at Noel. 'My parents too.'

Noel stared at her.

'Don't be so surprised, Noel.' Corinne almost laughed at his expression. 'I'm not a fool. I've disrupted their plans, that's what they think.' She challenged him. 'How come, Noel? How is it, when I'm the injured party in this, I'm made to appear as the villain?'

Relief flashed over Noel's face. 'I didn't say that, Cory.'

Corinne turned on him. 'That's right. I forgot. You never tell it like it is.' Her smile was tight. 'You make it up as you go along. Isn't that the truth! Well, I don't want to talk about this any more. These people,' she waved her hand, taking in the row of figures sitting on the jetty and the groups of hikers camped up on the stones. 'They don't care about me or Pallin-McCall, or even Noel Anderton,' she paused and added, 'whoever he might be.'

The agreeable expression faded from Noel's face.

Corinne saw the sudden hard clamp of his jaw.

He said pleasantly enough, 'Fine by me, baby. For tonight we'll shelve our differences. One big happy family, that's us.' He motioned towards the jetty. 'Now, let's go back.'

Corinne stared hard at her husband. There is no going back, she thought. But she kept the thought to herself.

As the evening wore on, the sun set over Loch na Duroir, a priceless gold droplet in a ruby streaked sky. Not even the sparking flames from the roaring fire could outdo its brilliance.

Joining the party, the Taylors were introduced to the Pallins and Noel Anderton.

Arms entwined, saying little, the couple stood back from the huge fire watching the party. Kim leaned tiredly on Alec. They did not sit down and after a short while, they went back to their cabin.

Falling into conversation with Phil, Noel was as good as his word. Not once did he allude to his writing, his publishers, or give his real reason for being beside the loch with a bunch of strangers.

184

Sitting side by side, Corinne's mother and father, polite but tight-lipped, refused the offer of beer and opted for red wine, poured into white plastic cups by Kate Menzies.

Jean Pallin did not keep the surprise out of her voice as she drank. 'Mmm... This is really nice.'

Kate Menzies told her, 'Ross, my husband, he chooses the wines.'

'You're not drinking?' Jean Pallin queried.

'No. I don't drink. I like to keep a clear head. Oh, not that there's anything wrong with it. It's... It's just... Well, I take medication you see...' Kate hesitated as if she'd given away a great secret and wasn't sure of the consequences. She looked about her vaguely.

Her husband was nowhere near.

On the opposite side of the bonfire, with Ryan and Louisa and a tall, lanky hiker with a strident Aussie accent who professed to have culinary skills, Ross was barbecuing strips of thin steak on a low grill over a smaller, purposely built fire.

Corinne saw Kate's struggle. 'I saw the smoke from the barbecue clear across the loch earlier. Who started it going?' she asked.

'Oh, it wasn't me.' Kate claimed no credit. 'No, no. It was Phil and Ryan. They got it going this afternoon. When Ross came to build the bonfire later, that was all done too,' she informed Jean Pallin. 'When the hikers heard what was planned they wanted to do their bit. Really I think they want to stay overnight.' When this explanation brought forth no response from the visitor, Kate fell silent.

'Well, that smell is making me hungry.' Corinne got up. 'Can I get anybody anything?'

'No. You stay.' It was her father. He stood up. 'I'll go. Perhaps you can come and help me?' He smiled down at a startled Kate Menzies.

'Oh,' Kate got off her cushion. 'Yes, of course.'

Pierre Pallin stepped forward and took her arm. He glanced

at his son-in-law. 'Noel can come with us too.' He threw glances at his wife and his daughter. 'We'll leave you two to chat.' He smiled at Kate. 'Shall we?'

Corinne watched them walk cross the pebbles. They deviated in a wide arc to avoid the bonfire that was spitting out sparks in all directions and forcing the onlookers to draw back.

There go three people with nothing in common, Corinne thought. Nothing – except *her*. Daughter, wife, friend? The last two had her wondering.

'You're day-dreaming,' Jean Pallin caught her. 'Where were you?'

'Sorry.' Corinne inhaled then exhaled deeply as if indeed emerging from a different world. 'You tend to do that a lot up here.'

'Have you managed yet to come to any more concrete conclusions while you've been on your own?'

'You know, Mum, I made a bargain with Noel earlier – no talk about us tonight.'

'You mean you and him. I'm talking about your father and me.'

'You're not going to let it drop, are you?'

'No. I'm not,' Jean Pallin said. 'You can take all the time you want to decide what changes to make in your life, Corinne. You have the luxury of years ahead of you to find out if those decisions you make now are the right ones or not. That's up to you. Your father and I, we don't have those years.'

Corinne blinked. 'What do you mean, you…?'

'Oh, for heaven's sake, nothing life-threatening. Good grief, with all the care we take of ourselves.'

'What then?' Relief made Corinne abrupt.

'Don't snap, Corinne. There are many things that can't be discussed easily over a camp-fire.'

'My sentiments exactly.'

'That's why,' her mother went on, 'I wanted to see you in

186

your lodge… oh… cabin!' She shifted on her carefully placed cushion. 'There are things I must tell you before we – any of us – can move on with our lives.'

'Have they anything to do with Noel and his little side-dish?'

'Oh, Corinne, don't be so predictable.'

'Have they?'

Jean Pallin stared straight ahead. She did not meet her daughter's eyes.

Laughter drifted across the pebbles on the back of the smell of food. The air was redolent with burning wood and singeing meat. It wasn't a bad smell, only meaty and earthy.

At last Jean Pallin answered, 'Indirectly.'

'Indirectly!' Corinne nodded. 'Am I supposed to guess? Because if so, I tell you now, Mum, I don't think there is anything left for me to surmise.'

'You think not?' When her mother fell silent, Corinne glanced at her. Her mother's eyes were glazed and watery.

The sight shocked Corinne. Her mother in tears just did not happen. 'Mum, whatever it is, I probably know already.' She gave a small dry laugh.

Jean covered her cheeks with her hands. She blinked rapidly as her husband came back towards the jetty. 'Oh, Pierre,' Ignoring Corinne, she got up to meet him.

Pierre Pallin dumped the food he had brought down on the jetty. He clasped his wife by the arms. 'I am sorry. I was talking to the young people. They are travelling.' He nodded at Corinne. 'You have been talking?'

His wife placed her hand on his face, forcing him to pay attention, not to his daughter but to her. She moved her head slightly. 'No.'

'But why?' Pierre Pallin was disbelieving.

'Now is not the time.' Jean removed her hand from his face. 'I would like to go now, please. Corinne is right; this is a place for thinking, not talking.'

Corinne stood up. 'You surprised me by coming here like

this. I'm sorry.'

Jean ignored her. She addressed her husband. 'Can we go home now?' Without waiting for an answer, she pulled her jacket straight and picked up her handbag and began to struggle over the pebbles.

Corinne knew there was no changing her mind. Whatever her mother had been about to say, would remain unsaid until Corinne was sitting in a comfortable arm-chair at some time in the future in her parents' sitting-room in Edinburgh.

She followed them across the pebbles to the dirt path.

'Wait. I'll drive you back to your car. I'll ask Ross for the Land Rover keys. I won't be a minute.' She left them standing silently beside the Land Rover.

At the barbecue she cornered Ross and put her mouth to his ear. 'Can I get your keys?' She motioned behind her. 'They want to go back. They're leaving now.'

Ross nodded. He drew the keys out of his pocket. Before he gave them to her, he lowering his head and warned her, 'Be careful. Take it slow.'

She nodded. 'I will.'

Edging her way back through the crowd around the bonfire, she came face to face with Noel.

'You bastard!' Over the laughing and singing she wasn't sure if he heard her.

'What?' He put his hand behind his ear.

'I said, you're a…'

He grinned.

Bubbling with rage, Corinne moved past him. Her fingers shook as she unlocked the doors of the Land Rover. Her parents in the back, she was alone on the front seat.

Starting the engine, she adjusted the rear view mirror and glimpsed the two of them sitting close together, her father's hand clamped firmly over her mother's. Already they were totally engrossed in each other, anxious to be away from this place.

Away from me, Corinne thought.

With Ross's whispered instructions lurking in her mind, she drove back through the woods.

Under the canopy it was almost black, only a dark sea-green light filtered down through the tops of the trees. With full headlights picking out every turn of the wheel, she eased the Land Rover up to the Menzies' shop. Relieved to have made it safely, she pulled on the handbrake and sat with her hands resting on the steering wheel. Not a single word had passed between her and her parents on the short journey. Now she couldn't bring herself to break the deadlock.

A tentative few minutes followed as they climbed down from the vehicle and slammed the door.

Her mother nodded, stony faced, and made for the car with no farewell.

Around the side of the Land Rover, her father came to Corinne. Standing very close, he said, 'Goodnight, Cherie.' His breath was warm on her face, his hands firm on her arms. 'Do not be so hard on her. She loves you very much.'

He bent and kissed her cheek. It was so very typical of her father.

CHAPTER THIRTEEN

Outside the Menzies' shuttered shop, the lone security light glowed dully orange.

Corinne watched until her father's car drove off.

Purring like a contented cat, and with all lights blazing, the sleek black vehicle moved away from her, down the narrow road leading to the railway station and then to the little town of Blairkeld. From there it would take them onto the B road before meeting up with the motorway. They would be home well in time for her father's regulation finger of whisky.

No response to her wave came from the dark inside the vehicle.

Corinne dropped her hand.

The luminous red rear lights disappeared within seconds.

She was left standing in the eerie mix of white light thrown out by the Land Rover's headlights and the orange security globe. Her cramped cabin was suddenly overwhelmingly inviting.

Quickly, she shelved the idea. There was no option but to go back to the barbecue. Ross would need his vehicle to get the gear back from the jetty.

Corinne leaned back against the Land Rover and viewed her surroundings.

Beyond the reach of the circle of light, it was impossible to see anything. The thick, solid trees on the perimeter screened the last slanting rays of the descending sun.

She stretched out her hand and touched the bonnet of the vehicle. The warmth from the engine made her fingers tingle, its strong, rough growl flooding her being. The beat of the mechanism drummed up through her like a second, reliable heart.

She placed both hands on the bonnet. If only there had been a tiny gesture, a sign from her mother that she was on her side. It would have gone a long way to fill the void growing steadily wider with every word that passed between them.

Corinne breathed deeply finding it hard to keep down the emotions about to burst to the surface. Closing her eyes, she steeped herself in the darkness.

Her parents' flying visit had done none of them any favours. At home, she and her mother would have argued, traded pointless barbs, and eventually reached a truce, albeit reluctantly and as usual highly compromised on both sides. It was the norm. Then they would have moved on.

But here, constrained by the unfamiliar dark, dominating loch, amid strangers who, while friendly enough, no doubt appeared alien to her mother, Corinne knew another thread in the fragile Pallin familial fabric had been destroyed.

Drawing a stuttering breath, she stood unmoving. It had happened again. The tiniest incident had widened the barren space opening between her and her mother. Did they understand each other? She wasn't sure they did. Sympathise? They both were too proud to accept that concession unconditionally from the other.

Corinne hated to think what would happen if her father were not there to keep them together. Peacemaker. It was a role he happily played time after time. He was always ready to step in between them. Why did he do it? Contrition for past transgressions?

Until this last week she had thought she knew her parents, accepting as she got older that they were emotional, changing beings, even at times fallible – but always truthful, open people.

Now, doubts were starting to creep in.

At first she'd blamed herself for these altered feelings but maybe, just maybe, it wasn't all down to her.

Corinne opened her eyes and removed her hands from the warm vibrating Land Rover.

At this moment, her life felt a complete sham. Nothing was as it appeared on the surface. She felt a fraud.

Giving out an agonized cry, she raised her head to the sky letting her hair whip across her face. She drilled her fingers through her hair and pushed it back from her face then ran her hands down the front of her body and straightened up.

She needed to keep herself together. Tonight, there was still Noel to face. With any luck she might get him to leave as well. Then she would be on her own again.

At this moment, the feel of being completely abandoned by the people closest to her was cruelly pleasurable.

Just what am I turning into?

Climbing into the driver's seat, she successfully eased the unfamiliar vehicle round in a wide circle. Not all caution gone, she drove back through the woods at a slightly faster speed than with her parents in the back.

On the path behind her cabin, she passed the walkway leading to her door.

For a second she felt a basic territorial connection. Her eyes travelled over the small square wooden building sitting in the semi-darkness, outlined by the deepening blue sky and glinting red-streaked water of the loch as the sun set. She wanted to be in there, with the door locked. On her own.

Hiding? She'd never hidden from anything in her life. Until now.

Fixing her eyes on the path ahead, she drove on.

At the jetty clearing, she manoeuvred the vehicle back where Ross had parked it earlier. Even before the engine was silent, he was at the driver's window.

'Everything all right?' He opened the door and held it wide.

'Yes. Everything's fine.' Corinne climbed out.

'You were missed.' Ross nodded over his shoulder towards the bonfire.

Yet more people had descended on the cove. They didn't know Corinne and she didn't know them. They'd been drawn by the noise and the flaming pyramid. In the last half hour, the congregation, as well as the bonfire, had grown considerably.

Phil Skinner was nervously urging people to stand well back from the flames.

Corinne remarked, 'Things are going well.' She threw the Land Rover keys to Ross. 'Thanks for that. They wanted to get back before it got too late.'

'You've not tried any food yet. Come on. Over this way.'

Following Ross, Corinne moved towards the white dusty ashes of the barbecue fire. Ryan was still hard at it. People she didn't recognise were drinking from plastic cups and eating with their fingers.

Her stomach felt hollow but up until this moment she'd put it down not to hunger but tension.

Ross reached across Ryan and got a plateful of food from a rack. He handed it to Corinne. 'We saved this for you.'

Ryan moved away and they were on their own.

'Did Ryan keep this for me or was it you?' Corinne didn't wait for an answer. 'I saw Louisa helping earlier. Is she still here?'

'Over there.' Ross pointed.

The girl stood near the loch's edge with Edwin and Tamzin Coburn. The three of them were laughing, dipping their greasy fingers into the cold water.

Upwards of twenty back-packers, were sprawled over a part of the cove which Ross had agreed could be used as a temporary camp-site. Their gear was spread about like a temporary township established without any specific intent or organization.

The sound of a harmonica, in the hands of one of the campers, cut across the babble of voices and a hesitant singing started up. It grew in strength as people recognised the tune and joined in trying to rival the haunting notes of the small silver instrument held lovingly to its owner's mouth.

Kate was sitting on the edge of the jetty, her long legs stretched out in front of her. Eyes half-closed, a detached smile covered her face as she listened to the music. Beside her, Noel was talking with Phil but Kate was not part of it.

Ryan, his stint at the barbecue over was at his partner's side.

Ross nodded towards the little group. 'Do you want to go and join them?'

Corinne was silent. She peered across at Kate then down at the food on her plate.

'I think I'll eat this first,' she said. 'To be honest, I'm not feeling very sociable right now.'

'Your parents, they seemed really anxious to see you,' Ross remarked. 'If I did the wrong thing bringing them down here, I'm sorry. I didn't have much option. Anderton knew where you'd be.'

'Don't worry. I know them all too well. They would have managed to get here somehow.' She licked her lips. 'Families! What you've got to do to keep them happy.'

The harmonica player was settling in. His audience wanted more and the music from his lone instrument grew louder and more raucous. People clapped in time and sang along. The noise built as each voice, un-noticed, un-criticised, mixed in with the rest of the crowd and floated out over the loch.

'They've got the right idea,' Ross jerked his thumb at the campers. 'Get right away from it all.'

'You can't, can you?' Corinne said. 'You're like me. Caught up so much in other people's lives you don't have one of your own.'

Ross turned his head sharply. 'You?' He seemed not to believe her. 'That's not how you come across.'

'No? Well, don't let outward impressions fool you.' Corinne nodded to the impromptu concert in full swing. 'What I wouldn't give right now to be one of them. Not a care in the world.' She smiled. 'No problems, no responsibilities. How great would that be?'

'Well!' Ross clapped his hands and made Corinne jump.

'Tonight, you're going to be one of them. Me too. Come, on.'

When Corinne grimaced doubtfully, he urged, 'I need you to cover for me. I'm no singer.'

Corinne caught sight of Louisa and the Coburns. They had moved into the crowd listening to the harmonica player. The numbers had grown like ripples in the disturbed water of the loch when Freddy threw his stones. Between Louisa and Tamzin was Noel. He was sitting cross-legged, not singing but swaying his shoulders back and forth in time with the chorus of voices. He seemed so completely at ease.

He shouldn't be enjoying himself. Not here. Not like that!

At that moment, Corinne hated her husband. He'd tracked her down, followed her and invaded her hideaway.

Ross followed her glance. 'All our problems in one tidy group.'

'Not all.' As she said it, Kate came towards them. Corinne's head swung in Ross's direction. 'Oh, I didn't mean…'

'Don't worry about it,' he said softly. 'You're right. We are two of a kind.' He reached out and took Kate's hand. 'Why aren't you sitting with the rest of them?'

It was a throwaway question but Kate's answer was deadly serious.

'I was helping Phil and Ryan. We were packing up the barbecue gear. The grill's still hot. Far too hot to move to-night. We'll have to leave that where it is until the morning. We could take the other bits and pieces now the Land Rover is back.'

She said to Corinne, 'Your family's gone?'

'Yes. They needed to get back.'

'Of course.' Abruptly, Kate suggested to Ross. 'I think we should tell Mr Anderton that he can't stay.'

Both Corinne and Ross were speechless.

Corinne could see Ross was thrown by his wife's sudden change of heart. It had come out of nowhere.

195

'Why? What's happened?' he wanted to know. 'What's brought this on?'

'I was wrong to tell him he could stay in the first place.' Kate was bravely adamant as she watched the little group that included Noel. Her voice was quivering as she said, 'You should take him back to his car, Ross. And Louisa, she must come home with us – now.'

A shadow of understanding crossed Ross's face.

'I'll speak to Mr Anderton and tell him we made a mistake. As for Louisa…' he shrugged. 'She's having a good time. Let her stay where she is. Don't let's break up the party just yet.'

'No!' Kate grabbed Ross's arm. 'I don't want her to stay.' Suddenly she was begging. 'Please, Ross. Get Louisa and let's all go home.'

'Kate, stop this.' Ross put his arm on his wife's shoulders. Holding her, he gave her a little shake. 'We'll all stay a little while longer.'

Kate's narrow frame seemed to shrivel in size. She leaned all her slight weight up against her husband. He held her firmly but gently like she was a small frightened child in need of reassurance.

Corinne felt overwhelming pity. It was painful to watch this beautiful woman disintegrate whenever she saw her daughter in the company of Edwin Coburn.

The little group with Louisa at its centre appeared less engrossed with each other than in the festival atmosphere that was steadily building.

Corinne joined in as they clapped when a pretty girl got to her feet and made a brave attempt to dance solo. Twirling, she stumbled on the pebbles and fell on top of her boy-friend. Jeers followed and the girl laughed but did not try again.

As she watched this little by-play, Noel leaned forward to speak to Louisa and at the same time caught Corinne's eye. He nodded in her direction and grinned.

196

Stony faced, she stared back.

Louisa followed Noel's glance and saw the acrimony flow between him and Corinne. Tugging at his arm, she whispered briefly in his ear. Their mouths widened and together they laughed. The words and the laughter were soundless among the noisy campers.

Corinne felt powerless. Her defences were weakening with every minute that passed. If she let a girl like Louisa intimidate her, what hope was there that she would get through this break-up with Noel unscathed?

Aware of Ross watching her, she said, 'I think I've had enough, too. I'm going to make tracks back to the cabin.'

Kate saw her chance. 'We'll all go. Please Ross.'

'I'll go and round up the others.' Ross patted his wife's arm. 'You stay here with Corinne.' He untangled himself from Kate's grasp. 'It'll only take a minute.'

Leaving Kate and Corinne at the jetty, Ross picked his way through the revellers. The haunting notes of the harmonica drifted over the crowd sitting sprawled across the pebbles. He avoided them all.

Corinne saw him crouch down behind Louisa, put his hand on her shoulder, and whisper in her ear. He got up and the Coburns and Noel scrambled to their feet. Louisa stayed where she was. Between them, Edwin and Noel persuaded her to get up. They each grabbed one of her hands and pulled her upright. They were laughing, Louisa wasn't.

Unable to hear Louisa's words, Corinne, nevertheless, could tell by the sulky pout on the girl's face that she wasn't happy about leaving.

When Edwin and Tamzin reached the jetty, they were laughing.

'Youth has many advantages.' Edwin stretched his back. 'Not the least of which is the ability to ignore one's comfort. Ouch!'

'You're not old, Edwin.' Louisa came up behind him. She had recovered her good humour. 'Well, not *that* old!'

The banter went on as Noel, too, eased his back.

Kate was watching. Abruptly, she said to Noel. 'You can't stay. I made a mistake, there is no room available.' She swallowed and put her hand to her neck. 'I am sorry.'

The banter stopped.

Noel swung his head from Kate to Corinne and back to Kate. 'Don't worry about it,' he said. 'I've got to get back, anyhow.' He addressed Ross. 'You'll give me a lift back to my car?'

'Yes, sure. As for the rest of you, how are we going to do this?'

'I'll go with Edwin and Tamzin,' Louisa cut in.

'Oh, sorry,' Tamzin shrugged. 'We didn't bring the car.'

'We can't all get in one vehicle,' Edwin reasoned. 'I should have thought. But Tamzin and I can easily walk back.'

Ross stood quiet for a minute. 'Edwin and Tamzin, I can take you two, and Mr Anderton and Louisa. I'll come back for Kate and Corinne.'

'I'll stay with Kate,' Edwin offered.

'I want to stay with you, Edwin!' It was Louisa.

'Right then,' Ross held up his hands, 'Louisa, you drive. Drop Edwin and Tamzin at their place first. Then take your mother and Mr Anderton back to the shop.'

'What about you?' Kate asked.

'I'll walk back with Corinne.' He nodded to Corinne. 'Is that all right with you?'

Everyone turned to Corinne as the arbiter of the plan.

'That suits me.' Anything to have it sorted. Anything to get Noel on his way was agreeable to her.

Ross opened the door of the Land Rover and retrieved a torch from the side pocket. He handed the keys to Louisa.

'Drive carefully now. Edwin and Tamzin, first, remember.'

'God! I heard you the first time.' Louisa grabbed the keys out of his hand and jumped into the driver's seat. Edwin got in beside her, while the others settled themselves in the back.

As Louisa reversed before heading onto the path, Noel glanced out of the vehicle window straight at Corinne. The smile he threw her was tight-lipped. It disappeared from his face even before he turned away. He'd put up no protest at his summary eviction, or at having little or no chance to say his good-byes to her in private. Despite his speedy departure there was no regret in that smile.

Watching the vehicle disappear along the path into the trees, Corinne couldn't shake the feeling that Noel was leaving the scene victorious.

Waving to Phil and Ryan, she stood at the edge of the path, saying goodnight to people she didn't know as small groups in the crowd began to break up and wander away.

Ross spoke to the campers. They could stay by the jetty for the night on the understanding that no more wood was fed onto the fire.

One last check and Ross was back.

'They seem a sensible lot. And Phil says he'll keep an eye out. Anyhow I think they've had enough for tonight as well.' Ross gestured to Corinne. 'Come on. You'll be home in twenty minutes.'

'Home? Oh, you mean my cabin.' Corinne laughed.

They stepped under the canopy of trees and at once the fading daylight disappeared. A white triangle of light spread out in front of them as Ross switched on the torch.

The air in the wood was moist, redolent with the thick scent of pine, and cool.

Corinne slowed and took her jacket from her shoulders and put it on. 'It's a different world in here.'

Beside her, Ross's face was just distinguishable. 'You're really not afraid of the dark, then?'

Corinne felt he was laughing at her. She didn't care.

'No, not me. I can get up in the middle of the night and wander about in the dark; no lights, no torch, nothing!'

'Interesting. Like this?' The torch went out.

Her eyes no longer focused on the beam of light, Corinne

found herself enveloped in complete darkness. Her heart began to race.

'Yes, like that,' she breathed.

She put out her hand to locate Ross. The cool air moved between her fingers but they did not come in contact with him. A small, tight knot of panic began to form in her stomach. She heard a thud followed by a muttered curse.

'Ross?'

A scrabbling went on over to her right. The tight knot gripped her whole body. Her breathing was shallow at the thought of being abandoned.

'Ross? Where are you?'

'Sorry.'

The torch beam hit her full in the face but immediately was aimed away. 'I dropped the bloody thing.'

The sound of his voice made her legs weak with relief. Her face flushed hot in the darkness. 'You certainly know how to make a point. I'll keep my mouth shut from now on.'

'Don't do that.' Again his face was in darkness. 'I like to hear you talk.'

Despite this claim, they walked side by side in silence. At length Ross said, 'You had a pretty hard time of it today.'

Corinne wasn't sure if it was a question or a statement.

'Life can be difficult.' She glanced sideways. Her eyes readjusting to the darkness, she could just make out the grooves and angles of his face, deepened by the shadows. 'You have to deal with it.'

'I agree. But with Anderton here and then your family arriving like that. That was tough.'

'I love them but they can be heavy going.'

'I'm sorry if we added to your problems.'

'You weren't to know that I had *escaped.*' She said it lightly.

'Is that what you were doing – escaping?'

Under cover of the cool green canopy, Corinne admitted, 'Well, I suppose I was. When you take off you don't stop to analyse if there is any sense in what you're doing. You just know that you need to get away.'

They were walking very slowly.

'What was it that made you pick Four Hills?' he asked.

'Oh, I wasn't running to Four Hills, if that's what you're thinking.' She laughed. The sound echoed thick and full in the tunnelled space under the trees. She grew serious. 'To be honest I have no idea why I came here. I didn't even know this place existed.'

'You came. You're here.'

'Yes. I saw it advertised in a magazine.'

'Are you glad you did? Do you like it?'

'I'm not sure.'

'Nothing decided yet, then?'

'I'm more confused than ever.' Corinne was amazed at her unplanned confession.

'You don't mind being on your own here?'

'It won't be for long.'

'You know that?'

'Oh, I know I have to get back to work.' She grimaced. 'Sooner rather than later, as well.'

'You don't have any kids to rush back for, do you?'

Corinne stared straight ahead at the beam from the torch. 'No. No kids.'

'Did you never want kids?'

Corinne was taken aback. The familiar stab of regret hit. 'The time was never right.'

'Is that why you're so involved with your business?'

'Ross… I'm not comfortable talking about this.'

The torch beam wavered. 'Sorry. I thought you might want to bounce it off an outsider.'

'What are you talking about?' She slowed down. 'Bounce what off an outsider?'

'Noel told Kate that you had problems at home. We assumed…' The torch beam hit her full in the face. 'Oh, sorry.' The light swung back to the path.

201

Corinne gasped. 'For God's sake stop saying you're sorry!' Her foot caught on a raised root and she stumbled. She regained her balance already regretting her rebuff. 'It's just that whenever it's my mother and me, she likes to make the decisions. I had to get away to make my own.'

'About you and Anderton?'

A long drawn-out breath escaped Corinne. 'About everything.' She stumbled again.

'Here.' Ross reached out to her. 'Hang on to me. We've not far to go now.'

Corinne clasped his hand. Close together, they walked in silence.

'It's getting cold.' Unlocking her hand from his, she stuck it in her pocket.

Ten minutes later Corinne stepped onto the walkway leading to her cabin door. 'I'll make it from here,' she said.

Ross swung the torch beam down the length of the walkway. 'You sure? It's pretty dark.'

She walked the few steps in the glare of the torch and put the key in the door. The lock clicked open. 'I told you, I'm not afraid of the dark.'

'I'll remember that.' He swung the beam of light away from her. They were standing in the gloaming, the torch casting a blue hazy reflection over the still water of the loch.

Ross stepped from the walkway. Seconds later he was on the path.

As he moved away, Corinne could make out the glint of the torch, but not much else. She followed the progress of the arc of light in and out of the trees, getting ever smaller. At last it disappeared.

Corinne toed off her shoes.

Low light flooded the room when she flicked the lamp switch. Walking barefoot to the bedroom, she threw her jacket on the bed.

A warm shower and a magazine to read might stop her

thinking about the day that had just passed. If she started going over every minute of tonight at the jetty she would drive herself crazy. She was glad it was over.

As for Noel, she had no idea if the reason he had come to Four Hills had been achieved. He'd certainly seemed pleased with himself.

God! She was at it already! Noel was back, crowding her brain. It was not the best omen for a good night's rest.

Her shower lasted ten minutes. She brushed her hair and put on a pair of white silk pyjamas.

In the kitchen, she filled the kettle and made coffee. Mug in hand, she went to the bedroom. About to draw back the cover on the bed, she hesitated. Her watch said ten to one. She stood still, considering, then, with her free hand she smoothed the cover back down, picked up her magazine and flicked the light switch off with her thumb as she left the bedroom.

The lamp was still burning in the living room. Pulling the cushions off one of the chairs she piled them high at her back on the sofa. With the unopened magazine on her lap, she drank her coffee.

Through the window, she could see nothing of the outside world. It was her reflection in stark black and white that the lamp threw back into the room.

Watching herself put the mug to her lips, she could see her neck tighten with every swallow. Slowly she raised her hand to her throat. Her fingers were cool on her skin; her face was flushed.

Putting the mug on the table she got up. With a flick she switched off the lamp. The scene outside her window revived instantly. A cold black and silver image of her – a misty ghost – shimmered in the dark night.

Unlocking the cabin door, she lay down again on the cushions and waited.

The knock that came was so soft it would have roused no

one if that had been its true purpose. It was followed by the handle being turned and the door pushed open slowly.

Facing the door, Corinne watched.

Ross Menzies entered the cabin and closed and locked the door behind him. He came to where she lay.

He leaned over her. 'Hi. You look relaxed.'

Corinne did not move. 'Looks can be deceiving.'

He crouched down at her side, his elbows resting on his knees and peered hard at her. 'Tell me I haven't got this wrong?'

The cold night air he brought into the cabin, hung over them.

'Both of us know nothing good can come of this,' she cautioned softly.

He scrutinised her face. 'Don't analyse it. I'll leave if you do.'

'No.' She put out her hand but didn't touch him. 'Stay. I just don't want anybody to get hurt.'

'You can't stop doing it, can you?' He brought his face closer to hers. 'You're looking for a reason. Well, don't. There isn't one. We both want to be here.' He laid his hand on her shoulder. 'That's got to be enough.'

Corinne heard it for what it was – a 'take it or leave it' proposition. He was offering her nothing. Through the dimness she gazed up at him able to make out his unblinking eyes, his serious face.

'How do you know it'll be enough for you?' she challenged him.

Through the silk pyjama top she felt his fingers tighten on her shoulder.

'Stop it,' he ordered. 'No games. We've both got too much going on.'

'And we're supposed to ignore it all?' Corinne gave a pathetic little laugh.

'For one night, yes.' He leaned over her and cupped her face in his cold hands. 'No baggage. Just you and me tonight.'

His face so close, Corinne lifted her hand and trailed her finger down his temple to his chin. 'If only it were that simple.'

CHAPTER FOURTEEN

Monday started cool.

Only half-awake, Corinne was aware of the sharp, white light streaming through the front windows of the cabin.

The belligerent rattle of children's voices as they played on the stones at the loch edge reached her. The animated sound made her open her eyes to the day and face what it would bring. Whatever, it couldn't be as bad as yesterday.

She glanced at her watch. Five minutes past nine. Until Four Hills, she'd never slept this late. Here she did things differently.

Her feet touched the floor. She was naked.

The night before hit her like a shower of freezing rain swept over the loch on a cold wind. She glanced over her shoulder at the crumpled sheets.

'In the dark,' she had insisted.

He had laughed indulgently in her ear, a low, rich rolling sound she couldn't remember having heard from him before. *She'd* done that.

Corinne could find not a single trace of his visit. No one would be able to tell of the hours she and Ross Menzies spent on the rumpled bed.

'No games,' he had said.

She'd known straight away he meant it. Like a vision conjured from that place in her head for wishful thinking, he had come to her bed, and went away as easily and as shadowy as a dream, leaving nothing of himself behind. What was that if it wasn't a game? She smiled. He'd wanted her. She'd been happy to play along.

Corinne threw back her head. Instantly, she regretted it. Her scull felt heavy and she couldn't focus for more than a second without blinking. She felt old and jaded; a far cry from the person of last night. But a little glow of satisfaction was compensation enough.

Grabbing the top half of her pyjamas, she covered herself and made for the bathroom.

In the shower, she stood under the streaming water, eyes closed tight, face taut. The buffeting little bullets of warmth pounded her skin. Even if she wanted to, there was no chance of cleansing the image from her head of her and Ross Menzies together. His words were as clear as if he were standing close and naked by her side in the tiny cubicle whispering in her ear. *No games, no baggage. No games, no baggage. No games, no baggage.* She had agreed. And then they had played…

Corinne backed off from the spray. Her eyes opened wide. God, what had she set herself up for?

Half an hour later, showered and dressed, she wandered out to the walkway and jumped down on to the pebbles.

At the water's edge Lucy and Freddy Coburn were quarrelling fiercely over a small piece of wet speckled rock.

'Hello, you two.' Corinne crossed the few metres to where Freddy squared up to his big sister, and called a halt to the argument. 'What have you got there?'

'I found it first!' Freddy laid claim to the rock now in the unyielding possession of his sister.

Lucy crinkled up her eyes against the brightness to address Corinne. 'Do you know anything about rocks?' The question was unequivocal, a clear answer expected.

'No, I'm afraid, I don't,' Corinne admitted.

The disputed rock clenched firmly in her hand, Lucy continued to stare hard at Corinne. 'Daddy says you are very clever.' The bright light reflected from the cabin window at last forced the little girl to lower her eyes to the rock nestled in the palm of her hand. 'But you don't know a lot of stuff.'

A muffled laugh made Corinne turn.

On a flat stone, her back resting against the wall below the cabin window, sat Louisa Menzies. Through half-shut eyes she was watching the little scene.

'For someone with a lot on their mind, you sure can sleep.'

She smiled like a lazy cartoon cat served up with a bowl of cream.

'I suppose it's the clear air up here.' Corinne moved away from the children to sit beside the grinning girl.

Her head propped back against the wooden wall, Louisa asked, 'Did you enjoy last night?'

'What?' Corinne's stomach contracted.

'Over at the jetty. The barbecue. What did you think of the lot that were there?'

For Corinne, the glare from the water was just too much. She eased her Bvlgari onto the bridge of her nose. Several seconds passed before she answered.

'Yes, it was fine. How about you?'

'Too many wrinklies there for my liking.' Louisa's eyes were closed, her pale face raised up, braving the growing strength of the morning sun on its climb into the sky. The languid smile was still there.

'My parents weren't invited.' Corinne hated being obliged to explain her family's presence. 'They just came up on a whim.'

'I went back later.' Louisa gave a little laugh. 'Much later, after you all went to bed.' Her eyes mere slits, she watched Corinne. 'Those hikers – the Australians – they know how to have a good time.' She did not elaborate on what went on after the barbecue had supposedly ended.

'Oh, how did you get back there?' Corinne was curious.

'I walked.'

'By yourself? In the dark?'

'You did. You walked back here from the jetty.'

'That was different. Your father was with me.'

'My father! Ha! You're real funny, you know that?'

Irritation rose up like a wave of hot, sour bile and lodged in Corinne's throat. Unwilling to reveal her present insecurity to this inquisitive girl, she clenched her hands but did not respond.

Louisa had the knack of knowing just how to scratch the

surface of her calm, agitating away at what lay beneath until it erupted like a weeping sore.

Her eyes fully open, Louisa stated bluntly, 'You know what? I think your Noel is nice. What stopped you from going home with him last night? He wanted you to. I'm positive. That's why he came, wasn't it?'

Unable to stop herself, Corinne snapped, 'None of your business!'

Louisa ignored the put-down. She sat forward. In a theatrical gesture she tossed her tumbled flaming hair back off her face. 'So what's keeping you here?' she asked.

Corinne studied Louisa's profile. The girl was taunting her. There was no way she could know anything about last night. Ross would have checked Kate and Louisa were asleep before he came back to her cabin… surely.

Corinne reflected on just how easy it had been to take another woman's husband. He'd made it easy for her. *Just you and me.* She'd gone no further than those four little words, needed no more reason than he wanted her, she wanted him. The thin justification was pushed firmly to the back of her mind.

'I could ask you the very same thing,' she ventured. 'Why are you still here, Louisa?'

'What do you mean by that?' Louisa straightened. Her voice was tight, the timbre that of a petulant child. '*I* belong here.'

Corinne slipped off her sunglasses and carefully folded the legs together.

'You live here because you like to think you're forced to.' She rubbed an imaginary smear from the lens. 'But that's not true. You're out of place here. The city is where you belong even if you can't face up to it. You're scared of putting yourself out there and being held to account for yourself.'

'You don't know anything about it!' Louisa was rattled.

Corinne felt the tables gradually turning. She was getting under Louisa's skin, digging, interminably scratching away, giving the girl a taste of the malice she dished out constantly.

'Kate told me all about it,' she said eyeing her own distorted reflection in the Bvlgari lenses.

'Oh, told you what exactly?'

'You know what. Why you were kicked out of college.'

Louisa sprang to her feet. 'You're a liar!' She glared down at Corinne. 'Why would she tell *you*? She wouldn't!'

Corinne sat still. She refused to meet Louisa's eye.

'Kate feels guilty,' she said. 'Mostly because she can't find any way to put things right between you two. She thinks it was all her fault.'

'That's all you know!' Louisa stood with legs apart, barring Corinne's view of the children. 'Whatever she told you, she doesn't feel guilty. No way! She's just jealous!' Her voice reached a manic high while her pale skin flushed. She threw a glance towards the loch.

At the water's edge, both Lucy and her smaller sibling, heads bent peering into the water, were oblivious to the conversation going on beneath the cabin window.

'Jealous of what?' Corinne asked.

Hands clenched, her tall body bent at an acute angle, Louisa stuck her face close to Corinne's. 'Edwin Coburn!' She spat out the name. 'That's what!'

'No, you're wrong about that,' Corinne said. 'He's an old friend; she told me. Besides, he has a wife and those two.' Corinne nodded briefly in the general direction of the children. 'She just doesn't want you to go there; get involved with him. She doesn't want you to go down that road and get hurt. You must know yourself it won't end well. It never does.'

'She doesn't want *me* to go there! Ha! That's a good one!' Ignoring the stones, Louisa threw herself back down. She drew her legs up and cuddled them in close to her body. 'She had him years ago. Yes. Like mother like daughter.' Abruptly, Louisa dropped her forehead on to her knees hiding her face.

Corinne said nothing.

The minutes passed. The only sound on the miniature beach was the murmur of the children's voices as they found then discarded rock after rock in the ongoing search for that special one.

Eventually, Louisa raised her head. She cupped her hands over her eyes to avoid meeting Corinne's gaze, squinting instead out across the length of the loch.

'You're probably right. About the city anyway. I should go back to Glasgow. Get myself a job there.' Louisa dropped her hands from her face. 'But she needs me,' she said intently.

The bare emotion on the girl's face disturbed Corinne. Louisa really believed her mother would not survive without her and yet there was so very little harmony whenever they were thrown together. There it was – like herself and her own mother – that's what Louisa could sense, why she came to talk.

Corinne shied away from the comparison. 'Kate has your father,' she reminded Louisa. 'You need your own life.'

'Like you, you mean!' The verbal armour was firmly back in place.

Corinne bit back a retort. She said candidly, 'I'm trying to sort my life out. I'm not expecting anybody else to do it for me.'

'But you'll take all the help you can get. Is that how it's done?' Louisa laughed. 'Huh, I should take notes. You've got them all running after you.' A facetious curiosity wrinkled her brow. 'How do you do that, then? Is there a sort of formula you use? Come on, give.'

Corinne flinched. What the girl said went deep. It was true. Or at least that's how it must appear. Noel, her mother, her father, they had all tracked her to Four Hills, to be with her. Then last night in the dark cabin, Ross Menzies. Why had she not seen it when Louisa had? Corinne was speechless.

'Forget it. Scrub what I said.' Louisa scrambled up. 'Who

211

am I? Big loser! What do I know?'

'No… you're right.' Corinne swallowed hard. 'One problem and I head for the hills.' She laughed weakly. 'Literally.' Unseeing, she stared past Louisa to where Lucy and Freddy were arguing over yet another fragment of ancient mountain scree.

'Hey, don't take any notice of me.' Beneath her thin top, Louisa shrugged her shoulders and put up her hands in a gesture of mock surrender.

Corinne was shaken. 'We're a right pair.' She forced a smile. She felt slightly sick.

'I should learn to keep my big mouth shut,' Louisa said. 'I've never been much good at that. I expect you've noticed.'

Corinne stood up. 'I think I'll take a walk. See you later.' She climbed back up onto the walkway and went inside the cabin.

She made straight for the bathroom. At the sink, she leaned her hands on its cold smooth edge. In the square mirror above it, she gazed hard and close at her reflection. Her family had come and gone with nothing resolved. So what had she done? Only added to her problems by sleeping with Ross Menzies, a man she barely knew. How easy it is to slip. Oh, Noel… Noel…

'Hey, Corinne. You there?' Louisa's voice brought Corinne up short. She suppressed a desire to scream at the top of her voice, to tell the girl to go to hell, to rant and rave and get it all out of her system. A silent helpless laugh passed between her and her glass image. Tears threatened and she forced them back. Louisa would like that – seeing her disintegrate.

A smile on her lips, her voice was easy as she called out, 'I'll be with you in a minute.'

She faced herself in the mirror. Who was that person? Outwardly she was confident and assured; inside she was confused and scared. Despite Louisa's assertion that everybody was running after her, she felt very much on her own.

Her head up, she walked to the living-room.

Louisa was holding open the cabin door.

'Do you want to walk up to the centre with us?' Her graceful body was arched inside the cabin, her feet still outside on the walkway. She hadn't actually crossed the threshold. 'I've got to get these two back before lunch time. Want to come?'

'Yes,' Corinne nodded. 'You three go on. I'll catch you up in a second.'

'You'll want these.' Louisa stretched out her arm.

The light bounced off the Bvlgari as they swung back and forth between her thumb and forefinger.

Corinne watched the shine of the swaying black lenses.

'You know what? Keep them. You always seem to end up with them.' She tried to smile at the girl but the lone feeling was back.

'You think I stole them!'

The sunglasses flew across the room. They hit Corinne on the chin and landed with an impotent clatter at her feet.

'*You* keep them!' The door rattled on its hinges as Louisa slammed it shut behind her.

'Louisa!' Corinne pulled the door open. Lucy and Freddy were standing on the walkway staring at the back view of Louisa as she ran onto the path and disappeared into the trees. Taken by surprise, the children both stood wide-eyed.

'You dropped them when you got up,' Lucy said. She turned to her brother. 'Come on, Freddy.' She held Freddy by the hand and led him to the path.

It was an hour later before Corinne convinced herself that she was not in the wrong.

Louisa had brought it on herself, reading too much into a simple, impulsive gesture that had come from Corinne's need to give of herself. The girl had an uncanny knack of putting people on the defensive. And she *had* stolen the sunglasses once.

Before she left the cabin, Corinne slipped the Bvlgari into the pocket of her jeans. On top of her head she stuck the cheap sunglasses Ross had brought to make amends for the first time the Bvlgari *'got lost'*. This simple act made her feel better which Corinne could not explain, because her stomach, as she walked to the craft centre, still churned and her hands trembled when she stretched them out as if she were recovering from an illness.

If this is what infidelity does for you, I must be allergic!

At the craft centre, she found a seat on the veranda and waited. Other tables were occupied but the place wasn't busy.

Monday must be a slow day, she reckoned.

A minute later, Edwin came out to take her order, a bright yellow pencil and a tiny square pad of paper at the ready.

'I'm surprised to see you today,' he said. 'What would you like?'

Corinne sat baffled.

'Coffee?' Edwin prompted.

'Yes. Please. Coffee,' Corinne agreed, and added. 'Why, surprised to see me?'

Edwin smiled. 'Husband, father, mother… All after you. Yet you're still here. Our local attractions must be stronger than I thought.'

Corinne pulled her hands from the table onto her lap. 'Does everyone here know my business?'

'Sorry,' Edwin bent his head and smiled. 'I for one am extremely happy you stayed on. There, I'm rumbled. I can't resist a pretty face.'

The old line fell on unreceptive ground. This morning Corinne was immune. But she made an attempt to smile at Edwin. 'No, it's me. I'm sorry. I'm too touchy. Don't take any notice.'

'One of my coffees and you'll be as right as rain.' With a practiced hand he propped the other two chairs on their front legs against the table. It was a pointless gesture for there was no one else wanting to use them.

On her own, the innocent action made Corinne feel completely isolated. Any company would be better than this.

'Did the kids get back from the loch?' she called after Edwin. 'I saw them down there earlier, outside my window.'

'Yes. They're back.' His face sobered. 'Down by your cabin? By themselves, were they?'

'Oh no, Louisa was with them.' She gave a short laugh. 'They were searching for stones.'

'Ah! Right. Only, they know they're not meant to hang around the cabins. She usually takes them to the little cove. I'll get you that coffee now.'

Corinne slumped back in her chair. So Louisa brought the children to her little bit of beach as an excuse to come herself. She sighed. Since last Wednesday she had been at Four Hills. Five days of doing nothing yet she felt exhausted, not through physical exertion but with the mind games that these people constantly played.

'Your coffee, *Madame*.' Tamzin Coburn, colourful in a brightly patterned shapeless dress, placed the small tray in front of her. She nodded in the direction of the few other customers.

'Not a lot of company for you here at this time of year, I'm afraid. Are you going to be staying much longer down at the loch?'

Corinne's shrugged. 'Oh, I'm not really sure yet.'

'You realise that little soirée last night was put on for your benefit, don't you?'

'For me? I don't understand. I got the impression you did that sort of thing now and then for the visitors.'

'Well, we do. Weather dependent of course. In July and August when there are more customers,' Tamzin was honest. 'But last night people came out of the bushes – from everywhere!' About to go, she hesitated. Her lips betrayed a mocking smile.

215

'Now don't go letting on to Ross and Kate that I gave away their little secret.' She edged her way between the tables and chairs and disappeared into the craft centre.

Her hands warmed by the coffee cup, Corinne gazed down into the hot liquid.

She couldn't believe it! The barbecue had been set up for her. Suddenly the vision of her parents and Noel sitting with Kate and Ross Menzies in the Land Rover burned in her head. Which of them had colluded to try and persuade her to pack up and go home?

Barricaded in at her table by the upturned chairs, the feeling of isolation consumed Corinne.

Lowering her head to hide the tears welling up, she sipped at the coffee. It tasted bitter. She reached out and dribbled a thin trail of cream across the dark brown surface, stirred it in, and drank again. The edge had been taken off the taste.

She pushed the cup away. Without a glance at either the other customers or the open door of the centre, she got up and left. She needed to get back; back to her own cabin where she could think straight. And talk.

She would talk to the one person she knew would listen.

Corinne heard the ring tone cut off as the call was picked up.

'Uncle Ian,' Corinne identified herself before he had a chance to speak. 'It's me.'

'What's been going on with you?' His deep voice was uncharacteristically sharp. 'You should be home by this time. Why didn't you hitch a lift back with Pierre and Jean last night?' It was an accusation.

Corinne's spirits slumped. He was never this curt with her. She had been counting on Ian McCall.

'I'm not ready to come back. Not just yet.'

'Corinne, Pierre and Jean went up there to see you to explain some things. Things – no, let me finish – things that needed to be said face to face not over the phone. Instead they found themselves at a sort of *al fresco* do, and, to crown

216

it all, in the company of Noel.'

'I didn't ask them to come up here. What did they think it was – a conference centre?' She defended the simplicity of Four Hills.

'Lass, what's happened to you?' Ian McCall levelled his voice 'Don't you want to get this problem between you and Noel sorted out?'

'Of course I do.'

'That place doesn't seem to be doing you much good. Jean said you weren't your usual self when they saw you.'

Corinne couldn't deny it.

Getting no response, Ian McCall went on, 'There are things that must be talked through which you don't know about. They could make a deal of difference to what you eventually decide to do about you and Noel.' He paused.

Corinne could hear him take in a thick nasal breath before he said, 'That's why Jean went all that way to talk to you.'

'Well, can't *you* tell me now?'

'No, no. It's not for me to take it upon myself to do that.'

'Is it about Noel? Because if it is… If there's more to come out about what he's been getting up to, I don't know that I could take it right now. My head is crammed full as it is.'

On the far end of the line there was no denial, or confirmation, from Ian McCall.

The silence between them was painful for Corinne. It scared her. There had never been a time in her life when she wasn't able to go to him and get a straight answer, to anything that troubled her.

'Why didn't Mum tell me what she came here to say? Why come all this way and then decide that it wasn't the right time?'

'She says there were far too many people around. And from all accounts, it would not have been the best time for a family chat anyhow.'

Corinne felt he was making light of her mother's sudden exit from Four Hills. She was even more convinced of it when he added, 'Besides, with Noel there… Well, what did you expect?'

'I didn't invite him either!'

'Did the two of you get to talk things through?' he asked. 'That's the important thing.'

'We talked all right,' Corinne confided. 'Basically, he thinks I should just lighten up. *Forget* his little fling and move on to a new life with him.'

'Is that so?'

'I thought Mum was on Noel's side. You make it sound as if his being here put her off talking to me. Uncle Ian?'

'She's not on his side as you put it. Neither is your father. None of us condones what he's put you through. But, Corinne, there are two sides to every story.'

'And it just depends on which one you want to believe,' she said.

'No, Corinne, no,' he scolded her. 'It depends on how much you love a person and how much tolerance you can give to their indiscretions.'

'You didn't think that when I rang you two days ago,' she accused him. 'Then, you agreed that Noel was just trying to wriggle out of his contract. All of a sudden you've changed your mind. What's brought this about?'

His breathy sigh reached her down the line. 'Don't be angry. You know fine I'm on your side.'

The laugh Corinne gave out trailed off pathetically. 'I don't know anything anymore.'

'Then why don't you come home?' Ian McCall counselled.

'Not yet. I can't.'

'It must be a special place, this Four Hills.'

'God knows why I came here! But I won't give in to them, Uncle Ian. Mum and Dad, they can beg or bully all they want. As for Noel, well, you know Noel.' Her laugh was scathing. 'He's not going to win me over this time. He can try all he likes. Believe me! When I make up my mind it's going to be for keeps, but the rules will be rewritten, and by

218

me. He'll just have to take it or leave it whatever I decide.'

'Corinne…'

'What?'

'Would you let me come and see you? Talk. Just the two of us.'

For once in her life Corinne held back from him. 'I don't see what that would achieve.'

'In the past you would never have said that.' He did not sound hurt by her reluctance, merely accepting that things had moved on.

'This is not about the past. It's about the future, my future.' She was anxious to explain away her easy rejection of him. 'I've got to make sure I get it right. Oh, there's somebody at the door. I have to go.'

She pressed the end-call button on her phone with the lightest of touches. Despite the gentle pressure, the connection was cut abruptly, ending any chance of further conversation.

For a while Corinne stayed where she was. Her phone cradled in her hand, she looked out of the cabin window. The high, bright sky of earlier had gone, giving way to a steely-grey ominous bank of cloud which, even as she watched, turned the sparkling water of the loch into a blue-black oily slick. Shivering, she realised the temperature in the room had dropped. The cabin was no longer light and airy but felt slightly damp, pervaded with the stifling smell of pine.

On the back of days of warm sunshine, the change surprised Corinne. It reminded her that it was still only May.

The summer had barely started.

CHAPTER FIFTEEN

About two o'clock in the afternoon, the drizzle started.

It crept, soft and gradual, like a cautious enemy, down through the pines and across the loch. It formed a thick, grey veil which was neither rain nor mist but a mixture of the two, silent and depressing.

Corinne scraped the last of the cheese from the pasta bowl. She placed it carefully in the sink (all evidence of destroyed dishes guiltily removed earlier), thinking as she did that very little food and many coffees was not a good combination.

She was a creature of habit. Not in all things but in most. At Four Hills the natural order had gone so completely from her life that it began to alarm her.

Without enthusiasm, and with the minimum of effort required, she gathered magazines and newspapers into a neat pile on the table. Out across the water she saw the high trees like vague grey spires, hardly distinguishable from the glowering sky pressing down on them. At the edge of the loch the pines merged with the drizzle into a dense sea-grey barrier.

The water itself was transformed. No glitter of light bounced off its surface. No dazzle had Corinne reaching for her Bvlgari to hide behind. The mist sat suspended over the still water much as clouds would sit in a steep valley, not moving, engulfing everything and everyone caught in its soft murk.

With narrowed eyes Corinne gazed hard down the loch. The jetty, with its canoes tethered cosily to its side was not visible, hidden behind the impenetrable grey mist.

She shivered and for the first time since arriving at Four Hills and taking possession of the cabin with its compelling view, she came away readily from the window. Less than a week and she had grown used to the scene, lulled by the shining calm waters every morning when she opened her eyes.

Today she felt let down.

In the bedroom she picked up her waterproof, the one Ross pressed on her the night Kate Menzies went missing. Worn reluctantly once, the dull green garment was lying folded neatly in a corner, unused since then.

Corinne pulled it on over her head and let it fall about her, reminding her of the cape they swathed her in at the hair salon. Reaching down to her knees, its odour was plastic, sweet and sickly.

She tried the hood up over her hair. It felt claustrophobic and she threw it back.

Feeling over-equipped and more than a tad self-conscious, Corinne opened the cabin door.

Not a drizzle any longer, the rain now was coming down straight and heavy. She laughed as she stuck her face out into it. Her unflattering garb was spot on.

Stepping onto the soaked walkway she went towards the path. The night she walked alone to the craft centre in the dark trying to locate Kate was fresh in her mind. Even in daylight, it would not be a comfortable walk to the shop with the drenched trees shedding their overload of water down on her. Having experienced it once, she was wary of going through it again.

She walked, hands deep in the side slits of the wide cape, the hood now pulled firmly down over her face.

She managed to reach the Menzies' shop in ten minutes. During that time she passed a small group of hikers trudging two abreast. After them came a young couple and several lone walkers.

Meeting so many people on the path temporarily diverted her and took her mind off herself.

Once she detected the Gallic purr of a French accent as two girls, carrying rucksacks that would have put a stoop on a healthy male, said hello as they came level. An elderly couple seriously kitted out for hill walking, stopped and

221

stuck their shooting sticks in the ground and chatted to her seemingly oblivious of the rain.

Soaked, yet in a strange way enthused by her transient association with these strangers, Corinne reached the shop to find that it too was experiencing a temporary up-surge.

The place was crowded. Edging her way through the dripping customers, she saw Kate and Ross behind the counter.

Corinne raised her voice. 'I was hoping to see Louisa.'

Kate finished with her customer and made her way from the counter and through the queue towards Corinne.

Over the heads of the customers, Ross caught Corinne's eye. 'Okay?' he mouthed.

Corinne hesitated. What was she supposed to say? *No, I'm not bloody okay! I've slept with a man I hardly know, I want to do it again, I will have to lie to his wife, and I've called his daughter a thief!*

She met his eyes and nodded briefly.

Ross's mouth curved upward as he nodded back at her.

He's relieved!

'Hi.' Kate was beside her.

'I was wondering where Louisa was.' Corinne decided not to let on about what went on that morning outside her cabin. Two of a kind, the trivia that so easily upset her daughter did exactly the same thing to Kate. She was learning fast to tiptoe around these people.

'You've just missed her, I'm afraid. She went up to the craft centre. It's her designs,' Kate confided. 'She's got her best pieces up there but they're not moving. Too expensive, maybe, for here. One can never tell with that sort of thing. What she's going to do with them, I have no idea, but she says she wants them back.'

She shepherded Corinne into the passageway to the house.

'Can I ask, did you tell her to go back to Glasgow?' Kate's hand swiped across her forehead. She did not wait or even seem to want an answer to her question. 'Since this morning all she can talk about is getting away.' The beautiful green eyes, turned falteringly on Corinne, were hurt and confused.

'I saw her down by the loch earlier,' Corinne said truthfully. 'We did talk – mainly about me.'

'You're not getting much peace, are you?' Kate drew her further into the passageway away from the door. Her face was very close to Corinne's. 'Was she all right when you saw her?'

'I think I may have upset her,' Corinne admitted. 'Oh, it wasn't anything much. My sunglasses; I said she should keep them. That's all. I'm afraid it didn't go down too well. That's why I'm here.'

'Yes…' Kate was trying to make sense of her daughter's latest outburst. As usual she seemed at a loss. 'Perhaps, I'd better go up to the Coburns.' Her eyes flicked briefly back and forth at Corinne. 'She shouldn't be up there.'

'But if Tamzin is trying to sell her designs?'

'It's not Tamzin.' Kate pursed her lips together. Her hands came up in an impatient gesture. Corinne had the impression she was going to grab hold of her. She was wrong.

Kate sank back against the wall, her tall thin frame falling naturally into a dramatic pose that harked back to her lost career.

'Ah, Edwin, I suppose,' Corinne guessed.

Kate's head drooped. 'Tamzin knows. I'm sure she does. Yet she still encourages Louisa to go up there. She gets her to look after the children. The idea to sell Louisa's designs was hers in the first place.'

'You think she's using Louisa?'

'Oh, don't you understand?' Kate cried.

'No! I don't. Kate, I'm a stranger here. A week ago I didn't know any of you even existed.'

'Of course. I know that.' Kate reached out to Corinne. 'You're not one of us. I think that's why she's really taken to you.' Her face softened. 'We all have in our own way.'

'Well, I don't know what I can do.' Corinne shrugged.

223

'We certainly don't bring the best out in each other, Louisa and I.'

'An independent, successful woman, that's how she sees you. Everything she wants to be,' Kate said honestly.

An exasperated little laugh burst from Corinne. 'My life is a mess right now. My head's as screwed up as anybody's.'

'You *are* strong, though. Even when your family confronted you last night, you didn't give in to them. Everybody saw it. And you're still here. That's what Louisa admires in you.'

'Ah, the barbecue.' Again Corinne laughed. 'What a fiasco. Sorry. But for me it was.'

'That was partly our fault,' Kate said. 'When they said who they were, naturally we thought you would want to see them.' She shrank back. 'Your husband too. I shouldn't have presumed.'

'So the barbecue wasn't put on just to get me and my family together?'

'What?' Kate was confused. 'No. They arrived without booking or anything. How could we know they were coming?'

'You wouldn't of course. It's just that Tamzin gave me the impression... Oh, never mind. It doesn't matter.' Corinne had nearly fallen for Tamzin's lie. She believed Kate; the Menzies had not set her up.

'Last night, Noel, what did he say to my mother when they met? How were they with each other? Did you notice?' Corinne asked.

Kate's brows came down and the pale skin of her eyes crinkled into gentle freckled lines.

'Well, it was all a bit strained. When your parents pulled up outside, your husband went very quiet. He had a strange expression on his face, defensive is the only way I can describe it. But he didn't seem all that surprised to see them.'

'Are you sure about that?'

'Yes,' Kate confirmed. 'Your mother and father didn't

224

seem too happy to see him either.'

'So it hadn't been arranged between them?'

'No, I don't think so. Your husband, well, he did mention your mother not having the nerve to tell you.'

'About what? Did they say?'

'No. They stood here, right in the shop, and when your husband said that, it all went rather awkward. After that your mother and father more or less ignored him.' Kate was uncomfortable. 'Is it important?'

'That's the thing. I don't know. With Noel involved, I get the feeling it could be very important.'

'I'm sorry if we did the wrong thing taking them to the jetty last night.'

'Oh, really it doesn't matter. Knowing my mother, she wouldn't have given you much option.'

Kate did not deny it.

Corinne knew she'd guessed right. 'I'm not giving mothers a very good press, am I?' she said. 'Mind you, as a daughter I wouldn't pick up any prizes either!'

They both stood silent. Corinne could feel Kate was itching to talk but unable to find the words.

At last it came. 'Do you think you could go up to the centre for me and bring Louisa home?' Kate asked. Corinne's problems were already forgotten.

'Bring her home, or get her away from Edwin?'

Kate's face went blank. 'I'm sorry. I shouldn't have asked. I'll do this another way.'

'Do what another way?'

'She mustn't get involved. Not with Edwin.'

'Kate…' But Kate was already making her way out of the passageway into the shop.

'Kate!' Corinne tried to call her back.

Edging between the customers Kate went straight to the far side of the shop.

Left standing in the doorway Corinne was suddenly faced with Ross.

He nodded towards his wife attending to three women. 'What were you two talking about?'

Without any prevarication, Corinne told him, 'She's worried about Louisa.'

'As ever,' Ross said.

'Doesn't it bother you that Louisa hangs around Edwin Coburn just to annoy Kate?'

'When Edwin gets fed up with her *"hanging around"*, he'll send her home like he would one of his own kids,' he stated confidently. 'Kate's getting herself all worked up about nothing.'

'You think so, do you?' Corinne's patience snapped. 'Well, I think you should stop making excuses for everything Louisa does and get to the bottom of what's really bothering your wife.'

He stared at her. 'What did she say? Was it about last night?'

'Last night?' The delicious dark hours came flooding back to Corinne. 'No, not that.' She breathed deeply and let it out in a rush. 'I think your wife is in love with Edwin Coburn.'

Ross's eyes went dark. 'No. That's been over for years. It was decades ago in London. They were together. I know all about it. They're just friends now, good friends. Kate looks to Edwin to…'

'To what, Ross? What does she expect from Edwin?' Corinne watched his strong jaw form a hard line.

'You're right,' he said. 'With Louisa, I tried to tell myself it was just a teenage phase. She never seemed that keen on Edwin until she came back from college. Then Kate started to get upset whenever Louisa was in his company.' He tilted his head toward Corinne as if to reassure himself she was there beside him.

'Ross,' Corinne touched his arm, wishing now she had kept her mouth shut. 'Don't do anything rash. About Edwin I mean. Speak to Kate first.'

Whether he heard her or not, Corinne got the feeling that

whatever was going on at Four Hills, it could only have a bad outcome.

'Yes. Yes, I'll do that.' He put his problem aside. 'You're all right, Corinne, yes?'

'Me?' She forced a laugh. 'I'm going to buy the best bottle of wine you have, find myself a good book, and spend the rest of the day with my feet up.'

He reached out and held her hand. 'You're a good person, Corinne.'

It was a strange thing to say.

Walking back to the cabin with her bottle of wine under her cape, the little impromptu compliment reverberated in her head. She could think of no other occasion when she had been called a good person. Slightly embarrassed by the accolade, she wasn't really sure what he meant by it.

At the cabin she carried out her promise to herself.

Pouring a large glass of the pricey wine, she rummaged and found a magazine. With her head back and her feet up, she lay and tried to read the glossy pages. But she couldn't settle. With her wine-glass in one hand and her arm along the back of the sofa, her eyes, as ever, were drawn to the loch.

The hazy mist was gone, replaced by gusts of wind-borne rain. Choppy waves, higher than normally seen from her window, scalloped the edge of the water with frothy white spume.

Away to the right, towards the jetty, the view improved. She could just make out the straight wooden structure sticking out into the water. Conditions on the loch were too rough to be inviting to any would-be canoeist other than the keen or the foolhardy. The little yellow craft, pulled up high on the pebbles gave the impression of having been abandoned.

As she watched, three figures appeared from one of the cabins and stood in the squally wind at the head of the jetty braving the weather. Their animated conversation, accompanied by the flailing hands of one of them, appeared accusing if not exactly threatening.

Corinne strained to make out the three. Two were dressed from head to toe in dark blue waterproofs. The third was dressed as if it were a warm summer's day.

Right away she knew. *That* was Louisa.

Intrigued, Corinne watched the trio continue to argue, heads pushed forward, arms gesturing through the falling rain. One blue figure tried to restrain the other, the taller Corinne could see, blatantly challenged Louisa.

The heated argument went on unabated for several minutes. It was fast deteriorating into a physical squabble when the tall blue figure snatched a small object out of Louisa's hand. Now things *were* threatening.

In her head Corinne heard the cry of anguish as Louisa lunged forward and tried to wrestle the object back but failed.

The shorter figure stepped forward apparently trying to put an end to the dispute and calm Louisa.

The girl thrust out her hands, gave a hard shove, and sent the person sprawling backwards onto the wet stones.

The movements of the little group by the jetty became frantic.

Corinne gasped and stretched up, her face so near the window it misted over with her warm breath.

With their partner's help, the person got up.

Louisa was on her knees, head down, waving her arms in the air.

Words followed and accusing gestures made.

Together the two waterproofed figures linked arms and walked away leaving the argument behind them, and Louisa, alone in the rain, squatting on the stones.

Corinne saw the pair walk from the side of the jetty to the nearest cabin. It was the one occupied by the Taylors.

The couple just reached the short wooden veranda before Louisa scrambled up and rushed after them. She was shouting. Her arms wrapped across her middle, she bent forward in a heart-rending display of entreaty.

Kim and Alec Taylor ignored her. They hurried inside the cabin and closed the door firmly on the girl's pleading.

Corinne pulled at her lip. She hadn't recognised the Taylors at first. Louisa was a different matter. Easy to make out, even at this distance across the loch, Corinne could see the flaming hair hanging loose and dank on the girl's shoulders and down her back. Louisa's appearance at the jetty, for whatever reason, had sparked off a row.

It disturbed Corinne to see her stand alone in the rain, her clothes drenched and sticking to her spare figure. There was no mistaking the dejection in the droop of her head or the slump of those thin shoulders.

She watched the girl drag herself up to the path at the edge of the woods, the desperate movement more telling than any words.

The effort to cover that short distance seemed to exhaust Louisa. She stopped to stare at the closed door of the Taylors' cabin. No movement came from there or any other quarter of the cove.

The place was deserted except for Louisa. The girl appeared lost and disorientated as if not really sure why she was there.

It was a painful thing for Corinne to witness. She screwed up her eyes to watch the lone figure. *Why* had Louisa walked all the way there in this weather? Kate said she'd gone to the craft centre to talk about her designs. As usual, with Louisa one was never sure what was true, and what part of the lies she told she wanted to be true.

Even as Corinne watched, Louisa tilted her head skyward and let the rain water pour down over her face and throat. The frustration evident in her even from a distance, she lifted both arms above her head, opened her mouth wide and screamed.

To Corinne listening to the drumming of the rain on the

229

cabin window, it was a silent, frustrated scream. Watching from across the water she felt helpless.

Nobody appeared in response to the agonized cry. Corinne wished she could help, if only to let the troubled girl know she'd heard or at least seen her anguish, even if she could not understand it or do anything to ease it.

Louisa stood still. Her hands at her sides, she stared straight ahead at the dark waters of the loch.

Corinne held her breath; her fingers gripped the edge of the window-sill. Her heart beat fast and hard in her chest as she watched. Scrambling onto her knees, she laid her hands flat on the cool glass of the window. 'No, Louisa... Don't.'

It was as though, through the rain, her plea had travelled across the water and been heard.

Louisa spun around and, as was her way of escaping, sprinted into the trees and out of Corinne's sight.

Relieved, Corinne sank back. Her hands were shaking. She was exhausted. Her mouth was dry and she felt weepy. Lying down she closed her eyes. If she slept she could obliterate the Menzies family from her head. Four Hills, the loch – it would all disappear into oblivion, at least for a while.

It was tempting. Corinne did not move. The thudding of her heart and her own breath coming fast and heavy was all she could hear. This place was not good for her. She should go home.

A sudden ache to be back doing what she did best, swept over her. Oh, for wind-blown Edinburgh streets, her office, her staff, her home, her family, Uncle Ian...

The cosy illusion disintegrated. She had to face reality. Never again would it be the same. Things were changing, had changed already. Whatever bound them all together was surely being undone by one person, and that one person was Noel.

At that moment, she felt as betrayed as Louisa.

Corinne stood up and pushed her hair back from her face.

She would get through this. She gazed out across the loch. Unlike certain others.

She saw the rain start to ease. The view across the loch to the deserted jetty was already much clearer.

Draping herself in the rubbery waterproof one more time, she stuffed her hair inside the hood and set out for the jetty.

She was glad of the clumsy garment. Walking head down, drops of water pelted her from above. She half expected to meet Louisa but there was no sign of the girl making for home.

She reached the entrance to the clearing and the jetty without coming across anyone.

Out from under the trees, she found the rain had stopped. A weak, watery sun made an attempt to shine through the fast thinning cloud.

The door of the Taylors' cabin opened before Corinne stopped knocking.

When he saw her, relief passed over Alec Taylor's face.

'Miss Pallin!' His eyes flicked over Corinne's shoulder, checking. 'Or should I say Mrs Anderton?'

Caught off guard, Corinne stared at him. Of course, everybody at the barbecue knew of her deception.

'Yes. You met my husband, Noel, last night, didn't you?'

'Interesting he was too.' The cabin door remained half-shut. 'Crime seems to pay in his case.'

'I'm sorry?'

'His novels. Kim says she's read all of them but I didn't know who he was. I haven't read any of his stuff.'

'Who is it, Alec?' Kim Taylor's voice reached Corinne.

Alec called over his shoulder, 'It's…' With a lift of his brows he smiled thinly at Corinne. 'Miss Pallin.'

'Let her come in, then.' The voice was shaky.

Corinne saw that Alec Taylor was about to deny his wife's wishes and close the door in her face. Putting her hand on the door-jamb she stepped in front of him.

A resigned Alec Taylor let her pass. The door was closed,

231

and he pushed past Corinne quickly to his wife's side.

Kim Taylor was lying on a sofa very much like the one in Corinne's cabin. A thick wool blanket was thrown over her legs. She, too, had a view out onto the loch only this time it filled the window from west to east while Corinne's narrow view from her cabin was from north to south.

Prompted by the sight of two small pill bottles on a table at Kim Taylor's elbow, Corinne asked, 'Are you all right?' The woman's usually perfect hair was slightly lopsided.

'Did Louisa Menzies ask you to come and find out?' Alec Taylor asked.

Kim raised her hand. 'Please, Alec. Give Miss Pallin a chance to catch her breath.' The fine almost translucent skin of Kim Taylor's face broke into a smile. She nodded beyond the window. 'You're much braver than I am coming out on a day like this.'

Corinne knew that neither Kim nor her husband were about to discuss what happened with Louisa. Fragile as she was, Kim Taylor always seemed to get her way.

'I came to see if everybody was all right,' Corinne said. 'I saw the scuffle earlier and wondered if anybody was hurt.' It was the best she could come up with on the spur of the moment. Also, it was true.

'Oh, it wasn't a scuffle, dear,' Kim said with authority. 'No, no. I slipped and twisted my ankle. It was ever so slight. Nothing that an hour with my feet up won't cure.' She gave a short laugh. 'It's one way I can get out of trailing about in this awful rain.'

Corinne kept her eyes away from Alec. 'And Louisa?' She left the question hanging.

'At home by this time, I should think,' Alec said.

Now holding his wife's hand, Corinne saw Alec Taylor was staring at her.

He wants me out of here. He wants to be alone with his wife.

She lowered her eyes to avoid him but as she did her eyes

skimmed over the table at Kim's side. The pill bottles were no longer there.

Kim said, 'The silly girl came out in those thin summer things that young people will wear nowadays never mind how cold it is. She ran off before we could fetch her a coat.' She gave a little tut of mock disapproval.

'Yes. That was stupid. Look at me!' Corinne watched Kim's exhausted face as the woman's hand slipped from her husband's grip.

'Very sensible,' Alec Taylor acknowledged Corinne's waterproof. 'The only thing for a day like this.' He was edging towards the door fully expecting Corinne to follow him.

Kim nodded. 'Goodbye, Miss Pallin. Thank you for popping in.' She smiled at Corinne.

At the open door, Alec said solicitously, 'You get back as fast as you can and dry off. This weather is enough to drive anybody crazy.'

He laughed but the sound held no vestige of levity.

CHAPTER SIXTEEN

Drips of water, icy on their descent from the overhead branches, went ignored by Corinne.

Away from the jetty and the Taylors' cabin, she walked in a bemused state, oblivious of her surroundings.

Their conversation had been surreal, all three of them avoiding the real reason for her visit: Louisa Menzies. And why, left on her knees on the rain lashed loch-side, she had been arguing with the Taylors in the first place.

The injured Kim – the *ill* Kim, despite all her efforts to conceal it – and a concerned Alec had put paid instantly to Corinne's less than subtle probing. The intimate touches and knowing glances between husband and wife were no less obstructive than a flat denial.

Angry at this clever act to exclude her, Corinne had to admit it worked. She had no option but to leave when she was as good as hustled out of the cabin by Alec Taylor on the pretext she should get back before the weather worsened.

Figuratively speaking she was as much in the dark now as before, no nearer to knowing why Louisa had been abandoned in such a state by two seemingly caring people.

Her frustration building, Corinne covered the sodden path at a panting pace. The damp air was heavy, her laboured breaths drawing a mixture of pine and green earthy smells deep into her lungs.

Her over-sized green water-proof flapped in time with her frenzied movements like a pre-historic bird exercising its fleshy wings for the first time. Only for a second did she slow down when she reached the point in the path where it turned down to her cabin. Fired-up, no sitting on her backside was going to get her any answers. Corinne marched on past.

She headed for the Menzies' shop. Her business or not, Ross and Kate were not going to stop her talking to Louisa.

She needed answers.

She was sweating and breathless when she pushed open the door of the shop.

Ross was there alone and came from behind the counter when he saw her. 'Why are you back out in this,' he said. 'It's not a day for walking.'

Corinne glared at him. She clenched her teeth. He was treating her like a passing tourist yet less than 24 hours ago they had made love like two souls drawn together, not just by accident or circumstance, for both she admitted had been in that tumultuous mix, but by raw attraction.

'Is Louisa in?' she asked curtly. Her breath was noisy, her chest heaving. Neither Louisa nor Kate, were anywhere in the shop.

'She's spending the day with the Coburn kids,' Ross answered.

Corinne turned on him. 'Really? Kate told me she went to get her designs.'

'Then why are you asking me?' Ross said defensively. 'What's all this about?'

Corinne waved it off. 'Forget it. It doesn't matter.'

'Oh, but I think it does.' Ross pulled her further into the shop. 'Stay there.'

Corinne waited by the door. Hot from her dash from the jetty, her clothes felt damp, not from the rain but from her own sweat. Gripping her waterproof on both sides she pulled it up over her head. At once she felt free, released from the stifling material, able to breathe normally again.

At the counter two customers, their purchases in baskets, waited to be served. Ross spent unhurried minutes taking their money and seeing them out without any outward sign of rushing them. As soon as they left, he closed the door and locked and bolted it.

'Through there.' He motioned to the passageway into the house.

'No. If Louisa's not here, I'll get back.' Corinne did not

move from her spot by the main door.

'What's going on, Corinne?' Grabbing her arm Ross forced her to walk the length of the shop. 'I can tell something's up just by your face. You're not leaving here until you tell me what's happened.'

As they reached the door to the passageway, Corinne stopped and faced him. His arms were folded across his chest. He filled the doorway effectively barring her escape.

Corinne was trapped. 'I'm not certain myself,' she admitted. 'I wanted to make sure Louisa was, well, that she was all right.'

'What makes you think she might not be?'

'I was worried. That's all.' She stepped back from him further into the passageway.

It made no difference. Ross was in front of her again, crowding her so close she was forced back against the wall.

'Very well, I'll tell you,' she gave in. Through the semi-darkness of the narrow space she could see his eyes fixed on her. That still, unmoving gaze…

In the next second she was held in a strong grip and lifted clean away from the wall.

For an instant Corinne stopped breathing. The rage that had brought her here seeped away and was replaced by trembling. 'Let go of me,' she pleaded. 'Please. Let go.'

His face was very close to her. 'I don't want to. That's the problem. You've done this to me.'

Corinne stayed very still, breathing in the warm smell of him through his thick work shirt. She drew her head back and met his eye. 'I'm sorry, Ross. For a minute there… I was scared.'

'What?' His expression clouded. 'Oh, God!' His head came down to meet her forehead. 'I wouldn't hurt you.' His hold slackened but he still held her. 'What's got you so worked up about Louisa? Come on, out with it.'

'Well. Maybe it's nothing but earlier she was over on the other side of the loch, you know, at the jetty. It was raining hard, she had no coat and she was arguing with the Taylors. I think she was disorientated.' It was all he needed to know.

Ross let his hands drop to his sides. He tipped his head back and gazed up at the ceiling.

'Ross,' Corinne put her hand on his chest. 'It could be nothing. But I know she's vulnerable. I was concerned.'

He was about to reply when the door at the far end of the passageway opened. Light flooded in engulfing them.

'Kate!' Ross left Corinne and went to his wife. 'Is Louisa in the house?'

'No.' Kate was staring at Corinne. 'Didn't you see her at the Coburns?'

'I've not been up to the centre,' Corinne said and glanced pointedly at Ross. 'I might take a wander up there now.'

'I'll come with you,' Ross said. 'There's not much doing right now so I've closed the shop. Kate, you stay and take it easy. I won't be long.'

'No!' The cry from Kate was immediate and pleading. She reached out her fingers and curled them around Ross's arm. 'We'll all go,' she implored him.

'You sure?' Ross was reluctant.

'Yes, I'm sure,' Kate nodded. She glanced at Corinne, 'I don't know what she's done to deserve it but my daughter seems to take up a lot of your time.'

'Kate!' Ross remonstrated with his wife gently.

Kate smiled ruefully at Ross. 'I'm sure she would make a much better mother than I do.'

'Me?' Corinne rejected the idea. 'I doubt it'

'Well, it seems that Louisa is able to talk to you,' Kate said.

'Argue more like.'

Kate asked suddenly, 'What's she done now?'

'Nothing,' Ross answered. 'She's done nothing.'

Corinne was first to hear the rattle of the shop door-handle. She glanced through the passage doorway, through the shop to the main door. Two figures were trying to get in. The outline of one, twisting the handle back and forth frantically, was unmistakeably Louisa. She was bent forward, shading her eyes close to the glass in an effort to see inside. Waiting just behind her was Edwin Coburn.

'It's her,' Corinne called down the passageway. 'She's back.'

Ross came past Corinne. He crossed the shop, unlocked the door and threw it open. 'We were just about to get up a search party for you.'

Corinne was aware of Kate moving at her back, coming to join her beside the counter. Together they waited for Louisa to come in.

The girl's legs buckled slightly as she walked. She dug Ross in the chest with her finger. 'Hello, there, Daddy!' She started to giggle.

Louisa advanced unsteadily towards Corinne and Kate. In the cold white glare of the overhead lights, it was obvious the girl was either drunk or stoned. A man's blue denim jacket, grotesquely oversized for her, hung from her thin shoulders. The arms of the jacket flapped empty and loose, the shoulders black with rain, as she staggered forward. Her thick, vibrant hair was soaked through. Flattened to her scalp it was like a chestnut coloured scarf, the darkened ends of which dripped water carelessly down to the shop floor.

Faced with first Corinne, then Kate behind her, Louisa stopped.

'The ladies of the jury!' She nodded eagerly at Corinne. 'That's a good title, right?' Her staccato giggle continued, harsh and unreal in the empty shop.

Kate stepped in front of Corinne. 'Have you had anything to eat?' she asked Louisa.

'Eat?' Louisa blinked. Her eyes were lazy, half-shut. She was having difficulty keeping them open. She peered over her shoulder at Edwin standing silently watching.

'Have I had anything to eat? No.' The giggling increased. 'No.' Her head swung fiercely sending little arcs of water to settle over nearby shelves. 'What I've had was a lot better than that!' She swayed sideways.

'Come on.' Ross held Louisa's arms and steered her toward the passageway. 'Let's get you dried out.' He beckoned with his head for Kate. 'Take her.'

'No!' Louisa shrank away from her mother. '*She* doesn't care. Not about me.' Like a stringed puppet, her hands waved uncontrollably in the air and Corinne, in line for a slap, stepped back.

Louisa was unsteady, her legs buckling under her. She collapsed bodily against Ross. 'Ross does. Don't you, Ross? Sure you do.' She reached up and for a second Corinne wondered if she were about to hit him.

Louisa gently stroked the side of Ross's face like a beloved pet. Again with the same shaky, uncoordinated movement, she whirled around, dangerously unbalanced on her sodden feet. 'Now that we're all here…' The giggling stopped. She blinked and in a stage whisper, said, 'We can let *her* in on the big secret.' She was staring at Corinne.

From the shop door, Edwin Coburn spoke. 'Talking can wait,' he said. 'A nice warm bath is what you need right now.'

'Ah! The man himself!' A huge grin on her face, Louisa waved at Edwin. 'In case you didn't know – and who doesn't – this is the man, the man it's all about.' She pushed Ross away and grabbed Edwin's hand and pulled him forward to face Corinne. 'My mother's lover!'

'That's enough!' Ross went to Louisa.

He wasn't fast enough. The long thin arm of Kate Menzies shot out. The flat of her hand slapped Louisa across her face. Not a crisp, crack of a hit, but soft and reluctant and clumsy.

Silence filled the shop.

'You see,' Louisa began to laugh pathetically. 'She won't face up to it.' She twisted abruptly to confront Corinne. 'Really she's got nothing to feel guilty about. Being faithful is not a high priority here.' She glanced over at the two men,

'Is it? You two should know!'

Tears were running unheeded down Kate's cheeks. Her eyes were fixed on her daughter's face. No words came from her pale lips. No denial, no excuses.

'Louisa, stop this.' It was Edwin. 'Right now you need food and sleep.'

'Yes, let's get you inside,' Ross said.

'Get off me!' Louisa threw out her arms. 'I'm not *his* you know.' Her head swung round to Corinne. 'Oh no. You kept saying *your father*. Ha! Big joke!'

That Louisa was not his appeared to be old news to Ross. He was ignoring Corinne, standing, arms at the ready, poised like a referee ready to step in between mother and daughter.

'Stop this!' Kate raised a quivering voice. 'Stop it!'

Corinne could see the cords standing out on Kate's neck, a cage for her taut, white, no longer graceful, ageing throat. Her thin body was rigid as she faced Louisa.

'What is it you want to do to me?' Kate asked. 'If it's to humiliate me you're nineteen years too late for that.'

Ross edged forward. 'Picking away at each other like this is not the answer.'

'You've found an answer, then!' Louisa screamed at him. 'You're answer to being cooped up in this god-forsaken place!'

'You don't know what you're talking about,' Ross said.

Louisa laughed. With a shaking hand, she pushed futilely at a lank strand of hair stuck to her cheek. 'Don't I?' She glared hard at Corinne. 'Her!'

Corinne stood speechless. Her face flamed red. She could find no words to defend herself from this girl she knew was so fragile in so many ways and so vicious in others.

Ross rescued her. 'Corinne has nothing to do with this.'

'No?' Louisa was moving in agitated little steps inside the confined circle made up of Corinne, the two men, and her mother. In a desperate voice she said, 'He tried it on with me, you know!'

240

'That's a lie!' Ross shouted.

Louisa ignored him. She was nodding vigorously at Kate. 'Oh, he was my dad all right. Until I grew up and became a newer version of you!'

The two men were standing side by side. Edwin edged in front of Ross and said urgently to Louisa, 'Do you know what you're saying?'

Corinne's body was taut. She watched Kate turn and face her husband and it struck at her heart to see the hurt in the woman's eyes. 'I for one don't believe that,' Corinne said. Her mouth was dry and her voice came out stilted and officious.

'Oh yes, you would know!' Louisa yelled. 'Spying and following me about.' The blinking of her eyelids was becoming more pronounced. 'You told them, didn't you, about finding me and Edwin together. You said you didn't but you're a liar!' She gazed, each in turn, at the faces surrounding her. 'You're all liars!'

'Shut up, Louisa.' Edwin tried to stem the abuse. 'Don't.'

He got no further. Suddenly, Kate put her hands over her ears and let out a high pitched scream. It was like a wounded animal in its death throes.

Everybody stood very still.

Slowly Kate lowered her hands. In a shaking voice, she asked Edwin, 'You and Louisa... you haven't been together?' She put her hand up over her mouth and through her fingers pleaded with him, 'Please tell me no, Edwin. Please.'

'Kate...' For once Edwin's self-assurance appeared to slip. 'She's so like you.'

A triumphant yell came from Louisa. 'There! You've heard it! It wasn't me he wanted. It was you! Are you happy now?' she screamed in Kate's face. Her shoulders slumped and her head arched forward. 'You couldn't stop me,' she cried triumphantly. 'Hard as you tired you couldn't keep me away from him.'

'There was a reason,' Kate said in a small distracted voice.

'Kate, don't do this here,' Ross said. 'Not while she's in this state.'

'A reason. Oh, good! Good! Good!' Louisa twirled in her confined little ring-a-ring o' roses circle. 'We all want to know the reason why I'm not allowed to have a life of my own.' She stopped and stared hard at Kate. 'Well, tell us then. Go on. We're all dying to hear.'

Corinne made a move away from the counter. 'I think perhaps I should go. You don't need me here.'

'No! You stay!' Louisa pointed a shaking finger at Corinne. 'You stirred this up. You! Running away with your secrets and your false name.'

'Corinne Pallin *is* my name,' Corinne said calmly. 'There's nothing false about it.'

'Don't you laugh at me!' Louisa screamed.

Corinne heard the desperation in Louisa. 'All right, I'll stay. But you realise this has nothing to do with me.'

Louisa laughed. 'Don't you want to know what makes me a non-person, a nobody? A second rate copy of *her.*'

Corinne didn't answer. She could see the girl was fast losing her reasoning. She staggered with every movement now, her equilibrium completely gone. Underneath the soaked denim jacket she was shivering violently. Like the challenging teenager she was, she stuck her face close to Kate's. 'Well?'

Kate's eyes swept over her daughter's rain-washed face. She reached up a hand to move a piece of dripping hair from Louisa's face but in the last instant she dropped her arm as if it would be too painful to touch her daughter.

'I didn't want Edwin,' she said slowly. Ignoring Louisa's rolling eyes, she went on. 'We were lovers. Decades ago, when we were young.' A ghost of a smile crossed her face. 'And then you were born.'

The silence that followed Kate's words was penetrated only by the sound of great drops of water falling from the tall pines onto the shop roof.

Corinne stole a look at Ross. There was no anger there. He appeared resigned.

Kate gave a pensive little chuckle as she smiled across at Louisa. 'You were a funny little thing. All arms and legs. And, oh, how you could scream. I used to feed you any time you wanted just to keep you happy. You fed and fed and still you screamed. And you were such a bean-sprout.' The memory brought a dreamy smile. 'When you came along to the fashion shows the girls were sure you were going to be on the catwalk when you grew up. They all said so. They helped me babysit you because I couldn't keep a nanny and Edwin went off to Italy for a year to do his own thing. It didn't really matter. It wasn't as if I needed anybody.' She paused. 'I was on my own yet there always seemed to be plenty of people around.' A little shake of her head showed she was still confused by this anomaly, decades later.

Edwin Coburn was rooted to the spot, his brows pulled so low that his eyes appeared closed as if trying hard to see in his mind's eye those early days he and Kate had shared.

'No!' Louisa had Kate by the shoulders. 'No, no, no!' She was shaking her back and forth like a rag doll she intended to tear apart. Her own head wobbled sickeningly, the ends of her hair flapping wetly about her neck. 'You should have told me!' she screamed into her mother's face. 'My father…' Louisa's hands slid up to Kate's neck.

'Stop that!' Grabbing Louisa's arms Ross forced them apart. 'That'll do, Louisa. Let go!'

Kate stared at her daughter. Her hand touched her throat where Louisa's fingers had circled it. Already angry red wheals marred her thin white skin.

'I tried to stop you,' Kate whispered. 'You wouldn't listen to me, Louisa. You never listen to me.' Her tall figure swayed forward.

Corinne put her hand out and steadied Kate.

'You knew,' Louisa struggled in Ross's grasp. He held her

243

back, her flailing arms now out of reach of Kate, but it did not stop the tirade. 'All the time, you knew I went up there to see him. You even made up excuses for me to save the truth from coming out.' She struggled again but in vain. 'You knew he was my father and you didn't tell me.' She glared at her mother. 'You let this happen!' she screamed.

'No. I didn't. I tried to stop you.' Kate held tight to Corinne. 'I thought you were only seeing him to get back at me.'

'I was!' Louisa danced with rage in Ross's arms. 'You stupid cow! I was!' Sheer exasperation sent her limp and she fell back against Ross.

In the lull that followed, Corinne edged Kate around, through the door, and led her down the passageway into the house without any resistance.

Nobody followed them. Corinne could hear nothing behind her in the shop. The place had fallen silent. She settled Kate in a chair and brought her a glass of water from the kitchen. 'Kate, will you be all right for a minute?'

The vague nod was all Corinne knew she was going to get. She touched Kate's shoulder and watched as, like an automaton, the woman calmly raised the glass of cold water to her lips and drank.

'I'll fetch Ross.' Corinne wondered what had stopped him following his wife to be with her.

She could now hear the low murmur of voices in the shop; male voices and, so low, that their whispering sounded furtive.

As she emerged into the shop, Corinne thought Louisa was no longer there. Ross appeared dazed by what had just been said between Kate and Louisa.

'Where is she?' she asked him.

He nodded down to the side of the counter.

Her back against the hard slats of the wooden counter, Louisa was sitting on the wet shop floor. Her head was tipped forward on her propped-up knees, her face completely hidden in her folded arms.

Corinne crouched down. 'Louisa,' she stroked the girl's bowed head. Words seemed pointless but she had to try; the girl was hurting. 'Louisa.'

'Get away from me!' Louisa's arm flew out and struck Corinne across her chest.

Corinne toppled back. She put her hands out to save herself from falling and righted herself on the balls of her feet. Above her she was aware of Ross about to intervene. He stopped when she raised her hand.

'Louisa, come back to my cabin,' she said. 'We can talk if you want to.' Her tone lightened. 'Or we could just drink coffee.' She touched Louisa's knee. 'Nobody will disturb us. I promise you.'

It was a promise she had no right to make but she couldn't leave Louisa and Kate under the same roof that night. The only other place would be the Coburns.

Her offer was about to be turned down but then Louisa lifted her head and Corinne was able to see her face. The girl was bewildered. With a weary hand she tucked a lank piece of hair behind her ear only to have it fall back. Her eyes were swollen and whatever she had taken earlier in the day was wearing off. She had the frightened face of a victim who realised that the thing she had tried so hard to escape from was still there, bigger in reality when not cloaked in stupor.

Louisa nodded. She held her hand out to Corinne.

Corinne helped her scramble up off the floor.

The girl was a pitiful sight. Her clothes clung, wet and creased, against her thin, hunched body while her glorious hair had begun to dry into a mass of unruly tangles. She was completely unaware of how she appeared. Docile now, she seemed content to be told exactly what to do.

Corinne linked arms with Louisa and as they began to make their way to the front of the shop she glanced back at the two men.

Edwin Coburn was appealing to Ross who told him firmly,

'Not now. It'll need to wait.'

Edwin appeared to accept this. But his stance and the exasperated shake of his head told another story.

The rain had let up. The huge branches above their heads moved in a light breeze. Penetrating between the trees, it caught gently at their hair and tugged ineffectively at their clothes.

Afraid that her charge would take to her heels and disappear, Corinne kept her arm curled tightly around Louisa's while they walked.

If the closeness brings the girl a little comfort all the better, Corinne thought, although she was not even sure if Louisa was aware of the restraint she kept on her.

While it wasn't her business, she was amazed and more than a little irritated that Kate Menzies had let things go so far. It seemed doubtful this fresh revelation between her and her daughter would end harmoniously, especially with Edwin Coburn always in the background.

At the cabin, Louisa collapsed on to her favourite end of the sofa. All the spark that had driven her earlier was gone.

'Do you want to talk?' Corinne asked.

Louisa said nothing.

'Right then,' Corinne accepted it. 'Why don't you stay where you are? I'll make us coffee.' She forced herself to smile down at the girl.

The pale features showed no emotion. The blue-black shadows under Louisa's eyes made them appear vague and innocent, their beautiful green depths cold and vacant. Corinne had no idea what was going on behind them.

Except for the sound of Corinne in the kitchen, the cabin was silent for the next few minutes. When she carried the coffee to the sofa, the girl lay on her side, eyes closed, her face pressed into the cushion at her head and her legs curled up to her body in a foetal position, her back acutely curved.

Corinne set down a mug on the table. If the girl was not

asleep she was pretending for a reason not to be intruded on. She crossed to the door and, as quietly as she could stepped out and clicked it shut behind her.

Outside, daylight lingered. The wind had transformed the view of the loch into a panorama of blue lapping waves above which a setting sun, that had not yet lost its fire, flirted with grey-white clouds.

Her mug in both hands, she watched as the light subtly began to change.

For an hour she sat there. Behind her in the cabin there was no movement. In front of her the water of the loch slid from deep blue to black as the day petered out and the light started to fade.

She jumped with a guilty start when she heard footsteps. Ross and Edwin came down the path towards her. She sat still, waiting. When they reached her she stalled them by speaking first. 'She's inside, sleeping. I'd leave her for now.'

'We've got to talk to her,' Ross said. 'There are things she's got to hear.'

Corinne sighed. 'Well, believe me, whatever it is she's in no fit state to take it in. Not right now.'

Ross sat beside her on the edge of the walkway.

'You know she was high,' Corinne remarked.

'That,' Edwin said sitting down on the other side of Corinne, 'was pretty obvious when she came to the centre. She was completely out of her head.'

'Whatever it was, Kate says she didn't get it from her,' Ross said firmly. 'She swore to me and I believe her.'

'Kate doesn't lie,' Edwin confirmed. 'But she can get confused.'

Corinne's head swung between the two men. Her eyes came to rest on Edwin. 'What do you mean? Confused about what?'

Edwin looked past Corinne to Ross. 'Go on. Tell her.'

'No. It's up to you. You were there.'

Corinne sensed Edwin Coburn straighten his back.

'Well, Kate thinks that what she says is true,' he began. 'But, like I said before, she's confused.' His eyes flicked away from the two listening. 'I'm not Louisa's father. I couldn't be. I was in Italy for over a year. When I came back to London, Kate was six months pregnant.' Edwin licked his lips. For a second he paused while Corinne and Ross waited.

'Maybe I shouldn't have gone but at the time she was happy with it. We didn't split up. It wasn't like that. I just had to try new jobs on my own. A chance came up and I jumped at it. She had her work by then and all her friends.' He laughed bitterly. 'Friends that lived off her and helped her score as much as she wanted.' Again Edwin glanced momentarily at Ross. 'She was a beautiful woman at the very pinnacle of her career. Everybody was clamouring for a piece of her. There were always plenty of men.'

'So you see, nobody knows who Louisa's father is,' Ross told Corinne. 'When we came here Kate got close again to Edwin. Those years in London, the men, the drugs, it all came back to her. Everything was stirred up again like it was only yesterday. I think she wanted to put it all right. In her head Edwin *was* that time. They had been together before he moved to Italy and he was there when Louisa was born and he's here now. To her it all added up to one thing. He was Louisa's father. The dates, the truth, she simply dismissed them from her mind.'

'If that's what she really believed, why on earth didn't she tell Louisa to begin with?' Corinne asked.

'She didn't want to hurt me,' Ross said. 'A woman like Kate, well, I knew there must have been other men. Edwin, she told me all about. Everything except that he was Louisa's father. She didn't mention that.'

'But he's not?'

'But Kate believes he is.'

'And now Louisa thinks he is,' Corinne said. 'Poor Louisa.'

CHAPTER SEVENTEEN

When she woke, Louisa was calm. Submissive, she let herself be led by Ross, down off the walkway outside Corinne's cabin up onto the path and through the trees and home.

Corinne lay on the same spot where Louisa had curled up trying hard to shut out the world behind closed eyes.

As the day reached its end, the air in the cabin turned cold. The throw from the bed was spread over Corinne's legs. While her mind skipped and jumped from question to question there was little chance of sleep. Her bedroom, out of sight of what she now thought of as *her* view of the loch, was too confining so she'd chosen the sofa.

The sky from the cabin window was dark, a deep, inky blue but still blue. Mid-night blue, her mother, so keen to give everything a definitive name, would no doubt call it. Corinne smiled in the semi-darkness. Mid-night blue really did exist. It was not a colour; it was a time and place and a state of mind. She must remember to tell her mother she had experienced mid-night blue.

The fanciful theory gave Corinne a near physical twinge of guilt. It felt an age since she'd talked with her mother. Yet they had seen each other only yesterday. The unforgettable Sunday barbecue had brought them together. Moot point, she thought. In the same place at the same time is not together. Her guilt was matched by predictable regret at the way things had ended yesterday.

Her head to one side, she let her gaze linger on her mobile phone. Black and shiny, it lay within touching distance on the table. Her mother, her father, Uncle Ian, they were only a press on the screen away from her and yet here she lay, alone, separated from them not just physically but isolated by her own reluctance to face the inevitable.

Reaching out she grabbed the thin, cold instrument. She

pulled herself further up on the cushion and tucked the throw tighter around her legs. Clearing her throat, she readied herself and made the call.

In seconds she was through to him. 'Papa, it's me.'

'Cherie. It is late.' He sounded as though he had just come across her in the middle of the night going through the contents of the fridge in the large kitchen of the family home. 'Are you not able to sleep?' he enquired softly.

'No. Too much on my mind. You weren't asleep were you?'

'No. Only reading. Your mother is watching television upstairs.'

'Papa, yesterday… why exactly did you come here? It wasn't because of Noel and me splitting up. Was it? You and Mum, Noel put you off didn't he?'

'Yes, Corinne, we did want to see you, but on your own.' He paused. 'We have decided that we are going ahead with our move to France.'

'I know that,' Corinne interrupted. 'But I've got the feeling that wasn't it, was it?'

'We are going soon, Cherie. We have made arrangements. You must come back and take up your position here. We need you to do that.' He did not sound angry with her. 'This disagreement with Noel, it is not for the best. Not for anyone.'

Noel again! Corinne's throat tightened. For nearly a day she had tried hard not to think about her husband, about the reason she was here, alone, miles away from her family. She had almost succeeded.

'Corinne, are you there?'

'Yes, I'm still here.' Corinne moved her hand away from her chest so she would not feel her heart pounding against her ribs. 'I'll be back in a couple of days. We'll discuss it then, all right?'

There was another pause. 'Papa?'

'Well, I must tell you,' her father said, 'we held a meeting this afternoon.'

'Who did?' Corinne shot upright.

'Your mother and I, and Ian. At the office,' he added.

Corinne felt her face grow hot. 'A meeting about what?'

'About this situation that has arisen with Noel.'

'You went ahead with a meeting about him without me there?'

'We all agreed that you would not be able to see it in a practical way. That is why we went ahead with it. And do not forget, Cherie, you did not want to talk to us about him. What were we to do?'

'A few days, Papa. Was that too much to ask?'

'Business does not stand still waiting for you to make up your mind, Corinne. I do not have to tell you that.' Pierre Pallin's voice was unusually brusque.

Corinne winced; this was not like her father.

Keep calm. Don't jump the gun.

'What was decided?' she asked. 'I take it you went over his contract?'

'Yes, of course it was discussed. We went over what remains of his contract,' he told her. 'That was the point of the meeting. Ian, already he had reviewed it, very well. And nothing for the moment has changed. Nothing has been put in writing yet. The lawyers and our accountants are coming in a couple of day's time to the office and then we will all meet again when it will be finalized and drawn up for all parties to sign.'

Alone in the cabin Corinne bristled. 'Am I allowed to ask what has been agreed so far, *in my absence?*'

'Cherie, we asked you to come home and sort this out with Noel. When you did not do that we had no option but to take matters into our own hands.'

'Are you going to tell me or do I have to ask Uncle Ian – or my mother for that matter, God forbid!'

'Do not be disrespectful, Corinne.' His words were clipped.

251

Corinne knew he was holding his temper in check. She went on quickly, 'What have the three of you decided about Noel? By the way, was he there at your *extraordinary* meeting?'

'No, of course he was not.' Corinne heard the faint sound of her father clearing his throat. 'We know that he wants to dissolve his present contract.'

'And replace it with what?'

'Well, with an agreement that will ease the separation between you both. Also to help things repair between Pallin-McCall and him.'

'Papa, that last is a business contract you're talking about,' Corinne reminded him. 'Our separation has nothing to do with it.'

'Do not be so naïve, Corinne. At least you must try to be honest with yourself. If you were still together it would not have occurred, this... this...' For the first time since she'd got through to him on her mobile, her father faltered, lost for easy words that wouldn't hurt.

'You're right of course,' she didn't want to argue, not with him. 'I'm sorry.'

'I do not think that you are sorry, Corinne.' He was angry now. 'You are piqued that a decision has been made without your agreement. That is all.'

'No, you're wrong about that. I just don't want our biggest name to walk out on us. Not because of me. Papa, it *is* the business I'm thinking of.'

'If you say so, Corinne.'

'What did you decide? Tell me. Please, I want to know.'

On the far end of the phone she heard her father take a deep breath, readying himself.

'We want him to complete the rewrites of A Stranger's Bullet by the end of next month,' he said. 'The draft he's been working on recently – Callum's Mask – will be completed perhaps before the end of the year and we will publish it here at Pallin-McCall.' He stopped talking and there was silence on the line.

Corinne pursed her lips together to stop herself from commenting. Her face now burning hot, she waited.

'After that all future transactions for practical purposes will be dealt with by our lawyers,' Pierre finished.

'And the other three books he's contracted to?' Corinne asked.

'No. Nothing after Callum's Mask. That will be the end of our association with Noel Anderton,' Pierre confirmed.

'You all agreed to this? Uncle Ian too?'

'Yes. And I think Noel will accept this as fair.'

'Fair! I can't believe this! You're letting him walk away.'

There was a protracted silence before Pierre came through to her again. 'We could hold him to his contract and get three more books out of him, yes. And when they are completed what will they be? Rubbish! Rehashes of old drafts he's got at the bottom of a discarded pile right now. We would have little option; we would have to accept them. What good would that do the company's reputation? None.' He sounded tired, drained of his normal spirit.

Corinne felt pushed into a corner. 'You have been busy. Have you put any of this to Noel?'

'No. Not yet. But we know he will happily accept it.'

'I'll say! And what if he and I were to get back together again?' Corinne held her breath.

'To keep his contract alive, you would do this?' Her father sounded genuinely astounded.

'Well, he's been living a lie these last two years. What would change? He could carry on as usual.' Suddenly Corinne's mind was clear. Business was business. She wasn't about to let fifteen years of hard work go down the drain dragged by her marriage going the same way. 'There would be no L.A. though. And definitely no Lynne Robertson. Our house is big enough. We could both still live under the same roof until his current contract is fulfilled.' She gave a little forced laugh. 'I am still his wife.'

'Corinne, I'm not sure that would work.'

'Why not? That's what he's been angling for. That's why he came up here because he wanted to get me back to Edinburgh with him. To restore the status quo.'

The pause that followed sent a cold shiver running the length of Corinne's spine.

'Papa?'

'I think things have gone beyond that,' Pierre said.

'How? What do you mean? It's only been a week. No, not even a week.' Corinne gripped the phone hard. 'Papa?'

He answered her slowly. 'You said you believed that Noel had been deliberately careless. He allowed this situation to develop between the two of you to make you feel guilty?'

'And to show how sorry I was, I would go out to L.A. with him for a new start, and everything would be forgiven and forgotten. I did think that. Yes.' Corinne forced herself to revisit old ground.

'Cherie, I think he will use any means he can now to get away.'

The cold shivers became hot suddenly and Corinne, clammy and uncomfortable, kicked off the throw. It concertinaed into a soft, dark pile on the floor. She stared hard at the neat wool bundle. 'I had Uncle Ian check. Noel's contract is solid. There's no way he can wriggle out of it just like that. He has no other leverage,' she said carefully.

'Yes, it is true. There is nothing weak about the contract,' Pierre agreed.

'What's he been saying then?' All at once alarm bells were ringing. 'Was it about me? Papa, I've never strayed. I've done nothing.' Corinne smothered the image of Ross Menzies in her bed.

Pierre was calm. 'A clean break will be the best for all concerned,' he said.

'Not necessarily. I could stand patching it up if it saves the business thousands.' Even to her own ears, it sounded reckless.

'Not everything is about profit, Cherie.' Pierre sighed. 'And would we want to publish what Noel writes in the future?'

'Oh, come on. You know he can come up with the goods when he really wants to.'

'A captured bird does not sing the sweetest, Cherie.'

'Old age is turning you into a philosopher.' Corinne attempted a laugh but it came out as a breathy gasp. She was near to tears. Ever since Noel's deception had surfaced, her father, inexplicably, was very slowly but surely holding himself back from her.

Suddenly, she was afraid. 'Does Uncle Ian think you should let Noel go this easily?'

'He agrees that there is nothing to be gained by dragging this out,' Pierre said.

Corinne felt helpless. And hurt. Excluded as she was by those she always felt were closest to her, arguing now to keep her husband would appear contrary and spiteful.

'So he is going to get away with it,' she said softly. 'Making a fool of me and skipping out on his obligations.'

'Everything has a cost, Corinne,' Pierre said.

With a vehemence that shocked her, Corinne challenged his acceptance of the situation. 'What if I started divorce proceedings right away and we did take him through the courts? He'd still be under contract to us and –.'

'No!' This half-baked idea was firmly scrapped by Pierre Pallin.

'Your marriage is your affair, Corinne, but the firm is not going to court over Noel's contract. That has been decided.'

'So I hear!'

'Cherie, we are not trying to hurt you. The opposite is true.' Pierre sounded weary. 'The business is in reasonable health. With your mother and me in France, you and Ian will find new business to open up.' His voice faltered.

'New horizons for us all, then,' Corinne replied slowly.

'I will always be there. *We* will always be there for you,

Cherie.'

'Have you decided when you're leaving? I take it you and Maman have a date in mind?'

'As soon as Noel's contract is re-written and signed. We will travel soon after that.'

'A couple of weeks then? Three at the most?'

'Yes, I expect that it will be so.' There was little joy in her father's voice at the prospect of the longed-for return to his birth place. She'd put paid to that. 'But you will be home by then, Corinne. We must spend time together before we leave, Cherie.'

Corinne couldn't stop tears flooding her eyes. She tipped her head back and blinked. 'Yes, yes. Two days, Papa. Two days at most and then I'll be back. I promise.' The tears rolled down the side of her face.

A stiff good-bye and her father rang off. Corinne lay back down, trying hard to make sense of what he had told her. She hadn't asked to speak to her mother and he hadn't suggested that she should.

The more she went over what he'd said, the more convinced Corinne was that things were not right. When the two of them had come up to Four Hills, her parents had barely acknowledged Noel. He had been watchful of them, she recalled, waiting she supposed for his opportunity to put his case to them again to get her back.

Apparently, she had been wrong about that. In the end he, too, had left without a word of their getting back together. There had been no mention of his contract between her parents and Noel, at least not that she had been privy to.

But we know that he will happily accept it. Her father had been confident.

If they hadn't been in touch with him since Four Hills, how did they know he would agree to the new terms? To Corinne it didn't make sense. Unless…

Corinne sat up and swung her feet to the floor. Unless these terms were Noel's terms, put forward by him to her parents who came up to the loch to put them to her.

They had already been agreed or at least discussed. Had she, too, been discussed like an option on his contract? If so, it seemed she was pretty worthless.

It grew dark in the cabin. Corinne examined the plainly furnished room and a feeling of loneliness descended on her like a cold loch mist. Nothing of her was here. Not one thing of any consequence would remain behind once she had packed up her few possessions and locked the door behind her. Would they even remember her name, the people of Four Hills? And if they did, what would be their verdict on the lone woman fleeing from her family to avoid facing the truth?

Corinne slid her hands up over her face. With great care she picked up the woollen throw and folded it into a neat square at one end of the sofa.

It was dark in the cabin now. She switched on the lamp and the mid-night blue beyond the window transformed instantly into a thick black curtain. Perched on the edge of the sofa she picked up her mobile phone and pressed the spot on the screen that held Ian McCall's code.

For the few seconds the tone buzzed at the end of the line. He was not going to answer. The feeling of helplessness came back a hundred fold. How easy it was to distance yourself, Corinne thought. When his voice came through to her, an overwhelming sense of relief flooded through her, leaving her feeling weak and tearful again.

'Now, here's a coincidence. I was just thinking about you,' he said.

'I've been speaking to Dad. He told me about your meeting.'

'Yes. I guessed as much. I'm sorry we didn't tell you about it beforehand.' His voice was even, forthright, but without any of his usual bluff heartiness. 'But it needed doing sooner rather than later.'

'It couldn't wait for another few days?' Corinne was

surprised at Ian McCall's matter-of-fact dismissal of the biggest decision in Pallin-McCall's calendar for the last few years. 'Dad said you were in full agreement, letting Noel get away with completing Callum's Mask and then after that, just walking away. Uncle Ian?'

The qualifying denial that Corinne hoped for didn't come.

'He's not the only name we have working with us, Corinne,' Ian said. 'Holding onto him wouldn't have solved anything.'

'Wasn't that for me to decide?'

'I think we made the right business decision.'

'Well, that decision – have you considered it won't stand up?' Corinne queried. 'Like you said, I wasn't informed the meeting was being held.'

The few seconds pause hung in the air like a thick vapour.

Ian McCall's gravelly voice was still calm when at last he answered. 'It will hold up, believe me. More to the point, it will call a halt to anything that Noel might be hatching.'

'What makes you think he's hatching anything?'

'Yon lad's not daft. He's learned a lot from you in the years the two of you've been together.' His matter-of-fact voice went on. 'He might not get the better of you in a legal battle over this contract but by God he would drag you through the gutter in the attempt – you and the lot of us for that matter.' He stopped and Corinne could visualize his heavy brows drawn down over his faded brown eyes, his large head nodding in conviction of what he believed was the best way forward.

'You're saying I should let this go to avoid embarrassment?' Corinne asked.

'I'm saying accept it, for in my opinion, doing anything else is going down the wrong road.'

'I thought you would be on my side.'

'I am. But this is for the best. I know what I'm talking about. You need to trust me on this.'

'All right. If you say so.' Corinne hadn't the heart to argue

258

any further. Her father had stepped away. Now it seemed her one sure ally had taken the support she needed so badly away from her. 'I'll be back maybe tomorrow or the next day.'

Ian McCall did not press her. 'I'll be here, whenever,' he said. 'You know that, lass.'

'Yes. Goodnight.' Corinne shut her mobile to cut the connection between Four Hills and Edinburgh.

Tired as she was, when she eventually went to bed, Corinne slept restlessly. Waking often she slipped back into uneasy shallow dozes shot through with implausible dreams.

Beyond the cabin walls, the weather was just as capricious, spattering vicious little gusts of rain against the window, easing then building noisier and yet more persistent. Twice, she stared bleary-eyed at her watch; once at ten to three and again at twenty past four. She did not check again but continued to toss from side to side in an evermore frantic search for sleep. At last she could stand it no longer. Sitting up, she drew her fingers brutally through her tangled hair. Drained and listless she regretted not staying on the sofa for the night.

Eyes closed, shoulders hunched forward, hands limp on the covers, she felt beaten. Staying in this place was doing her no good. Today, she decided, was it. She would shower and dress, pack her bags, and walk to the train station if necessary. But, definitely, she would get out of here today.

It was just before six, and light enough in the cabin not to need the lamps on. She stepped into the shower and stayed under the warm spray, standing still and letting the warm water run down through her hair and over her shoulders and limbs.

Out from the heat of the shower into the coolness of the bathroom, she shivered. She towelled herself hard until her skin was pink and her body warm. This little self exorcism went a little way to reviving her spirits as well as her body

259

and suddenly she felt buoyed up.

When she packed her bags she did it with a certain amount of care and attention which her few crumpled clothes did not need but once completed, the simple task had the effect of making her feel back in control.

At seven o'clock she made coffee and toast and went to the front window. When she'd first dragged herself out of bed the day had been grey but dry. Now great drops of rain began to pattern the glass with shimmering, artistic streaks. As she watched, the rain gathered in strength and the stretch of loch faded into a grey, rain-pelted water-basin collared by the tall pines that were as dark as the water itself.

Drawn by the mesmeric pounding on the loch's surface, Corinne continued to watch the rain pour relentlessly as she ate her breakfast. She was finished before she became aware of the movement on the far side of the loch, the make-shift barbecue side. The last time she'd been over there had been to find Louisa and see if the girl was all right. Her search had been futile.

The same sense of helplessness started to take hold of Corinne again as she gazed out. She did not try to shrug it off nor did she question it. Instead she sipped at her coffee and focused on the figures moving at the near side of the jetty.

She peered through the heavy rain now strafing the surface of the loch like jagged arrows.

At first she thought it might be a fishing party she was watching. She skipped this idea when it became obvious there were no boats out on the water only one canoe pulled just clear of the water's edge, the rest upside down in their usual position high up on the stones beyond the end of the jetty.

Corinne counted seven or eight figures. Hooded and bulky and colourless through the downpour, they appeared identical in wet weather gear. She watched them stay close and moving as one, bend and lift an object clear of the stones. Together they walked in short disjointed, stuttering steps away from the jetty.

It was too far away for Corinne to see what they carried. She began to tense up as she followed the dark little procession with her eyes. No damaged light-weight canoe would need so many hands to move it. Gripping the edge of the windowsill, she made out the close knit gathering turn again, in unison, and carry their burden to the nearest cabin. Still she could not see what it was they carried so carefully, but her instincts rushed to the only viable reason for the early morning, misty assembly – an accident. On the jetty? On the water? She was guessing.

A sour taste formed in Corinne's mouth. She swallowed a mouthful of coffee but the sourness was still there. Suddenly, her disturbed night's sleep made sense. Whatever had happened, it had happened during the night. In the woods, in the loch, mishap, accident, tragedy – one of these had played out and she had been totally unaware of it. Nobody had come to her cabin to let her know, or ask for her help.

With an increasing feeling of dread, Corinne slipped the now hated green waterproof over her head. She pulled the hood up and over her hair and tightened it closely around her face. No make-up on, she felt pale and exposed. She didn't care. Now was no time for vanity.

She found her trainers and put them on and then checked the room. What did you take with you when you went expecting to find an accident? Corinne suddenly stopped. How ridiculous was this! She laughed and tried to make it loud so she could hear herself and be comforted in her isolation. What came out of her mouth was a pitiful, distorted sound that scared her. Rushing out she slammed the door but did not stop to lock it.

She plunged off the walkway and onto the path. Her trainers sank deep into the soft puddled dirt as she took the direction to the jetty. There was only one likely way the group of huddled figures would come back from the side of

261

the loch. If she stayed on the path she would meet them. Soon, she would know what happened.

She tried to run. In the constricting green waterproof, impractical. She slowed and walked through the rain slanting through the pines. Vehicle tyres had gouged deep tracks in the sodden earth of the path and it wasn't easy to dodge the rain filled pools. Corinne made slow progress.

With every step she expected to come face to face with the people she'd seen at a distance. But she met up with no one until she reached the clearing which led down to the jetty.

The man she recognised as the taxi driver who had driven her in his vintage car from the train station, barred the way.

For him, it was the same. He recognised her instantly.

'Now then, you'd be better to go back to your cabin, Miss,' he told her. 'I can't let you go any further.'

'What happened? Has anyone been hurt?' Corinne tried to see behind him. He shifted his bulk purposely in an effort to block her view.

'There's been a wee bit bother out on the loch, that's all,' he said. 'It's all sorted.'

Corinne backed away from him. 'What is it? Who's been hurt?' Again she tried to see what went on behind him but again he moved in tandem with her. They did a bizarre side-step of a dance, neither of them giving or gaining any ground.

'It's all been taken care of.' He stared into her face. 'There's nothing to see.'

His tone was dismissive, not to be challenged. He was in charge.

Corinne shut her mouth tight on the angry words that sprang readily to mind. Instead, 'It's been a really bad night, hasn't it. I couldn't sleep myself because of the rain. That's why I'm out so early. I needed to walk off the stiffness.' She smiled at him.

'Aye, it was a bad one, all right,' he agreed readily with her.

Corinne nodded over his shoulder. 'Is that Ross Menzies' Land Rover? Maybe I can get a lift back with him.'

The man opened his heavy lids wide to show clearly the yellowish whites of his eyes. 'I don't think that would be a very good idea. Turn back. There's no point in you waiting.'

Corinne wondered at the tenacity of the man. 'I'm not just a sightseer,' she injected a modicum of authority into her voice. 'Perhaps I could help?'

'Oh, I know.' He nodded. His manner warmed, sympathetic to her position on the outside of the incident, over which, at this point, he stood guard. 'But there's nothing for you to be bothering yourself with,' he said. 'It's all over and done with now.'

CHAPTER EIGHTEEN

Corinne backed away from the taxi driver. She did not know him but bizarrely despised him at that precise moment for not including her in the incident.

No sirens, no shouting, no chaos. Nothing was there to hint what drama had played itself out on the far side of the loch in the early hours. And the taxi driver gave nothing away.

Everything was peaceful.

The wind started to ease down. Blue-white cloud was being teased into straggling impotent strands. The air was soft and thin. Sucked in deep through Corinne's nostrils it was cool and clean and fresh. Another day, ordinary, normal, as if the turbulent night had never happened.

Still wrapped in her waterproof she backtracked through the woods unwilling to make the effort to stop and remove the garment. Her first instinct was to get back to her cabin and change clothes. But she was already packed and ready to leave. If she went back to the cabin now there would be no reason not to pick up her bags and vacate Four Hills right away. The incident at the jetty she would never have to worry her head about. She would never know, never be involved. So be it.

She stalled. Instead of heading to her cabin, she followed the path that appeared on her left She'd never been this way before but she could do what she wanted, nobody to say yes, no, go, stay.

Anger bubbled up inside her. The faster she walked the more it built. It was not just anger, it was exasperation. She was useless, unable to help, and so unable to leave.

Without knowing it, the taxi driver in his guise of guard over the early morning incident had brought home to her how much she had begun to care about the people at Four Hills. An outsider, yes, she didn't deny it, but with her own life in turmoil she was able to empathise. Obviously, the taxi driver didn't think so.

Breathing hard, Corinne slackened her pace. Maybe he was right.

Angling her watch face she caught what light there was flickering through the trees. The time, ten minutes past ten. Almost an hour since she started out. Here the tall pines, dripping last night's rain on her, were exactly like those growing near the loch close to her cabin. With no idea where she was, the one thing she knew for certain was that she had been going steadily up-hill. Gradually, the path had narrowed. Now it was only a couple of metres wide. From its soft unbroken, relatively smooth surface, it appeared no vehicles ever came this way.

Reluctant to abandon her walk without reaching any definitive point, she knew she would soon have to turn back. Her bags sat ready for her to pick up and head for the station. What was it that kept her going, what she couldn't face? Leaving?

More effort was needed when the path became a climb. She'd slowed down more than a little with the gradual ascent. The further she climbed the more the light began to find its way through the trees. First it filtered between the thick top branches and then through the brown needle-less limbs hanging low down on the huge trunks. She was walking in what was now semi-shade.

The path became so steep she had to retrace her last few steps in order to achieve a run-up a short slope.

At the top, a small plateau opened out almost in line with the tops of the trees. Breathless, she stood for a minute, amazed at this hidden viewing platform.

Struggling out of the waterproof, she let it fall away. With the release came elation. Corinne threw out her arms and inhaled, consciously pulling the clear air into her lungs. No gym exercise gave you this cold, clean rush. Heart pounding fast, she stood motionless in the middle of the natural mound. Slowly she moved her head from east to west taking in the full vista.

It was intensely quiet. The blood throbbed in her head. She was aware of her own noisy breathing. The tops of the pines swayed and little puffs of wind lifted and tossed her hair across her face.

A small bird cackled nearby and settled momentarily on a branch below her. The great branch dipped and rose with the minute disturbance. The bird spread its wings and flew out of sight. The plateau was hers once more, and silent.

Corinne crossed the twenty metres of soft earth to the opposite side of the clearing. To her left she could see the gouged-out, sunken track with parallel silver train lines that would take her back home, and half of the brown painted roof of the small railway station. Further east was a scattering of cottages. Blairkeld village, she guessed. Squat, solid, grey stone buildings with a few larger houses higher up the hill, were built haphazardly on a curving hillside, facing south. She could make out neat patches of gardens with lines of green growth, straight and military neat that screamed vegetables in this frugal highland place.

Panning from left to right, Corinne saw the craft centre roof and the shining glass-topped plant house tacked on at its back.

From where she stood at the edge of the plateau, Corinne discovered she had not come as far as she first estimated. The path circled the plateau and came at it from behind putting another half a kilometre on to her walk.

Suddenly, the reason the place was called Four Hills became obvious. From her high vantage point, she saw them, two on either side of the loch.

The four hills sat like squat upside-down soup bowls decorated in misty grey and green. The top half of their slopes were bare, the bottom half wooded. There, the trees grew so tall that, down at the lochside, they had made it impossible to see the shape of the four hills or even tell they were there.

Corinne felt her throat tighten and tears threaten. Four Hills at least had not been a fabrication. There they were, ancient and solid, for anyone who made the effort to see them.

Narrowing her eyes, she followed the line from the craft centre and picked out the clearing where the Menzies' shop was obliterated by trees. She couldn't make out her cabin but others at the loch's edge were in full view.

She saw the jetty. Blurred but unmistakeable, the wooden structure stuck out into the water shining gun-metal grey and very smooth in the morning light.

Her eyes lingered on the crescent of stony beach. The party in waterproofs had disappeared. Evidence of this morning's incident remained only in the shape of two dark suited men, heads down, searching.

One, a big, bear-like figure, stood on the pebbles, head bowed, gazing at the neatly beached canoes. His companion, less ursine, of average height and girth, dressed much the same, wandered slowly to the end of the jetty. Hands in his pockets, he focused long and hard on the loch. Minutes later, and without any sign of urgency, he wandered back to his colleague. They pointed fingers, first in one direction then another, as if measuring up the pros and cons of water versus land.

Corinne watched the little mime show. She felt cut off from this morning's incident. Anger seared through her. Damn the taxi driver! She should have stayed at the clearing. By now she would have known what the raft of figures had carried between them across the stones; or if anyone was hurt.

More than two hours had gone since the *thing* had been picked up and carried away. During that time Corinne had managed to keep any negative images firmly to the back of her mind. All her effort had been channelled into putting one foot in front of the other. Now, tired out, cracks began to make themselves felt in her armour. Bit by bit her resistance started to crumble. At last they came freely, the grim thoughts, the unthinkable images, swarming up to the fore of her mind.

Screwing up her eyes she tried to focus on the Menzies' place. Nothing and nobody moved. No sign of any of the family. No sign of *him.*

She closed her eyes and his face was clear in her mind, strong and serious, telling her, for one night, to forget her problems. And as he held her and loved her, she had.

Please, don't let it be him.

She had allowed herself to be thwarted so easily, *too easily,* in her effort to get to the loch and see him, speak to him.

Corinne rolled up her waterproof into a bundle and hitched it under her arm. She knew where she was now in relation to her cabin. Easy enough to retrace her steps to get back there. Plus, it was all downhill.

The meandering route of the path firmly in her head, she started back. The aerial view from the plateau gave her direction and distance and, like all return journeys it felt shorter by knowing her destination. Even so, the fork in the path leading to the craft centre emerged from the thick undergrowth before she was ready for it.

She hesitated before deciding to take the turnoff. No doubt the Coburns would know what had happened down at the loch.

Corinne saw Tamzin first. The woman's slight figure seemed to have shrunk. Her face for once was not cloaked in the interminable smile. In stark contrast with her bright yellow and blue dress, she was sickeningly white.

As Corinne made her way past the few customers, Tamzin saw her.

'Where the hell have you been?' she demanded. 'Edwin went to every cabin but he couldn't find you.'

Caught off guard, Corinne faced her accuser. 'I've been up the hill – that way.' She gestured vaguely in the direction of the plateau. 'Why? What did he want with me?'

Tamzin drew back. She seemed to regret her initial attack. Her small, neat hands were clasped tightly in front of her chest. 'There's been an accident.' Her words were clipped but still her voice quivered. 'We've managed to tell everyone, except you.'

Corinne could see it was taking all her strength for the woman to talk rationally.

A cold shiver pricked at Corinne's skin.

Whatever it is, I will stay calm; these people are not my family.

The arm that held her rolled-up waterproof tightened comfortingly on its bundle.

'I saw the men from my window,' she said evenly. 'I went to the jetty but that man, the taxi driver, he wouldn't let me any further than the path.' She knew she was waffling. 'My packing's all done, so I went for a last walk.'

'Yes… Well then… you won't know.' Tamzin Coburn, too, was dancing around the incident, reluctant to say the words.

The two women stood eyeing each other.

'What happened?' At last Corinne managed to say it.

Tamzin was like a bewildered child, more innocent than her own two lively offspring, who at that moment were nowhere to be seen.

'Is anyone hurt?' Corinne managed to keep *his* name at bay.

Tamzin didn't answer.

Corinne could have struck the woman. 'Tell me!'

Tamzin tugged at her fingers. She pulled her slight shoulders straight as if gathering her meagre strength before saying, 'Edwin's taken it upon himself to tell the other guests.'

'Edwin? Why Edwin?' Corinne could feel her subsiding anger rush back. 'The Menzies' Land Rover was there. Was it Ross? Is he hurt? Is it him?' she asked curtly.

Tamzin put her hand over her mouth.

269

'If you're not going to tell me, I'll go to the shop,' Corinne threatened and turned to leave.

It worked. Tamzin stuck out her hand but did not touch Corinne. 'No. It wasn't Ross,' she said. 'Don't go down there. He doesn't want anybody at the shop. Not right now.' Her hand fell to her side and her shoulders slumped.

Corinne wanted to shake Tamzin until the words were forced out of her. She was stopped by Tamzin herself, strangely aloof now, accusing her with dry, bright eyes.

'It was Kate.'

'Kate?' The one person not figured in Corinne's guess. 'No... What happened?'

'I don't know,' Tamzin said. 'She wasn't discovered until Ryan Teacher went to check on the canoes.'

Corinne went cold. 'What do you mean, discovered?'

Tamzin's small hand went up to cover her mouth. Corinne tensed herself for what was coming.

'Kate drowned,' Tamzin whispered. 'During the night.'

'Oh God! No!' Corinne's stomach lurched.

The words out, Tamzin resumed her normal voice. 'We've been trying to tell everybody, to keep them away from the shop.'

With Corinne told, Tamzin assumed an air of efficiency. 'We've got Louisa here with us, in the house. Right now, Edwin is with her. I've managed to give the police an idea of everyone staying in the cabins. They'll want to speak to you, of course.'

Corinne stood stunned. While she had been walking through the woods feeling miffed at the taxi driver, Louisa was being told her mother was dead. And she had taken herself off like a huffy child not let in on the heartbreak which, as soon as she saw the huddle of figures at the side of jetty, she knew in her heart was unfolding. She'd walked away not knowing.

'The police? Yes, right. Where are they?'

Tamzin led her to the back of the centre.

A very large police detective was sitting on a small wooden chair with his legs propped open wide. His unbuttoned jacket revealed a blue shirt straining over his bulging stomach. At a table, his colleague, younger, neater, was scribbling in a small notebook. The scribbling halted and he glanced up as Corinne appeared.

'Come in. Sit down. You are?' The young man's face was expressionless.

'Corinne Anderton.'

'No Anderton on the list.' He informed the large detective.

'Sorry, Pallin. Anderton is my married name.'

'Right.' A tick went into the notebook. 'Ah. Cabin one.'

The big detective was abrupt. 'You know Mrs Menzies?' he said.

'Yes.'

'When did you last see her?'

'Ah… Last night. Yes, that's right. Last night.'

'Don't be nervous.' The voice was soft and smooth, like double cream; it didn't match its owner. 'Where was that?'

'In the Menzies' shop.'

'What time?'

'Six. Six thirty.'

'Who else was there?'

'Umm… Mr and Mrs Menzies. Their daughter. Edwin Coburn from the centre here. I… I think that was all.'

'What did you talk about?'

'I… I can't remember. Nothing special.'

'What did you buy?'

'Sorry?'

'In the shop… You bought…?'

'Oh! Nothing.'

The detective nodded, silent. Another scribbled line was added to his notes by his colleague.

'Mrs Menzies,' the detective emphasised the name. 'Would you say she seemed… normal let's say, when you spoke to her?'

Corinne felt cold. 'I don't think we spoke.'

'No? Did you speak to anybody else?' The detective actually smiled.

'Louisa. The Menzies' daughter. She came back to my cabin for coffee.'

'When did she leave again?'

'About eight, I think it was.'

'On her own?'

'No. Her father was there. He'd come to get her.'

'They left together?'

'Yes.'

Another line went into the notebook.

'You didn't see Mrs Menzies after you left the shop?'

'No.'

A short scribble and the note-taker raised his eye-brows at his colleague.

'That's fine.' The big detective shifted his bulk on the small chair. 'Thank you, Miss... Pallin, wasn't it. That's everything for now.'

'Yes. I should tell you. I intended to leave this afternoon.'

The small wooden chair creaked as the detective moved. 'No problem. Leave your address and your number. If we need anything else we'll be in touch.'

Corinne had answered truthfully. Still she felt guilty.

At the counter she asked Tamzin, 'Do you think I could see Louisa?'

Tamzin seemed about to refuse then she shrugged. 'I don't know what good you think it'll do.' She pointed to a corridor at the far corner. 'I've got to stay here. People need drinks and things and what with the shop closed...'

'Yes, of course.' Corinne gestured toward the corridor and Tamzin nodded.

Corinne's mind was the antithesis of the cold white-washed corridor she walked through. Her head buzzed. Kate Menzies was dead. Ross would be suffering.

And Louisa? What could she say to Louisa when she saw her?

She was through the chilly corridor and out into the glass plant house before she had formed any solid words. What words would be enough for the two bereaved Menzies, father and daughter? For a second Corinne stopped as it hit her. *Step*-father, *step*-daughter. That stark little correction said a lot about why the Coburns had brought Louisa back to their place while her mother lay lifeless elsewhere with her husband watching over her.

The conservatory-like structure stretched out in front of Corinne. Through the glass on the right hand side she could see a smaller, more robust wooden room which was part of the original building. At the door, and without hesitating, she rapped five or six times. While she waited, she glanced at the untidy rows of herbs and heathers growing on wooden trestle tables across the full length of the plant house. She had seen them for sale in the centre. Tamzin was a woman of many talents, Corinne thought, but not equipped for dealing with heartbreak.

When the door opened Edwin Coburn gave her a swift, grim nod. His cheeks were drawn, his eyes red-rimmed. Without a word he held the door wide for her.

Corinne stepped into a square fussy, over furnished living-room. At first she didn't see Louisa. About to ask the whereabouts of the girl, Corinne was silenced by Edwin already holding his index finger to his lips.

'She's asleep,' he whispered and pointed to an old battered leather sofa drawn up by the fire.

Louisa lay covered with a red tartan rug, her long legs childishly zigzagged as ever up towards her body. Her face was half-hidden in her temporary refuge.

'Oh!' Corinne was taken aback. 'How is she?' She kept her voice low as if asking after a patient in ICU. She avoided looking at Edwin. Should she sympathise with this man, this special friend of Kate's, for his loss?

273

'Tamzin told me what happened.'

She jumped when he touched her arm. Motioning her to follow, Edwin went to the window at the far side of the room out of earshot of the sleeping Louisa.

'We really don't know what happened yet,' he said in the same hushed tones. 'Louisa went to pieces when Ross told her.' He cast a worried glance at the leather sofa before going on. 'She can't be left on her own. Tamzin couldn't handle it. That's why I'm here.'

'Yes, of course. She shouldn't be alone.' Corinne's thoughts swung from Louisa to Ross and finally to Kate. Kate, dead, being driven through the woods, along the shaded paths, back to her home.

She pulled herself back to Edwin. 'Is there anything I can do? I was going to leave today but I can stay if…'

'Go!' Louisa's cracked voice cut through Corinne's hushed words like a jagged razor through tender flesh. 'Get out!' Her legs, tangled in the tartan rug, swung to the floor. 'Who needs you?'

The girl struggled to escape the rug and stand. Her eyes were puffy and narrowed with crying, her face swollen from its normal sharpness. She blinked trying to focus on Corinne and attempted an unsteady step towards her. 'Why did you have to come here? Why? Wasn't it enough that your own life was rubbish? You had to take him, didn't you? Right in front of my mother!' Louisa staggered a little sideways and then righted herself. 'Was it good? Eh? Did it make everything all right for you? Being able to get him that easy?' She made a face of mock surprise. 'Oh, you thought I didn't know?' Her voice rose. 'Ha! We all knew. Everybody knew!' She threw her arms out wide and lunged forward. 'Even my mother!' she screamed into Corinne's face.

Corinne felt Edwin's hand on her back urging her toward the door. But she was frozen to the spot. *She thinks I contributed to Kate's death.*

Edwin dropped his hand and moved to Louisa's side.

274

The girl, standing steady now, ignored him. Oblivious of her rumpled clothes and hair, but fully awake, she faced Corinne. 'Don't deny it. I saw you.'

Corinne flushed. It all began to fall into place; the shadowy figure flitting through the trees away from her cabin; Kate's face when she came across her and Ross in the passageway of the shop.

'I wasn't going to deny it,' she said. 'I am sorry about your mother.' She stepped away. 'I can see you don't need me here. I'll get out of your way.'

'You do that!' Louisa shouted.

The venom in the simple words hit Corinne like shards of shattered glass as she turned for the door. But she didn't get far. Louisa collapsed onto the sofa. Her face hidden in her hands, noisy sobs wracked her body.

'My mother loved me!' she screamed at Corinne. With shaking fingers, she made a futile attempt to wipe her wet face. 'You wouldn't know what that feels like, a bitch like you!'

Edwin tried to calm her. 'Come on, stop this. This is no good.'

'No?' Louisa rounded on him. 'Good? How would you know what's good? *I* was good enough for you.' She let out a weak, jerky laugh. 'Just like my mother.' She started to cry again, her face twisted and wretched.

Edwin, his face haggard, accepted the verbal blows unflinching.

Corinne came back into the room and eased herself down beside the quivering girl.

'Louisa, if you want someone to blame, go ahead. It won't bring her back.' Louisa jerked away from her.

Corinne went on, 'Your mother was very beautiful, maybe too beautiful. It must be hard to live up to that image everyone has of you every single day of your life.'

Louisa stared straight down into her lap. 'She was beautiful, wasn't she?' she whispered.

'Yes, she was. Very. She put all the rest of us in the shade.' Corinne smiled. 'When I was a teenager the one thing I wanted was high cheekbones.'

Louisa scanned Corinne with swollen eyes. 'You're all right.'

'I make do,' Corinne said. 'Most of us eventually learn to. I didn't know your mother all that well but... she had a life and family that most people would envy.' She put her hand out and placed it on Louisa's arm. 'Good fortune doesn't visit us all the time, but Kate had had a wonderful career that she loved. And she was so proud of you.'

Louisa's face was strained. 'I said things.'

'She knew you were just sounding off,' Corinne said gently.

'No, I said things to *you*.' Louisa stared at Corinne as if seeing her not as a passing visitor but as a leading player in this horrible chapter of her life. 'You came here at the wrong time. Things were going on before you arrived. Me and Edwin...' She caught Edwin's eye. 'You knew it was just to get at her.' It was a statement of fact.

Edwin did not contradict her.

Louisa's head went from side to side as if trying to clear it of jumbled images. 'If I'd known it would lead to this...' Her swollen eyes were on Corinne. 'This is my fault.'

'You can't think like that,' Corinne said. 'Accidents happen.'

Louisa lifted her hands from her knees and brought them together. 'You really think this was an accident?' She sighed. 'God, if only I'd said nothing about you and him, she might never have found out.'

Corinne was stung into silence. Not once since she had seen what she now knew was the body of Kate Menzies being carried from the loch had Corinne felt she'd played any part in it. She glanced at Edwin. He was gazing angrily at Louisa.

Half to himself, he muttered, 'Yes, you should have kept

your mouth shut. She might still be alive.'

Corinne saw Louisa about to dissolve again. She glared at Edwin to shut him up.

'Will they believe that?' Louisa asked Corinne fretfully. 'That it was just an accident. In the middle of the night, in a canoe?' She leaned back drawing away from Corinne but her eyes stayed fixed on Corinne's face.

'How do you know that?' Corinne asked. 'That she was in a canoe? I didn't see any canoe in the water.'

Louisa stared hard at her. 'Were you there?' she demanded. She half rose and then fell back. 'My God, you get everywhere!'

'No, Louisa.' Corinne cursed her clumsiness. 'I saw the commotion from my window when I got up this morning. I wasn't at the jetty. I didn't see Kate.'

'She didn't like the water,' Louisa said vaguely.

'She liked the loch though? Yes?'

'Not really. To get her to go down to the loch took a lot of persuasion.' She leaned nearer Corinne. 'Do you really believe it was an accident?'

'I don't know,' Corinne played safe. 'But the police will tell you as soon as they've checked over everything.' She glanced up at Edwin. He was standing back, remote from their conversation, and she was doubtful his being there was doing any good.

'Louisa, why don't you come down to my cabin with me and stay there?' she asked. 'There's bound to be a lot of questions. Perhaps it would be better if you have more privacy.'

'Not at the shop?'

'No, not the shop.' Corinne squeezed the girl's cold hand but there was no return reflex. 'And there's something I think I must tell you.'

On the way from the craft centre, Louisa said very little to Corinne, walking as if she were on her own with an

277

uninviting destination ahead.

Corinne had no idea what effect seeing where her mother had died, even from a distance, would have on Louisa.

She made no mention of the shop or where Kate Menzies may have been taken by the ambulance that no doubt had been summoned by the doctor in attendance. These practical details did not seem to have occurred to Louisa. Corinne decided it was better to leave her in ignorance of what was being done. At the moment the girl was consumed by her own feelings.

In the cabin, she placed the girl at the end of the sofa where she would have to turn her head purposely if she wanted to see the jetty. Corinne sat at the opposite end facing her.

'You're leaving today,' Louisa said sulkily. 'Is that what you wanted to tell me?'

Corinne watched the girl's grey tinted face and guessed she was suffering from shock. It had been a long morning. If Louisa had taken anything earlier its effects were not obvious now.

'Would a paracetamol help?' Corinne asked.

Louisa drew up her lips in imitation of a smile. 'If that's all you've got.'

Corinne got up and brought the paracetamol and a glass of water. She handed them to Louisa. 'What I'm going to tell you might take a bit of believing, but I think you should hear it.' She sat down.

'If you don't think I'll believe it why bother?' Louisa said.

'Because I think you've got to hear this. It doesn't in any way concern me. But what with Ross and Edwin, well, I've taken it on myself.'

'Oh, go on.' Louisa was losing patience. 'Get it over with.'

Corinne steeled herself. 'Edwin is not your father.'

Louisa stopped drinking. She lowered the glass and cradled it in her hand on her lap. Little drops splashed out onto the back of her hand. She left them there. Through narrowed eyes, she watched Corinne.

Corinne kept her voice even. 'At the time Kate fell pregnant with you Edwin was already in Italy. He'd been there for six months.' There it was done.

'Why would she lie?' Louisa screwed up her face. 'Why?'

'No, Louisa, you don't understand. She didn't lie. Edwin remembers the time perfectly. You mother was at the height of her career then. She was so successful, so beautiful.' Corinne decided to sugar the pill. 'Life was one great job after another. Lots of love, lots of men, no doubt all wanting to marry her.' She paused and smiled. 'Kate had you but she didn't marry anyone. But she found it hard. When Edwin came back home he seemed to make it all right for her. From then on, always, in her mind you were Edwin's child. She didn't lie, Louisa. Over the years Kate convinced herself that it really was true.'

Louisa said, 'She wanted it to be true.'

'Maybe she wanted you to have a father.'

'She should have told me!'

'Your mother was a complicated person. She didn't want to hurt you, or Ross. Or the Coburns for that matter.'

'If she'd just said, Edwin could have told me the truth,' Louisa insisted. 'And none of this would have happened.'

'I'm sorry,' Corinne said. 'It wasn't really for me to tell you. But after this morning, you needed to know. It might make things easier between you and Ross and the Coburns.' She inclined her head to catch Louisa's eye. 'Nobody is to blame.'

'I guess not,' Louisa said slowly. She had stopped crying and seemed to be weighing up the undeniable consequences of what she had just heard. 'I'm back to having no father and now my mother's gone.'

'Once he's over the shock, Ross will be there for you,' Corinne said. 'Maybe even get you settled back in college again. Your mother would like that.'

'God! He's not going to trust me to try that again.' Louisa

279

was silent for a time. Then, 'I'm sorry I told on you and him, you know, sleeping together.'

'*That* was a mistake.' Corinne smiled shortly. 'One of my many!'

'You hurt my mother.'

'I'm sorry.' Corinne sighed. 'One way or another I think we've all hurt your mother.'

Louisa wanted to go back to the craft centre. Corinne saw no point in arguing with her and telephoned Edwin to come for her.

After they left Corinne carried her bags to the end of the walkway. She set them down on the edge and went back to the cabin, placed the key in the door and locked it for the last time.

It was a little after three o'clock. Corinne was slightly dazed, bombarded with a tragedy that relegated her own problem to a lower league. What lurked in the remaining hours of the day for Louisa, she couldn't imagine, but *she* had to get away now.

Taking a final moment at the loch, dark and slick, immune to any tragedy, she felt in tune with the blackness. It brought out conflicting feelings. One part of her wanted to run to the station and forget everything she had seen in the last week; another part very badly wanted to stay.

A bag in each hand, she walked steadily to the shop. She shied away from the short ride to the station on the creaking cream leather seats of the vintage taxi. The eyes of the driver would be watching her in his rear-view mirror, sharing yet not sharing what they both knew. The alternative, carrying her bags the entire distance to the train station, seemed eminently preferable.

Several times she stopped to reposition the bags in her hands before she reached the shop. No surprise, the place was deserted. Knowing what lay behind the silence, she was reluctant to knock on the closed door or even try the handle.

There was no need. A sheet of white A4 paper, stuck at eye level on the outside of the door, was hard to miss.

The curt hand-written message gave instructions to leave cabin keys in the box. Unambiguous, meant not just for her, it gave no apology for this unconventional check-out.

The stiff red plastic box at the bottom of the door had no lid. All traces of its original contents had been eradicated. She marvelled at this incongruous colourful container placed at the door of a household going through so much pain.

Dropping her cabin keys, she stared at the red plastic box. She had not paid for her stay. Six nights she had been living in the cabin down by the loch. For six nights and seven days she had been privy to heart-wrenching disclosures about the Menzies family, been drawn reluctantly into their world, witnessing the ties between mother and daughter so close and binding that they inevitably became unyielding and brittle, to the point of disintegration.

And what had she done? Slept with Ross Menzies in an attempt to forget the troubles that brought her to the shores of Loch na Duroir.

Her own relationship with her mother had taken a hammering in the last few days. The usual equilibrium, so delicate, so carefully nurtured by them both, tipped off its axis last Wednesday when she boarded the train and left Edinburgh.

That the status quo would never be restored to its former level of tolerance, gnawed away at Corinne. It frightened her in a way she could not recognise. Things had changed. The balance of her life had slid out of kilter.

Tearing her eyes away from the red box, she noticed several cars parked to one side of the shop along with Ross's Land Rover. The police? Probably. She should leave. Get out of Ross's way. Making up a bill for her would be the last thing on his mind.

Corinne rifled through her bag. She would leave him her details and get going.

Her name and address made a neat block of five lines. Finished, she hesitated. It was impersonal and she could maybe add a note of sympathy. The small piece of paper was creased now; she flipped it over and stared, pen poised, at the white blankness of it. What could she say? She was sorry. Leave it at that? No. There were too many things she was sorry about. Sorry for him, sorry about Kate. Sorry she was leaving. It sounded trite and insincere.

Turning the scrap of paper face up, Corinne smoothed it out between her fingers. She read her own address. It was all he needed.

She retrieved the keys from the box. Rolling up the scrap of paper into the shape of a not very well executed roll-your-own she stuck it through the short chain that joined the key to the wooden disc carved with the number 1. Nicely done, she noticed for the first time, and rubbed her thumb over the workmanship. A feeling of guilt tugged at her at the trivial action. She rationalised it; mundane things take on a heightened degree of attention at a time of crisis.

Was she in crisis?

She dropped the key into the box. Done. On your way, she said to herself.

It was a movement on the other side of the closed door that stopped her leaving.

Behind the glass, an outline. Corinne stayed still. The key rattled in the lock and the metal bolt was shot back with a nerve-wracking slam.

Ross, his hand on the door edge, gazed at her. 'You're ready to go.' Unshaven, he was red eyed and unkempt.

'Yes.' Corinne indicated the red plastic box. 'The keys are there.'

For what seemed to Corinne an age, his eyes drilled into her. She couldn't smile. If she kept her face straight and serious she was less likely to cry. When she opened her mouth, her voice was deceptively normal.

'Is Louisa…?'

'Louisa…' he said at the same time, cutting her short. 'Thanks for taking care of her this morning. Edwin told me. Phil and Ryan have taken her for a while.' He motioned over his shoulder. 'I have to get back.'

'Ross, I'm so sorry about Kate.'

283

At last his eyes slid away from her face to the empty space behind her. 'The ambulance went to Glasgow about half-an-hour ago with her. The police are still here.' His eyes were back on her again. 'They might want to speak to you. They're having a word with everybody. It's just routine.'

'I've already seen them. If they want me again, my address is there.' Corinne indicated the crudely rolled up paper sticking through the key-chain.

'A holiday to remember?' His words were forced.

Corinne saw his lips press hard together to stop more trivia from forming.

'Say good-bye to Louisa for me.'

'Yes.' He picked up the cabin keys. He pulled the note from the chain without unrolling it and curled it in his fingers, hiding it so completely in the palm of his hand that no part of it could be seen. He tried to connect with Corinne but his eyes were heavy-lidded and not properly focused.

She imagined he might step out from the doorway and come to her, kiss her. Nothing.

He was struggling. Corinne could see it. Feeling for him, she did the one thing that she could to lessen the turmoil that he was obviously going through; she picked up her bags and started her walk to the train station.

By eight o'clock that night Corinne was in the back of a black cab passing through the damp, windswept streets of Edinburgh.

Rearing up on every side, buildings, shops, monuments, all reassuringly grey, solid and familiar. She felt emotional as though she had been away for a very long time.

At the house, she paid the taxi driver and stood gazing at her home. The face of the house was dark; no sign of a welcoming light showed at any window. Except for her car, parked in its usual place, the drive was empty.

Ignoring the front door she went around to the back of the house. At the garden room her key opened the sliding glass doors smoothly and with hardly any effort. Inside, she dropped her bags to the floor, switched on the overhead lights and went straight to the kitchen.

Beside the shiny coffee-maker, was the answer-phone. She pressed the play button. Twelve messages. While the water in the kettle boiled and she made tea, she listened.

All were short, a couple garbled and unintelligible, others clear and to the point. She heard them through. Ignoring the need to respond to one or two, she deleted every one. None had been from her mother or her father or Uncle Ian. None from Noel.

She felt let down by this lack of contact.

With Ross Menzies large in her head all day, she had spared little time on wondering what would be waiting for her. She'd had no real expectation. Just home. But not this. Not this loneliness.

The place was tidy. The room smelled sharply of lemon, clean and sterile, a touch acerbic. After the cabin at Four Hills the house appeared spacious and cold and, she tried to analyse it and could only come up with, *bare.* She shivered and blamed her first mouthful of hot tea for the hair-raising effect on her arms and legs.

Upstairs the same order had been restored to her bedroom after her shambolic escape. A powdery, floral smell permeated through from the bathroom. Emma must have been there very recently to make sure everything was in its proper place for whenever Corinne decided to come home.

Only a week ago, she'd left so abruptly. Yet the place felt different; less comfortable, less pleasant than her memory persisted on telling her it should be. She couldn't pin it down. It was still her home. Even the fading daylight coming through the bedroom window seemed greyer, less sharp and true.

I'm comparing it to the cabin!

With the bedside lamps switched on, the room softened. A creamy glow sketched evening shadows prematurely down into the corners. The room felt marginally better.

Sitting on the edge of the bed, Corinne picked up the telephone. Who first? Her parents? Uncle Ian?

The buttons clicked rhythmically under her fingernail. When the last ring changed to a recorded invitation to leave a message she hung up. Her parents must be out, visiting friends before they left for France, she guessed.

She tapped another well-remembered number. The ringing this time sounded only twice before Ian McCall answered. 'Hello.'

'It's me.'

'Ah! And how are you?'

'I'm back. At home. I've just got in.'

'Good! Good! That's what I've been wanting to hear.'

'Are Mum and Dad with you?'

'No. They're not here.'

'Will you be seeing them tonight?'

'No.'

'Oh, I just thought… Oh, I don't know,' Corinne said frankly. 'I rang them just now. There was no answer. I had the idea we maybe could have dinner together.'

'Feeling deserted, are you?' Ian said. 'Well, there's no need for that. Get yourself over here and I'll give you dinner.'

About to refuse, Corinne visualized him sitting in the staid old-fashioned house packed with books and mementos of a life lived honestly and openly. The blunt invitation, tossed so casually down the phone was, nevertheless, sincere.

'See you shortly,' she told him and hung up.

By the time Corinne arrived at his house, Ian McCall had grilled fillets of salmon and put together a bowl of green salad.

Corinne refused his offer of wine and drank water instead. As they ate the meal, she relayed to him every moment of her day from first waking and witnessing the huddle of figures at the jetty on the far side of the loch, to being dropped off at home and finding her car exactly where she'd left it.

'It was like I'd just stepped out this morning. But then inside everything was so, oh, impersonal, I suppose.'

'You used to love that house,' Ian reminded her. 'That can't have changed. Not in a week.'

'Oh, I don't know. I honestly don't. It's not the house; that's the same, so it must be me.'

'Corinne,' Ian leaned forward, his thick forearms, hidden under a crisp white shirt, pressed heavily on the edge of the table, 'you can't feel guilty about everything, you know. And by God, there's no good reason why you should.' His index finger tapped the table top. 'You've got to learn to accept that the things happening around us are not always within our control.' He stopped his tapping and went back to his meal, his great bushy brows shadowing his eyes so that Corinne could not see them.

'When things go wrong, I should turn the other way?' she said. 'Is that what you're saying?'

'Well, at times it's better for all concerned.'

'Oh no! That's one thing I don't accept.' With the tines of her fork, Corinne picked at the flakes of pink fish on her plate. 'If people shut their eyes to the truth and pretend they don't see it, well, that's not just wrong – it's dishonest.'

'Dishonest it might be, but, tell me, what good is the truth if all it does is wound folk. What's so righteous about that, eh?' Ian's knife clattered down onto his plate.

They both stared at it.

Corinne placed her knife and fork carefully together. 'The woman who died this morning – Kate Menzies – her life was based on a lie, a lie that ultimately destroyed her.' She reached out and removed his plate. 'What price is that to pay for not facing the truth?' She rose from the table and carried the dishes to the kitchen.

Ian McCall stayed in his chair. His eyes were half-closed,

his face, creased as if in pain, sank forward onto his broad chest.

'Uncle Ian!' Corinne was back. Alarmed by the slumped head and stillness of the broad shoulders, she threw the cheese board she was carrying onto the table. Cuts of cheese and precisely stacked columns of biscuits slid across the highly polished surface.

'Uncle Ian!'

His head came up. 'I was thinking.'

'Ohhh…' Corinne laughed weakly. She flopped down into her chair. Her heart was pounding and heat flooded her face. For a moment she sat watching him. With shaking fingers, she gathered the cheese and biscuits and began to heap them back onto the board. 'What were you thinking about?'

'Leave that. Leave it.' Taking both her hands in his, Ian McCall forced Corinne to turn and face him. 'This past week,' he began, 'you've struggled with the truth as you saw it. No, don't talk. I don't want you to talk. Don't say anything at all until I'm finished. I just want you to listen.' He put both her hands together and patted them before letting go.

'Those things you've just said about truth, well, it brought home to me that there are people who need to know the truth no matter what it does to them. You're one of that breed, lass. You faced Noel and his little secret and – no, let me talk – taking yourself off like you did? I know fine why you did that. So we wouldn't see the hurt you were going through. Oh, we knew it all right.' He tipped his head back. 'In your hurry to hide your grief you forgot your mother and father and me, we've lived too. We've had our time. And, I might add, a time when most of the world was upside down with war and a good few of its men found themselves hunkered down in foreign soil thinking their days were numbered.' The faded hazel eyes glazed over with the memory.

Corinne gave him a thin smile. 'I know the story.'

'Awe lass…' He smiled back at her, a cheerless, sad

attempt. 'It's not just about us. It's about you as well.' He was watching her closely.

'If it's got anything to do with the war, remember I wasn't born then,' Corinne tried to lighten the mood.

'No. It's not just about the war. After the war and later on besides. What I have to say might change things.'

'Like what for instance? Tell me. I'm all ears.'

'Yes. It needs to be said. When you hear what it is, I don't want you to judge us too harshly. Any of us.'

Corinne drew her head back. '*Us*?'

He ignored the question as though it had never been put to him.

She saw his chest, broadened by age, expand as he drew in an invigorating breath in readiness for what he was about to tell her. The sheer deliberation of his action smothered in her any further questions.

Despite the warm room, Corinne began to feel cold. Placing her hands together in her lap she pressed her spine against the soft padded back of the upright chair and waited.

When he continued the story, Ian McCall's voice was low and flat. His words were clipped and, Corinne heard, selective.

'We were young. Too young by far for what we went through. When the war ended it was like everyone's life restarted. The world began to turn again. To begin with, times were hard. The folk that survived were happy, happy at least to be able to give life another go. Me, I was one of them. Pierre was another. When he came to Scotland it was like finding a long lost brother we were that close. It wasn't easy but the business did all right by us. We weren't rich but we were well enough off, compared with a lot of other people that is.'

Corinne had heard all this before, told in slightly different versions by her father and her mother as well as Ian McCall. But always the nub of the past remained the same.

She now found herself listening to the familiar history. But

289

her insides began to quiver as if she were sitting in a cold draught from an open window. She shivered and knew by his glower that Ian had seen the involuntary shudder. He did not remark on it but went on with his story.

'It was a while but eventually Pierre found his Jean. From the very start I knew fine that they were meant for each other. He used to make up excuses to visit her at least once, sometimes twice a day. I let him get away with it. I made out I didn't know like.' His accent became thick and burred as he slipped back over the years.

'One time she came to tea in a green spotted frock. My, she was a lovely girl.' The memory edged a smile onto his lips and deepened the lines on either side of his mouth.

Corinne's stomach stopped fluttering; her body flushed hot. She had the uneasy feeling of being a voyeur into a window on the past but she couldn't find the courage to pull down the shutters on that window and tell him to stop.

'It happened when Pierre went off to France to see his family one time. He wanted them to know about Jean first hand. She couldn't go because she couldn't get the time off her work.' He was reciting details as they came to mind. They were clear and crisp as if he had reflected on them very recently and swept the dust from them for this very occasion.

'By then she was coming to the printers for her tea every day. And those weeks he was away she went on doing that very same thing. Just her and me it was. Biscuits and tea. Oh, I knew she was missing him.' A little laugh travelled the space between him and Corinne. 'And I was lonely…'

Corinne covered her mouth with her fingers to keep from shouting at him to stop, not to tell her any more. Biscuits and tea and loneliness… Stop there! She'd heard enough.

He went on. 'Only the one time it happened. To her it didn't mean anything. And she said it could never happen again and that we were to forget it.' Pain on his face, a small explosion of breath left him. 'Forget it!' He appeared to remember suddenly that Corinne was there. 'How could I do that? Seeing her every day? Making out when Pierre got back that things were normal, that nothing had happened. Then when I saw them back together… Well, somehow, I found the strength.'

The room was still. Ian was watching Corinne with calm resignation. He smiled sadly. 'After that I threw myself even more into my work. For a while Jean stopped coming for her tea.' The sadly comic consequence of their love-making was told with stuttering breath. 'Then one day she came when Pierre was out on a delivery.' He paused anxious to get it right. 'That's right, I remember; a delivery down to the bank headquarters on St Andrew's Square.' He paused, pleased at recalling the exact details.

Corinne sat transfixed.

'That was the day Jean told me she was pregnant.'

Unable to form the words that she wanted to shout at him, Corinne could only shake her head. Eyes wide, she stared at him.

The twinkling chandelier above their heads cast down a sharp bluish light, giving his ruddy face a grey marble pallor, making his jowls appear heavy and unappealing.

He did not try to reach out to her, but went on with the same detached, painfully detailed recounting of the story.

'She told me it couldn't be Pierre's since they hadn't been sleeping together for that long – only since he got back from France. She'd worked it out, you see. I told her to make the decision. If she wanted me to I would marry her. Oh, I didn't ask her in so many words but I hoped she would. If she didn't want to she had the choice of telling Pierre or keeping it to herself. Whichever way it went, somebody was bound to get hurt.' Ian stretched his shoulders. 'And that was down to me.' He leaned hard into the padded back of the chair forcing his considerable bulk upright. 'Jean thought a lot about it, but in the end she decided she loved Pierre too much to lie to him. So, one day when they were in the park together, she told him. Told him everything. Without a word, he got up and walked away from her. Left her sitting there all by herself he did.

'He made a bee-line straight to the print shop. We fought, fought like a couple of wild animals that knew no better. When it was over, hardly a stick of furniture was left standing in the place.'

'No!' The appeal rang in Corinne's ears unaware she shouted the word.

Ian's eyes on her, he reached out. 'Lass…'

Pulling her hands away, Corinne slumped in her chair unable to summon up enough energy to dispute this horrendous lie about her family. The air in the room all at once seemed thick and cloying preventing her from saying more than that one condemning word over again. 'No!'

'We lived with it,' Ian said softly. 'All three of us, for Jean wouldn't let Pierre give up his livelihood with me at the printers. It was the only way she could see of making up for what we'd done – both of us.'

At that Corinne found her voice. 'I was bartered?' she gasped. 'For half your company?' She stared at him. A rage-induced surge of adrenalin had her head spinning. 'To sort out your little problem, you gave *my father* half your business. My God! He got the best of that deal.'

'Don't talk like that!' Ian was angry. 'There was no deal. Not like that anyhow.' He leaned forward, his hands clasped tight on the thin carved arms of his chair.

'Pierre loved your mother so much. It was heart-breaking to see his reaction. Jean said if he still wanted her she would marry him but he had to take the child and stay in the business.' Ian leaned further forward, his chest almost touching the table-top in his eagerness to make her understand. 'That way she believed she could make it up to him. She didn't want him to lose everything he'd worked for. They were her terms, nobody else's.'

The adrenalin drained away from Corinne, leaving her weak and confused. 'But him and me, we've always been so close, so alike.' Avoiding his face she glanced down the length of the table, half of which was bare and shone dully in the light from the chandelier overhead.

'Me and Mum, we're forever arguing,' she said. 'We can never agree on anything. And you...' The food she'd eaten was threatening to come back up into her throat and choke her.

'I know,' he said. 'The three of us did our best for you. We settled it between ourselves and got our lawyer, William Greyson, to draw up the agreement giving Pierre half the business.'

Like ripples from a launched stone on the smooth waters of the loch at Four Hills, the consequences of this decades old pact began gradually to penetrate Corinne's brain. 'Who else knew about this?'

'Except for us three and old Willie, we thought nobody else knew.'

Her brows rose. 'You *thought?*'

Ian McCall shifted heavily in his chair. 'Yes. That's right. Apparently we were wrong.' He sucked in a breath. 'Noel found out.'

'Noel!'

He was quick to justify it. 'It could only have been from Jimmy Greyson, old Willie's son. Nobody else knew about you.'

'How long has he known – Noel?' she demanded. 'How long?'

'Just a matter of days.' Ian McCall appeared defeated. 'We asked him not to tell you until we had discussed it between ourselves.'

'You did *what?*'

'We talked it over and your mother didn't want to tell you but your father did.'

'You mean Pierre Pallin.'

Ian was silent for a second then very slowly he continued. 'You might as well know the rest. I don't know how your

293

mother and *your father* are going to take me telling you all this but things have gone too far for you not to know.'

'My God! There's more?'

Ian ignored her. 'Noel did, and still does, want out of your marriage,' he told her. 'He wants to walk away with no forfeit, no lingering ties of any kind.' He glanced at her to see how she was taking this bald bit of information. 'I'm not saying this to hurt you.'

'Go on, I'm listening.'

'Of course we wouldn't agree to it. Then he said he was going to tell you everything he'd found out. That's when we tried to make a bargain with him.' Ian was rushing his words. 'But he kept pushing and pushing. That was his biggest mistake. You know your mother. Jean dug her heels in. She said no, he was not going to just walk away from everything. She decided. Pierre drove her to Four Hills to tell you the truth themselves. Even then Noel wouldn't back down. He threatened he would get in there first if we didn't tear up his contract and let him go. He didn't care about the damage to you or to them.'

Her face flat and expressionless, Corinne listened in silence as Ian recounted what he learned from Jean and Pierre when they got back from Four Hills.

'What with a bunch of strangers as well as Noel hanging about all the time, and you not exactly making it easy for them to talk to you, they couldn't do it. They couldn't tell you. When they got home we talked it over again. We drew up the new contract and told Noel that was it. If he didn't like it he could do what he wanted with his information – he could tell you or not.' Ian smiled grimly to himself. 'It sort of put the boot on the other foot for he had no reason to land a vicious blow on you when he was getting off relatively lightly. I suppose he was really thinking of the damage to his reputation if it ever got into the papers.'

'So I was bartered again. I'm a thirty-eight year old woman, not a foundling bastard!' Corinne spat out.

'Although at this precise moment the two seem quite compatible.'

'Act like a woman then!' Ian exploded. 'Think about Jean and Pierre. Do that for just one minute, will you? They're on their way to the airport right now. Yes.' He saw her start. 'They've left for France already because they didn't think it would do any good to wait around to talk to you now.'

Corinne blinked. 'They've gone?'

'They're going to tell your grandparents.'

'What? No, no…' Corinne got to her feet. The chair scraped back. 'They mustn't do that!' she shouted. 'We've go to stop them. It'll kill them!'

Ian McCall didn't move. He stared hard at his daughter. 'What price now your truth?'

CHAPTER TWENTY

The late summer breeze down Princes Street was light.

The grey mist that had the early morning commuters shivering, lifted by lunch time. It vanished away to taunt them with a last glimpse of summer sun.

Corinne unbuttoned her jacket and let it hang loose. She walked slowly glancing into one shop window after another. At a display of fine cheeses dotted about with French wines set out with a romanticised rustic touch, she stopped and smiled. Her grandparents, too, would be amused at the idyllic pastoral image of all things Gallic.

She started to walk again. People dodged past her, all seeming at the height of the day, to have somewhere to go, urgent things to do, possibly important.

Her mind still in France, she went with the crowd. The bustle of people carried her over the wide pedestrian crossing to the far pavement and left her there, ignorant of having played a part in deciding where Corinne went that lunchtime.

Across the street, hanging just above the Scott Monument, the sun's rays struck the side of her face. She half-closed her eyes, shutting out the dazzle. Today, Edinburgh's kind weather lessened her envy of her mother and Pierre seeking shade from the heat under the trees in the garden of her grandparents' house.

Her grandparents. When she thought of Genevieve and Jean-Luc Pallin, that's how she saw them. That would never change. And for them she would always be their *petite-fille*. For Pierre Pallin's aged parents *she* was the same. Corinne truly believed it.

Too late to stop her, her mother had not held back. She cleared her conscience and exposed them all. To them it didn't matter. In their hearts nothing was altered even now that they knew Corinne's life had started with deceit.

On the telephone, they insisted she used English to them as always. Every conversation ended with them begging her to come to see them.

Never did a call finish without Corinne promising she would go soon, the reorganizing of her workload her excuse for repeatedly putting it off. A deadline was due; the time was not right, not yet.

Corinne never mentioned Pierre. The few short minutes tête-à-tête with them, she managed to get through without actually ever referring to their son.

Corinne paused at the corner of a large department store and hitched her bag higher on her arm. A man in a football top, his woollen cap pulled down low over his eyes, bumped his solid shoulder into hers. Grunting an apology, he was on his way before she could say it was probably her fault.

This half-dreaming state was nothing new. Over the last few months her staff had become used to it. Now when she left the office for lunch, they never bothered to ask when she would be back. Too many times she had shrugged, 'I'm not sure.' Casual enquiries as to where she had been were also dropped. Likewise any mention of Noel and her parents. The changed relationship between Ian McCall and Corinne was now common knowledge.

One week after her return from Four Hills, she had told her assistant, Sarah, the bare facts, adding, 'There's no reason to keep it a secret.'

The woman nodded. She did not pretend to understand what had forced this carefully buried secret suddenly to the surface but she asked no questions. Time had a way of revealing everything. The others in the office were told. If they bulked it out with idle detail, Corinne never knew and Sarah never said. She got on with her job of supporting her boss as usual.

She did it well. Corinne, at her desk, would find notes from Ian McCall on one side, separate and obvious from the rest of her work. Messages which needed her personal attention stacked up on her desk while she was out. Even the most urgent of these she would put to the side until she dealt first with those from Ian McCall.

Some of it was trivial. It made no difference; she did not want to appear to be avoiding him. On the other hand, it might make her seem too eager. Corinne was caught in the middle. Since that night in mid-May she had not been able to call him by his name, not once. Struggling to work normally, avoiding him in the corridor, taking the stairs in case he was in the lift, became the norm.

She hated herself for keeping him at arm's length.

"Dad", "Father". Ian McCall had not suggested she call him either of these relative attachments – both knew that would never happen. The comfortable tag of "uncle", spurious as it had always been, now had a mocking ring to it. Corinne couldn't bring herself to utter it.

At the far end of Princes Street Corinne stopped. Sheer habit made her glance in the bookshop there. Her eye went immediately to the display in the very centre of the shop floor.

The cardboard portrait of a dark figure in glossy black on a blood red back-ground was familiar. *A Stranger's Bullet.*

The thriller had taken off even faster than Noel had rattled through it to get it finished, thrown the memory stick across her desk like a grenade with the pin removed, and headed for the airport.

Corinne had put on her business head and reasoned that not to get it out fast onto the shelves would, as Ian McCall was fond of saying, be like cutting off her nose to spite her face. Also, it would cost them money. She pulled out all the stops.

Early figures showed it to be one of Noel's best efforts to date; and its success proved cathartic in getting him out of Corinne's system.

As she surveyed the carefully arranged display she felt a tiny frisson of pride. The emotion was not for the success of *A Stranger's Bullet.* It was for her and her alone. She had kept herself together these last three months. While the pieces of her life deconstructed then started to reassemble, like a child's toy, into a new and unpredictable form, she had no idea what the end result would turn out to be. She had emerged out of this remodelling. Wiser? Certainly that, she told herself. Stronger? She wasn't convinced. There was a little core, deep down inside her, hidden away from even her most perceptive friends, which wept constantly for the woman she had been, and for the life she once thought perfect.

Through the shop window an assistant caught her eye and waved, her hand going back and forth like a solitary window-wiper on fast speed.

Corinne nodded her head briefly. She didn't know the young girl. It had been a good night the book-signing Noel had carried out at the launch of *A Stranger's Bullet*. Probably, they'd crossed paths then.

The friendly little exchange over, she gazed at the bold black and red display. People seemed to be taken with the enigmatic figure.

She gave herself a shake; it was a cardboard cut-out. Real life versus fiction.

Pushing the door open Corinne went in. Over the heads of people at the counter, she tried to locate the young assistant who had waved so spontaneously to her. Too late. The girl was no longer there. Someone else had taken her place.

It was after 3 a.m. when friends dropped Corinne back home that night after dinner.

The food had been good, the conversation undemanding, and the company at a mutual friend's home, easy going.

Corinne had drank one glass of wine too many. At the end of the night she was pleasantly light-headed but not so uninhibited as to have said anything regrettable, she was pretty sure.

A mixed bunch, couples, and singles, her own age and

older, she knew everybody at the dinner table. They all knew about her split with Noel. Not one person offered any sympathy about her current marital situation. The reverse was the case.

'Now that Noel's gone do you intend to stay where you are, Corinne? That's a fine house you have there,' an elderly man, a cartoonist Corinne worked with from time to time, commented.

Her host's partner jumped in before Corinne could answer. 'Whatever you do, don't give it up, Corinne,' the woman said. 'Your own bit of space can be a God send. And think of the cost of finding another place.'

The conversation drifted casually from the size of homes to the price of property in the capital city.

It was all very civilized and very open.

Getting ready for bed, Corinne went over the evening's conversations in her head. She tried hard to remember what, eventually, she had replied to the cartoonist's blunt query. She couldn't remember if she *had* answered him. Anyway, it didn't matter what response she'd come up with; she had been wined and dined and handled with studied care by her friends all evening. They had played it just right. Or nearly.

Corinne lay down, her eyes wide open.

In the early hours the party had ended. She had been seen safely home and now was surrounded by silence.

On Monday Corinne's office was closed for a day's holiday.

The city's annual Festival had come to an end with a spectacular fireworks display watched by her and the other dinner guests last night from an attic window in her friend's home. Buskers would still hang about to entertain the tourists for a while but the majority of the Festival acts as well as the Fringe already were headed back south of the border. It was the northern English towns that were about to get a taste of their widely varying talents.

The city was gradually easing its way back to normal.

Corinne felt the same about her life. With nothing on the agenda for that night, there was no need to plan her day. She would go where her mood dictated.

Her second cup of coffee of the morning in her hand, last night's talk over the dinner-table, came back to her.

"Don't sell it!' A man urged about the house.

His wife advised, "Get yourself a new bed." Everybody laughed knowing what she meant.

Maybe she would do just that.

Corinne wandered from room to room trying to see the house as a stranger would see it; high ceilings, discreet lighting, modern, expensive furniture.

Then it struck her, just as on the day she got back from her stay in the spartan cabin at Four Hills, the cool formality of it all. Everything was functional and efficient, very efficient. Noel had liked it that way.

There was nothing warm about the house, nothing embracing or *comforting.*

It's a reflection of our marriage, Corinne thought bitterly, a true collaboration that had lost its initial excitement and become routine if no less efficient in the process.

Surprisingly, thinking of Noel did not upset her.

Her hostess last night had been right. This was now her space. She could do what she pleased in it.

A euphoric sense of freedom made Corinne abandon her coffee mug on the nearest table and sprint upstairs. Pulling out a coat at random, she grabbed her handbag and left the house by way of the garden room door. For a second she considered taking her car into town but then ditched the idea.

Walking between the avenue of old stone houses she soon began to regret her decision. The wind was strong. It whipped her hair across her face and snatched her breath away.

Heading for Princes Street, she passed by the front of her office. She dawdled. With watering eyes, and breathless, she felt an untidy mess and slightly out of control. The scary urge to throw back her head and laugh out loud welled up.

She was saved this humiliation by a gentle pull on her shoulder.

The hysterical feeling disappeared.

She turned to face Ian McCall.

'I've just done a couple of hours at the office,' he told her. 'Want to join me for a bite of lunch?'

The invitation came, issued in the same casual, undemanding way he'd used previously – when he was her 'Uncle Ian'.

For Corinne it was hard to think of him as anything else. Neither could she think back to a time when it had not been acknowledged that she was to get his part of the company. The normal inheritance scenario was now reversed. Another bit of her life that had tipped upside-down. The half of Pallin-McCall which she felt entitled to, would not come from Pierre Pallin but from Ian McCall. Pierre Pallin's share would be passed on to her out of the goodness of his heart – allowing that he did not have a change of heart – and not from any sense of legitimacy.

Corinne knew that Ian McCall was waiting for her answer.

His thick, course hair defied the blustery wind and sprung back into place. He had a touch of blue biro on his cheek. 'How about it?' He was acting as if everything had righted itself and was now in its proper order.

For the second time that morning, an urge to laugh came over Corinne. She held it back, knowing the situation between them to be rather pathetic. And it was much too early for lunch.

A sharp nod of her head and she accepted his invitation.

Ian McCall touched her arm and walked her over the pedestrian crossing at the top of Princes Street. He let her go in front of him up the stairs of the hotel opposite the bookshop, and through the smooth swing-door.

Neither of them said a word until they were sitting at a table in the empty dining room with a menu placed in front of them, the waiter having warned them they would have to wait.

'What was it you were doing this morning?' Corinne forced herself to speak first. Low key – that was the answer. Keep it low key. 'Was it anything urgent?' It was like talking to a not very close work colleague.

'No, not urgent. Just a clear up. That's all.'

'It's meant to be a long week-end away from work for everybody,' Corinne pointed out.

'Well, since your mother and Pierre went back to France I pop in most weekends. I like to make sure we're not falling behind with anything.'

'I didn't know you did that.'

'You've had a lot on your mind lately.'

'Don't make excuses for me. I don't need it.'

'I'm not.'

'If I haven't been pulling my weight, you should have told me.'

'Why? Am I not allowed to cover for you nowadays?'

'Cover for me?'

'Oh, you know what I mean. Lend a hand. Make sure everything's in order.' Ian McCall would not back down. He dismissed it as no big thing. 'You've done it for me in the past when we were busy. I was always grateful for it. I thought you would be too.'

Corinne leaned back. Her anger evaporated. He was right. 'Things are a lot different now.' Her lips curled. 'Anyway, you could probably run the company with your eyes shut.'

'You're probably right.'

They glanced at one another, the trace of a smile on both their faces. A mild silence followed. The tension that had been building slipped away.

Ian raised his bushy brows at Corinne. 'I'll do whatever it takes to get things running smoothly again. No,' he wagged a finger at her. 'I don't mean the business. I mean you. You've had a rough deal. And none of it, *none* was of your own making.' He stretched out his hand but in the next instant thought better of it. He fell back in his seat. 'You've stood up well to it.'

Across the corner of the table, Corinne watched him. She was his daughter. He cared, it was obvious, but he had not said he was happy. But then she had not given him much opportunity to say how he felt. He had not pressed her, not once. Instead, she realised, he had been at her back, making sure her work was completed on time and that she did not blunder while her mind was shredded by so much revelation.

'Ian...' She smiled again at him.

Ian walked half way back to Corinne's house with her. The wind still swirled along the streets. Walking side by side was not easy. Their snatched talk was of taxis and road-works and new trams and the coming Tuesday morning meeting. No mention of Noel, or Pierre and Jean Pallin, entered their limited conversation.

Only when he was about to leave her did Ian bring up the notion of her parents and, even then, not directly.

'You ought to take time off.' He stood with his back to the wind giving her a narrow corridor of protection from the buffeting. 'Think on it,' he said. 'A month in the sun will set you to rights.'

He did not say where or with whom. With his archaic turn of phrase, Corinne knew he was trying to give her back the last pieces needed to rebuild her life.

She nodded. 'I will. I'll think about it.'

That early morning feeling of freedom was still with Corinne that night. But now she felt, not the initial euphoria that had hit her like a tornado making her hurry down the street like a demented woman let loose, but a calm contentment which itself was frighteningly unfamiliar. It brought home to her that she had not been happy for a very long time. Immersed in work, she hadn't even realized it.

Just after eight o'clock she switched on the television and began to make a simple dinner of rice and vegetables.

Beyond the great swathe of window she glanced out onto the fast darkening wind-whipped garden. The watery sun of the afternoon had disappeared behind a bank of grey cloud. Huge boughs, hanging low on the old trees, were in danger of snapping they bent so low in the wind. Dipping and weaving like little boats braving turbulent seas, they rose up only to be caught again in the next fierce gust and drawn back down. The lawn was strewn with bits of twigs and rolling leaves, spoiling its smooth neatly cropped cut and obliterating the straight, unnaturally pristine man-made edges.

Gazing dejectedly at nature's unwarranted destruction, Corinne gave a start. Her whole body tightened and she stood very still.

A figure had detached itself from the hedge at the side of the garden and was walking slowly towards her. Even through the gloom, the tall, thin shouldered slouch of Louisa Menzies was unmistakeable as she neared the window.

Corinne unlocked the door and slid it open. 'God! Where did you spring from? You gave me one hell of a fright!'

Louisa stopped short of stepping inside. 'I wasn't sure if you were on your own or not.'

'Come in.' Corinne stood aside. 'Come on.' She motioned Louisa into the room.

As usual the girl was under-dressed for the cold, blustery evening. A grey cardigan was wrapped tightly around her skeletal body and tied clumsily at the side in a huge, ugly knot. The garment reached to just above her knees. Bright green tights covered her legs and on her feet were white ankle-boots.

From high in the ceiling the bright artificial spotlights shone down stark and white on Louisa's pale face. She had lost weight and was thinner than when Corinne last saw her, the beautiful green eyes deeper and wider, the untidy red hair a dull copper against her colourless skin.

For a brief moment Corinne felt she was about to turn and run back the way she had come. 'There's nobody else here,' she said. 'Just me.'

Louisa stepped further into the room.

'How did you know where to find me?' Getting no answer, Corinne moved to the cooker. 'Would you like something to eat? You should have warned me you were coming. I would have done something better than this.' She glanced up from the boiling pot as Louisa came closer.

Louisa was reluctant to engage with her. She slowly scanned the entire room. 'It wasn't hard to find you. I wasn't sure about coming though.'

'What are you doing in Edinburgh? Here this should do. Hand me those plates will you?'

'I've got a place on an arts and design course that's started up.' Louisa handed over the plates. She gave a little grimace. 'Ross is paying. It's costing him plenty, I guess.' She watched Corinne but did not offer to help. 'They let me in out of sympathy.'

Corinne ignored this last. She slid the two plates of food onto the glass counter and they each climbed onto a high stool on opposite sides. 'Worth it if it gets you a job at the end of it,' she commented.

'That's if I stay on.' Louisa played with the rice on her plate.

'Why wouldn't you now that you've decided to give it a go?' Corinne asked. 'You've got the talent. If you want to succeed you're going to have to put in the effort.'

A sardonic smile flashed over Louisa's face and just as quickly faded. 'You don't change, do you?'

'If you came for sympathy, sorry, I'm all out.'

Louisa swallowed a mouthful of food. 'Huh! Thanks for this at least.'

'Louisa, I've had a lot to deal with recently.'

'Your husband not here then?'

Corinne stopped eating. She glanced across at Louisa. The girl's head was down concentrating on her plate. She seemed alert but not wound too tight. She hadn't taken anything, at least not recently; Corinne was as sure as she could be. She answered curtly, 'No, he's not.'

Louisa's head came up. 'Can I stay then? Just for the night?'

After a moment, Corinne nodded. 'Oh, all right. You can take the spare room.'

Louisa pointed to the sofa near the television. 'I could sleep there.' She gave a grin, and then fixed Corinne with a coaxing smile. 'If that's okay with you?'

'Oh, if that's what you want,' Corinne agreed. 'Where are you staying while you're on this course of yours?'

'They've got a house for students up Gorgie.' Louisa shrugged. 'I've only been there a couple of nights. It's not up to much.'

'Well, remember, this is just for tonight.'

'Thanks.'

'How is Ross?'

Louisa put down her fork. She drew her bony shoulders up to her ears like a bird about to take off. 'Glad to get rid of me I expect.'

'Don't say that. He was devastated by losing Kate.'

'Yeh, right!'

'Oh, Louisa, you know he was. With her gone, and now you…'

'You forget *we* were nothing to each other, him and me.'

'You don't mean that.'

Louisa picked up her fork. 'Oh, forget it!' She stabbed at the soft mounds of rice.

'No, I won't forget it. Ross cared for your mother the best way anyone could. He was always there for her. Kate knew it. She needed him. Who do you think she went to every time you slapped her down? It was Ross.' She was angry now. 'When you got into trouble, who sorted it out? Ross. And not

307

once did he say anything against you.'

'How would you know?'

'Kate told me so herself.'

'What?'

'You know she did, Louisa. She confided in me. You once said I went to Four Hills at the wrong time. But I didn't. I went at the right time. Right, for Kate at least. And I felt right for you too at the time.'

'Ross, too,' Louisa said slowly, 'he *confided* in you as well.' She curved her lips in a bland smile at Corinne. 'Just like the rest of us, he was using you.'

Corinne stared hard at the young, white face. 'You are cruel, Louisa, and vindictive. It's not attractive.'

'I'm honest. That's what. You think you are. But you can't handle the truth.' Louisa's face went blank. She stared at Corinne. 'And don't talk about my mother like you knew her. There was no one else there that's the only reason she talked to you.'

'Yes, I suspect you might be right about that,' Corinne nodded. 'But at least I listened. I tried to understand how she believed everything *you* did was down to her.'

'Well, why not? She screwed me up to start with. Getting dragged all over the world with a lot of conceited dolls. No real home. No real family. What do you think that does to a person's head?' Louisa's thin jaw clamped shut.

'Is that why you tried to get your own back,' Corinne asked softly.

A smile flitted across Louisa's lips. Carefully she set her fork at the side of her plate and placed her hands flat on the cool glass of the table. 'I did it too. Oh, yes, I got my own back all right. I made sure I never have to compete with her ever again.'

Corinne stopped eating. 'Louisa?' Her heart thumping hard against her ribs, Corinne kept her voice level. 'What are you saying?'

'I was there! I was there!' Louisa's hand banged down

308

hard on the table.

'Louisa,' Corinne grabbed her wrist. 'Look at me. Were you with Kate when she died?'

Louisa pulled her hand away. '*You* know it was no accident.' Her lips curled with the suggestion of a smile. 'I followed her to the jetty. At four in the morning? Oh, I knew what she was going to do. When it came to it though, she didn't have the nerve to do it herself. So... I gave her a helping hand.' Louisa sucked hard on her bottom lip. Her expression was uncertain. 'I thought there would be more splashing about. And screaming...' She stopped, bewildered. 'There was none of that. She just looked up at me in the boat and stopped begging. Then it was over.' Louisa's dry, glassy eyes fixed on Corinne.

Slipping off her stool, she said, 'Show me where the pillows are. I'll make up my bed.'

During the night the wind dropped. The occasional gentle spatter of rain against Corinne's window petered out. Twice she got out of bed and parted the curtains to see fast moving snatches of blue-white cloud scurry over the face of a full moon, the silver light almost too bright to linger on.

But it was not the moon that kept her awake. The reason she could not sleep was laying one floor below on the sofa in the garden room.

At six o'clock it was no more than half light. Picking up her mobile Corinne made one short call. Seconds later, she got up and went into the bathroom. She slipped her arms into the bathrobe hanging behind the door and tied the belt at her waist.

Moving carefully she went down the main stairs without making a sound. Near the bottom she turned down the little flight that led into the garden room. There was no need for her to put on the overhead lights. Grey, cold morning light seeped in through the wall of tinted glass. A cursory glance showed her the carnage the wind had caused the previous night. The garden was battered and bruised.

She turned away from the depressing sight to the opposite wall. The bedcovers were bundled high on the sleeping figure. Her tousled head sticking out, the girl had pulled them right up under her chin.

Corinne wondered if she was actually asleep. She watched the girl's gentle, even breathing for a moment.

Louisa's mouth hung slightly open, slack and vulnerable, childlike in its wet pinkness. An involuntary flicker of her eye-lids made Corinne turn away. The girl *was* asleep. She was dreaming.

Corinne sighed. Why had Louisa come to her? They were nothing to each other, acquaintances of a few days, no more. What was it that had prompted her to seek out Corinne and blurt out her crime?

From the first moment they'd met, she was wary of Louisa. Everything she said, every gesture she made had Corinne delving to find a hidden meaning.

Once before she had seen Louisa exactly as she was now. It had been after Kate told her daughter that Edwin Coburn was her father. That night, Louisa had slept in her cabin like a child beaten beyond endurance, trying hard to shut out a world that she found too demanding. There was so much turbulence, so much raw emotion in her that no amount of reasoning could assuage it. No wonder she was so unpredictable, and volatile. Always it was the same. The eruption over, the regret came, the recriminations, and a strenuous defence of what she had done wrong or what she had said out of place. It was always someone else's fault, never hers.

Corinne glanced back at the sleeping figure. There was no defiance in the young face now.

She's an innocent, Corinne thought, an innocent trying to shape the world to her own needs. Then, don't we all, she smiled grimly. It's exactly what Kate tried to do. And it had been a lie, a shameful mistake that crushed Louisa, pushing her to the point of…

Corinne gazed out through the glass window to the ravaged garden. The image of the tall beauty, now dead, flashed across her mind. She knew why Louisa had searched her out. Without Kate, Louisa was lost. She had no one to blame.

And Ross? Her call would have him knocking at her door any time now. Together they would have to decide…